AUG 2 7 2001

12

Stories for an Enchanted Afternoon

KRISTINE KATHRYN RUSCH

With a Foreword by Kevin J. Anderson

GOLDEN GRYPHON PRESS • 2001

"Burial Detail," copyright © 2000 by Kristine Kathryn Rusch. First appeared in *Realms of Fantasy Magazine,* February 2000.
"Coolhunting," copyright © 1998 by Kristine Kathryn Rusch. First appeared in *Science Fiction Age,* July 1998.
"Echea," copyright © 1998 by Kristine Kathryn Rusch. First appeared in *Asimov's Science Fiction Magazine,* July 1998.
"The Gallery of His Dreams," copyright © 1991 by Kristine Kathryn Rusch. First appeared as a limited edition short novel published by Axolotl Press, June 1991.
"Going Native," copyright © 1998 by Kristine Kathryn Rusch. First appeared in *Amazing Stories,* Fall 1998.
"Harvest," copyright © 1990 by Kristine Kathryn Rusch. First appeared in *Amazing Stories,* July 1990.
"Millennium Babies," copyright © 2000 by Kristine Kathryn Rusch. First appeared in *Asimov's Science Fiction Magazine,* January 2000.
"Monuments to the Dead," copyright © 1994 by Kristine Kathryn Rusch. First appeared in *Tales from the Great Turtle,* edited by Piers Anthony, Richard Gilliam, and Martin H. Greenberg, Tor Books, 1994.
"Skin Deep," copyright © 1988 by Kristine Kathryn Rusch. First appeared in *Amazing Stories,* January 1988.
"Spirit Guides," copyright © 1995 by Kristine Kathryn Rusch. First appeared in *Heaven Sent,* edited by Peter Crowther, Daw Books, 1995.
"Strange Creatures," copyright © 1999 by Kristine Kathryn Rusch. First appeared in *Earth, Air, Fire, and Water,* edited by Margaret Weis, Daw Books, 1999.

Copyright © 2001 by Kristine Kathryn Rusch
Foreword © 2001 by Kevin J. Anderson

Edited by Marty Halpern

LIBRARY OF CONGRESS CATALOGUING-IN-PUBLICATION DATA
Rusch, Kristine Kathryn.
Stories for an enchanted afternoon / by Kristine Kathryn Rusch ; with a foreword by Kevin J. Anderson — 1st ed.
p. cm.
ISBN 1-930846-02-9 (hardcover : alk. paper)
1. United States—Social life and customs—20th century—Fiction. I. Title.
PS3568.U7S76 2001
813'.54—dc21 00-053574

All rights reserved, which includes the right to reproduce this book, or portions thereof, in any form whatsoever except as provided by the U.S. Copyright Law. For information address Golden Gryphon Press, 3002 Perkins Road, Urbana, IL 61802.

Printed in the United States of America.
First Edition

Contents

This book is dedicated to Dean Wesley Smith and Gardner Dozois,
who encouraged me to return to short fiction writing.
Thank you both for helping me make one of the best decisions
of my life.

Acknowledgments

This book would not exist without the help, support, and encouragement of these fine people:

The writing teachers who helped me understand the craft: Daniel Hodnick, Virginia Kruse, Algis Budrys, Michael Bishop, Kate Wilhelm, Damon Knight, Elizabeth Lynn, Joe Haldeman, Gaye Haldeman, Jack Williamson, Fredrick Pohl, and Gene Wolfe.

The editors who showed me how to make a good short story into a better one: Gardner Dozois, Shawna McCarthy, Sheila Williams, Mike Resnick, Stan Schmidt, Patrick L. Price, Kim Mohan, Charles C. Ryan, Scott Edelman, Ellen Datlow, Terri Windling, and Dean Wesley Smith.

The friends who gave me their time and their excellent critiquing skills: Paul Higginbotham, Nina Kiriki Hoffman, Harlan Ellison, Jerry Oltion, Kathy Oltion, Christina F. York, J. Steven York, Loren Coleman, Ray Vukcevich, Kent Patterson, Mark Budz, Marina Fitch, Kevin J. Anderson, and of course, my husband, Dean Wesley Smith.

And finally, many thanks to Marty Halpern and Gary Turner for approaching me about publishing the collection.

Foreword
Kevin J. Anderson

SHE COULD HAVE GONE through life as a waitress at the Top Hat restaurant, dressed all in phony tux and skimpy tails (but she didn't get along with the manager). She could have continued to be a reporter and news director at Madison, Wisconsin's local listener-sponsored station (WORT—"Stick it in your ear"). Or she could have continued in the picture-framing business she and her former husband established in a strip mall. On weekends, she could have continued as the dungeon master in a long-running game of D&D for a local group of misfits, myself included.

But instead of doing any of these things for keeps, Kristine Kathryn Rusch became a writer. And we've all benefited greatly from that choice.

When Kris first decided she wanted to be a writer, she made the mistake of signing up for an advanced creative writing class at the University of Wisconsin, Madison. I say "mistake," because creative writing classes have probaby done more to sidetrack and muddle the careers of potential writers than just about any other thing I can imagine. Fortunately for me, I happened to make the same mistake, and that class is where I first met Kris.

* * *

At the time (1981, I think), I was a naive (and probably obnoxious) college sophomore who had also been bitten by the writing bug. Our professor, a writer-in-residence named Lawrence O'Sullivan, was a gruff, cigar-chewing caricature of a tough guy who bragged about the fact that, although he had another book under contract, he was years past the deadline.

Kris was a quiet student sitting on the other side of the conference table, who didn't realize that her short stories were really fantasy fiction. She was surprised when I approached her and complimented her on stories that had genuine ideas and real plots—a rarity in creative writing classes, where most stories tend to involve tired relationships breaking up during dull conversations over dirty breakfast dishes.

O'Sullivan grumbled every time I attempted to steer the classroom conversation toward practical matters, such as marketing fiction, finding agents, proper manuscript format, etc. Apparently, an advanced fiction writing workshop was no place to learn about the (shudder) *commercial* aspects of becoming an author. Kris, though, was listening, and after the semester was over, we kept in touch and continued to work toward our shared goal. She was even the first person I knew who purchased a word processor.

Five years later (writing and publishing stories all along), Kris and her husband Dean Wesley Smith founded the influential Pulphouse Publishing and she became the editor of *Pulphouse: The Hardback Magazine*, wherein she helped to establish the careers of many currently prominent authors. Nineteen ninety-one was a watershed year for Kris: her first novel, *The White Mists of Power*, saw publication, as did her excellent novella "The Gallery of His Dreams" (nominated for the Nebula, Hugo, and World Fantasy Awards, and winner of the Locus Award); she also took on the mantle as editor of *The Magazine of Fantasy & Science Fiction*, for which she won the Hugo Award in 1994.

While being *F&SF* editor allowed Kris to leave her mark on the field, the time-consuming task unfortunately diminished her writing output. Since finishing her tenure at that magazine in 1997, however, she has come back like a comet.

In addition to writing ambitious science fiction (if you haven't read *Alien Influences*, go do so), creepy horror (try *Sins of the Blood*), and heart-wrenching fantasy (read all of the books of the Fey), Kristine Kathryn Rusch has also cultivated her own batch of pen names. She writes popular media fiction as Sandy Schofield and Kathryn Wesley (usually collaborations with Dean Wesley Smith), more literary fiction under just Kris Rusch (*Hitler's Angel*), humorous romance as Kristine Grayson (*Utterly Charming*), and critically acclaimed mysteries as Kris Nelscott (*A Dangerous Road*). Even I can't keep track of them all, although I remember standing at a grocery store paperback rack not long ago and finding books by four of her different incarnations all in the same place.

No one is going to question Kris's choices for the stories included in this book, but I'm saddened that you won't have the opportunity to read some of her innovative early work, such as "Winter Fugue," or "Sing," or "Stained Black," or "Death in a Minor Key," or the story about a Civil War battlefield surgeon who was actually a vampire (sorry, neither of us can even remember the title of that one).

Kris has always had a keen eye for details and characters, little incisive descriptions that suddenly bring into focus perspectives that most other people would never notice. While I was writing stories that involved blowing up planets or battling dragons with magic swords, Kris was comparing tear streaks on a man's face to the tracks of melted snowflakes.

Unlike a lot of others, Kris approached writing with persistence and determination. She dove in headfirst and never stopped striving to improve here skills. She must have heard a Darth Vader-like whisper in the back of her mind that told her, "Kris, this is your destiny!"

She has published so many novels under her own name and under various pseudonyms that even she can't give a ready answer as to where the current total stands. She has won or been nominated for practically every award in the field, from the Hugo and the Nebula to the Bram Stoker Award, the HOMer, the World Fantasy Award, the John W. Campbell Award, and a fistful of "Readers' Choice" awards from various magazines.

Kristine Kathryn Rusch is a Writer with a capital W. She and her husband Dean Wesley Smith have surrounded themselves not only with their own projects, but have worked hard to comprehend the mysterious business of writing, a rather nonsensical industry that would make executives of large corporations shake

Introduction: Old Friends

A FEW YEARS AGO, an old friend of mine found my e-mail address. We had been close since the second grade. We had lost touch after high school—we had gone to different universities and my family had moved out of the old hometown. So she initiated what became a long daily correspondence, trying to catch up on the missing years.

In the middle of this intense rebuilding, my mother died, and that sent my friend and I on a string of reminiscences which led, ultimately, to a comparison of memories.

Here's what I remembered: I had been the tomboy in the relationship—always climbing trees, jumping out of swings, getting in trouble. She had been good at everything she tried from music (she ultimately went to Oberlin on a music scholarship) to home ec (which I used to call Home Ick). I still have a stuffed animal that she made for me after I had a fairly serious bike accident—a stuffed animal she sewed without a pattern when she was ten years old.

So imagine my surprise when she wrote in one of our correspondences that she felt I had always been the feminine one of the two of us—the one who excelled at "girl" things.

She was evaluating girl things on a different scale, apparently.

My mother had stressed appearances above all else, so my clothing always matched and my hair was neatly trimmed. I had poise (which hid a shaking insecurity) and I guess I noticed boys before she did.

I don't remember that. I always thought she was the better girl. We laughed about these memories together because it showed another side of our relationship that we both remembered exactly the same way: we were highly competitive, always striving to best each other at everything—including, I guess, being a girl.

Her comment, about me being good at "girl" things, has stuck with me over the last few years. If you were to ask me at any given moment if I thought myself feminine, I would tell you I am not. That tomboy is still indelibly inked in my psyche as the dominant persona.

And yet. . . .

I look at the stories in this collection, and I realize that most of them are written from a female perspective. Not a feminist perspective necessarily and not always from a woman's point of view. But many of the stories in here deal with hearth and home, children and relationships. And until I revisited these tales while I was putting together this collection, I hadn't realized that thematic element existed in my own writing.

I'm proud of the stories in this collection. Most of them have their own pedigree: "Skin Deep," my first published story, is also the short story of mine that's been reprinted the most, including in two year's best collections; "Harvest" and "Monuments to the Dead" have also been reprinted as the best stories of the year; "Echea," "Coolhunting," and "The Gallery of His Dreams" are all award-winners, and "Going Native" is an award nominee.

I have a lot of other stories with pedigrees that aren't in this volume. Some of them are mystery stories with no science fiction or fantasy element. (I wanted this collection to focus on science fiction and fantasy.) The remaining stories are science fiction and fantasy, but after rereading them, I chose to exclude them. Let me explain why.

I became a short fiction editor shortly after selling my first short stories. For years, my colleagues in the business told me that someday I would have to choose between writing and editing. I was young then and arrogant (I am no longer young), and I believed that I could do both as long as I wanted to.

I was wrong.

In my bibliography, there's a disturbing trend. Between 1990 and 1995, I published between twelve to thirteen short stories a year. In 1996, I published just one. Since it usually takes anywhere from one to two years for a story to go from completion to publication, most of the stories published in 1994 and 1995 were written in 1992 and 1993. In other words, I had only written one short story from 1994 to 1996, and that I had done as a favor to a friend. It became increasingly clear that I was making my choice between writing and editing, and writing was losing.

During this period, I was getting crankier and crankier. (I think my husband would use harsher words than that.) I was not happy with the subconscious choice. Finally, my husband challenged me to return to short story writing.

In order to do that, we both knew, I had to quit editing.

So, after a particularly difficult evaluation of my life and finances, I did.

I was fortunate. All during my editing career, the staff at *Asimov's Science Fiction Magazine*—Gardner Dozois and Sheila Williams in particular—continued to ask me for my short stories. When I kept promising and not delivering, Gardner reminded me of the choice that I would one day have to make between writing and editing. Very few people understand the difficulties of that choice. Gardner is one of them. Our discussions were extremely valuable to me because of his insights.

When I quit my editing job, Gardner provided a home for my work. He did not accept everything I wrote, but instead gave me advice on how to start again—what he was looking for, and what the market needed. Editing taught me the importance of listening, and so I took the advice he gave me.

Gardner said to write more science fiction. So I did.

One of the first stories I wrote after I quit was "Echea." Gardner helped me fine-tune it, and then he published it in *Asimov's*. It won the *Asimov's* 1998 Readers Choice Award, and the HOMer award, given by SF readers on CompuServe. It became a finalist for the Nebula, Sturgeon, Locus, and Hugo awards, and was chosen as one of the top five novelettes of the year by *Tangent Magazine*.

The validation meant more to me than it ever had before.

It meant I made the right choice. It also showed me that all those years of short fiction editing had taught me more than I could have learned anywhere else. In addition to learning that editors often have advice worth taking, I absorbed the short story form into my subconscious. In my non-objective opinion, the short stories I have written since I quit editing are stronger than many of the ones I wrote before.

I'm still proud of the older stories, and I would love to see them collected some day. But I'm happier with the new ones. I want to share "Strange Creatures" because it's set in a world that means a lot to me: the magical, mystical Oregon Coast. I want to share "Millennium Babies"—certainly one of the stranger ideas I've had—and "Burial Detail" because it's a modern cousin to the story I'm best known for, "The Gallery of His Dreams."

Reviewing my short stories as I put this collection together was like e-mailing my old friend from school. My memories of the stories were not the same as the stories themselves.

When I think of "The Gallery of His Dreams," I remember writing it in my one-bedroom apartment, sneaking away from my editing job so that I could finish the novella in a blinding white heat. I remembered only a few scenes from the story itself. I was surprised to see how much "Spirit Guides" has in common with the mystery stories I'm currently writing. I had forgotten how strong a presence my grandmother is in "Harvest," and how my background in journalism influenced both "Going Native" and "Monuments to the Dead." Going through these stories has been as much a journey of self-discovery as that e-mail correspondence had been.

I'm happy to be back writing short stories, and I'm very pleased that people want to read them. Short stories form the basis of all of my writing: I get my novel ideas from them, and I experiment in them. But most of all, I like to share them.

Here are eleven of my best.

Enjoy.

—Kristine Kathryn Rusch
January 25, 2000

Stories for an Enchanted Afternoon

Skin Deep

"MORE PANCAKES, COLIN?"

Cullaene looked down at his empty plate so that he wouldn't have to meet Mrs. Fielding's eyes. The use of his alias bothered him more than usual that morning.

"Thank you, no, ma'am. I already ate so much I could burst. If I take another bite, Jared would have to carry me out to the fields."

Mrs. Fielding shot a glance at her husband. Jared was using the last of his pancake to sop up the syrup on his plate.

"On a morning as cold as this, you should eat more," she said as she scooped up Cullaene's plate and set it in the sterilizer. "You could use a little fat to keep you warm."

Cullaene ran his hand over the stubble covering his scalp. Not taking thirds was a mistake, but to take some now would compound it. He would have to watch himself for the rest of the day.

Jared slipped the dripping bit of pancake into his mouth. He grinned and shrugged as he inclined his head toward his wife's back. Cullaene understood the gesture. Jared had used it several times during the week Cullaene worked for them. The farmer knew that his wife seemed pushy, but he was convinced that she meant well.

"More coffee, then?" Mrs. Fielding asked. She stared at him as if she were waiting for another mistake.

"Please." Cullaene handed her his cup. He hated the foreign liquid that colonists drank in gallons. It burned the back of his throat and churned restlessly in his stomach. But he didn't dare say no.

Mrs. Fielding poured his coffee, and Cullaene took a tentative sip as Lucy entered the kitchen. The girl kept tugging her loose sweater over her skirt. She slipped into her place at the table and rubbed her eyes with the heel of her hand.

"You're running late, little miss," her father said gently.

Lucy nodded. She pushed her plate out of her way and rested both elbows on the table. "I don't think I'm going today, Dad."

"Going?" Mrs. Fielding exclaimed. "Of course, you'll go. You've had a perfect attendance record for three years, Luce. It's no time to break it now—"

"Let her be, Elsie," Jared said. "Can't you see she doesn't feel well?"

The girl's skin was white, and her hands were trembling. Cullaene frowned. She made him nervous this morning. If he hadn't known her parentage, he would have thought she was going to have her first Change. But the colonists had hundreds of diseases with symptoms like hers. And she was old enough to begin puberty. Perhaps she was about to begin her first menstrual period.

Apparently, Mrs. Fielding was having the same thoughts, for she placed her hand on her daughter's forehead. "Well, you don't have a fever," she said. Then her eyes met Cullaene's. "Why don't you men get busy? You have a lot to do today."

Cullaene slid his chair back, happy to leave his full cup of coffee sitting on the table. He pulled on the thick jacket that he had slung over the back of his chair and let himself out the back door.

Jared joined him on the porch. "Think we can finish plowing under?"

Cullaene nodded. The great, hulking machine sat in the half-turned field like a sleeping monster. In a few minutes, Cullaene would climb into the cab and feel the strange gears shiver under his fingers. Jared had said that the machine was old and delicate, but it had to last at least three more years—colonist's years—or they would have to do the seeding by hand. There was no industry on the planet yet. The only way to replace broken equipment was to send to Earth for it, and that took time.

Just as Cullaene turned toward the field, a truck floated onto the landing. He began to walk, as if the arrival of others didn't concern him, but he knew they were coming to see him. The Fieldings seldom had visitors.

"Colin!" Jared was calling him. Cullaene stopped, trying not to panic. He had been incautious this time. Things had happened too fast. He wondered what the colonists would do. Would they imprison him, or would they hurt him? Would they give him a chance to explain the situation and then let him go?

Three colonists, two males and a female, were standing outside the truck. Jared was trying to get them to go toward the house.

"I'll meet you inside," Cullaene shouted back. For a moment he toyed with running. He stared out over the broad expanse of newly cultivated land, toward the forest and rising hills beyond it. Somewhere in there he might find an enclave of his own people, a group of Abandoned Ones who hadn't assimilated, but the chances of that were small. His people had always survived by adaptation. The groups of Abandoned Ones had grown smaller every year.

He rubbed his hands together. His skin was too dry. If only he could pull off this self-imposed restraint for an hour, he would lie down in the field and encase himself in mud. Then his skin would emerge as soft and pure as the fur on Jared's cats. But he needed his restraint now more than ever. He pulled his jacket tighter and let himself into the kitchen once more.

He could hear the voices of Lucy and her mother rise in a heated discussion from upstairs. Jared had pressed the recycle switch on the old coffee maker, and it was screeching in protest. The three visitors were seated around the table, the woman in Cullaene's seat, and all of them turned as he entered the room.

He nodded and sat by the sterilizer. The heat made his back tingle, and the unusual angle made him feel like a stranger in the kitchen where he had supped for over a week. The visitors stared at him with the same cold look he had seen on the faces of the townspeople.

"This is Colin," Jared said. "He works for me."

Cullaene nodded again. Jared didn't introduce the visitors, and Cullaene wondered if it was an intentional oversight.

"We would like to ask you a few questions about yourself," the woman said. She leaned forward as she spoke, and Cullaene noted that her eyes were a vivid blue.

"May I ask why?"

Jared's hand shook as he poured the coffee. "Colin, it's customary around here—"

"No," the woman interrupted. "It is not customary. We're talking with all the strangers. Surely your hired man has heard of the murder."

Cullaene started. He took the coffee cup Jared offered him, relieved that his own hand did not shake. "No, I hadn't heard."

"We don't talk about such things in this house, Marlene," Jared said to the woman.

Coffee cups rattled in the silence as Jared finished serving everyone. The older man, leaning against the wall behind the table, waited until Jared was through before he spoke.

"It's our first killing in *this* colony, and it's a ghastly one. Out near the ridge, we found the skin of a man floating in the river. At first, we thought it was a body because the water filled the skin like it would fill a sack. Most of the hair was in place, hair so black that when it dried its highlights were blue. We couldn't find any clothes—"

"—or bones for that matter," the other man added.

"That's right," the spokesman continued. "He had been gutted. We scoured the area for the rest of him, and up on the ridge we found blood."

"A great deal of it," Marlene said. "As if they had skinned him while he was still alive."

Cullaene had to wrap his fingers around the hot cup to keep them warm. He hadn't been careful enough. Things had happened so swiftly that he hadn't had a chance to go deeper into the woods. He felt the fear that had been quivering in the bottom of his stomach settle around his heart.

"And so you're questioning all of the strangers here to see if they could have done it." He spoke as if he were more curious than frightened.

Marlene nodded. She ran a long hand across her hairline to catch any loose strands.

"I didn't kill anyone," Cullaene said. "I'll answer anything you ask."

They asked him careful, probing questions about his life before he had entered their colony, and he answered with equal care, being as truthful as he possibly could. He told them that the first colony he had been with landed on ground unsuitable for farming. The colonists tried hunting and even applied for a mining permit, but nothing worked. Eventually, most returned to

Earth. He remained, traveling from family to family, working odd jobs while he tried to find a place to settle. As he spoke, he mentioned occasional details about himself, hoping that the sparse personal comments would prevent deeper probing. He told them about the Johansens whose daughter he had nearly married, the Cassels who taught him how to cultivate land, and the Slingers who nursed him back to health after a particularly debilitating illness. Cullaene told them every place he had ever been except the one place they were truly interested in—the woods that bordered the Fieldings' farm.

He spoke in a gentle tone that Earthlings respected. And he watched Jared's face because he knew that Jared, of any of them, would be the one to realize that Cullaene was not and never had been a colonist. Jared had lived on the planet for fifteen years. Once he had told Cullaene proudly that Lucy, though an orphan, was the first member of this colony born on the planet.

The trust in Jared's eyes never wavered. Cullaene relaxed slightly. If Jared didn't recognize him, no one would.

"They say that this is the way the natives commit murder," Marlene said when Cullaene finished. "We've heard tales from other colonies of bodies—both human and Riiame—being found like this."

Cullaene realized that she was still questioning him. "I never heard of this kind of murder before."

She nodded. As if by an unseen cue, all three of them stood. Jared stood with them. "Do you think Riiame could be in the area?" he asked.

"It's very likely," Marlene said. "Since you live so close to the woods, you should probably take extra precautions."

"Yes." Jared glanced over at his well-stocked gun cabinet. "I plan to."

The men nodded their approval and started out the door. Marlene turned to Cullaene. "Thank you for your cooperation," she said. "We'll let you know if we have any further questions."

Cullaene stood to accompany them out, but Jared held him back. "Finish your coffee. We have plenty of time to get to the fields later."

After they went out the door, Cullaene took his coffee and moved to his own seat. Lucy and her mother were still arguing upstairs. He took the opportunity to indulge himself in a quick scratch of his hands and arms. The heat had made the dryness worse.

He wondered if he had been convincing. The three looked as if they had already decided what happened. A murder. He shook his head.

A door slammed upstairs, and the argument grew progressively louder. Cullaene glanced out the window over the sterilizer. Jared was still talking with the three visitors. Cullaene hoped they'd leave soon. Then maybe he'd talk to Jared, explain as best he could why he could no longer stay.

"Where are you going?" Mrs. Fielding shouted. Panic touched the edge of her voice.

"Away from you!" Lucy sounded on the verge of tears. Cullaene could hear her stamp her way down the stairs. Suddenly, the footsteps stopped. "No! You stay away from me! I need time to think!"

"You can't have time to think! We've got to find out what's wrong."

"Nothing's wrong!"

"Lucy—"

"You take another step and I swear I'll leave!" Lucy backed her way into the kitchen, slammed the door, and leaned on it. Then she noticed Cullaene, and all the fight left her face.

"How long have you been here?" she whispered.

He poured his now-cold coffee into the recycler that they had set aside for him. "I won't say anything to your father, if that's what you're worried about. I don't even know why you were fighting."

There was no room left in the sterilizer, so he set the cup next to the tiny boiler that purified the ground water. Lucy slid a chair back, and it creaked as she sat in it. Cullaene took another glance out the window. Jared and his visitors seemed to be arguing.

What would he do if they decided he was guilty? He couldn't disappear. They had a description of him that they would send to other colonies. He could search for the Abandoned Ones, but even if he found them, they might not take him in. He had lived with the colonists all his life. He looked human, and sometimes, he even felt human.

Something crashed behind him. Cullaene turned in time to see Lucy stumble over her chair as she backed away from the overturned coffee maker. Coffee ran down the wall, and the sterilizer hissed. He hurried to her side, moved the chair, and got her to a safer corner of the kitchen.

"Are you all right?" he asked.

She nodded. A tear slipped out of the corner of her eye. "I didn't grab it tight, I guess."

"Why don't you sit down. I'll clean it up—" Cullaene stopped as Lucy's tear landed on the back of his hand. The drop was heavy and lined with red. He watched it leave a pink trail as it rolled off his skin onto the floor. Slowly, he looked up into her frightened eyes. More blood-filled tears threatened. He wiped one from her eyelashes and rolled it around between his fingertips.

Suddenly, she tried to pull away from him, and he tightened his grip on her arm. He slid back the sleeve of her sweater. The flesh hung in folds around her elbow and wrist. He touched her wrist lightly and noted that the sweat from her pores was also rimmed in blood.

"How long?" he whispered. "How long has this been happening to you?"

The tears began to flow easily now. It looked as if she were bleeding from her eyes. "Yesterday morning."

He shook his head. "It had to start sooner than that. You would have itched badly. Like a rash."

"A week ago."

He let her go. Poor girl. A week alone without anyone telling her anything. She would hurt by now. The pain and the weakness would be nearly intolerable.

"What is it?" Her voice was filled with fear.

Cullaene stared at her, then, as the full horror finally reached him. He had been prepared from birth for the Change, but Lucy thought she was human. And suddenly he looked out the window again at Jared. Jared, who had found the orphaned girl without even trying to discover anything about the type of life form he raised. Jared, who must have assumed that because the child looked human, she was human.

She was rubbing her wrist. The skin was already so loose that the pressure of his hand hadn't left a mark on it.

"It's normal," he said. "It's the Change. The first time—the first time can be painful, but I can help you through it."

The instant he said the words, he regretted them. If he helped her, he'd have to stay. He was about to contradict himself when the kitchen door clicked shut.

Mrs. Fielding looked at the spilled coffee, then at the humped skin on Lucy's arm. The older woman seemed frightened and vulnerable. She held out her hand to her daughter, but Lucy didn't move. "She's sick," Mrs. Fielding said.

"Sick?" Cullaene permitted himself a small ironic smile. These people didn't realize what they had done to Lucy. "How do you know? You've never experienced anything like this before, have you?"

Mrs. Fielding was flushed. "Have you?"

"Of course, I have. It's perfectly normal development in an adult Riiame."

"And you'd be able to help her?"

The hope in her voice mitigated some of his anger. He could probably trust Mrs. Fielding to keep his secret. She had no one else to turn to right now. "I was able to help myself."

"You're Riiame?" she whispered. Suddenly, the color drained from her face. "Oh, my God."

Cullaene could feel a chill run through him. He'd made the wrong choice. Before he was able to stop her, she had pulled the porch door open. "Jared!" she called. "Get in here right away! Colin—Colin says he's a Riiame!"

Cullaene froze. She couldn't be saying that. Not now. Not when her daughter was about to go through one of life's most painful experiences unprepared. Lucy needed him right now. Her mother couldn't help her, and neither could the other colonists. If they tried to stop the bleeding, it would kill her.

He had made his decision. He grabbed Lucy and swung her horizontally across his back, locking her body in position with his arms. She was kicking and pounding on his side. Mrs. Fielding started to scream. Cullaene let go of Lucy's legs for a moment, grabbed the doorknob, and let himself out into the hallway. Lucy had her feet braced against the floor, forcing him to drag her. He continued to move swiftly toward the front door. When he reached it, he yanked it open and ran into the cold morning air.

Lucy had almost worked herself free. He shifted her slightly against his back and managed to capture her knees again. The skin had broken where he touched her. She would leave a trail of blood.

The girl was so frightened that she wasn't even screaming. She hit him in the soft flesh of his side, then leaned over and bit him. The pain almost made him drop her. Suddenly, he spun around and tightened his grip on her.

"I'm trying to help you," he said. "Now stop it!"

She stopped struggling and rested limply in his arms. Cullaene found himself hating the Fieldings. Didn't they know there would be questions? Perhaps they could explain the Change as a disease, but what would happen when her friends began to shrivel with age and she remained as young and lovely as she was now? Who would explain that to her?

He ran on a weaving path through the trees. If Jared was thinking, he would know where Cullaene was taking Lucy. But all Cullaene needed was time. Lucy was so near the Change now that it wouldn't take too long to help her through it. But if the others tried to stop it, no matter how good their intentions, they could kill or disfigure the girl.

Cullaene was sobbing air into his lungs. His chest burned. He hadn't run like this in a long time, and Lucy's extra weight was making the movements more difficult. As if the girl could read his thoughts, she began struggling again. She bent her knees and jammed them as hard as she could into his kidneys. He almost tripped, but managed to right himself just in time. The trees were beginning to thin up ahead, and he smelled the thick spice of the river. It would take the others a while to reach him. They couldn't get the truck in here. They would have to come by foot. Maybe he'd have enough time to help Lucy and to get away.

Cullaene broke into the clearing. Lucy gasped as she saw the ridge. He had to bring her here. She needed the spicy water—and the height. He thought he could hear someone following him now, and he prayed he would have enough time. He had so much to tell her. She had to know about the pigmentation changes, and the possibilities of retaining some skin. But most of all, she had to do what he told her, or she'd be deformed until the next Change, another ten years away.

He bent in half and lugged her up the ridge. The slope of the land was slight enough so that he kept his balance, but great enough to slow him down. He could feel Lucy's heart pounding against his back. The child thought he was going to kill her, and he didn't know how he would overcome that.

When he reached the top of the ridge, he stood, panting, looking over the caramel-colored water. He didn't dare release Lucy right away. They didn't have much time, and he had to explain what was happening to her.

She had stopped struggling. She gripped him as if she were determined to drag him with her when he flung her into the river. In the distance, he could hear faint shouts.

"Lucy, I brought you up here for a reason," he said. Her fingers dug deeper into his flesh. "You're going through what my people call the Change. It's normal. It—"

"I'm not one of your people," she said. "Put me down!"

He stared across the sluggish river into the trees beyond. Even though he had just begun, he felt defeated. The girl had been human for thirteen years. He couldn't alter that in fifteen minutes.

"No, you're not." He set her down, but kept a firm grasp of her wrists. Her sweater and skirt were covered with blood. "But you were born here. Have you ever seen this happen to anyone else?"

He grabbed a loose fold of skin and lifted it. There was a sucking release as the skin separated from the wall of blood. Lucy tried to pull away from him. He drew her closer. "Unfortunately, you believe you are human and so the first one to undergo this. I'm the only one who can help you. I'm a Riiame. This has happened to me."

"You don't look like a Riiame."

He held back a sharp retort. There was so much that she didn't know. Riiame were a shape-shifting people. Parents chose the form of their children at birth. His parents had had enough foresight to give him a human shape. Apparently, so had hers. But she had only seen the Abandoned Ones who retained the shape of the hunters that used to populate the planet's forests.

A cry echoed through the woods. Lucy looked toward it, but Cullaene shook her to get her attention again. "I am Riiame," he said. "Your father's friends claimed to have found a body here. But that body they found wasn't a body at all. It was my skin. I just went through the Change. I shed my skin just as you're going to. And then I came out to find work in your father's farm."

"I don't believe you," she said.

"Lucy, you're bleeding through every pore in your body. Your skin is loose. You feel as if you're floating inside yourself. You panicked when you saw your form outlined in blood on the sheets this morning, didn't you? And your mother, she noticed it, too, didn't she?"

Lucy nodded.

"You have got to trust me because in a few hours the blood will go away, the skin you're wearing now will stick to the new skin beneath it, and you will be ugly and deformed. And in time, the old skin will start to rot. Do you want that to happen to you?"

A bloody tear made its way down Lucy's cheek. "No," she whispered.

"All right then." Cullaene wouldn't let himself feel relief. He could hear unnatural rustlings coming from the woods. "You're going to have to leave your clothes here. Then go to the edge of the ridge, reach your arms over your head to stretch the skin as much as you can, and jump into the river. It's safe, the river is very deep here. As soon as you can feel the cold water on every inch of your body, surface, go to shore, and wrap yourself in mud. That will prevent the itching from starting again."

The fear on her face alarmed him. "You mean I have to strip?"

He bit back his frustration. They didn't have time to work through human taboos. "Yes. Or the old skin won't come off."

Suddenly, he saw something flash in the woods below. It looked like the muzzle of a heat gun. Panic shot through him. Why was he risking his life to help this child? As soon as he emerged at the edge of the ridge, her father would kill him. Cullaene let go of Lucy's wrists. Let her run if she wanted to. He was not going to let himself get killed. Not yet.

But to his surprise, Lucy didn't run. She turned her back and slowly pulled her sweater over her head. Then she slid off the rest of her clothes and walked to the edge of the ridge. Cullaene knew she couldn't feel the cold right now. Her skin was too far away from the nerve endings.

She reached the edge of the ridge, her toes gripping the rock as tightly as her fingers had gripped his arm, and then she turned to look back at him. "I can't," she whispered.

She was so close. Cullaene saw the blood working under the old skin, trying to separate all of it. "You have to," he replied, keeping himself in shadow. "Jump."

Lucy looked down at the river below her, and a shiver ran through her body. She shook her head.

"Do—?" Cullaene stopped himself. If he went into the open, they'd kill him. Then he stared at Lucy for a moment, and felt his resolve waver. "Do you want me to help you?"

He could see the fear and helplessness mix on her face. She wasn't sure what he was going to do, but she wanted to believe him. Suddenly, she set her jaw with determination. "Yes," she said softly.

Cullaene's hands went cold. "All right. I'm going to do this quickly. I'll come up behind you and push you into the river. Point your toes and fall straight. The river is deep and it moves slow. You'll be all right."

Lucy nodded and looked straight ahead. The woods around them were unnaturally quiet. He hurried out of his cover and grabbed her waist, feeling the blood slide away from the pressure of his hands. He paused for a moment, knowing that Jared and his companions would not shoot while he held the girl.

"Point," he said, then pushed.

He could feel the air rush through his fingers as Lucy fell. Suddenly, a white heat blast stabbed his side, and he tumbled after her, whirling and flipping in the icy air. He landed on his stomach in the thick, cold water, knocking the wind out of his body. Cullaene knew that he should stay under and swim away from the banks, but he needed to breathe. He clawed his way to the surface, convinced he would die before he reached it. The fight seemed to take forever, and suddenly he was there, bobbing on top of the river, gasping air into his empty lungs.

Lucy's skin floated next to him, and he felt a moment of triumph before he saw Jared's heat gun leveled at him from the bank.

"Get out," the farmer said tightly. "Get out and tell me what you did with the rest of her before I lose my head altogether."

Cullaene could still go under and swim for it, but what would be the use? He wouldn't be able to change his pigmentation for another ten years or so, and if he managed to swim out of range of their heat guns, he would always be running.

With two long strokes, Cullaene swam to the bank and climbed out of the water. He shivered. It was cold, much too cold to be standing wet near the river. The spice aggravated his new skin's dryness.

Marlene, gun in hand, stood next to Jared, and the two other men were coming out of the woods.

"Where's the rest of her?" Jared asked. His arm was shaking. "On the ridge?"

Cullaene shook his head. He could have hit the gun from Jared's hand and run, but he couldn't stand to see the sadness, the defeat in the man who had befriended him.

"She'll be coming out of the water in a minute."

"You lie!" Jared screamed, and Cullaene saw with shock that the man had nearly snapped.

"No, she will." Cullaene hesitated for a moment. He didn't want to die to keep his people's secret. The Riiame always adapted. They'd adapt this time, too. "She's Riiame. You know that. This is normal for us."

"She's my daughter!"

"No, she's not. She can't be. This doesn't happen to humans."

A splash from the riverbank drew his attention. Lucy pulled

herself up alongside the water several feet from them. Her skin was fresh, pink and clean, and her bald head reflected patches of sunlight. She gathered herself into a fetal position and began to rock.

Cullaene started to go to her, but Jared grabbed him. Cullaene tried to shake his arm free, but Jared was too strong for him.

"She's not done yet," Cullaene said.

Marlene had come up beside them. "Let him go, Jared."

"He killed my daughter." Jared's grip tightened on Cullaene's arm.

"No, he didn't. She's right over there."

Jared didn't even look. "That's not my Lucy."

Cullaene swallowed hard. His heart was beating in his throat. He should have run when he had the chance. Now Jared was going to kill him.

"That is Lucy," Marlene said firmly. "Let him go, Jared. He has to help her."

Jared looked over at the girl rocking at the edge of the riverbank. His hold loosened, and finally he let his hands drop. Cullaene took two steps backward and rubbed his arms. Relief was making him dizzy.

Marlene had put her arm around Jared as if she, too, didn't trust him. She was watching Cullaene to see what he'd do next. If he ran, she'd get the other two to stop him. Slowly, he turned away from them and went to Lucy's side.

"You need mud, Lucy," he said as he dragged her higher onto the bank. She let him roll her into a cocoon. When he was nearly through, he looked at the man behind him.

Jared had dropped his weapon and was staring at Lucy's skin as it made its way down the river. Marlene still clutched her gun, but her eyes were on Jared, not Cullaene.

"Is she Riiame?" Marlene asked Jared.

The farmer shook his head. "I thought she was human!" he said. Then he raised his voice as if he wanted Cullaene to hear. "I thought she was human!"

Cullaene took a handful of mud and started painting the skin on Lucy's face. She had closed her eyes and was lying very still. She would need time to recover from the shock.

"I thought they were going to kill her," Jared said brokenly. "There were two of them and she was so little and I thought they were going to kill her." His voice dropped. "So I killed them first."

Cullaene's fingers froze on Lucy's cheek. Jared had killed

Lucy's parents because they didn't look human. Cullaene dipped his hands in more mud and continued working. He hoped they would let him leave when he finished.

He placed the last of the mud on the girl's face. Jared came up beside him. "You're Riiame too, aren't you? And you look human."

Cullaene washed the mud from his shaking hands. He was very frightened. What would he do now? Leave with Lucy, and try to teach the child that she wasn't human at all? He turned to face Jared. "What are you going to do with Lucy?"

"Will she be okay?" the farmer asked.

Cullaene stared at Jared for a moment. All the color had drained from the farmer's face, and he looked close to tears. Jared had finally realized what he had done.

"She should be," Cullaene said. "But someone has to explain this to her. It'll happen again. And there are other things."

He stopped, remembering his aborted love affair with a human woman. Ultimately, their forms had proven incompatible. He wasn't really human, although it was so easy to forget that. He only appeared human.

"Other things?"

"Difficult things." Cullaene shivered again. He would get ill from these wet clothes. "If you want, I'll take her with me. You won't have to deal with her then."

"No." Jared reached out to touch the mud-encased girl, but his hand hovered over her shell, never quite resting on it. "She's my daughter. I raised her. I can't just let her run off and disappear."

Cullaene swallowed heavily. He didn't understand these creatures. They killed Abandoned Ones on a whim, professed fear and hatred of the Riiame, and then would offer to keep one in their home.

"That was your skin that they found, wasn't it?" Jared asked. "This just happened to you."

Cullaene nodded. His muscles were tense. He wasn't sure what Jared was going to do.

"Why didn't you tell us?"

Cullaene looked at Jared for a moment. Because, he wanted to say, the woman I loved screamed and spat at me when she found out. Because one farmer nearly killed me with an axe. Because your people don't know how to cope with anything different, even when *they* are the aliens on a new planet.

"I didn't think you'd understand," he said. Suddenly, he grabbed Jared's hand and set it on the hardening mud covering

Lucy's shoulder. Then he stood up. There had to be Abandoned Ones in these woods. He would find them if Jared didn't kill him first. He started to walk.

"Colin," Jared began, but Cullaene didn't stop. Marlene reached his side and grabbed him. Cullaene glared at her, but she didn't let go. He was too frightened to hit her, too frightened to try to break free. If she held him, maybe they weren't going to kill him after all.

She ripped open the side of Cullaene's shirt and examined the damage left by the heat blast. The skin was puckered and withered, and Cullaene suddenly realized how much it ached.

"Can we treat this?" she asked.

"Are you asking for permission?" Cullaene could barely keep the sarcasm from his voice.

"No." The woman looked down and blushed deeply as some humans did when their shame was fullest. "I was asking if we had the skill."

Cullaene relaxed enough to smile. "You have the skill."

"Then," she said. "May we treat you?"

Cullaene nodded. He allowed himself to be led back to Jared's side. Jared was staring at his daughter, letting tears fall onto the cocoon of mud.

"You can take her out of there soon," Cullaene said. "Her clothes are up on the ridge. I'll get them."

And before anyone could stop him, Cullaene went into the woods and started up the ridge. He could escape now. He could simply turn around and run away. But he wasn't sure he wanted to do that.

When he reached the top of the ridge, he peered down at Jared, his frightened daughter, and the woman who protected them. They had a lot of explaining to do to Lucy. But if she was strong enough to survive the Change, she was strong enough to survive anything.

Cullaene draped her bloody clothes over his arm and started back down the ridge. When he reached the others, he handed the clothes to Marlene. Then Cullaene crouched beside Jared. Carefully, Cullaene made a hole in the mud and began to peel it off Lucy. Jared watched him for a moment. Then he slipped his fingers into a crack, and together the alien and the native freed the girl from her handmade shell.

Echea

I CAN CLOSE MY EYES and she appears in my mind as she did the moment I first saw her: tiny, fragile, with unnaturally pale skin and slanted chocolate eyes. Her hair was white as the moon on a cloudless evening. It seemed, that day, that her eyes were the only spot of color on her haggard little face. She was seven but she looked three.

And she acted like nothing we had ever encountered before.

Or since.

We had three children and a good life. We were not impulsive, but we did feel as if we had something to give. Our home was large, and we had money; any child would benefit from that.

It seemed to be for the best.

It all started with the brochures. We saw them first at an outdoor café near our home. We were having lunch, when we glimpsed floating dots of color, a fleeting child's face. Both my husband and I touched them only to have the displays open before us:

The blank vista of the Moon, the Earth over the horizon like a giant blue and white ball, a looming presence, pristine and healthy and somehow guilt-ridden. The Moon itself looked barren, as it always had, until one focused. And then one saw the pockmarks, the shattered dome open to the stars. In the corner of the first brochure I opened, at the very edge of the reproduction, were blood-splotches. They were scattered on the craters and boulders, and had left fist-sized holes in the dust. I didn't need to be told what had caused it. We saw the effects of high velocity rifles in low gravity every time we downloaded the news.

The brochures began with the Moon, and ended with the faces of refugees: pallid, worn, defeated. The passenger shuttles to Earth had pretty much stopped. At first, those who could pay came here, but by the time we got our brochures, Earth passage had changed. Only those with living relatives were able to return. Living relatives who were willing to acknowledge the relationship —and had official hard copy to prove it.

The rules were waived in the case of children, of orphans and of underage war refugees. They were allowed to come to Earth if their bodies could tolerate it, if they were willing to be adopted, and if they were willing to renounce any claims they had to Moon land.

They had to renounce the stars in order to have a home.

We picked her up in Sioux Falls, the nearest star shuttle stop and detention center to our home. The shuttle stop was a desolate place. It was designed as an embarkation point for political prisoners and for star soldiers. It was built on the rolling prairie, a sprawling complex with laser fences shimmering in the sunlight. Guards stood at every entrance, and several hovered above. We were led, by men with laser rifles, into the main compound, a building finished almost a century before, made of concrete and steel, functional, cold and ancient. Its halls smelled musty. The concrete flaked, covering everything with a fine gray dust.

Echea had flown in on a previous shuttle. She had been in detox and sick bay; through psychiatric exams and physical screenings. We did not know we would get her until they called our name.

We met her in a concrete room with no windows, shielded against the sun, shielded against the world. The area had no furniture.

A door opened and a child appeared.

Tiny, pale, fragile. Eyes as big as the moon itself, and darker than the blackest night. She stood in the center of the room, legs spread, arms crossed, as if she were already angry at us.

Around us, through us, between us, a computer voice resonated:

This is Echea. She is yours. Please take her, and proceed through the doors to your left. The waiting shuttle will take you to your preassigned destination.

She didn't move when she heard the voice, although I started. My husband had already gone toward her. He crouched and she glowered at him.

"I don't need you," she said.

"We don't need you either," he said. "But we want you."

The hard set to her chin eased, just a bit. "Do you speak for her?" she asked, indicating me.

"No," I said. I knew what she wanted. She wanted reassurance early that she wouldn't be entering a private war zone as difficult and devastating as the one she left. "I speak for myself. I'd like it if you came home with us, Echea."

She stared at us both then, not relinquishing power, not changing that forceful stance. "Why do you want me?" she asked. "You don't even know me."

"But we will," my husband said.

"And then you'll send me back," she said, her tone bitter. I heard the fear in it.

"You won't go back," I said. "I promise you that."

It was an easy promise to make. None of the children, even if their adoptions did not work, returned to the Moon.

A bell sounded overhead. They had warned us about this, warned us that we would have to move when we heard it.

"It's time to leave," my husband said. "Get your things."

Her first look was shock and betrayal, quickly masked. I wasn't even sure I had seen it. And then she narrowed those lovely chocolate eyes. "I'm from the Moon," she said with a sarcasm that was foreign to our natural daughters. "We have no things."

What we knew of the Moon Wars on Earth was fairly slim. The news vids were necessarily vague, and I had never had the patience for a long lesson in Moon history.

The shorthand for the Moon situation was this: the Moon's economic resources were scarce. Some colonies, after several years of existence, were self-sufficient. Others were not. The shipments from Earth, highly valuable, were designated to specific places and often did not get there. Piracy, theft, and murder occurred to gain the scarce resources. Sometimes skirmishes broke out. A few times, the fighting escalated. Domes were damaged, and in the worst of the fighting, two colonies were destroyed.

At the time, I did not understand the situation at all. I took at face value a cynical comment from one of my professors: colonies always struggle for dominance when they are away from the Mother country. I had even repeated it at parties.

I had not understood that it oversimplified one of the most complex situations in our universe.

I also had not understood the very human cost of such events.

That is, until I had Echea.

We had ordered a private shuttle for our return, but it wouldn't have mattered if we were walking down a public street. I attempted to engage Echea, but she wouldn't talk. She stared out the window instead, and became visibly agitated as we approached home.

Lake Nebagamon is a small lake, one of the hundreds that dot Northern Wisconsin. It was a popular resort for people from nearby Superior. Many had summer homes, some dating from the late 1800s. In the early 2000s, the summer homes were sold off. Most lots were bought by families who already owned land there, and hated the crowding at Nebagamon. My family bought fifteen lots. My husband's bought ten. Our marriage, some joked, was one of the most important local mergers of the day.

Sometimes I think it was no joke. It was expected. There is affection between us, of course, and a certain warmth. But no real passion.

We had no passion. Of that, I'm sure. Just a warm affection. The passion I once shared with another man—a boy actually—was so long ago that I remember it in images, like a vid seen decades ago, or a painting made from someone else's life.

When my husband and I married, we acted like an acquiring conglomerate. We tore down my family's summer home because it had no potential and historical value, and we built onto my husband's. The ancient house became an estate with a grand lawn that rolled down to the muddy water. Evenings we sat on the verandah and listened to the cicadas until full dark. Then we stared at the stars and their reflections in our lake. Sometimes we were blessed with the northern lights, but not too often.

This is the place we brought Echea. A girl who had never really seen green grass or tall trees; who had definitely never seen lakes or blue sky or Earth's stars. She had, in her brief time in North Dakota, seen what they considered Earth—the brown dust, the fresh air. But her exposure had been limited, and had not really included sunshine or nature itself.

We did not really know how this would affect her.

There were many things we did not know.

Our girls were lined up on the porch in age order: Kally, the twelve-year-old, and the tallest, stood near the door. Susan, the middle child, stood next to her, and Anne stood by herself near the porch. They were properly stair-stepped, three years between them, a separation considered optimal for more than a century now. We had followed the rules in birthing them, as well as in raising them.

Echea was the only thing out of the norm.

Anne, the courageous one, approached us as we got off the shuttle. She was small for six, but still bigger than Echea. Anne also blended our heritages perfectly—my husband's bright blue eyes and light hair with my dark skin and exotic features. She would be our beauty some day, something my husband claimed was unfair, since she also had the brains.

"Hi," she said, standing in the middle of the lawn. She wasn't looking at us. She was looking at Echea.

Echea stopped walking. She had been slightly ahead of me. By stopping, she forced me to stop too.

"I'm not like them," she said. She was glaring at my daughters. "I don't want to be."

"You don't have to be," I said softly.

"But you can be civil," my husband said.

Echea frowned at him, and in that moment, I think, their relationship was defined.

"I suppose you're the pampered baby," she said to Anne.

Anne grinned.

"That's right," she said. "I like it better than being the spoiled brat."

I held my breath. "Pampered baby" wasn't much different from "spoiled brat" and we all knew it.

"Do you have a spoiled brat?" Echea asked.

"No," Anne said.

Echea looked at the house, the lawn, the lake, and whispered. "You do now."

Later, my husband told me he heard this as a declaration. I heard it as awe. My daughters saw it as something else entirely.

"I think you have to fight Susan for it," Anne said.

"Do not!" Susan shouted from the porch.

"See?" Anne said. Then she took Echea's hand and led her up the steps.

* * *

That first night we awakened to screams. I came out of a deep sleep, already sitting up, ready to do battle. At first, I thought my link was on; I had lulled myself to sleep with a bedtime story. My link had an automatic shut-off, but I sometimes forgot to set it. With all that had been happening the last few days, I believed I might have done so again.

Then I noticed my husband sitting up as well, groggily rubbing the sleep out of his eyes.

The screams hadn't stopped. They were piercing, shrill. It took me a moment to recognize them.

Susan.

I was out of bed before I realized it, running down the hall before I had time to grab my robe. My nightgown flapped around me as I ran. My husband was right behind me. I could hear his heavy steps on the hardwood floor.

When we reached Susan's room, she was sitting on the window seat, sobbing. The light of the full moon cut across the cushions and illuminated the rag rugs and the old-fashioned pink spread.

I sat down beside her and put my arm around her. Her frail shoulders were shaking, and her breath was coming in short gasps. My husband crouched before her, taking her hands in his.

"What happened, sweetheart?" I asked.

"I-I-I saw him," she said. "His face exploded, and the blood *floated* down."

"Were you watching vids again before sleep?" my husband asked in a sympathetic tone. We both knew if she said yes, in the morning she would get yet another lecture about being careful about what she put in her brain before it rested.

"No!" she wailed.

She apparently remembered those early lectures too.

"Then what caused this?" I asked.

"I don't *know!*" she said and burst into sobs again. I cradled her against me, but she didn't loosen her grip on my husband's hands.

"After his blood floated, what happened, baby?" my husband asked.

"Someone grabbed me," she said against my shirt. "And pulled me away from him. I didn't want to go."

"And then what?" my husband's voice was still soft.

"I woke up," she said, and her breath hitched.

I put my hand on her head and pulled her closer. "It's all right, sweetheart," I said. "It was just a dream."

"But it was so *real*," she said.

"You're here now," my husband said. "Right here. In your room. And we're right here with you."

"I don't want to go back to sleep," she said. "Do I have to?"

"Yes," I said, knowing it was better for her to sleep than be afraid of it. "Tell you what, though. I'll program House to tell you a soothing story, with a bit of music and maybe a few moving images. What do you say?"

"Dr. Seuss," she said.

"That's not always soothing," my husband said, obviously remembering how the House's *Cat in the Hat* program gave Kally a terror of anything feline.

"It is to Susan," I said gently, reminding him. In her third year, she played *Green Eggs and Ham* all night, the House's voice droning on and on, making me thankful that our room was at the opposite end of the hall.

But she was three no longer, and she hadn't wanted Dr. Seuss for years. The dream had really frightened her.

"If you have any more trouble, baby," my husband said to her, "you come and get us, all right?"

She nodded. He squeezed her hands, then I picked her up and carried her to bed. My husband pulled back the covers. Susan clung to me as I eased her down. "Will I go back there if I close my eyes?" she asked.

"No," I said. "You'll listen to House and sleep deeply. And if you dream at all, it'll be about nice things, like sunshine on flowers, and the lake in summertime."

"Promise?" she asked, her voice quavering.

"Promise," I said. Then I removed her hands from my neck and kissed each of them before putting them on the coverlet. Then I kissed her forehead. My husband did the same, and as we were leaving, she was ordering up the House reading program.

As I pulled the door closed, I saw the opening images of *Green Eggs and Ham* flicker across the wall.

The next morning everything seemed fine. When I came down to breakfast, the chef had already placed the food on the table, each on its own warming plate. The scrambled eggs had the slightly runny look that indicated they had sat more than an hour—not even the latest design in warming plates could stop that. In addition, there was French toast, and Susan's favorite, waffles. The scent of fresh blueberry muffins floated over it all, and made me smile. The household staff had gone to great lengths to make Echea feel welcome.

My husband was already in his usual spot, e-conferencing while he sipped his coffee and broke a muffin apart with his fingers. His plate, showing the remains of eggs and ham, was pushed off to the side.

"Morning," I said as I slipped into my usual place on the other side of the table. It was made of oak and had been in my family since 1851, when my mother's people brought it over from Europe as a wedding present for my many-great grandparents. The housekeeper kept it polished to a shine, and she only used linen placemats to protect it from the effects of food.

There wasn't a scratch on it.

My husband acknowledged me with a blueberry stained hand as laughter made me look up. Kally came in, her arm around Susan. Susan still didn't look herself. She had deep circles under her eyes, which meant that *Green Eggs and Ham* hadn't quite done the trick. She was too old to get us—I had known that when we left her last night—but I hoped she hadn't spent the rest of the night listening to House, trying to find comfort in artificial voices and imagery.

The girls were still smiling when they saw me.

"Something funny?" I asked

"Echea," Kally said. "Did you know someone owned her dress before she did?"

No, I hadn't known that but it didn't surprise me. My daughters, on the other hand, had owned only the best. Sometimes their knowledge of life—or lack thereof—shocked me.

"It's not an unusual way for people to save money," I said. "But it'll be the last pre-owned dress she'll have."

Mom? It was Anne, e-mailing me directly. The instant prompt appeared before my left eye. *Can you come up here?*

I blinked the message away, then sighed and pushed back my chair. I should have known the girls would do something that first morning. And the laughter should have prepared me.

"Remember," I said as I stood. "Only one main course. No matter what your father says."

"Ma," Kally said.

"I mean it," I said, then hurried up the stairs. I didn't have to check where Anne was. She had sent me an image along with the e-mail—the door to Echea's room.

As I got closer, I heard Anne's voice.

". . . didn't mean it. They're old poops."

"Poop" was Anne's worst word, at least so far. And when she used it, she put all so much emphasis on it the word became an epithet.

"It's my dress," Echea said. She sounded calm and contained, but I thought there was a raggedness to her voice that hadn't been there the day before. "It's all I have."

At that moment, I entered the room. Anne was on the bed, which had been carefully made up. If I hadn't tucked Echea in the night before, I never would have thought she had slept there.

Echea was standing near her window seat, gazing at the lawn as if she didn't dare let it out of her sight.

"Actually," I said, keeping my voice light. "You have an entire closet full of clothes."

Thanks, Mom, Anne sent me.

"Those clothes are yours," Echea said.

"We've adopted you," I said. "What's ours is yours."

"You don't get it," she said. "This dress is *mine.* It's all I have."

She had her arms wrapped around it, her hands gripping it as if we were going to take it away.

"I know," I said softly. "I know, sweetie-baby. You can keep it. We're not trying to take it away from you."

"They said you would."

"Who?" I asked, with a sinking feeling. I already knew who. My other two daughters. "Kally and Susan?"

She nodded.

"Well, they're wrong," I said. "My husband and I make the rules in this house. I will never take away something of yours. I promise."

"Promise?" she whispered.

"Promise," I said. "Now how about breakfast?"

She looked at Anne for confirmation, and I wanted to hug my youngest daughter. She had already decided to care for Echea, to ally with her, to make Echea's entrance into the household easier.

I was so proud of her.

"Breakfast," Anne said, and I heard a tone in her voice I'd never heard before. "It's the first meal of the day."

The government had fed the children standard nutrition supplements, in beverage form. Echea hadn't taken a meal on Earth until she joined us.

"You name your meals?" she asked Anne. "You have that many of them?" Then she put a hand over her mouth, as if she were surprised she had let the questions out.

"Three of them," I said, trying to sound normal. Instead I felt defensive, as if we had too much. "We only have three of them."

The second night, we had no disturbances. By the third, we had developed a routine. I spent time with my girls, and then I went into Echea's room. She didn't like House or House's stories. House's voice, no matter how I programmed it, scared her. It made me wonder how we were going to link her when the time came. If she found House intrusive, imagine how she would find the constant barrage of information services, of instant e-mail scrolling across her eyes, or sudden images appearing inside her head. She was almost past the age where a child adapted easily to a link. We had to calm her quickly or risk her suffering a disadvantage for the rest of her life.

Perhaps it was the voice that upset her. The reason links made sound optional was because too many people had had trouble distinguishing the voices inside their head. Perhaps Echea would be one of them.

It was time to find out.

I had yet to broach the topic with my husband. He seemed to have cooled toward Echea immediately. He thought Echea abnormal because she wasn't like our girls. I reminded him that Echea hadn't had the advantages, to which he responded that she had the advantages now. He felt that since her life had changed, she should change.

Somehow I didn't think it worked like that.

It was on the second night that I realized she was terrified of going to sleep. She kept me as long as she could, and when I finally left, she asked to keep the lights on.

House said she had them on all night, although the computer clocked her even breathing starting at 2:47 A.M.

On the third night, she asked me questions. Simple ones, like the one about breakfast, and I answered them without my previous defensiveness. I held my emotions back, my shock that a child would have to ask what that pleasant ache was in her stomach after meals ("You're full, Echea. That's your stomach telling you it's happy.") or why we insisted on bathing at least once a day ("People stink if they don't bathe often, Echea. Haven't you noticed?"). She asked the questions with her eyes averted, and her hands clenched against the coverlet. She knew she should know the answers, she knew better than to ask my older two daughters or my husband, and she tried ever so hard to be sophisticated.

Already the girls had humiliated her more than once. The

dress incident had blossomed into an obsession with them, and they taunted her about her unwillingness to attach to anything. She wouldn't even claim a place at the dining room table. She seemed convinced that we would toss her out at the first chance.

On the fourth night, she addressed that fear. Her question came at me sideways, her body more rigid than usual.

"If I break something," she asked, "what will happen?"

I resisted the urge to ask what she had broken. I knew she hadn't broken anything. House would have told me, even if the girls hadn't.

"Echea," I said, sitting on the edge of her bed, "are you afraid that you'll do something which will force us to get rid of you?"

She flinched as if I had struck her, then she slid down against the coverlet. The material was twisted in her hands, and her lower jaw was working even before she spoke.

"Yes," she whispered.

"Didn't they explain this to you before they brought you here?" I asked.

"They said nothing." That harsh tone was back in her voice, the tone I hadn't heard since that very first day, her very first comment.

I leaned forward and, for the first time, took one of those clenched fists into my hands. I felt the sharp knuckles against my palms, and the softness of the fabric brushing my skin.

"Echea," I said. "When we adopted you, we made you our child by law. We cannot get rid of you. No matter what. It is illegal for us to do so."

"People do illegal things," she whispered.

"When it benefits them," I said. "Losing you will not benefit us."

"You're saying that to be kind," she said.

I shook my head. The real answer was harsh, harsher than I wanted to state, but I could not leave it at this. She would not believe me. She would think I was trying to ease her mind. I was, but not through polite lies.

"No," I said. "The agreement we signed is legally binding. If we treat you as anything less than a member of our family, we not only lose you, we lose our other daughters as well."

I was particularly proud of adding the word "other." I suspected that, if my husband had been having this conversation with her, that he would have forgotten to add it.

"You would?" she asked.

"Yes," I said.

"This is true?" she asked.

"True," I said. "I can download the agreement and its ramifications for you in the morning. House can read you the standard agreement—the one everyone must sign—tonight if you like."

She shook her head, and pushed her hands harder into mine. "Could you—could you answer me one thing?" she asked.

"Anything," I said.

"I don't have to leave?"

"Not ever," I said.

She frowned. "Even if you die?"

"Even if we die," I said. "You'll inherit, just like the other girls."

My stomach knotted as I spoke. I had never mentioned the money to our own children. I figured they knew. And now I was telling Echea who was, for all intents and purposes, still a stranger.

And an unknown one at that.

I made myself smile, made the next words come out lightly. "I suspect there are provisions against killing us in our beds."

Her eyes widened, then instantly filled with tears. "I would never do that," she said.

And I believed her.

As she grew more comfortable with me, she told me about her previous life. She spoke of it only in passing, as if the things that happened before no longer mattered to her. But in the very flatness with which she told them, I could sense deep emotions churning beneath the surface.

The stories she told were hair-raising. She had not, as I had assumed, been orphaned as an infant. She had spent most of her life with a family member who had died, and then she had been brought to Earth. Somehow, I had believed that she had grown up in an orphanage like the ones from the nineteenth and twentieth centuries, the ones Dickens wrote about, and the famous pioneer filmmakers had made flats about. I had not realized that those places did not exist on the Moon. Either children were chosen for adoption, or they were left to their own devices, to see if they could survive on their own.

Until she had moved in with us, she had never slept in a bed. She did not know it was possible to grow food by planting it, although she had heard rumors of such miracles.

She did not know that people could accept her for what she was, instead of what she could do for them.

My husband said that she was playing on my sympathies so that I would never let her go.

But I wouldn't have let her go anyway. I had signed the documents and made the verbal promise. And I cared for her. I would never let her go, any more than I would let a child of my flesh go.

I hoped, at one point, that he would feel the same.

As the weeks progressed, I was able to focus on Echea's less immediate needs. She was beginning to use House—her initial objection to it had been based on something that happened on the Moon, something she never fully explained—but House could not teach her everything. Anne introduced her to reading, and often Echea would read to herself. She caught on quickly, and I was surprised that she had not learned in her school on the Moon, until someone told me that most Moon colonies had no schools. The children were home taught, which worked only for children with stable homes.

Anne also showed her how to program House to read things Echea did not understand. Echea made use of that as well. At night, when I couldn't sleep, I would check on the girls. Often I would have to open Echea's door, and turn off House myself. Echea would fall asleep to the drone of a deep male voice. She never used the vids. She simply liked the words, she said, and she would listen to them endlessly, as if she couldn't get enough.

I downloaded information on child development and learning curves, and it was as I remembered. A child who did not link before the age of ten was significantly behind her peers in all things. If she did not link before the age of twenty, she would never be able to function at an adult level in modern society.

Echea's link would be her first step into the world that my daughters already knew, the Earth culture denied so many who had fled to the Moon.

After a bit of hesitation, I made an appointment with Ronald Caro, our Interface Physician.

Through force of habit, I did not tell my husband.

I had known my husband all my life, and our match was assumed from the beginning. We had a warm and comfortable relationship, much better than many among my peers. I had always liked my husband, and had always admired the way he worked his way around each obstacle life presented him.

One of those obstacles was Ronald Caro. When he arrived in St. Paul, after getting all his degrees and licenses and awards, Ronald Caro contacted me. He had known that my daughter Kally was in need of a link, and he offered to be the one to do it.

I would have turned him down, but my husband, always practical, checked on his credentials.

"How sad," my husband had said. "He's become one of the best Interface Physicians in the country."

I hadn't thought it sad. I hadn't thought it anything at all except inconvenient. My family had forbidden me to see Ronald Caro when I was sixteen, and I had disobeyed them.

Every girl, particularly home schooled ones, have on-line romances. Some progress to vid conferencing and virtual sex. Only a handful progress to actual physical contact. And of those that do, only a small fraction survive.

At sixteen, I ran away from home to be with Ronald Caro. He had been sixteen too, and gorgeous, if the remaining snapshot in my image memory was any indication. I thought I loved him. My father, who had been monitoring my e-mail, sent two police officers and his personal assistant to bring me home.

The resulting disgrace made me so ill that I could not get out of bed for six months. My then-future husband visited me each and every day of those six months, and it is from that period that most of my memories of him were formed. I was glad to have him; my father, who had been quite close to me, rarely spoke to me after I ran away with Ronald, and treated me as a stranger.

When Ronald reappeared in the Northland long after I had married, my husband showed his forgiving nature. He knew Ronald Caro was no longer a threat to us. He proved it by letting me take the short shuttle hop to the Twin Cities to have Kally linked.

Ronald did not act improperly toward me then or thereafter, although he often looked at me with a sadness I did not reciprocate. My husband was relieved. He always insisted on having the best, and because my husband was squeamish about brainwork, particularly that which required chips, lasers and remote placement devices, he preferred to let me handle the children's interface needs.

Even though I no longer wanted it, I still had a personal relationship with Ronald Caro. He did not treat me as a patient, or as the mother of his patients, but as a friend.

Nothing more.

Even my husband knew that.

Still, the afternoon I made the appointment, I went into our bedroom, made certain my husband was in his office, and closed the door. Then I used the link to send a message to Ronald.

Instantly his response flashed across my left eye.

Are you all right? he sent, as he always did, as if he expected something terrible to have happened to me during our most recent silence.

Fine, I sent back, disliking the personal questions.

And the girls?

Fine also.

So you linked to chat? again, as he always did.

And I responded as I always did. *No. I need to make an appointment for Echea.*

The Moon Child?

I smiled. Ronald was the only person I knew, besides my husband, who didn't think we were insane for taking on a child not our own. But I felt that we could, and because we could, and because so many were suffering, we should.

My husband probably had his own reasons. We never really discussed them, beyond that first day.

The Moon Child, I responded. *Echea.*

Pretty name.

Pretty girl.

There was a silence, as if he didn't know how to respond to that. He had always been silent about my children. They were links he could not form, links to my husband that could not be broken, links that Ronald and I could never have.

She has no interface, I sent into that silence.

Not at all?

No.

Did they tell you anything about her?

Only that she'd been orphaned. You know, the standard stuff. I felt odd, sending that. I had asked for information, of course, at every step. And my husband had. And when we compared notes, I learned that each time we had been told the same thing—that we had asked for a child, and we would get one, and that child's life would start fresh with us. The past did not matter.

The present did.

How old is she?

Seven

Hmmm. The procedure won't be involved, but there might be

some dislocation. She's been alone in her head all this time. Is she stable enough for the change?

I was genuinely perplexed. I had never encountered an unlinked child, let alone lived with one. I didn't know what "stable" meant in that context.

My silence had apparently been answer enough.

I'll do an exam, he sent. *Don't worry.*

Good. I got ready to terminate the conversation.

You sure everything's all right there? he sent.

It's as right as it always is, I sent and then severed the connection.

That night I dreamed. It was an odd dream because it felt like a virtual reality vid, complete with emotions and all the five senses. But it had the distance of VR too—that strange sense that the experience was not mine.

I dreamed I was on a dirty, dusty street. The air was thin and dry. I had never felt air like this. It tasted recycled, and it seemed to suck the moisture from my skin. It wasn't hot, but it wasn't cold either. I wore a ripped shirt and ragged pants, and my shoes were boots made of a light material I had never felt before. Walking was easy and precarious at the same time. I felt lighter than ever, as if with one wrong gesture I would float.

My body moved easily in this strange atmosphere, as if it were used to it. I had felt something like it before: when my husband and I had gone to the Museum of Science and Technology in Chicago on our honeymoon. We explored the Moon exhibit, and felt firsthand what it was like to be in a colony environment.

Only that had been clean.

This wasn't.

The buildings were white plastic, covered with a filmy grit and pockmarked with time and use. The dirt on the ground seemed to get on everything, but I knew, as well as I knew how to walk in this imperfect gravity, that there wasn't enough money to pave the roads.

The light above was artificial, built into the dome itself. If I looked up, I could see the dome and the light, and if I squinted, I could see beyond to the darkness that was the unprotected atmosphere. It made me feel as if I were in a lighted glass porch on a starless night. Open, and vulnerable, and terrified, more because I couldn't see what was beyond than because I could.

People crowded the roadway and huddled near the plastic

buildings. The buildings were domed too. Prefab, shipped up decades ago when Earth had hopes for the colonies. Now there were no more shipments, at least not here. We had heard that there were shipments coming to Colony Russia and Colony Europe, but no one confirmed the rumors. I was in Colony London, a bastard colony made by refugees and dissidents from Colony Europe. For a while, we had stolen their supply ships. Now, it seemed, they had stolen them back.

A man took my arm. I smiled up at him. His face was my father's face, a face I hadn't seen since I was twenty-five. Only something had altered it terribly. He was younger than I had ever remembered him. He was too thin and his skin filthy with dust. He smiled back at me, three teeth missing, lost to malnutrition, the rest blackened and about to go. In the past few days the whites of his eyes had turned yellow, and a strange mucus came from his nose. I wanted him to see the colony's medical facility or at least pay for an autodoc, but we had no credit, no means to pay at all.

It would have to wait until we found something.

"I think I found us free passage to Colony Latina," he said. His breath whistled through the gaps in his teeth. I had learned long ago to be far away from his mouth. The stench could be overpowering. "But you'll have to do them a job."

A job. I sighed. He had promised no more. But that had been months ago. The credits had run out, and he had gotten sicker.

"A big job?" I asked.

He didn't meet my gaze. "Might be."

"Dad—"

"Honey, we gotta use what we got."

It might have been his motto. *We gotta use what we got.* I'd heard it all my life. He'd come from Earth, he'd said, in one of the last free ships. Some of the others we knew said there were no free ships except for parolees, and I often wondered if he had come on one of those. His morals were certainly slippery enough.

I don't remember my mother. I'm not even sure I had one. I'd seen more than one adult buy an infant, and then proceed to exploit it for gain. It wouldn't have been beyond him.

But he loved me. That much was clear.

And I adored him.

I'd have done the job just because he'd asked it.

I'd done it before.

The last job was how we'd gotten here. I'd been younger then and I hadn't completely understood.

But I'd understood when we were done.

And I'd hated myself.

"Isn't there another way?" I found myself asking.

He put his hand on the back of my head, propelling me forward. "You know better," he said. "There's nothing here for us."

"There might not be anything in Colony Latina, either."

"They're getting shipments from the U.N. Seems they vowed to negotiate a peace."

"Then everyone will want to go."

"But not everyone can," he said. "We can." He touched his pocket. I saw the bulge of his credit slip. "If you do the job."

It had been easier when I didn't know. When doing a job meant just that. When I didn't have other things to consider. After the first job, my father asked where I had gotten the morals. He said I hadn't inherited them from him, and I hadn't. I knew that. I suggested maybe Mother, and he had laughed, saying no mother who gave birth to me had morals either.

"Don't think about it, honey," he'd said. "Just do."

Just do. I opened my mouth—to say what, I don't know—and felt hot liquid splatter me. An exit wound had opened in his chest, spraying his blood all around. People screamed and backed away. I screamed. I didn't see where the shot had come from, only that it had come.

The blood moved slowly, more slowly than I would have expected.

He fell forward and I knew I wouldn't be able to move him, I wouldn't be able to grab the credit slip, wouldn't be able to get to Colony Latina, wouldn't have to do the job.

Faces, unbloodied faces, appeared around me.

They hadn't killed him for the slip.

I turned and ran, as he once told me to do, ran as fast as I could, blasting as I went, watching people duck or cover their ears or wrap their arms around their heads.

I ran until I saw the sign.

The tiny prefab with the Red Crescent painted on its door, the Red Cross on its windows. I stopped blasting and tumbled inside, bloody, terrified, and completely alone.

I woke up to find my husband's arms around me, my head buried in his shoulder. He was rocking me as if I were one of the girls, murmuring in my ear, cradling me and making me feel safe. I was crying and shaking, my throat raw with tears or with the aftereffects of screams.

Our door was shut and locked, something that we only did

when we were amorous. He must have had House do it, so no one would walk in on us.

He stroked my hair, wiped the tears from my face. "You should leave your link on at night," he said tenderly. "I could have manipulated the dream, made it into something pleasant."

We used to do that for each other when we were first married. It had been a way to mesh our different sexual needs, a way to discover each other's thoughts and desires.

We hadn't done it in a long, long time.

"Do you want to tell me about it?" he asked.

So I did.

He buried his face in my hair. It had been a long time since he had done that too, since he had shown that kind of vulnerability with me.

"It's Echea," he said.

"I know," I said. That much was obvious. I had been thinking about her so much that she had worked her way into my dreams.

"No," he said. "It's nothing to be calm about." He sat up, kept his hand on me, and peered into my face. "First Susan, then you. It's like she's a poison that's infecting my family."

The moment of closeness shattered. I didn't pull away from him, but it took great control not to. "She's our child."

"No," he said. "She's someone else's child, and she's disrupting our household."

"*Babies* disrupt households. It took a while, but you accepted that."

"And if Echea had come to us as a baby, I would have accepted her. But she didn't. She has problems that we did not expect."

"The documents we signed said that we must treat those problems as our own."

His grip on my shoulder grew tighter. He probably didn't realize he was doing it. "They also said that the child had been inspected and was guaranteed illness free."

"You think some kind of illness is causing these dreams? That they're being passed from Echea to us like a virus?"

"Aren't they?" he asked. "Susan dreamed of a man who died. Someone whom she didn't want to go. Then 'they' pulled her away from him. You dream of your father's death—"

"They're different," I said. "Susan dreamed of a man's face exploding, and being captured. I dreamed of a man being shot, and of running away."

"But those are just details."

"*Dream* details," I said. "We've all been talking to Echea. I'm sure that some of her memories have woven their way into our dreams, just as our daily experiences do, or the vids we've seen. It's not that unusual."

"There were no night terrors in this household until she came," he said.

"And no one had gone through any trauma until she arrived either." I pulled away from him now. "What we've gone through is small compared to her. Your parents' deaths, mine, the birth of the girls, a few bad investments, these things are all minor. We still live in the house you were born in. We swim in the lake of our childhood. We have grown wealthier. We have wonderful daughters. That's why we took Echea."

"To learn trauma?"

"No," I said. "Because we could take her, and so many others can't."

He ran a hand through his thinning hair. "But I don't want trauma in this house. I don't want to be disturbed anymore. She's not our child. Let's let her become someone else's problem."

I sighed. "If we do that, we'll still have trauma. The government will sue. We'll have legal bills up to our eyeballs. We did sign documents covering these things."

"They said if the child was defective, we could send her back."

I shook my head. "And we signed even more documents that said she was fine. We waived that right."

He bowed his head. Small strands of gray circled his crown. I had never noticed them before.

"I don't want her here," he said.

I put a hand on his. He had felt that way about Kally, early on. He had hated the way an infant disrupted our routine. He had hated the midnight feedings, had tried to get me to hire a wet nurse, and then a nanny. He had wanted someone else to raise our children because they inconvenienced him.

And yet the pregnancies had been his idea, just like Echea had been ours. He would get enthusiastic, and then when reality settled in, he would forget the initial impulse.

In the old days we had compromised. No wet nurse, but a nanny. His sleep undisturbed, but mine disrupted. My choice, not his. As the girls got older, he found his own ways to delight in them.

"You haven't spent any time with her," I said. "Get to know her. See what she's really like. She's a delightful child. You'll see."

He shook his head. "I don't want nightmares," he said, but I heard capitulation in his voice.

"I'll leave my interface on at night," I said. "We can even link when we sleep and manipulate each other's dreams."

He raised his head, smiling, suddenly looking boyish, like the man who proposed to me, all those years ago. "Like old times," he said.

I smiled back, irritation gone. "Just like old times," I said.

The nanny had offered to take Echea to Ronald's, but I insisted, even though the thought of seeing him so close to a comfortable intimacy with my husband made me uneasy. Ronald's main offices were over fifteen minutes away by shuttle. He was in a decade-old office park near the Mississippi, not too far from St. Paul's new capitol building. Ronald's building was all glass on the riverside. It stood on stilts—the Mississippi had flooded abominably in '45, and the city still hadn't recovered from the shock—and to get to the main entrance, visitors needed a lift code. Ronald had given me one when I made the appointment.

Echea had been silent during the entire trip. The shuttle had terrified her, and it didn't take long to figure out why. Each time she had traveled by shuttle, she had gone to a new home. I reassured her that would not happen this time, but I could tell she thought I lied.

When she saw the building, she grabbed my hand.

"I'll be good," she whispered.

"You've been fine so far," I said, wishing my husband could see her now. For all his demonizing, he failed to realize she was just a little girl.

"Don't leave me here."

"I don't plan to," I said.

The lift was a small glass enclosure with voice controls. When I spoke the code, it rose on air jets to the fifth floor and docked, just like a shuttle. It was designed to work no matter what the weather, no matter what the conditions on the ground.

Echea was not amused. Her grip on my hand grew so tight that it cut off the circulation to my fingers.

We docked at the main entrance. The building's door was open, apparently on the theory that anyone who knew the code was invited. A secretary sat behind an antique wood desk, dark and polished until it shone. He had a blotter in the center of the desk, a pen and inkwell beside it, and a single sheet of paper on top. I suspected that he did most of his work through his link, but the illusion worked. It made me feel as if I had slipped into a place wealthy enough to use paper, wealthy enough to waste wood on a desk.

"We're here to see Dr. Caro," I said as Echea and I entered.

"The end of the hall to your right," the secretary said, even though the directions were unnecessary. I had been that way dozens of times.

Echea hadn't, though. She moved through the building as if it were a wonder, never letting go of my hand. She seemed to remain convinced that I would leave her there, but her fear did not diminish her curiosity. Everything was strange. I suppose it had to be, compared to the Moon where space—with oxygen—was always at a premium. To waste so much area on an entrance wouldn't merely be a luxury there. It would be criminal.

We walked across the wood floors past several closed doors until we reached Ronald's offices. The secretary had warned someone because the doors swung open. Usually I had to use the small bell to the side, another old-fashioned affectation.

The interior of his offices were comfortable. They were done in blue, the color of calm he once told me, with thick easy chairs and pillowed couches. A children's area was off to the side, filled with blocks and soft toys and a few dolls. The bulk of Ronald's clients were toddlers, and the play area reflected that.

A young man in a blue worksuit appeared at one of the doors, and called my name. Echea clutched my hand tighter. He noticed her and smiled.

"Room B," he said.

I liked Room B. It was familiar. All three of my girls had done their post-interface work in Room B. I had only been in the other rooms once, and had felt less comfortable.

It was a good omen, to bring Echea to such a safe place.

I made my way down the hall, Echea in tow, without the man's guidance. The door to Room B was open. Ronald had not changed it. It still had the fainting couch, the work unit recessed into the wall, the reclining rockers. I had slept in one of those rockers as Kally had gone through her most rigorous testing.

I had been pregnant with Susan at the time.

I eased Echea inside and then pulled the door closed behind us. Ronald came through the back door—he must have been waiting for us—and Echea jumped. Her grip on my hand grew so tight that I thought she might break one of my fingers. I smiled at her and did not pull my hand away.

Ronald looked nice. He was too slim, as always, and his blond hair flopped against his brow. It needed a cut. He wore a silver silk shirt and matching pants, and even though they were a few years out of style, they looked sharp against his brown skin.

Ronald was good with children. He smiled at her first, and then took a stool and wheeled it toward us so that he would be at her eye level.

"Echea," he said. "Pretty name."

And a pretty child, he sent, just for me.

She said nothing. The sullen expression she had had when we met her had returned.

"Are you afraid of me?" he asked.

"I don't want to go with you," she said.

"Where do you think I'm taking you?"

"Away from here. Away from—" she held up my hand, clasped in her small one. At that moment it became clear to me. She had no word for what we were to her. She didn't want to use the word "family" perhaps because she might lose us.

"Your mother—" he said slowly and as he did he sent *Right?* to me.

Right, I responded.

"—brought you here for a check-up. Have you seen a doctor since you've come to Earth?"

"At the center," she said.

"And was everything all right?"

"If it wasn't, they'd have sent me back."

He leaned his elbows on his knees, clasping his hands and placing them under his chin. His eyes, a silver that matched the suit, were soft.

"Are you afraid I'm going to find something?" he asked.

"No," she said.

"But you're afraid I'm going to send you back."

"Not everybody likes me," she said. "Not everybody wants me. They said, when they brought me to Earth, that the whole family had to like me, that I had to behave or I'd be sent back."

Is this true? he asked me.

I don't know. I was shocked. I had known nothing of this.

Does the family dislike her?

She's new. A disruption. That'll change.

He glanced at me over her head, but sent nothing else. His look was enough. He didn't believe they'd change, any more than Echea would.

"Have you behaved?" he asked softly.

She glanced at me. I nodded almost imperceptibly. She looked back at him. "I've tried," she said.

He touched her then, his long delicate fingers tucking a strand of her pale hair behind her ear. She leaned into his fingers as if she'd been longing for touch.

She's more like you, he told me, *than any of your own girls.*

I did not respond. Kally looked just like me, and Susan and Anne both favored me as well. There was nothing of me in Echea. Only a bond that had formed when I first saw her, all those weeks before.

Reassure her, he sent.

I have been.

Do it again.

"Echea," I said, and she started as if she had forgotten I was there. "Dr. Caro is telling you the truth. You're just here for an examination. No matter how it turns out, you'll still be coming home with me. Remember my promise?"

She nodded, eyes wide.

"I always keep my promises," I said.

Do you? Ronald asked. He was staring at me over Echea's shoulder.

I shivered, wondering what promise I had forgotten.

Always, I told him.

The edge of his lips turned up in a smile, but there was no mirth in it.

"Echea," he said. "It's my normal practice to work alone with my patient, but I'll bet you want your mother to stay."

She nodded. I could almost feel the desperation in the move.

"All right," he said. "You'll have to move to the couch."

He scooted his chair toward it.

"It's called a fainting couch," he said. "Do you know why?"

She let go of my hand and stood. When he asked the question, she looked at me as if I would supply her with the answer. I shrugged.

"No," she whispered. She followed him hesitantly, not the little girl I knew around the house.

"Because almost two hundred years ago when these were fashionable, women fainted a lot."

"They did not," Echea said.

"Oh, but they did," Ronald said. "And do you know why?"

She shook her small head. With this idle chatter he had managed to ease her passage toward the couch.

"Because they wore undergarments so tight that they often couldn't breathe right. And if a person can't breathe right, she'll faint."

"That's silly."

"That's right," he said, as he patted the couch. "Ease yourself up there and see what it was like on one of those things."

I knew his fainting couch wasn't an antique. His had all sorts of diagnostic equipment built in. I wondered how many other people he had lured on it with his quaint stories.

Certainly not my daughters. They had known the answers to his questions before coming to the office.

"People do a lot of silly things," he said. "Even now. Did you know most people on Earth are linked?"

As he explained the net and its uses, I ignored them. I did some leftover business, made my daily chess move, and tuned into their conversation on occasion.

"—and what's really silly is that so many people refuse a link. It prevents them from functioning well in our society. From getting jobs, from communicating—"

Echea listened intently while she lay on the couch. And while he talked to her, I knew, he was examining her, seeing what parts of her brain responded to his questions.

"But doesn't it hurt?" she asked.

"No," he said. "Science makes such things easy. It's like touching a strand of hair."

And then I smiled. I understood why he had made the tender move earlier. So that he wouldn't alarm her when he put in the first chip, the beginning of her own link.

"What if it goes wrong?" she asked. "Will everybody—die?"

He pulled back from her. Probably not enough so that she would notice. But I did. There was a slight frown between his eyes. At first I had thought he would shrug off the question, but it took him too long to answer.

"No," he said as firmly as he could. "No one will die."

Then I realized what he was doing. He was dealing with a child's fear realistically. Sometimes I was too used to my husband's rather casual attitude toward the girls. And I was used to the girls themselves. They were much more placid than my Echea.

With the flick of a finger, he turned on the overhead light.

"Do you have dreams, honey?" he asked as casually as he could.

She looked down at her hands. They were slightly scarred from experiences I knew nothing about. I had planned to ask her about each scar as I gained her trust. So far, I had asked about none.

"Not anymore," she said.

This time, I moved back slightly. Everyone dreamed, didn't they? Or were dreams only the product of a linked mind? That couldn't be right. I'd seen the babies dream before we brought them here.

"When was the last time you dreamed?" he asked.

She shoved herself back on the lounge. Its base squealed from the force of her contact. She looked around, seemingly terrified. Then she looked at me. It seemed like her eyes were appealing for help.

This was why I wanted a link for her. I wanted her to be able to tell me, without speaking, without Ronald knowing, what she needed. I didn't want to guess.

"It's all right," I said to her. "Dr. Caro won't hurt you."

She jutted out her chin, squeezed her eyes closed, as if she couldn't face him when she spoke, and took a deep breath. Ronald waited, breathless.

I thought, not for the first time, that it was a shame he did not have children of his own.

"They shut me off," she said.

"Who?" His voice held infinite patience.

Do you know what's going on? I sent him.

He did not respond. His full attention was on her.

"The Red Crescent," she said softly.

"The Red Cross," I said. "On the Moon. They were the ones in charge of the orphans—"

"Let Echea tell it," he said, and I stopped, flushing. He had never rebuked me before. At least, not verbally.

"Was it on the Moon?" he asked her.

"They wouldn't let me come otherwise."

"Has anyone touched it since?" he asked.

She shook her head slowly. Somewhere in their discussion, her eyes had opened. She was watching Ronald with that mixture of fear and longing that she had first used with me.

"May I see?" he asked.

She clapped a hand to the side of her head. "If it comes on, they'll make me leave."

"Did they tell you that?" he asked.

She shook her head again.

"Then there's nothing to worry about." He put a hand on her

shoulder and eased her back on the lounge. I watched, back stiff. It seemed like I had missed a part of the conversation, but I knew I hadn't. They were discussing something I had never heard of, something the government had neglected to tell us. My stomach turned. This was exactly the kind of excuse my husband would use to get rid of her.

She was laying rigidly on the lounge. Ronald was smiling at her, talking softly, his hand on the lounge's controls. He got the read-outs directly through his link. Most everything in the office worked that way, with a back-up download on the office's equivalent of House. He would send us a file copy later. It was something my husband insisted on, since he did not like coming to these appointments. I doubted he read the files, but he might this time. With Echea.

Ronald's frown grew. "No more dreams?" he asked.

"No," Echea said again. She sounded terrified.

I could keep silent no longer. *Our family's had night terrors since she arrived,* I sent him.

He glanced at me, whether with irritation or speculation, I could not tell.

They're similar, I sent. *The dreams are all about a death on the Moon. My husband thinks—*

I don't care what he thinks. Ronald's message was intended as harsh. I had never seen him like this before. At least, I didn't think so. A dim memory rose and fell, a sense memory. I had heard him use a harsh tone with me, but I could not remember when.

"Have you tried to link with her?" he asked me directly.

"How could I?" I asked. "She's not linked."

"Have your daughters?"

"I don't know," I said.

"Do you know if anyone's tried?" he asked her.

Echea shook her head.

"Has she been doing any computer work at all?" he asked.

"Listening to House," I said. "I insisted. I wanted to see if—"

"House," he said. "Your home system."

"Yes." Something was very wrong. I could feel it. It was in his tone, in his face, in his casual movements, designed to disguise his worry from his patients.

"Did House bother you?" he asked Echea.

"At first," she said. Then she glanced at me. Again, the need for reassurance. "But now I like it."

"Even though it's painful," he said.

"No, it's not," she said, but she averted her eyes from mine.

My mouth went dry. "It hurts you to use House?" I asked. "And you didn't say anything?"

She didn't want to risk losing the first home she ever had, Ronald sent. *Don't be so harsh.*

I wasn't the one being harsh. He was. And I didn't like it.

"It doesn't really hurt," she said.

Tell me what's happening, I sent him. *What's wrong with her?*

"Echea," he said, putting his hand alongside her head one more time. "I'd like to talk with your mother alone. Would it be all right if we sent you back to the play area?"

She shook her head.

"How about if we leave the door open? You'll always be able to see her."

She bit her lower lip.

Can't you tell me this way? I sent.

I need all the verbal tools, he sent back. *Trust me.*

I did trust him. And because I did, a fear had settled in the pit of my stomach.

"That's okay," she said. Then she looked at me. "Can I come back in when I want?"

"If it looks like we're done," I said.

"You won't leave me here," she said again. When would I gain her complete trust?

"Never," I said.

She stood then and walked out the door without looking back. She seemed so much like the little girl I'd first met that my heart went out to her. All that bravado the first day had been just that, a cover for sheer terror.

She went to the play area and sat on a cushioned block. She folded her hands in her lap, and stared at me. Ronald's assistant tried to interest her in a doll, but she shook him off.

"What is it?" I asked.

Ronald sighed, and scooted his stool closer to me. He stopped near the edge of the lounge, not close enough to touch, but close enough that I could smell the scent of him mingled with his specially blended soap.

"The children being sent down from the Moon were rescued," he said softly.

"I know." I had read all the literature they sent when we first applied for Echea.

"No, you don't," he said. "They weren't just rescued from a

miserable life like you and the other adoptive parents believe. They were rescued from a program that was started in Colony Europe about fifteen years ago. Most of the children involved died."

"Are you saying she has some horrible disease?"

"No," he said. "Hear me out. She has an implant—"

"A link?"

"No," he said. "Sarah, please."

Sarah. The name startled me. No one called me that anymore. Ronald had not used it in all the years of our reacquaintance.

The name no longer felt like mine.

"Remember how devastating the Moon Wars were? They were using projectile weapons and shattering the colonies themselves, opening them to space. A single bomb would destroy generations of work. Then some of the colonists went underground—"

"And started attacking from there, yes, I know. But that was decades ago. What has that to do with Echea?"

"Colony London, Colony Europe, Colony Russia, and Colony New Deli signed the peace treaty—"

"—vowing not to use any more destructive weapons. I remember this, Ronald—"

"Because if they did, no more supply ships would be sent."

I nodded. "Colony New York and Colony Armstrong refused to participate."

"And were eventually obliterated." Ronald leaned toward me, like he had done with Echea. I glanced at her. She was watching, as still as could be. "But the fighting didn't stop. Colonies used knives and secret assassins to kill government officials—"

"And they found a way to divert supply ships," I said.

He smiled sadly. "That's right," he said. "That's Echea."

He had come around to the topic of my child so quickly it made me dizzy.

"How could she divert supply ships?"

He rubbed his nose with his thumb and forefinger. Then he sighed again. "A scientist on Colony Europe developed a technology that broadcast thoughts through the subconscious. It was subtle, and it worked very well. A broadcast about hunger at Colony Europe would get a supply captain to divert his ship from Colony Russia and drop the supplies in Colony Europe. It's more sophisticated than I make it sound. The technology actually made the captain believe that the rerouting was his idea."

Dreams. Dreams came from the subconscious. I shivered.

"The problem was that the technology was inserted into the brain of the user, like a link, but if the user had an existing link, it superseded the new technology. So they installed it in children born on the Moon, born in Colony Europe. Apparently Echea was."

"And they rerouted supply ships?"

"By imagining themselves hungry—or actually being starved. They would broadcast messages to the supply ships. Sometimes they were about food. Sometimes they were about clothing. Sometimes they were about weapons." He shook his head. "Are. I should say are. They're still doing this."

"Can't it be stopped?"

He shook his head. "We're gathering data on it now. Echea is the third child I've seen with this condition. It's not enough to go to the World Congress yet. Everyone knows though. The Red Crescent and the Red Cross are alerted to this, and they remove children from the colonies, sometimes on penalty of death, to send them here where they will no longer be harmed. The technology is deactivated, and people like you adopt them and give them full lives."

"Why are you telling me this?"

"Perhaps your House reactivated her device."

I shook my head. "The first dream happened before she listened to House."

"Then some other technology did. Perhaps the government didn't shut her off properly. It happens. The recommended procedure is to say nothing, and to simply remove the device."

I frowned at him. "Then why are you telling me this? Why didn't you just remove it?"

"Because you want her to be linked."

"Of course I do," I said. "You know that. You told her yourself the benefits of linking. You know what would happen to her if she isn't. You know."

"I know that she would be fine if you and your husband provided for her in your wills. If you gave her one of the houses and enough money to have servants for the rest of her life. She would be fine."

"But not productive."

"Maybe she doesn't need to be," he said.

It sounded so unlike the Ronald who had been treating my children that I frowned. "What aren't you telling me?"

"Her technology and the link are incompatible."

"I understand that," I said. "But you can remove her technology."

"Her brain formed around it. If I installed the link, it would wipe her mind clean."

"So?"

He swallowed so hard his Adam's apple bobbed up and down. "I'm not being clear," he said more to himself than to me. "It would make her a blank slate. Like a baby. She'd have to learn everything all over again. How to walk. How to eat. It would go quicker this time, but she wouldn't be a normal seven-year-old girl for half a year."

"I think that's worth the price of the link," I said.

"But that's not all," he said. "She'd lose all her memories. Every last one of them. Life on the Moon, arrival here, what she ate for breakfast the morning she received the link." He started to scoot forward and then stopped. "We are our memories, Sarah. She wouldn't be Echea anymore."

"Are you so sure?" I asked. "After all, the basic template would be the same. Her genetic makeup wouldn't alter."

"I'm sure," he said. "Trust me. I've seen it."

"Can't you do a memory store? Back things up so that when she gets her link she'll have access to her life before?"

"Of course," he said. "But it's not the same. It's like being told about a boat ride as opposed to taking one yourself. You have the same basic knowledge, but the experience is no longer part of you."

His eyes were bright. Too bright.

"Surely it's not that bad," I said.

"This is my specialty," he said, and his voice was shaking. He was obviously very passionate about this work. "I study how wiped minds and memory stores interact. I got into this profession hoping I could reverse the effects."

I hadn't known that. Or maybe I had and forgotten it.

"How different would she be?" I asked.

"I don't know," he said. "Considering the extent of her experience on the Moon, and the traumatic nature of much of it, I'd bet she'll be very different." He glanced into the play area. "She'd probably play with that doll beside her and not give a second thought to where you are."

"But that's good."

"That is, yes, but think how good it feels to earn her trust. She doesn't give it easily, and when she does, it's heartfelt."

I ran a hand through my hair. My stomach churned.

I don't like these choices, Ronald.

"I know," he said. I started. I hadn't realized I had actually sent him that last message.

"You're telling me that either I keep the same child and she can't function in our society, or I give her the same chances as everyone else and take away who she is."

"Yes," he said.

"I can't make that choice," I said. "My husband will see this as a breach of contract. He'll think that they sent us a defective child."

"Read the fine print in your agreement," Ronald said. "This one is covered. So are a few others. It's boilerplate. I'll bet your lawyer didn't even flinch when she read them."

"I can't make this choice," I said again.

He scooted forward and put his hands on mine. They were warm and strong and comfortable.

And familiar. Strangely familiar.

"You have to make the choice," he said. "At some point. That's part of your contract too. You're to provide for her, to prepare her for a life in the world. Either she gets a link or she gets an inheritance that someone else manages."

"And she won't even be able to check to see if she's being cheated."

"That's right," he said. "You'll have to provide for that too."

"It's not fair, Ronald."

He closed his eyes, bowed his head, and leaned it against my forehead. "It never was," he said softly. "Dearest Sarah. It never was."

"Damn," my husband said. We were sitting in our bedroom. It was half an hour before supper, and I had just told him about Echea's condition. "The lawyer was supposed to check for things like this."

"Dr. Caro said they're just learning about the problem on Earth."

"Dr. Caro." My husband stood. "Dr. Caro is wrong."

I frowned at him. My husband was rarely this agitated.

"This is not a technology developed on the Moon," my husband said. "It's an Earth technology, pre-neural net. Subject to international ban in '24. The devices disappeared when the link became the common currency among all of us. He's right that they're incompatible."

I felt the muscles in my shoulders tighten. I wondered how my husband knew of the technology and wondered if I should ask. We never discussed each other's business.

"You'd think that Dr. Caro would have known this," I said casually.

"His work is in current technology, not the history of technology," my husband said absently. He sat back down. "What a mess."

"It is that," I said softly. "We have a little girl to think of."

"Who's defective."

"Who has been used." I shuddered. I had cradled her the whole way back and she had let me. I had remembered what Ronald said, how precious it was to hold her when I knew how hard it was for her to reach out. How each touch was a victory, each moment of trust a celebration. "Think about it. Imagine using something that keys into your most basic desire, uses them for purposes other than—"

"Don't do that," he said.

"What?"

"Put a romantic spin on this. The child is defective. We shouldn't have to deal with that."

"She's not a durable good," I said. "She is a human being."

"How much money did we spend on in-the-womb enhancement so that Anne's substandard IQ was corrected? How much would we have spent if the other girls had had similar problems?"

"That's not the same thing," I said.

"Isn't it?" he asked. "We have a certain guarantee in this world. We are guaranteed excellent children, with the best advantages. If I wanted to shoot craps with my children's lives I would—"

"What would you do?" I snapped. "Go to the Moon?"

He stared as me as if he had never seen me before. "What does your precious Dr. Caro want you to do?"

"Leave Echea alone," I said.

My husband snorted. "So that she would be unlinked and dependent the rest of her life. A burden on the girls, a sieve for our wealth. Oh, but Ronald Caro would like that."

"He didn't want her to lose her personality," I said. "He wanted her to remain Echea."

My husband stared at me for a moment, and the anger seemed to leave him. He had gone pale. He reached out to touch me, then withdrew his hand. For a moment, I thought his eyes filled with tears.

I had never seen tears in his eyes before.

Had I?

"There is that," he said softly.

He turned away from me, and I wondered if I had imagined his reaction. He hadn't been close to Echea. Why would he care if her personality had changed?

"We can't think of the legalities anymore," I said. "She's ours. We have to accept that. Just like we accepted the expense when we conceived Anne. We could have terminated the pregnancy. The cost would have been significantly less."

"We could have," he said as if the thought were unthinkable. People in our circle repaired their mistakes. They did not obliterate them.

"You wanted her at first," I said.

"Anne?" he asked.

"Echea. It was our idea, much as you want to say it was mine."

He bowed his head. After a moment, he ran his hands through his hair. "We can't make this decision alone," he said.

He had capitulated. I didn't know whether to be thrilled or saddened. Now we could stop fighting about the legalities and get to the heart.

"She's too young to make this decision," I said. "You can't ask a child to make a choice like this."

"If she doesn't—"

"It won't matter," I said. "She'll never know. We won't tell her either way."

He shook his head. "She'll wonder why she's not linked, why she can only use parts of House. She'll wonder why she can't leave here without escort when the other girls will be able to."

"Or," I said, "she'll be linked and have no memory of this at all."

"And then she'll wonder why she can't remember her early years."

"She'll be able to remember them," I said. "Ronald assured me."

"Yes." My husband's smile was bitter. "Like she remembers a question on a history exam."

I had never seen him like this. I didn't know he had studied the history of neural development. I didn't know he had opinions about it.

"We can't make this decision," he said again.

I understood. I had said the same thing. "We can't ask a child to make a choice of this magnitude."

He raised his eyes to me. I had never noticed the fine lines around them, the matching lines around his nose and mouth. He was aging. We both were. We had been together a long, long time.

"She has lived through more than most on Earth ever do," he said. "She has lived through more than our daughters will, if we raise them right."

"That's not an excuse," I said. "You just want us to expiate our guilt."

"No," he said. "It's her life. She will have to be the one to live it, not us."

"But she's our child, and that entails making choices for her," I said.

He sprawled flat on our bed. "You know what I'll choose," he said softly.

"Both choices will disturb the household," I said. "Either we live with her as she is—"

"Or we train her to be what we want." He put an arm over his eyes.

He was silent for a moment, and then he sighed. "Do you ever regret the choices you made?" he asked. "Marrying me, choosing this house over the other, deciding to remain where we grew up?"

"Having the girls," I said.

"Any of it. Do you regret it?"

He wasn't looking at me. It was as if he couldn't look at me, as if our whole lives rested on my answer.

I put my hand in the one he had dangling. His fingers closed over mine. His skin was cold.

"Of course not," I said. And then, because I was confused, because I was a bit scared of his unusual intensity, I asked, "Do you regret the choices you made?"

"No," he said. But his tone was so flat I wondered if he lied.

In the end, he didn't come with Echea and me to St. Paul. He couldn't face brainwork, although I wished he had made an exception this time. Echea was more confident on this trip, more cheerful, and I watched her with a detachment I hadn't thought I was capable of.

It was as if she were already gone.

This was what parenting was all about: the difficult painful choices, the irreversible choices with no easy answers, the second-guessing of the future with no help at all from the past. I held her hand tightly this time while she wandered ahead of me down the hallway.

I was the one with fear.

Ronald greeted us at the door to his office. His smile, when he bestowed it on Echea, was sad.

He already knew our choice. I had made my husband contact him. I wanted that much participation from Echea's other parent.

Surprised? I sent.

He shook his head. *It is the choice your family always makes.*

He looked at me for a long moment, as if he expected a response, and when I did nothing, he crouched in front of Echea. "Your life will be different after today," he said.

"Momma—" and the word was a gift, a first, a never-to-be-repeated blessing "—said it would be better."

"And mothers are always right," he said. He put a hand on her shoulder. "I have to take you from her this time."

"I know," Echea said brightly. "But you'll bring me back. It's a procedure."

"That's right," he said, looking at me over her head. "It's a procedure."

He waited just a moment, the silence deep between us. I think he meant for me to change my mind. But I did not. I could not.

It was for the best.

Then he nodded once, stood, and took Echea's hand. She gave it to him as willingly, as trustingly, as she had given it to me.

He led her into the back room.

At the doorway, she stopped and waved.

And I never saw her again.

Oh, we have a child living with us, and her name is Echea. She is a wonderful vibrant creature, as worthy of our love and our heritage as our natural daughters.

But she is not the child of my heart.

My husband likes her better now, and Ronald never mentions her. He has redoubled his efforts on his research.

He is making no progress.

And I'm not sure I want him to.

She is a happy, healthy child with a wonderful future.

We made the right choice.

It was for the best.

Echea's best.

My husband says she will grow into the perfect woman.

Like me, he says.

She'll be just like me.

She is such a vibrant child.

Why do I miss the wounded sullen girl who rarely smiled?

Why was she the child of my heart?

Coolhunting

FIFTEEN DIFFERENT WAYS to fasten a shoelace and she was sitting on the porch steps of a refurbished brownstone, watching a boy barely old enough to shave tie knots in an ancient pair of Air Jordans. Steffie pushed her hair out of her face, opened her palmtop and used the tiny lens in the corner to shoot the boy's hands. They were long, slender, unlined, with wide knuckles and trimmed nails. A person couldn't do what he was doing with short stubby fingers or InstaGrow™ nails that curved like talons.

He took all six multi-colored laces, wrapped them around three fingers, and created bows of differing sizes. Then he tied them at the tongue, and created a flower that blossomed from the ancient shoe like a rose in the middle of rubble.

When he was done, she flipped him a plastic. He caught it between his thumb and forefinger, glanced at it, and raised his eyebrows.

"Mega," he said.

She was glad he thought so. She only paid him half the going rate for a style that would be all over the streets in the next two hours, then all over the stores in the next two weeks.

"Thanks," she said, and slipped her palmtop back in her pocket.

Then she grabbed one of his extra laces, tied her brown hair back, and headed down the gum-covered sidewalk toward the park.

Shoelaces. Who'd have thought? When shoes could zip, Velcro, and seal themselves, who'd've thought the arbiters of cool would go back to the lace?

Hers was not to ask why. Hers was to record, market, and change.

Coolhunting was still a strange profession, but thirty years after the first coolhunters hit the streets, it had worked its way into a mini science.

A science only a person with an eye for beauty and a sense of people could spot.

She resisted the urge to open her palmtop and check her own credit account. She'd sent the vid to seven laces companies, two shoe manufacturers, and one hundred resale outlets. Each of them should have sent a fee into her current account. It should have doubled with the laces bit. If she hit her quota today, she'd have enough for a two-week flop.

Lord knew she needed it. Her own boots were worn thin from all the walking. Twenty-one successful hunts in seven days, not to mention eight busts, and one illegal.

She still held the record for the most shifts in one day. Steffie Storm-Warning, they called her, because in her wake lay turmoil and destruction. Entire companies folded on the basis of her vids. Entire companies replaced them. And credits flowed back and forth like a river covered in Mediterranean sludge.

No one knew who she was. She had forty different legal identities, and more than enough credits stashed in various accounts to live expensively for the rest of her life. But she liked coolhunting. It was purposely anonymous—if people knew who she was, they would chase her, try to convince her they were cool—and it carried no responsibility. She didn't answer to a boss, she didn't answer to a company, she didn't even answer to the people she sold her vids to. She was as independent as independent got, a loner in every sense of the word.

And she liked it like that.

On the corner a hot dog vender floated his cart over a hot air grate. The dogs weren't like the ones she'd had as a kid. These were all meat, registered and certified lean cuts from prime portions of pig. The taste was similar but not the same.

A taste gone from her life.

Everything changed.

Nothing remained the same.

Life on the street had taught her that.

Coolhunting had reinforced it.

She took an unmarked plastic from her pocket, checked the credit level, and decided to launder it through the vendor. She stopped, ordered two dogs slathered in mustard, sweet catsup, and pickle relish, and handed the man the plastic.

He was skinny, unshaven, with an apron that had grime on it as old as she was. Vendors had always looked like that. Even in the ancient black 'n' white vids available for free download on any TV set, the vendors looked like that.

A hundred years hadn't changed them. Just their carts and their product.

He took her plastic, ran it through his machine, then frowned. "That's a lot of change," he said.

"Just run it through the machine." She took one of the dogs off his countertop, and took a bite. A little too juicy, a little too ham-flavored, but enough to still an appetite that had been building for the good part of a day.

"Don't do that anymore," he said. Anyone caught recharging too much plastic, running too many credits, was brought in.

"Sure you do, for an extra five," she said around the dog.

He grunted, then slammed the plastic into his machine. No one said no to an extra five, and she could afford it. She could afford anything if she were willing to spend credits instead of accumulate them.

Somehow, knowing how fast tastes changed, made her unwilling to commit to her own.

She ate the rest of the dog, nearly swallowing the last piece whole. Maybe it had been two days since she'd eaten. Maybe only a few hours. She couldn't remember. She'd been hunting.

It always took all of her energy.

As she picked up the second dog, he handed the plastic back to her.

"I won't do it again," he said.

"Your loss." She sprayed a bit of bun at him, and automatically covered her mouth with her left hand. "Sorry."

He shrugged, turned away. A lot of basically honest people did that when she asked them to violate their own rules. Made her ashamed sometimes. Made her realize how different her world was from theirs.

She had the luxury of eating the second dog more slowly, then cleaning her mustard-covered hands and face in the stand's laser wipe. She grabbed a napkin and wiped for good measure: public cleaners always left her feeling a bit gritty.

"Good dogs?"

She hadn't seen the guy approach. She glanced up as he spoke, registered him as someone she'd seen before, and a shudder ran down her back. He wasn't young like most of her subjects, but then her early subjects weren't young anymore either. Still, his clear gray eyes slanting in a coffee-colored Slavic-featured face looked familiar.

The wrong kind of familiar.

She shrugged, kept it light. "Dogs are as good as any these days."

"You ever had the old ones?" He brushed a hand over his silver suit. Three weeks old, worn Detroit style, with a red cummerbund instead of a tie and pierce chain. "The ones they made of sawdust and pig's feet?"

"That's not how they made 'em," she said and stepped away from him.

For a minute, she thought he'd keep up, but he didn't. He stayed at the stand, bought himself a dog, and watched her walk away.

Maybe that was how her subjects felt when she watched them. As if they were suddenly on public display, as if their entire selves were being exposed to the world.

Watchers shouldn't be watched.

She rounded a corner, then slipped into the park.

The air was fresher here, the trees budding. Tulips bloomed in special garden circles maintained by a crew of city employees who were determined to make Central Park look as cultivated as possible. She liked to spend spring here. It made her feel alive.

It also allowed her to watch the cools bloom.

She went to her bench. It was newly painted—green this time—to give the illusion of newness despite its great age. Around her, couples threw balls for their dogs, and kids went by in groups, deep in conversation.

She watched:

Clothes.

Shoes.

Jewelry.

Always alert for a new combination, a new look. But it wasn't as easy as all that. The look was a sense, a third eye, a way of seeing that most people didn't have.

She wasn't looking so much for the new trend as she was for the person who would set that trend.

Back when coolhunting started in the hype-filled '90s, the coolhunter's goal was to find the cool kid, the one who would be the innovator, the one all the other kids wanted to copy. But what the early coolhunters never realized was that cool itself was a transient state: a cool kid one week would be passé the next.

Cool was easy to spot.

Pre-cool was hard.

And she had the hardest job of all. She was in New York, not Phoenix or Dallas or Santa Fe, those hotbeds of the newest trends. Here she had to work harder because everyone knew that fashion moved north and east. It started in the southwest and traveled, slowly through the south, up the middle, then over to the eastern seaboard.

Coolhunting in New York was like deep-sea diving in the Arctic: not recommended.

Which made it all the more challenging.

Which meant it was for her.

She settled onto the iron bench. It was still a bit cold to be sitting still, but she had two dogs to settle and that encounter to put in place. Strangers rarely spoke to her. She put up an invisible barrier: if she was noticed it was in passing. If she wasn't, even better.

Casual people didn't speak to her on the street.

This guy knew her.

And if he knew her, he'd be here, sometime soon.

In the meantime, she'd hunt.

The nice thing about New York in the spring was that everyone came to her. After the winter cooped up in high heat flats, ThermalTemp All-Weather Gear™, and Footsnugger Boots™, the city's residents wanted to strut their stuff. Cool happened fast here in the spring: trends among the setters ran hourly. The early adapters spent only days in the new styles before moving onto something else. Even the herd, the followers, only spent a few weeks in the style before changing, and the laggers never caught the spring rush.

Last spring, she'd cleared thirty million credits in one month.

This spring, she hoped to do better.

She leaned back on the bench, feeling its chill penetrate her '01 vintage sweater. Her stomach churned restlessly, disturbed by too much food and that stranger's face.

Teenagers walked in front of her, laughing, the girls with their hair short and spiky, the boys with theirs down to their knees. Two-year-old fashions: these were laggers who really didn't care about their position. They were not the architects of cool that she wanted.

Sometimes, though, sometimes she envied them their easy walk, their uncaring laughter. Her life had become so focused on trends and styles, on the way that clothing—appearance—reflected thought that she wondered if she ever made decisions all on her own anymore. She wouldn't think of wearing spiky hair, nor would she walk in a crowd, laughing.

She missed the laughter.

Coolhunting made close companionship impossible. Friendships difficult. More and more lately she'd been thinking of retiring, of finding a flat in the city and actually having contact with people.

Making friends.

Establishing ties.

A boy, no more than ten, air-shoed past, running six inches off the ground. His shoes, early models, formed a cushion of air that was as dangerous as it was once thought safe: the air cushion acted like a super high platform. One false step and the wearer would fall.

To run in air-shoes required guts and a certain amount of I-don't-care.

She almost got up and followed him. Almost.

His spirit was unique, but she saw nothing that could be duplicated. Nothing that she could vid and sell. Air-shoes had been on the market since the teens, and had had their moment six months ago when the nets declared them unsafe.

Still, she had never seen anyone run in them before.

"I'd've thought you'd have followed him." The man from the hotdog stand sat next to her. He smelled faintly of spicy cologne, and he had a touch of mustard on the corner of his mouth. It made him seem more real, somehow.

"Why would I follow him?" she asked, then wished she hadn't. She knew better than to engage.

"I'd've picked him," the man said, "if I were coolhunting."

"Which you're not," she said.

"Who says?" He touched the shoelace in her hair.

She stood. "I do."

Her hands were shaking. She shoved them in the pocket of her tweed pants, then headed down the asphalt walk. He hurried behind her, his feet scuffling. She could smell him before he reached her.

That cologne was beginning to annoy.

"You know," he said softly, his torso brushing hers, his legs keeping pace with her legs, "there's a ten million credit reward for anyone who identifies you."

"Ten million?" she asked, a bit startled at the amount. Last she had heard it was two million. "That low?"

He laughed, not fooled. "You're hot, girl, and some cools want to find you."

He spoke softly as he walked with her, his words like a caress in her ear. She didn't know how he found her, didn't know who he worked for, didn't know what he wanted.

The not knowing terrified her.

But she didn't show it. She didn't allow anything to show on her face.

"Such a strange creature you make me out to be," she said.

"They don't call you Steffie Storm-Warning for nothing."

He had her name. Other corporate headhunters had found her before—a coolhunter always revealed herself in the moment of payment—but none of them had known who she was.

They had been dumb and obvious and she'd been able to give them the slip.

She couldn't slip him. He was still pressed against her, as if they were lovers on a midday stroll.

She kept walking, but her breath was coming shallowly now. She hoped he didn't notice.

"You know," she snapped, "there are about eighteen laws you're breaking touching me like that."

"You want to go to the cops?" he asked and she could hear the smile in his voice.

"No," she said. "I want you to back off."

She stopped suddenly and he slammed into her, nearly losing his balance. She shoved with her elbow, and he fell hard enough on the grass to let out a small grunt.

A girl stopped beside her and peered down. "He all right?" the girl asked. She was wired. Small chips dotted her face like jewelry. In the quick glance that Steffie got, she recognized audio, video, and net chips.

"He doesn't need to be," Steffie said.

"Ooo," the girl said. "Want me to get someone?" She tapped

a chip on her chin. Security system too. The girl had money.

"Naw," Steffie said. "I think he got the idea."

The girl laughed and continued, but not before Steffie caught a glimpse of her shoes. Scuffed Air Jordans with six laces tied in a flower bow.

An early adapter.

The vid had already hit the street.

The man was sitting up, a hand to his head. Steffie pushed him back down and put a foot on his chest. She got the distinct sense he was humoring her, that he could shove her aside with a flick of the wrist.

She didn't care. It was the look that counted. And right now it looked as if she were in control.

"I don't know who you are or what you want," she said. "But leave me alone."

"Can't do that." He put a hand on her boot. "Italian leather. Nice. They don't make stuff this soft anymore."

She yanked her foot away. "What do you want?" she asked.

"Well, I don't want to broadcast your ID," he said. "If I wanted that, I could have done it by now."

He was right. He had obviously seen her long before she saw him. The thought made her even more uneasy.

"You're one of those stalkers, aren't you?" she asked, yanking her foot away. "Interested in the hunt, in toying with your prey, in killing slowly."

He smiled as he sat up, and rubbed the grass stains out of his sleeve. "You have a vivid imagination."

"I want to know why you're bothering me," she said. *And how you know who I am.* But she didn't say that. She had already said too much.

"It's not enough to say that I'm an admirer?"

"No," she said.

"Well, I am."

"Then admire from a distance."

"And let you dive away like you did before, only to come back with a new look, a new style."

"Maybe I'll retire," she said.

"Maybe," he said. "But you haven't yet. And you have more than enough to live on. You don't need to be on the streets, but they're in your blood."

She was so thoroughly chilled now that gooseflesh had risen on her arms. No one knew this much about her. No one. She had made certain there wasn't much information about her anywhere. Sometimes she wasn't sure she had that much information about herself.

"What do you want?" she asked for the third and final time.

He spread out his hands. They were empty. "Let me up?" he asked.

She took her foot off his chest. He stood, brushed himself off, and adjusted the silver jacket. His cummerbund had twisted so that the self-sealing seam showed.

This time he kept his distance, and eyed her warily.

"Fashions have come and gone in the time it's taking you to answer this question," she said.

He wiped the mustard stain from the side of his mouth, glanced at his fingertips, winced and rubbed them together as if he could make the mustard go away.

"Your family sent me," he said.

She went hot, then cold, then hot again. She hadn't thought of her family in years.

Not true.

She thought of them every day.

She hadn't spoken to them in years.

"Really?" she asked, with the right amount of sarcasm.

His smile was patient. "I didn't expect you to believe me," he said. "And neither did they. They set up a home site accessible only to you, with names and numbers you'd know, they said. And the only way you can locate it is with this chip."

He held out his palm. In it was a red chip case the size of a sequin.

She stared at it. "For all I know that could scramble my system or blow me away."

He didn't move. "They told me to tell you that KD is dying."

Those hot/cold flashes ran through her again. "KD?" she said before she could stop herself. "That's not possible."

"That's what they said."

She squinted, unsure whether to trust, unsure whether to try. "And you are?" she asked.

"Unimportant," he said and flipped the chip case toward her.

She caught it in her left hand as he disappeared into the park.

She put the chip in the special nip pouch she'd had carved below her belly button. Nip pouches were expensive, because they were for the criminal or paranoid. Hers was big enough to hold a wrist-top and the surgeon had been good enough so that the pouch's opening looked like part of her belly button itself.

Then she went back to work.

—Caught a middle-aged woman topless, showing off surgically enhanced breasts. Micropoodles—dyed pink and gold—were leashed to her nipple chains. Steffie hated it, but knew it would catch on with the fifty and older crowd, the aging Gen-Xers who loved to torture their already burdened flesh.

(The chip lay cold against her skin, irritating, like a grain of sand in her eye.)

—Found a young man playing guitar beside a fountain, who looked as if he'd been dipped in gold. Gold hair, gold skin, gold eyes. As the light shifted, his colors deepened. She filmed a while, catching his transition from gold to bronze, bronze to brown. She didn't know what he used, and didn't ask when she flipped him his plastic. Someone would know, and someone would pay—several someones—depending on how she put it across the nets.

(The chip tingled, as if it were a live thing. Reminding her . . .)

—Had the palmtop out, already filming an androgen's roped fingernails when she saw the identical twins, captured in miniature, holding their keeper's hand. They strolled through the park wearing frilly white, their eyes old and bored and—

She shut the vid off, slid her hand across her belly, and pressed the chip.

KD's dying.

She shoved the palmtop in her pocket, and headed out of the park.

To Leo's.

Leo worked out of his apartment in a rundown condominium complex at the cross of Riverside and West Ninety-fourth. The building dated from the 1980s when it was posh. A lot of the original owners still lived in the buildings, but children and grandchildren who inherited had no respect for history. Leo was one of those. He liked the space and the old charm, but he hated the snobbishness that went with it.

Hence the little dive shop he ran out of his first floor apartment's kitchen.

She used the code he'd given her five years before to subvert the security system. It too was once state-of-the-art, in the post-doorman, high tech days, but even with updates, a street kid could get in with a few security chips and a beeper. Most of the residents wore their own security these days and didn't care, but a handful of the elderly ones had no idea how people like Leo compromised their safety.

People like Leo, and people like Steffie.

She knew a few electronic tricks of her own, and had used them often enough to gain a flop in a high security building. She never took anything except a little space and a little privacy, and she was sure the residents never noticed.

They always had space and privacy to spare.

Leo kept his door unlocked. After her fifth visit to him, she realized he didn't live in the apartment, only worked there, and didn't really care about the credits he made. Someone could—and often did—rip him off, and he continued, as if nothing had changed. She finally realized he was like her. The credits didn't matter; the challenge did.

She slid through the oak door and ran a hand over the motion detector that controlled the lights.

"Leo?"

"Kitchen, babe," he said, voice floating past the vintage mid-twentieth century furniture. His tastes ran to chrome and plastic, stuff once considered cheap by the very people who initially lived in this building. Not cheap any longer. His couch, with its chrome legs that swooped into uncomfortable arms, and orange plastic seat, ran in the range of several thousand credits.

She slipped through the remodeled arch doorway into his dark and dingy kitchen. It smelled of oranges. Peels littered the floor. Her boots made small sucking sounds as she walked.

Leo hunched over the oak table he'd inherited with the apartment, using a welding tool as old as his couch to solder some metal together. She watched him work, seeing the small shield before his face shimmer in the old-fashioned light.

Then he shut off the torch, turned and the shield faded to nothing.

He grinned. "Been a while, babe."

She knew his name, but he didn't know hers. She liked it that way; he didn't mind. She suspected he wasn't named Leo at all, suspected it was as much an affectation as the rest of the place.

She shrugged. "Been busy."

With a wave of a hand, he raised the lights. They didn't cut the gloom, but they illuminated his face and hers. His was mid-forties, careworn, no enhancements or lines. His eyes were a faded blue, his lips painted a pale maroon.

"Whatcha got?"

She was clutching the chip in her hand, and had been since she left the park. He didn't need to know about the nip pouch.

She came closer and opened her fist. The chip case gleamed in the odd light. "A man gave this to me. Said it was important."

"And you took it?" Leo raised a scarred eyebrow. He leaned over her palm, stared at the case, then reached behind himself and grabbed a tweezers. He picked the case up using the tweezers and set it on a clear sheet of glass.

"You should know better than to touch something like this, babe," Leo said.

"I do," she said.

"But he gotcha, right? What'd he do, tell you it's full of credits?"

"No," she said, unwilling to say anymore.

Leo shook his head. "I'll check it out for you. Want me to siphon the information off it?"

"Tell me what's there first," she said, "and if it's booby-trapped."

He grinned. "You give me all the fun jobs."

She shrugged. She'd never given him a job like this before.

"Head into the main room, wouldja? And can you wait? This might take some time."

"I can wait," she said, and left the kitchen.

The main room of his apartment overlooked Riverside, but the windows were so streaked with grime, she could barely see through them. His vid equipment was old and obviously for client use.

She sat on the couch, put her hand in her hair, and found the shoelace. She yanked it out, let her hair fall into her face, and wrapped the lace around her fingers. It was worn and old, fraying on the sides. Like the laces of the first pair of tennis shoes she'd had when she was a child.

KD had loved those shoes.

Big people shoes, she had said, wistfully.

"Big people shoes," Steffie murmured. She didn't want to think about KD. She leaned back, put an arm over her eyes, and let herself drift. This was as good a place to flop as any. Besides, she needed the rest.

It was dark when Leo woke her. He was wearing a personal light on each shoulder. They illuminated his face and a small circular area around him. The couch, the stained wood floor, and part of a ripped rug stood out in sharp relief.

He was holding the chip case between his thumb and forefinger—a good sign.

"It performs an instant download from a prearranged site," he said. "It forces the computer it's in to go to that site, and remain there until the download's complete. Theoretically, the site is rigged so that only the people who can answer certain questions can get it, but I circumvented it. The site's computer is in Nebraska. It links to a system in Kansas City, then links to another system in Austin. All checked out clean. No traps. And no real traps built into this thing except the instant download."

"Which someone could trace to my system."

"In a nanosecond," he said. His grin increased. "But not to mine."

She took the chip from him. "You got something like that for me?"

"I thought you'd never ask," he said. Then his smile disappeared. "Although I don't know why you'd want to. The site is your basic family crap. Genealogies, old photographs, histories, loss of former holdings, that sort of thing."

She rubbed the sleep off her face, hoping to keep any fleeting expression from him. "That's okay," she said.

"Your family?" he asked.

"I doubt it," she said. "Just some weirdness with my work."

"You sure, babe?" and this time his voice held concern. "I wouldn't want to give you something that'll get you in trouble. Of any kind."

"You found more trouble on there?"

He shook his head. "But folks don't normally bring this kinda stuff to me, you know? They bring me—" he paused, as if considering his words "—well, you know, stuff I would expect. Illegals, traps, listings no one should see. Not something this tame."

"And that scares you?" she asked.

"Different. Anything different. It's not good, you know."

She smiled. "Actually," she said. "I thrive on different."

The equipment weighed her down. She was used to a palmtop, some plastic and nothing more. Leo gave her a laptop the size of a purse and told her to dump it when she was done.

She took an aircab to Chinatown, found a basement restaurant where no one seemed to speak English, and took a booth in the back. The decor was as old as the stuff in Leo's apartment. If it weren't for the singletops for sale at the front desk, the tiny access ports built into the centers of the tables, and the program-it-yourself wall displays beside each booth, she'd have thought she'd entered some old flat black-and-white.

The lighting was dim, the booth ripped, and the soy sauce bottle so old that the red words were scraped off the glass. She ordered by pointing to three numbers on the wall display instead of talking to a waitress as she usually would have done. She liked having the opportunity to practice her Mandarin. It wasn't one of the recommended languages. She was fluent in eight non-recommended, and all seven recommended. It made the hunt easier, being able to speak the language of the people she came across.

There wasn't much hunting here. She checked it out the moment she sat down. An elderly woman wore a red silk dress that looked like it belonged at a pre-turn luau. Two businesswomen came in sporting cat's-eye glasses that had been in fashion on Wednesday three weeks before. A middle-aged man had staked out a table, and was eating slowly from six different plates. He wore the big jeans and oversized shirt that had been in style when he was a boy. She called people like that the fashion careless.

She didn't need to work. She'd had a profitable day despite the interruptions. She could continue to hunt, or she could see what this chip was all about.

She set the laptop on the table, and plugged the chip into the slot Leo had showed her. Instantly the 'top booted up, logged on, and started a download. She took a sip of tea and watched as her family history scrolled across the screen. A waitress set down a plate of egg rolls, and Steffie grabbed one, even though her stomach was churning.

Fifteen generations of history, then her own face flashed across the screen, aged ten, the last known formal full family portrait. Steffie didn't need to look. She already knew the image: parents in the back, her father's crewcut looking dated even now, her mother's nose ring catching the light. Grandparents behind them, looking staid, her paternal grandfather's long hair a mass of gray curls. Five children, various ages, Steffie the apparent oldest, with the baby Lana cuddled in her mother's arms. Her twin brothers flanking Steffie, and of course, KD.

KD.

She sat on Steffie's lap, wearing a ruffled white dress and patent leather shoes that had belonged to their great-grandmother Svetlana. Her unnaturally blonde hair was combed in ringlets, and her rosy cheeks blended into skin that past generations had once described as porcelain.

But her eyes. Her eyes belied it all.

Hooded and rebellious, they caught and reflected all the anger that no one else in the shot expressed. Steffie remembered holding the tiny body, remembered its tension, remembered how the anger molded each underdeveloped muscle.

KD is dying.

That's not possible.

But it was. Only not yet. Not for another three, maybe four decades.

Impossible.

A ploy to get her to contact the family?

Maybe.

But there were better ones.

Only her parents had never thought of them.

It took her a while to find the message embedded in the coding. They used the standard questions, the ones everyone answered easily—birthdate, along with city, state, and county code. Taxpayer identification number, resident identification number, and working resident identification number. Following that was a retinal scan (she wondered how Leo had gotten around that one) and a left thumbprint match.

Most of the questions she subverted as well. She hadn't typed her personal numbers in nearly fifteen years. She couldn't remember her resident number, and she didn't have a working resident number. Even if she did, she wouldn't have given it up. She liked her privacy, and required it for the most part so that she could do her job. Her on-line identities were multiple and clear to her: her real one was lost in the haze of memory.

When she found the hidden message, the machine gave her an instant hardcopy. She wondered if it had done that for Leo, as well. Only he wouldn't have understood the message.

> KD DYING. WANTS TO SEE YOU. COME BACK. YOU DON'T HAVE TO TALK TO US. BUT SEE HER THIS ONE LAST TIME.
>
> WE HIRED SEVERAL DETECTIVES AND A BOUNTY HUNTER. THE DETECTIVES COULDN'T LOCATE YOU. THE HUNTER DID BUT WOULD NOT GIVE YOUR LOCATION. HE DID, HOWEVER, VOLUNTEER TO DELIVER THIS CHIP.

> WE WOULD HAVE INCLUDED A PRE-PAID TICKET ON A SAME HOUR SHUTTLE, BUT WE DON'T KNOW YOUR CITY OF ORIGIN. WE ARE STILL WILLING TO PAY YOUR WAY HOME.
>
> NOTHING HAS CHANGED HERE. YOU KNOW WHERE TO FIND US.

There was no signature. There didn't need to be. She recognized her father's abrupt tones in the words. Amazing how deep those memories went, how deep the effect of the lives that first touched hers. She hadn't spoken to her father in years, and yet she could still hear his voice in her mind, feel his presence as clearly as if she had left him yesterday.

She logged off, closed the laptop and ripped up the hardcopy, stuffing the pieces into her nip pouch for later disposal. Then she closed her eyes and leaned her head back, wishing her life could be as simple as it had been only ten hours ago.

"Are you all right?" the waitress asked in Mandarin.

"Fine," Steffie replied in the same language. Then she sipped the rest of her tea, paid with unmarked plastic, grabbed the laptop, and left.

She took the first shuttle she could grab. It departed from the rooftop pad at Sixty-third and Lex an hour after she left the restaurant. It had taken her nearly as long to get to the pad as it would take her to get to Ann Arbor.

It had been ten years since she'd been outside of Manhattan. Ten years since she'd arrived, fresh from Austin, then the coolhunting capitol of the country. She'd arrived with a few credentials and a lot of balls, ready to take the plunge that most hunters fail:

Staking out her own hunting grounds, making her place the secret center of cool.

Austin lost its spot because everyone knew that coolness originated there. So early adapters arrived, followed by the trend-followers, and the cool-wanna-bes. Inundated by copycats, hunters, and wanna-bes, the truly cool left, and it took hunters almost a year to find the next center.

Phoenix.

Only no one advertised it.

Steffie didn't want to follow the cool ones. She wanted to find them. So she had come here, figuring that many of the cool were among the poor and unable to afford same-hour shuttles or even day transport. Every city in America, she figured, maybe even every city in the world had cool. She only had to find it.

And she knew none of the other hunters would come here, the heartland of American misery, the decaying edge of the known universe, where trends had not been set, really set, since the early part of the last century.

No one would come here.

Except her.

The shuttle was sleek and small. It sat on the rooftop like a black bird, wings permanently outstretched. A pilot sat up front and three other passengers were stepping into the back.

She punched her ticket code into the monitor, and watched as the electronic security shield shimmered into nothingness. She stepped across and heard a hum as it started up again.

As she climbed into the shuttle, she saw only ten passenger seats, and only five were full. Not much cause to go to Michigan in the late evening. She sank into the leather chair, fastened her belt and closed her eyes.

It would take five minutes from take-off to landing. Barely enough time to rest her eyes. Certainly not enough time to rethink the trip.

The shuttle landed on a concrete quad behind brick dorms on the University of Michigan campus. Steffie was the first to exit. She crossed the quad and entered the security gate, using one of her alias's codes to get through the scanning equipment.

She stopped when she made it outside. Snow still covered the ground although the sidewalks were bare. The air was cool and dry, and had a familiar smell, one she couldn't identify as anything more than childhood, than Ann Arbor.

Than home.

At the last word, she winced. She hadn't had a home for fifteen years, and she had liked it like that. Coolhunting suited her, with its insistence on anonymity, the constant need to keep trolling, the lack of attachments.

But here, here she was Stephanie Wyton-Brew, the second daughter of Andrew Wyton and Jennifer Brew, granddaughter of Elmer and Elise Wyton and Anthony and Josephine Brew.

And sister of KD.

She squared her shoulders, hoping they were strong enough to handle all that weight of the past, of an identity long lost. The house was just past the university, up on a hilly avenue whose name was lost in the fogs of her memory, near trees so old their canopied tops shrouded streets that had been built wide enough for carriages.

She had forgotten the name, but she hadn't forgotten how to get there. The way to the house she had grown up in was embedded as deeply into her memory as her father's voice.

Her stomach churned. She had nothing to say to these people. Nothing to say to anyone, really, even KD.

KD.

The reason for it all.

Steffie trudged along the sidewalk, wishing she had stopped long enough to get real boots instead of these dated Italian things. The thin leather did not protect her feet. And she wasn't wearing a coat. She looked like a homeless person in the pre-dawn darkness, and she knew if any of the residents of the Old Westside neighborhood peered out of their windows, they would wonder who was breaking curfew and why.

The walk to the house took three times longer than the shuttle ride. She stopped outside, astonished at how something that had loomed so large in her memory could look so small now.

The house had been built in 1910. It had two stories, a wide front porch, and a garage that had once been a barn tucked around the back. The large oak tree that covered the front lawn was half dead now. She and her brothers used to play around it.

KD had watched from the porch.

Lana hadn't even been born yet.

Steffie sighed, ran a hand through her messy hair, and walked up the path. It was cracked and smaller than she remembered. Her feet barely fit on the stones that her father had so carefully laid during the summer of her thirteenth year.

The memories were coming back.

She hated that.

She had thought she was beyond them.

She paused in front of the glassed-in front door and raised a hand. But she didn't knock. No one should have to knock on the door to their childhood home. She brought her hand down, bypassed the primitive security system, and let herself in.

The house smelled of banana bread, lemon furniture polish and her father's cigars. The cigar scent was faint—almost a memory—as if he hadn't lit up in a long time. A small shudder ran down her back. How many times had she come home from school to these smells? Sometimes the baked goods overlaying the polish were cookies, sometimes it was cake, but the house always smelled of baking. Her mother worked at home, and she always took a break by making something sweet.

It was a wonder she wasn't fat. She didn't know about her brothers. She hadn't seen them since she left home, and of course, hadn't heard from them.

KD couldn't get fat.

The grandfather clock that had sat in Wyton households since the mid-nineteenth century bonged the half hour. The sound was familiar and unfamiliar.

Steffie jumped.

The household was asleep. She could feel it in the stillness, almost as if a part of her could hear the uneven breathing from a floor away.

The main staircase with its newel posts and wooden banisters (now worth such a fortune that her parents actually should update their security system) wound toward the upstairs bedrooms. She wondered if hers was still as she remembered it, or if her parents had turned it into a guestroom.

She gazed up the steps into the darkness. KD was up there. If Steffie had any courage, she would wake KD, have a short visit, and then leave.

If she had any courage.

But she had none. She wanted to put off seeing KD as long as possible.

She avoided the staircase, and crossed beside the built-in bookshelves. The living room's layout hadn't changed in fifteen years. She sank onto the couch, fluffed a pillow and leaned back.

Let them be surprised in the morning.

She woke to her mother's face centimeters from hers. Her mother had aged naturally, with lines and age spots and skin blotchy from uneven sun exposure. Her hair had gone completely gray, and she wore glasses instead of having her eyes enhanced.

Enhancements had lost their charm, after KD.

Her nose ring remained, though, the tiny diamond stud Steffie's father had given her in lieu of an engagement ring.

"Stephanie?" Her mother asked, voice rising. "Sweetheart?"

Steffie blinked as if she were waking out of a sound sleep when in fact she had awakened the instant her mother sat down. One of the benefits of flopping, an instant wakefulness.

"Mother." She kept her voice cool, as if she had awakened to her mother's touch every day for the last fifteen years.

"He found you then."

The answer was obvious, so Steffie did not grace the remark with a reply.

"Why didn't you contact us? We'd have booked your ticket."

"No need," Steffie said. She yawned and stretched. The couch was the best bed she'd had in weeks. "Can I use the shower?"

"Sure," her mother said. "Towels are—"

"Where they always are, I know," Steffie said. And so were the extra clothes, and the special linens, and KD.

KD.

"How is she?" Steffie asked.

"Dying," her mother said. The response was curt, as if it held both anger and embarrassment.

Or maybe Steffie was just reading that in.

"I didn't think that was possible," Steffie said, although she had suspected it was. She had suspected from the beginning.

"It was—you know—a long time ago. The technology was new."

Early adapters. She had never thought of her parents that way, but that's what they were.

Early adapters.

She wondered who set the trend. She wondered who had coolhunted it.

She shivered.

"So what's happening?"

"Nothing you'd notice," her mother said. "It's all internal organ decay. On the cellular level, which makes sense, of course. Outside nothing has changed. She's still quite pretty. It's all so very Victorian—"

"The skin is an organ," Steffie said.

"But it's the most real of all of her parts," her mother said. "It didn't need much . . ."

She let her voice trail off. "Tampering," Steffie said, and stood up. She was, for the first time, conscious of how filthy she was. How long had it been since she bathed? How long since she changed clothes? It didn't matter in New York. People were people were people there. But here, a single stain on the couch was an international incident.

"She wants to see you," her mother said. "You're all she's been asking for."

Steffie didn't want to hear that. She ran a hand through her hair, noticing this time not just the mess, but the grease as well. "After I clean up," she said. "She can wait one more hour."

"I guess," her mother said, although she sounded doubtful.

Steffie froze. "How long does she have?"

Her mother was still kneeling beside the couch. She looked like a supplicant in St. Patrick's. Her mother leaned her head on the couch's arm.

"I don't know," she said. "A month. Maybe more. We've been looking for you for a long time, Stef."

"It's amazing you found me at all," Steffie said, *and even more amazing that I showed up,* she thought, but the words didn't leave her mouth. There were some things, no matter how old she got, that she could never ever say.

The shower was a time warp. The same rusted showerhead, the same hard water, the same glass double doors. The soap was different, modern, softer and better for her skin.

She wondered if they had bought it for KD.

She found some of her old clothes in the extra clothes closet and put them on. They were too big, but the fabric was still good. The look wasn't even dated—not that it meant anything, since dated happened within an instant these days.

When she looked in the steamed mirror, she saw a face that she thought had disappeared when she left Ann Arbor the first time. Freshly scrubbed, innocent, eyes wide and blue and younger, it seemed, than KD's had been in that ancient family portrait.

She leaned her head against the silvered glass. She couldn't put it off any longer.

KD.

She had to see KD.

It was harder than it sounded. She hadn't been able to look at KD for years. Not since she understood what her parents had done to her older sister.

Steffie walked down the wide hallway, the thinning carpet hard and rough beneath her feet. She paused outside KD's door. How often she used to go into this room, first for comfort and then simply to be with her sister. As a child, Steffie had never understood KD's unchanging face. Only that KD was always as she expected, always as she had known she would be.

Until the anger started.

Maybe it had always been there. Maybe it became, in Steffie's tenth year, too much for KD to close in. But suddenly the beautiful perfect little girl had become every parent's nightmare: the tantrum-throwing screaming monster child. The child that was an embarrassment; the child that made the parents look like monsters themselves.

It was, Steffie realized much later, KD's only revenge.

Steffie pushed the door open. The room was filled with morning light. The white ruffled curtains were open to the backyard, the window closed because of the last of winter's chill. The canopied bed still sat against the north wall, but the ruffles were white now instead of pink. A comforter covered the bed, nearly hiding the small form in it.

KD.

Her ringlets were fanned across the pillow, her long lashes gracing her chubby cheeks. Her skin was, as her mother had said, still the color of porcelain, her small mouth still formed a perfect bow. KD had the face of a perfect child: the features that had been used by white portrait painters to portray angels and cherubs and saintly children for over a hundred and fifty years.

KD had been damned by fashion, by advertising, by perfection. Their parents had gotten caught up in the enhancement craze in the early teens, and had thought it would be wonderful to have a child forever. Not a child that would grow to become a rebellious teenager and then an angry adult. But a child, a real human child, forever.

The doctors hadn't even tried to talk them out of it. They had pushed for it, in fact, probably seeing all the credits multiplying in their accounts, not realizing that lawsuits, years later, would pull those credits right back out again.

Steffie grabbed the white straight-backed chair with a little heart carved in its back, and pulled it beside the bed. Then she touched her sister's hand for the first time in years.

KD's skin was soft, a child's skin. Steffie half expected it to smell of talcum. Instead, the room had a vague sweet odor, the odor of decay.

"KD," she said softly.

KD did not open her eyes. Steffie felt pain slice through her heart. Had she come too late then? She hadn't even known twelve hours ago that her sister was dying. It wouldn't be fair.

"KD," she said again, this time raising her voice slightly.

KD's eyelids flickered, then opened, revealing those round eyes of startling blue. Steffie had forgotten how rich the color was, a color that could not be duplicated by human beings, no matter how hard they tried.

Those eyes filled with tears. "Stef?"

Steffie nodded.

"They said they couldn't find you," KD said.

Steffie smiled, shrugged. "They were wrong." She left off the "as usual." She felt the familiar—and old—incongruity she had always felt with her sister, the desire to protect a child, and the knowledge that KD was savvier than most people gave her credit for.

KD's hand slipped out from under hers, and grabbed Steffie's first and middle fingers. "I'm glad you came," she said.

"Me, too," Steffie lied.

"No you're not," KD said. "You have a life. I've been trying to follow it, on the net, seeing which style change is yours. They never make it here, you know."

"I know," Steffie said.

"I think I found your trademark. You like flamboyance, don't you? No elegance for you. Someone taking risks. Someone willing to take that extra step that might be a success or a mistake."

Steffie smiled. That was her trademark. She had never thought of it in those terms before.

"I saw a woman talking about coolhunting on the TV," KD said. "She said you couldn't pick a cool person without talking to them first, without knowing their attitudes, but I bet you can. I bet—"

"KD," Steffie said, not wanting to talk about herself. "I've got over four hundred million credits stashed in various accounts. I can get you treatments, things Mother and Dad can't afford. Maybe we can find a way to reverse this, or change it. Growth hormones, neuro-triggers, enhancement removal therapy, they're all expanding industries. There might be some solutions you don't know about—"

"So that I can grow big and strong like you?" KD's voice was dry. Steffie hadn't forgotten the anger, but she had forgotten the manifestation of it. The soft tones, the deceptively calm way KD had of speaking.

"So that you don't die." The words came out easier than Steffie had expected, given the pain that was slicing through her heart had moved into her throat.

KD removed her grip from Steffie's hand. "You know," KD said, "Mother and Dad never thought this through. They had the most perfect little girl, you know, but once their friends' children were grown, they stopped showing me off. I became a burden. It was like a failure on their part, that they had enough money to stop me here. We never left the house."

That was after Steffie had run away. "No," she said. "I didn't know."

"It didn't matter," KD said. "I didn't like playing anymore which confused children, and adults didn't want to hold a conversation with me. They would turn away like I was a doll come to life."

Which was what she looked like. Permanent child enhancements were still done, but rarely now, and almost always by people whose kids would only make them a fortune when they were young. Child-models, child-actors, child-singers all had their bodies frozen in form, but not permanently anymore. Even permanent child enhancements lasted only as long as the child was worth something. Once the tastes changed—and they did, even in film, netvid, and advertising—then the child hyphens were able to grow up.

No one did child-child enhancements.

The common consensus now was that it was cruel.

"So I've been living on the nets. I thought I'd find you."

Steffie's throat was dry. She didn't know KD had been looking for her.

"I did find you, you know," KD said. "Only a ghost. Only a flicker. But I did find you. And you helped me. I wanted to tell you that."

Steffie shook her head. "I didn't do anything."

"Sure you did. Fashion betting. I kept wagering on you. It took some time, some net watching, but I had the time. I saw the style introduced and I bet on the adaptation time. I was good at it, Stef. Almost as good as you."

Steffie swallowed. She'd heard of fashion betting, but never practiced it. It seemed to her like a pastime of the rich, the idle, the people who could never do anything with their lives.

Like KD.

KD lowered her voice. "I have five million credits in an account in your name, Stef. It'd been more but for the doctors."

"The doctors?" Steffie asked.

KD nodded. Then she smiled. "Enhancements like mine don't reverse. It's too old."

It took a moment for Steffie to understand what KD had said. "Then you were trying—"

"To grow up," KD said. She closed her eyes, and for a moment it seemed as if she had gotten her wish. Her cheekbones were more prominent than they had ever been, her skin sallow. She looked like a tiny old lady on her deathbed.

Steffie ran a hand through her damp hair. She didn't want to walk through this emotional thicket. She had left because dealing with KD had torn her up. Because her family had focused only on KD the child, not KD the unhappy child-woman.

"You made this happen?" Steffie asked.

KD opened her eyes. Her smile was tiny, girlish, like a child who'd been caught playing with the wrong toys. "Growth hormones."

"How did you buy them? Don't you need Mom's permission?" Permanent children were always considered children in the eyes of the law. The assumption was that these beings were designed not to grow up, so no matter how much experience they accumulated, no matter how many years they had lived, they would never achieve adult status in the eyes of the world.

KD scrunched her pillow back. The movement looked difficult. The bones of her arms stuck out of what once had been plump cherubic flesh. "That's why I had to see you," she said, her voice at a whisper. "I used your name."

"What?" All the muscles in Steffie's back went rigid.

"I used your name." KD's eyes were wide. Her lower lip was trembling. "You weren't using it. And I needed a legal adult to fill out the forms, to give permissions and send in the e-papers. That's why the money's in your name."

"You used my name to what?" Steffie asked.

"To get me the appointments. To get me the treatments."

Steffie swallowed. If she had been here, she might have helped. But she hadn't been here. She had left long ago. "All right. Why is that a problem?"

"Because I lied," KD said. A tear trembled at the tip of one of her lashes. "I said I got the enhancements less than twenty years ago."

"And that's important because—"

"The growth hormones don't work on enhancements like mine." Her voice rose into a wail. She did sound young. She acted young. But Steffie didn't know if that was because KD had been in this room for the past thirty years or because the enhancements did indeed keep her young.

"But you tried anyway."

"I read on-line that they just said that the hormones didn't work to keep us older ones in line. So I thought I could try it. But—" she rubbed the tear away with one small fist "—what no one said was that the hormones worked on people like me. They just worked wrong."

"Wrong?" Steffie asked. Her stomach was queasy. From the kitchen below rose the scents of coffee mixed with waffles.

"Wrong," KD said. "I'm aging, inside. Steffie, I have the heart of a ninety-five-year-old woman, and it gets older every day. All the other organs are changing like that too."

"Except your skin."

"Even my skin, but not as fast. The enhancements didn't have to touch it much because it would stay young if the rest of me did."

"Isn't there something they can do to reverse this?" Steffie asked. "More enhancements, maybe? Something to block the hormones?"

"No," KD said. "Not with this kind of destruction. The thing is, three weeks ago, I got legal notification for you that as my sister, you should have known the year I got enhanced. If I die, they'll go after you."

"After me? How?"

KD shrugged. "Misuse of information. Lying on government forms. Enough to hound you. To take your money. To freeze your identity."

Steffie kept her expression neutral. It didn't matter. She had enough identities. All it meant was that she would formally lose Stephanie Wyton-Brew. Whom she had already lost.

KD took her response for anger. She looked away.

"I wanted to grow up, Steffie." KD's voice was soft, plaintive. "You got to go out and see the world, all by yourself. I've never gone farther than Ann Arbor. I'm not even supposed to cross the street alone."

The complaint made the skin on Steffie's back crawl. She'd heard it all her life.

She was wrong about everything changing.

Here, nothing did.

She couldn't pay attention to that. She couldn't or she would go mad.

"Okay," Steffie said. "First things first. We see if we can find you some solutions. I know folks in companies with experimental treatments. Since we've already broken a few laws, we may break a few more and see if they'll send us some stuff that'll reverse this aging process. Then we'll find a doctor who'll work with you. We'll take it one step at a time."

"Will that work?" KD asked. Her voice was curious, but her eyes weren't. There was something in them, something Steffie didn't recognize.

She shook it off. She hadn't seen KD in a long time. How could she pretend to understand her?

"There's only one way to find out if it'll work," Steffie said.

"Are you willing to try?" KD asked.

Steffie felt it, that familiar sensation that she had just been outmaneuvered, outthought by a girl who couldn't get out of bed. But she didn't see how.

"I don't know," Steffie said.

"I won't beg," KD said.

"I'm not asking you to," Steffie said. But deep down, she almost wished KD would.

Steffie needed time to think. She let her mother serve her waffles with fresh strawberries and real butter, coffee and fresh-squeezed orange juice, just as if this were a Sunday morning and Steffie had never left home. The kitchen was still the center of the house, and on this morning, it had on electric lights against the winter gloom. The cabinets were white, done in 1990s kitsch, the stove a flattop with a conventional interior. Only the refrigerator was new: a compact model that miniaturized food and expanded it upon removal.

Steffie said nothing about her family's penchant for keeping things small.

Her father sat at the head of the table, an e-paper open but unread beside him. Her mother was still making waffles in the stove's waffle-maker attachment. Dozens of waffles for only four people.

Steffie wondered how much food her mother discarded every day.

Her father was staring at her.

Fifteen years had diminished her father. His shoulders had hunched forward, his face had gone flabby, and his crew cut was an inch long, making him look as if he wore a brush on the top of his head. The hair had gone gray, just as his skin had gone a pale white. He looked like an old man, even though he wasn't.

She found herself staring back at him, chewing as she did so. She had forgotten that cooking was one of her mother's best skills. The waffles were wonderful; it was a shame most of them would be discarded. She knew half a dozen people in the park alone who could have lived on these waffles for a week.

"You shouldn'ta left," her father said finally, his voice grating on his throat, as if he didn't want the words to come out.

She shrugged, chewed a bit more, and swallowed. "I didn't want to stay here."

"KD needed you. She loved you. You were the only one she talked to."

"Maybe she'd have more friends if you let her out of the house," Steffie snapped.

"She's too ill," her mother said.

"She wasn't fifteen years ago," Steffie said.

Her father looked down at his e-paper. Her mother poured more batter into the waffle maker. Steffie took a sip of her orange juice, her heart pounding.

She set the glass down. "Look," she said, unable to stand the silence. She had grown up in this silence. It was a powerful thing, a wall she couldn't breach. Every time she brought up a topic that was forbidden, her parents would greet that topic with silence, pretending as if she hadn't even spoken, yet making her feel guilty for opening her mouth.

"Look," she said again. "You know what KD did."

"Some of it," her mother said.

"And you knew she implicated me to do it."

"Yes." That was her mother again, in a whisper. She shot a furtive glance at her husband, but he didn't look up. He was going to ignore this conversation if he could.

"And you still sent for me?" Steffie clenched a fist. "Why don't you take care of her? Or did you want her to die?"

"She won't die," her father said.

"Oh, just like she won't grow up?" Steffie asked. "Did you arrange that too?"

"No." Her mother put her hand on her father's shoulder. He covered it with his own. Steffie had forgotten that gesture, the gesture of unity from her childhood.

"We were hoping," her mother said, and her voice broke. She swallowed to cover the emotion, and then took a deep breath. "We were hoping you could help her."

"Me?" Steffie asked. "Why me?"

"Because she won't take our help."

Steffie looked at both of them. "Why not?"

Steffie's mother bit her lower lip. "She wants to take too many risks."

Obviously, Steffie thought. But said nothing. "So you want me to take the risks with her?"

"No," her mother said. "We thought you could talk her out of them."

"Me? Why me?"

"Because you love her," her father said. "At least you did once."

"I felt sorry for her," Steffie said.

"You adored her," her mother said. "You followed her everywhere. And then when you got bigger, you carried her with you. She was your advisor, your best friend, your sister. Surely you remember."

Steffie remembered. And she remembered the late night conversations, the pounding of tiny fists against her chest, the way KD's cruel small fingers pinched Steffie's developing body, the symbol of the difference between them. She remembered it all, and the pain of it, the confusion she felt when her beloved sister had turned all her rage on Steffie because Steffie would grow up.

"I was a child," Steffie said.

"KD still is," her father said.

Steffie shook her head. "That's the thing you two never got, did you? The treatment you gave her did not leave her a child. She's an adult, but the law doesn't recognize it. Her appearance doesn't allow it. But her mind has grown, and changed, and learned. Just like yours has."

"You haven't spent these years with her," her mother said. "You don't know—"

"Of course I know," Steffie said. "It was happening even as I was growing up. It's hard when your sister, who is supposed to be a perpetual three-year-old has a better vocabulary and more knowledge of human nature than you do."

"The doctors said that would happen," her father said. "There'd be some learning, of course, but other things would always be beyond her."

"Like making a living? Like thinking for herself?"

Her mother nodded.

"How do you think she paid for the treatments?" Steffie said. "She didn't just implicate me. She broke into my systems, used my name and ID."

"There've been movies about that," her mother said. "I could do that."

"Could you fashion gamble?" Steffie asked.

"What?" her mother said.

"Fashion gamble," Steffie said. "KD made five million credits fashion gambling. That's how she planned to pay for everything. She has her own money. She wants out of here. And the only way she can get out is to grow up."

"It's too late for that now," her mother said.

Steffie sighed. Fifteen years, fifteen years of independence, of no contact with these people, and the instant she walked in the door, the old irritations returned. Her parents refusal to acknowledge what they had done to their own daughter and the consequences of it. The effect it had on the family.

The effect it had on KD.

"No," Steffie said. "It might not be too late. We have five million credits to work with and that buys a lot of treatments."

Steffie didn't tell them about her credits. She would probably need those, if she did something wrong, if she made a wrong move.

"The problem is," she continued, "that KD won't try any treatment, not as long as she stays small."

"She wouldn't be KD if she grew," her father said.

Steffie turned toward him. His head was still bent. There were dandruff flakes in his bristly hair. The food Steffie had eaten sat like a lump in her stomach.

"You would rather have KD die?" Steffie asked.

"Seems to me," her father said, "that KD will die either way."

"Childhood was never meant to be permanent," Steffie said. "*Nothing* in this world is meant to be permanent."

Her father did not answer. He drew his silence around him like a blanket, a shield against Steffie's words.

"You can help her, then," her mother said, ignoring the interchange. "You know what to do."

"I can try," Steffie said, regretting the words the instant that she spoke them. "But you'll have to help me in return."

"Anything," her mother said.

"I won't even do anything until you agree to let KD grow up."

"No," her father said.

Her mother squeezed her father's shoulder. Steffie saw him wince in pain. "Whatever it takes," her mother said. "Whatever it takes."

Her parents' computer was in the den. Her mother hovered behind her as she went inside, and faced a machine the size of a mirror, an antique she remembered from her childhood. She wondered if this was the machine KD had used to track her coolhunting, to make her five million credits, to gamble on fashion. She hadn't seen anything in KD's room, but that meant nothing. Computers could be small as a fingernail these days. Steffie had even coolhunted a couple of full body interfaces and tiny tattoos that were full performance machines. The craze had lasted ten days, one of her longest and best.

"Codes and passwords?" Steffie asked as she put her hand on the leather chair. It felt the same, cool to the touch, the leather softened with age.

"They're programmed in."

Steffie wanted to warn her, to say that such things were irresponsible. But when had her parents been sensible or responsible? They had only appeared so. And appearances were so important to them all.

"Scans?" Steffie asked.

"Retinal, palm, full face for some things," her mother said.

Steffie sighed. She could go around the scans, but she didn't want to. She didn't know who was monitoring the house, if anyone, but she didn't want to do anything too suspicious. Looking for a cure for KD was probably unusual enough, but easily explainable. Going around security systems, well, that was a felony, and one they would most certainly blame on her.

"Okay," Steffie said, not sitting down. "Get me on."

Her mother glanced at her, then went to the chair. It sagged under her weight. She put her hands on the keyboard, typing in codes. "What system?" her mother asked.

"Excuse me?" Steffie said.

"What net do you want?" Her mother asked, clarifying the question.

"Anything," Steffie said. She wasn't going to search for research—her family could do that—she was going to hunt. What she did best. Only she had never done it this way. "On second thought, go to one of the difficult ones. Better to have too much security than not enough."

Her mother typed. The machine was old enough to have a clicking keyboard, something that sounded grated on Steffie. She preferred silence, required silence in fact when she typed anything. If she had to have sound, she used a voice-activated system.

Then her mother eased out of the chair. The ancient monitor blurred a tunnel that should have been an automatic VR view. Steffie sat down. The chair was warm from her mother.

"Thanks," Steffie said, and began to work.

The medical boards were encoded and filled with garbage: people discussing their symptoms, asking for help with common problems, debating the financial practicalities of curing old age. The fundamental arguments, the ones she had heard all her life. Only she had known, as did anyone with a brain, that if they could create children like KD, they could stop people from dying. They could arrest them at any age—thirty-five, fifty, it didn't matter—but they refused because of the burden it would place on society.

Funny how perpetual children were not a burden when older, more experienced people were.

Hunting in here was not like walking the streets. It was more complex. But like streets, the attention to detail was the same. She wasn't looking for a paper on KD's arrested development or on growth hormones. Steffie was searching chat areas, listening to live conversations while she was digging through the research boards.

Listening for that single comment, looking for the silence that implied more knowledge than the user was willing to admit to. Whenever she found a name, she cross-referenced it with the Copyright Office's annual publication of the names of people who applied for patents.

By evening she had a headache, and her eyes ached from looking at material designed for systems that lasted hours instead of years. Her mother, who had apparently left the room sometime that morning, brought in three sandwiches, some homemade potato chips, and a mochachino, something that no one had made in so many years the taste actually invoked childhood—a small dinner party where Steffie at age three, the only time she was KD's contemporary, got to taste her first caffeinated beverage.

And hated it.

She smiled at the memory, took a sandwich, and felt her mouth water at the prospect of eating choice-cut beef. Her parents had never skimped on food. They had skimped on other things, but never food.

Her mother returned some time later to take the plate.

"Steffie," she said softly.

Her voice sounded like an explosion in the tight room. Steffie, who'd been following two chats and cross-reading patents, listening to on-line medical radio, and searching the drug listings, jumped.

"KD?" she asked.

"No change," her mother said. "How are you doing?

"Fine," Steffie said, in a tone that brooked no more interruption.

Her mother watched her for a moment. When it became clear that Steffie wasn't going to say anything more, her mother took the empty mochachino glass, and left the sandwiches. Steffie grabbed another as she returned her attention to her work.

Twelve non-stop hours later, she had learned a lot of things, some she didn't want to know. Not surprisingly, but something she had not thought of, was that KD was not alone. Large groups of "children" haunted net space, some in groups, some individually. Most were using their parents' systems illegally, using illegal identities, and playing the same tricks KD had.

Steffie wondered how much of this KD knew, and how much she had used before she got ill.

Or even if some of these groups had helped her take Steffie's identity, helped her find the doctor who had been willing to work on her without a certified adult present.

But all of those were questions for later, questions Steffie might never get answered. And although they were irritating, they weren't really relevant.

Not considering what else she found.

Ninety-seven patents had been issued to help the "children" grow. Another fifty-two had been issued to cope with diseases of the non-aging, and twenty-five had been issued to deal with the effects of growth hormones on the early adapters.

Twenty-five.

And of those twenty-five, twenty had received permission to do experiments on humans.

Of those twenty, ten had completed the studies.

Of those ten, only one had "children" who survived.

Only one.

At that point, Steffie had stopped and put her face in her hands. His treatment had been effective, but it had done something the parents opposed, and they had shut him down.

It had left the growth hormones intact.

The early adaptive child had arrived at his office, sickly on the edge of death, just like KD, and had left a full adult, with years ahead of them. The legal problems had been startling. The new adults had no legal standing since they were registered as permanent children, and their parents, who had uniformly not approved the treatment (the "children" had gotten it as they had gotten the growth hormones, through theft of adult documentation), had sued.

The doctor was no longer practicing. His bio said that he worked in the CUNY system as a biology teacher, and saw no one.

Especially not people like KD.

It seemed a bit too pat.

Steffie ate the last sandwich, and stared at the screen. Her eyes hurt, her head ached, and her shoulders were so tight that she pulled a muscle.

The sandwich was stale, the bread hardened by its exposure to air.

Her father would never approve. He would rather have KD die. Steffie closed her eyes.

KD, of course, would be excited about it.

Her mother would not take a stand, and Steffie would be in the middle, as always.

And that was assuming the doctor would work with them, that he would give up his safe little job in the CUNY system, and break the law to help KD.

Why had Steffie come back here?

Why did she think she could save her sister's life?

She had never been able to before.

The house was asleep when she finally stood up. She stretched and her spine cracked. It had been a long time since she spent a day in a chair, not moving. Usually she was always on the move, always doing something different, always finding a way to keep herself busy, to be creative

But not to think.

Never to think.

Or remember.

She remembered so much about this house. She remembered its rhythms, the silent hush it got when all the occupants but her were sleeping. She remembered the way the ceiling groaned in a harsh wind, the soft spot in the center of the fifth stair up, the wobbly spindle near the top of the banister.

And most of all, she remembered KD.

—You gotta help me. You're bigger. You could take me on the shuttle—

—I'm not old enough.

—They won't have to know. And then when I'm on my own, I'll find a way to repay you.

—You can't be on your own, KD.

—Then you can live with me. You'll be my adult. Only you won't have to supervise me because I won't need it. You'll do that, won't you, Stef? Think of all the times I helped you . . .

And most of all, she remembered the night she ran away. KD was still an accepted oddity, then. A member of an elite group, a prized possession, a status symbol not unlike expensive jewels or a house in the country. KD had given one of her best performances at dinner: a combination of precocious intelligence, and nauseating cuteness. She had conversed with the visiting German professor in his own language about the upcoming celebration of thirty years of his country's unity, and then, by request, she had lisped her way through a lullaby. She had cuddled on command with their father's boss, a childless woman who always treated KD like a stray animal, and then she had graciously accepted the small gifts of toys some of her parents' regular visitors had brought.

The toys got tossed into the corner of her room, and she had run to Steffie's, sobbing in her arms. Steffie had held her, understanding KD's humiliation for the first time, and the futility of it all.

And she had confronted their parents like she would have to confront them now, and they had told her she would never understand.

Never.

They were right.

Oh, she knew the history, but it never made sense to her. They had lost their first child, a girl, of some sudden onset disease that she should have been inoculated for, but somehow wasn't. (They always skipped over this part, as if it were someone else's fault, not their own.) By then, they had already had KD. Shortly after their first child died, they decided to prevent KD's loss. They decided to have a child forever, so they not only inoculated her against all childhood diseases, they also inoculated her against adulthood.

And the treatment had been so awful, they decided not to do it to the rest of their children. But KD had given them courage to have other children. She had given them their life back.

So they used to say, back when KD was their status symbol, their performing monkey.

Before society decided what they did was no longer fashionable, and just a little bit wrong.

By the time Steffie finished the sandwich, she knew what she had to do. She couldn't run this time. She had chosen to come back on her own. She had chosen to face the heartache, to see KD this last time. And in seeing her sister, in seeing what she had become, what she had done to herself just to try to have a normal life, Steffie could no longer leave.

KD deserved the chance to live her life, any life, on her own terms. Not on her parents' terms. Not on Steffie's.

On her own.

In her searches, Steffie had found the exact costs of the doctor's legal bills, and the extent of his garnishment at CUNY. He had never made much money. He had done this for a reason not covered in the gossip trades, a reason known only to him. But he was in deep and severe debt, and he could no longer practice his real trade. He had taken the job at CUNY out of desperation, wasting his talents teaching children for less than one-fiftieth of what he made before.

It bothered her that the information had been easy to find. It made her leery. But not leery enough to ignore him.

She offered to pay his legal bills, current and future, if he promised to treat KD. She sent this to him in encrypted e-mail, routed through half a dozen sources, and out of one of her dormant names.

Traceable, she supposed, but she doubted it. The amount of work would keep him busy for the next two weeks.

And that was if he were an expert in computers, which he clearly was not.

His response was startlingly immediate.

He accepted.

Some things became clear. The doctor was not what he seemed. The credits he wanted were too high; the address he gave was far from CUNY, and he offered to provide the adult KD with proper identification.

Steffie accepted it all. She had worked the seamier sides of the street too long to be shocked at the lengths people went to in order to get their work done.

Maybe her parents would have been shocked.

Maybe KD would have.

But Steffie knew:

Sometimes you had to do whatever it took.

Her parents no longer slept in the same room. That was a change, and one Steffie had not expected. Her mother had taken the twins' room for herself. Only one bed remained, and a few of the twins' things, but her mother's presence there did not look temporary. Her books were piled on the nightstand, her clothing littered the floor. A small entertainment unit with everything from computer remote to VR to good old-fashioned television was hooked to the foot of the bed.

The faint nightlight, a glass ball that had a phosphorescent glow, which Steffie had always associated with her parents' room, was on the dresser.

Steffie had stumbled into this room by accident, looking for her old penlight to carry into her parents' bedroom, not expecting her mother to be inside.

Her mother slept on her back with one arm flung above her head. She looked younger than Steffie had ever seen her—a combination of the soft light and the relaxation of sleep. Steffie saw herself in her mother's features, the long narrow face, the small mouth. She saw KD too, the promise of what KD would be.

Would have been.

Steffie went to her mother's side, crouched, and touched her mother's shoulder. When she didn't wake, Steffie's heart started to pound. She knew her mother was all right; she could hear the rhythmic breathing. But she wondered if her mother had taken anything to help her sleep, and felt the old frustration rise even though she didn't yet have proof.

The impracticality of it. A sick child—a sick person—Steffie still had to mentally correct herself, and she hated it—in the house, and her mother took some kind of chemical to help her sleep.

Steffie shook her mother's shoulder harder than she initially intended. Her mother's eyes blinked, and her eyebrows came together in a frown.

"Stephanie?" Her mother's voice was slurred with sleep.

"Wake up, Mother, I need to talk to you," Steffie said.

"KD. Is she—?"

"I haven't been in her room yet. I've come to see you."

Her mother was waking up more completely now. She slid back toward the pillows and pushed her hair out of her face. "You found something," she said in a normal voice.

"Yes," Steffie said. "A doctor who knows how to help KD."

"How much will it cost?"

More than Dad wants to pay, Steffie nearly answered, but decided at that moment not to say anything. "I'll worry about the cost."

"She's still our responsibility," her mother said.

Steffie shook her head. "You involved me."

"We'll take care of it," her mother said.

"No." Steffie was adamant. Her mother looked confused. Steffie wasn't about to admit the real reason for her generosity.

She didn't want her parents to interfere.

When it became clear that her mother would not accept Steffie's argument, Steffie said simply, "I guess I owe her for running away."

Her mother said nothing to that. She adjusted the blankets, then reached over and clicked on the bedside light. Steffie blinked at the sudden brightness.

"What do we do?" her mother asked.

"We get her out of here," Steffie said.

Her mother stared at her. "I'd like to take her."

"And what will you tell Dad?"

Her mother looked away.

"What is it?" Steffie asked. "Why is he so unwilling to let her grow up?"

"I don't know," her mother whispered. But Steffie could tell she lied.

After she left her mother's room, Steffie stood in the hallway for a moment. If she was going to back out, this was her only chance. Her only chance to escape the house, and never be seen again.

But KD's skeletal face would haunt her. KD's voice had, over the years, bemoaned Steffie's freedom, Steffie's size, Steffie's life. Steffie didn't sleep much as it was. She wouldn't be able to sleep at all if she abandoned KD now.

She opened the door to KD's room—and thought for a moment that KD had given her a reprieve.

The silence was odd. And almost terrifying. Then KD took a loud shuddery breath, and Steffie realized that her sister was still alive.

Steffie sat on the bed and touched KD's shoulder, much as she had touched her mother's.

KD's eyes opened immediately. "I thought you'd be gone," she said.

"I found someone to help you," Steffie said, a bit more rigidly than she had planned.

"Dr. Doom?" Then when Steffie frowned, KD added, "The guy who holds the patent?"

"You knew about him?"

"Sure. I know my way around the boards."

Steffie felt a trembling deep inside. Nothing changed. KD was playing her again, touching her sympathies and then throwing them back in her face.

"I spent hours searching for him," Steffie said, wondering how she managed to keep her voice so soft when all she wanted to do was scream at KD.

"Took me three days," KD said. "You are better than me."

"You could have saved me the time," Steffie said, "and just told me about him."

"Wouldn'ta worked," KD said. "You never believe anything you don't find on your own."

There was too much truth in that statement.

"We have a date to meet him," Steffie said. "And a place. Are you willing to go through with this?"

"I won't do it," KD said, "Unless it allows me to grow."

"It's one of the side effects," Steffie said. "But you already knew that."

KD smiled. "I already knew that."

"That's why you brought me here. Not to inform me of anything, but to take you to this man."

"Yes," KD said.

"Why? Mom would have taken you."

"No, she wouldn't," KD said. "I'm all she has left."

Steffie felt the world spin into place. She had left, run away. Her brothers and Lana were gone, too. Steffie had noted, on that family page, that none of them had been home in years either. Her parents' children grew up and away, and didn't just leave the nest.

They had abandoned it.

KD couldn't, not legally and not physically.

"I asked Mom to help me smuggle you out of here. Was that wrong?"

KD shook her head. "Unlike Dad, Mom still has a sense of what's right. She only acts on it when pushed, but she can be pushed."

Somehow that didn't reassure Steffie. "How do I push her?"

KD smiled. "I think you already did."

Steffie snuck around the house, preparing for the trip. The first shuttle didn't leave until 6 A.M. She couldn't sleep, so she went through her own closet with an eye for cool. Most of the clothes brought back memories: the blue and white dress with the sailor collar that she had bought with her own money; the silk sweater that had been too hot for her first date; a pair of Levi's, true Levi's, that dated from the mid-1950s and were worth their weight in gold. She wondered how many other treasures she'd find in this house, old once-fashionable things that had been out of style so long that they had become valuable antiques.

Probably nothing from the modern era would become an antique. Fashion came and went too quickly. It didn't have time to linger; the word antique was slowly beginning to mean something over a month old.

She chose an outfit from her closet to wear back to New York. The top was a pale peach tent shirt with a faux paisley pattern; the bottoms were a pair of brown gauze pants. She kept her boots—she couldn't walk far without them—but she tossed a pair of sandals into her stuff for safe keeping. She grabbed an old shoulder pouch, filled it, and slipped it over one arm. Then she pinned her hair on both sides of her head with matching ribbon barrettes.

For a day, at least, she wouldn't be Steffie Storm-Warning. She'd be KD's sister and the responsible adult for an important operation.

All they had to do was get out of the house before her father woke up.

Steffie had asked KD why their father didn't want her to change, didn't want her to grow. Their father, more than their mother. And KD had looked at her with those old, old eyes in that still-young face: *Don't you see what a failure he is? I remind him of the days when the world still had possibilities.*

Steffie had been thinking about that statement since she had come to her old room. It rang something within her; it made an emotional kind of sense. It was hard for her to think of her father as a failure: he had a job, he had this wonderful home, and he had a family. But his job was inherited, a tenured position he had taken from his father at the University of Michigan. The house was inherited too, and paid for. It had never cost their family a dime to live inside. Her parents hadn't remodeled. They hadn't even bought new furniture, except for the children's rooms.

The only thing they had spent money on was KD and she had been a victory for a time. A fashionable statement, a symbol of wealth and power—look! we can stop time!—and a luxury.

But it got him nothing except a bitter woman in a child's body, a woman tied to him and his inadequate life forever. His family was in ruins: his wife no longer slept with him, his second oldest daughter had run away the night before she graduated from high school, and the remaining children were gone, never to return.

When he died what would he have to show for his life but KD? She was the only stable thing in it.

KD, the house, and the job.

Only KD was his own.

His very own.

Steffie stood. She didn't know what it felt like to have something of her own. She flopped, bought clothes when she needed them, and discarded them when she was done. The only things she owned were her names, her accounts, and her contacts.

Her brains.

And her eye.

Nothing else.

It was strange to return to this place of history and see clothes so old that she could remember the first time she wore them, remember being fourteen and full of hope.

Even then she had sensed her parents' bitterness. Both of them, bitter at growing older, at living their lives like their parents had, at not stepping out of the confines of this simple house.

Much like KD.

Did their father want KD to be stuck here because he was?

She glanced at the room with its off-white walls and familiar cracks. She couldn't imagine what the last fifteen years would have been like here, staying through the harsh winter, seeing the same people.

Watching KD remain the same.

Day after day after day.

Time passed and no one noticed.

No one noticed at all.

Steffie made her way down the stairs like she had as a teenager on that last night, walking along the wooden sides, avoiding the creaks. Her mother sat at the base of the steps, cradling KD in a blanket. KD was too large for her mother. Large and heavy, like any three-year-old. Big enough to walk on her own.

But KD could no longer do that.

For the first time, Steffie saw fear in her mother's eyes.

"She'd found this guy on her own," Steffie whispered.

"Stop," KD said.

"KD?" Her mother's voice held very real pain. "Is this true?"

Over the edge of her blanket, KD shot Steffie a killing look. "Yes," KD said.

"Why didn't you tell me? I'd have taken you. We wouldn't've had to wait."

Steffie's mouth opened slightly. She hadn't expected this, her mother willing to do anything, even something vaguely illegal, to keep KD alive.

"Shh," KD said. "Dad will hear you."

But Steffie understood now. KD was using their father as a way not to answer the question. "Why did you wait?" Steffie asked.

KD closed her eyes. "You wouldn't have taken me, Mom. Dad would have stopped you."

Her mother put her head against KD's. "I want you to live."

"I know," KD said, in a resigned voice. "You want me to stay the same."

"Is that so wrong?" her mother asked.

KD didn't answer. Steffie couldn't. She cleared her throat.

"Do you want to call this off?" Steffie asked, her mouth suddenly dry, not knowing if she was addressing the question to her mother or her sister.

KD's eyes opened, large circles on her tiny face. "This is my only chance, Steffie," she said.

Steffie knew that. Their mother cradled KD closer. "We don't have much time," she said. "Your father will be down shortly after sun-up, wanting his coffee."

Like he had ever since Steffie could remember.

"All right," Steffie said, the knot in her stomach growing. "Let's go."

The family had bought their car before Steffie had been born. It was an old gas model, its combustion system redesigned in the mid-aughts to accommodate new fuel regulations. Steffie's parents had kept the car in pristine condition; like KD its value came in preserving its appearance.

Steffie's mother handed KD to Steffie, and climbed in the driver's seat. KD was heavier than Steffie expected, all dead weight and rubbery skin. No natural skin felt that way, as if it were made of stuffed plastic, but then nothing about KD was natural.

Steffie slipped into the passenger side, unwilling to put her sister in the special seat in the back. KD was so weak she could no longer sit on her own. No sense in even trying.

The drive to the shuttle stop on the quad would be short. But not as short as the shuttle ride itself. KD closed her eyes. Her face looked drawn. It had that translucent quality that Steffie had only seen before in the homeless who slept in the park.

The ones who were about to die.

Steffie shuddered. What had she gotten herself into? She felt absurdly guilty, found herself thinking if she had been more accessible, then her family would have found her sooner and she would have arrived before KD got so sick.

But much of KD's illness, all of it in fact, had been caused by KD. KD and her desire to be like everyone else. When she could never ever be.

Steffie looked down to see KD staring at her. KD smiled weakly. Steffie made herself smile back, even though she didn't want to. Even though she felt trapped, alone, and completely out of her depth.

Her mother backed the car up and drove the few short blocks to the university. The three of them traveled in silence. Amazing how, after being family, after not seeing each other, after facing such a crisis, they still had nothing to say to one another. Since she returned they had never once asked Steffie about the particulars of her work, or even if she enjoyed her job. They didn't ask where she lived, if she had a lover, if she had children.

Everything was lost in the focus on KD.

As usual.

Her mother pulled the car into the shuttle parking area. The shuttle was already on the ground, perched like a black bird in the quad, barely visible through the gap between the forty-year-old dorms. When the designers of the college residential area had designed the space, they hadn't realized that all of the pleasant, green, parklike land would eventually be multi-purposed: shuttle landing spots, aircar maneuvers, and regularly scheduled volleyball games between the students.

KD pushed herself up on her thin arms and stared at the shuttle. She coughed once, and swallowed hard, but not before Steffie saw blood.

"Looks like it's ready," their mother said.

Steffie looked at the new reddish tint to KD's lips. "You know," she said to her mother, "that there are no guarantees."

"I know," her mother said. She ran a hand over KD's thinning hair. "I'll miss you, baby."

"She means I might die, Mom," KD said. "She doesn't want you to blame her."

Their mother looked at Steffie over KD's head. It was too late: they already blamed her. They blamed her for leaving, for growing up, for being a different person from them. Her parents had kept KD the way they wanted her, and they couldn't do that with their other children.

Now Steffie was taking KD away.

Maybe forever.

"You could come with us, Mom," Steffie said. "You might get back before Dad even knows you're gone."

Her mother shook her head.

"KD could use the support."

"I don't need it," KD said. "This is an adventure."

"You go," her mother said. "Do what you can." Then she kissed KD on the top of the head, and pushed Steffie's arm. Away from her. Get out of the car, the movement said. There was no affection, no attempt at it.

Steffie got out, cradling KD.

"KD," their mother said, and there was desperation in her voice. "I love you."

KD sighed silently. Steffie felt her body move. "I love you too, Mom," KD said, her words sweet, her tone in complete contradiction to the sudden tension in her body. "Thanks for bringing us here."

"We're going to miss the shuttle," Steffie said.

"Send us news," their mother said.

Steffie nodded and headed for the shuttle. She mounted the small ramp, punched her ticket code, and climbed inside without turning to wave at their mother. Steffie didn't want another look at her, or at the quad, or at Ann Arbor itself.

This time, as in the time before, she hoped she would never have to go back. If this treatment worked, KD could come home on her own.

If she chose to come home at all.

This shuttle had twenty-five seats and all but two were full. New York was still a business hub, although not as important as it had once been, and more people were willing to take five minutes out of their day to head there first thing in the morning.

Steffie kept KD's head covered in the blanket, not wanting people to gawk at her older sister. Not wanting people to remember them.

Or her.

She slipped into one of the empty seats, only to have KD croak, "Window."

Steffie sighed and moved to the other seat. "You can't really see out of these things," she said. "They're only for being on the ground."

"Don't tell me any more," KD said. She eased out of the blanket, letting it fall aside, and peered out the window, looking, for the first time since Steffie returned, like the little girl she was meant to be. "You know all this stuff. I want to discover it."

The words were strong, but the voice wasn't. Steffie wondered how much the trip had already taken out of KD, and how much more there was to take.

One more passenger arrived and took the last vacant seat. Then the automatic straps buckled them all into place, including KD, holding her against Steffie's chest. They took off.

Steffie closed her eyes, but she didn't really doze. Five minutes wasn't long enough for an effective nap. Besides, it was hard with KD squirming on her lap, trying to see everything, trying to memorize everything, not afraid to show her complete and total awe at her surroundings.

Steffie had never shown such awe, not even on her first shuttle ride. In those days, it had been too important for her to keep her own aura of cool, not to let anyone know that she was interested in something, frightened of something, enjoying something.

KD had no sense of propriety, no sense of how she appeared in public.

Steffie guessed it didn't matter. People perceived KD as a child. She could get away with anything.

Except the things she wanted to get away with.

The shuttle landed on its own pad on top of Grand Central Station. Steffie cursed silently. She had forgotten to ask for a specific landing point, one closer to the address the doctor had given her. The restraints came off, and KD still leaned against her.

"Wow," KD whispered. "We're here?"

"Yes," Steffie said. She'd need another aircab, and she'd have to decide how close she wanted to be let off. She couldn't submit KD to too much of New York. It was difficult for those with strong constitutions.

KD didn't have much strength left.

Steffie waited until the other passengers got off the shuttle, then she carried KD out. KD's blanket trailed slightly, and KD had her arms around Steffie's neck. Her eyes were too bright, her cheeks had an unnatural flush, and she was looking around as if she had been invited to heaven and was being given a tour by God himself.

The landing platform was hot. Two more shuttles, probably the L.A. and Dallas ones, were resting nearby, passengers disembarking. A man, slender and tan, glanced at Steffie and smiled.

She did not smile back.

The crowd made her nervous. She didn't know how to be

around a crowd when she wasn't coolhunting, when she wasn't working. She cradled KD close, and made her way to the aircab stand.

Five men in business suits complete with pocket watch/computer/phone attached to their ample waists waited at the stand. Three women in platforms two feet high, and an elderly person whose gender Steffie couldn't identify also waited. A woman in an official green uniform used a soundless whistle to summon the taxis.

If Steffie didn't gain her sympathy, they'd waste ten minutes here.

She approached cautiously, then pulled the blanket down from KD's head. "Ma'am," Steffie said, doing her best to sound like she still was from Michigan. "My daughter—"

"Get in line!"

"Who do ya think you are?"

"We were here first!"

The shouts came from behind her. She knew then that she had a chance. Those people would not have yelled if they didn't already feel as if they had lost a position in line.

"My daughter is ill," Steffie said. "I'm trying to get her to a specialist."

The woman looked at both of them. KD was obviously ill. Steffie could see that reflected in the woman's eyes. "Shoulda told the shuttle to set you close."

"I didn't know you could," Steffie said.

The woman shook her head. Then she whistled for an aircab, held one of the large men back, and let Steffie and KD slide in.

"Thanks," KD said, voice a rasp.

"Get better," the woman said and signaled the taxi to move with her arm.

Steffie leaned back in the seat then gave the driver an address on the Lower East Side. He circled Grand Central and then took off as if an entire raft of police were after him.

KD watched from the comfort of Steffie's arms. "Is it always like this?" she asked.

"No," Steffie said. "Usually people aren't that friendly."

Then she realized that she didn't have to lie to KD. KD would never return here. She would never be a tourist alone on these mean streets. KD could know that New Yorkers generally were friendly. The problem was that you sometimes couldn't tell the friendly ones from the unfriendly ones.

"There's no trees," KD said.

"We're going the wrong way for trees." Steffie cradled her sister close. She had never expected KD here. Suddenly she felt as if KD were a three-year-old child, subject to all the horrors the city could present.

"And it's old. Those buildings are older than the ones in Ann Arbor."

"Dirtier," Steffie said.

Her responses didn't diminish KD's enthusiasm. "I've never been in an aircab before."

Or on a shuttle.

Or in a state outside of Michigan.

Or in a city that was a world unto itself.

KD had never had sex, never held a job, never fallen in love. KD hadn't lived a life at all.

And she was dying.

"Why do they call him Doctor Doom?" Steffie asked, afraid of the answer.

For the first time, KD took her eyes off the city. She looked at Steffie, and Steffie got a hint of what KD in an adult's body would look like. Beautiful, menacing, intimidating as hell.

"Because," KD said. "No one ever comes back."

Steffie's stomach flopped. She was taking her sister to meet death. KD had known it all along.

"I can't do this," Steffie said.

"Sure you can," KD said. "He doesn't always kill people. A lot of them never return to their parents because they're cured. And big. They can have their own lives."

"I'm not liking what I hear," Steffie said.

"It's not your choice," KD said. But there was a bravado in her voice. It was Steffie's choice. She was the legal adult even though she was the younger of the two. It was a fiction between them that KD had any control at all.

"You don't care what he does to you?" Steffie asked.

KD leaned against her. She was tiring visibly, the pallor of her skin growing. "I care," KD said. "I care very much."

The address Dr. Doom had given her was on one of those narrow sidestreets with so many rules about aircabs that most avoided the place. The driver let them off on a corner, and Steffie walked the rest of the way.

KD was too tired to move. Once Steffie looked down at her, and KD had smiled weakly, but she had said nothing. When they reached the address, a man came out a steel doorway. He stopped in the middle of the sidewalk, and his gaze met Steffie's.

He seemed to know who they were, but then, how could he miss? How many other women walked through this part of the city with a three-year-old child—or someone who looked like one—in their arms?

"You're going to go through with this?" he asked, and he sounded almost disappointed.

"Yes," Steffie said.

He sighed and went to the door. "I am no miracle worker," he said. He was looking at KD.

"They call you Doctor Doom," she said hoarsely.

For the first time, he smiled. It made him look younger, in his mid-forties, a cascade of laugh lines forming on his careworn face. "They do," he said. "And they are right."

The front of his rented space served as a reception area. From the makeshift kitchen in the corner and the ratty look of the couch, Steffie suspected it also doubled as his home. He never did give them his real name, although Steffie knew it. Instead, he led her to the back room, which looked shinier, newer, and cleaner than any hospital she had ever been in.

Now the doubts she had felt when she discovered him made sense. That had only been his screen persona, designed to scare away those who were not serious. This was not a man who taught at CUNY, who had exorbitant legal bills. This was a man who made a living off people like KD.

"The authorities know about me," he said. "They will have your e-mail by now."

"Then why don't they come for you?"

He smiled again. "They tried. But there is no law yet against saving lives, now is there? Only a lack of courage on the part of the government and the normal facilities."

"Do you save lives?" Steffie asked.

"Sometimes," he said. A man came out of a side room that Steffie hadn't even realized was there. This man was slender and younger than Steffie. He took KD from her, and placed her on a steel table in the center of the room.

"There are no legal bills, are there?" Steffie asked.

Dr. Doom smiled at her. "There are always legal bills," he said.

She no longer wanted to leave KD there. She no longer trusted him with KD, if she ever had.

KD was scanning the room, her small head turning.

"This is a mistake," Steffie said to her.

KD eased up on her elbows. The whites of her eyes were a dull yellow, and the blood was back in the corner of her mouth. "It's a chance, Steffie," she said. And then, with a last burst of strength, she added, "It's my choice."

Her choice.

Steffie crossed her arms. KD was right, no matter what the law said. It was her choice. And she had stated it over and over. If she had to remain the way she was, she wanted to die. If there was no chance of change, there would be no survival.

"Can you help her?" Steffie asked.

Dr. Doom looked at her. His mouth was a thin line, his eyes wide. He did not have the blustery confidence that most doctors had.

"We can only try," he said.

During the operation, she went outside. The day was sunny with a hint of muggy; the city smelled of garbage as it always did.

She was surprised to realize that she had missed it.

Spring was in full swing. Soon it would be summer.

Summer was her best time of year.

She sat down on a stoop at a nearby building, and brought her knees up to her chest. She wrapped her arms around them, trying to seek comfort from herself. What would she do with KD? If KD died, then Steffie'd have to take the body back to Ann Arbor, and admit to her parents that she had failed. She knew her mother would be upset, but she wasn't certain about her father. He hadn't wanted an adult KD, and he had already resigned himself to her death. He might simply accept it as a matter of course.

No. That seemed straightforward. It was what she would do if KD lived that bothered her.

Steffie had no apartment, and her job required her to move around a lot. To constantly be in a different place at a different time. She had enough credits stored away that she could quit working altogether, but what was the point of that? Although she might have to, if she were responsible for KD.

At least Dr. Doom had guaranteed identification along with the successful surgery. That way, Steffie wouldn't have to brave the underground bureaucracy for her sister. All she had to concentrate on was teaching KD how to live in the real world.

It would fall to her. Her parents would never do the job. They might even try to keep the adult KD as imprisoned in their home as they had the child.

Steffie would have to warn KD of that.

Steffie brushed a strand of hair out of her face. She no longer felt clean from that shower she'd had at her parents' home. That was one disadvantage of flopping. She allowed herself to look as if she had been sleeping on the street more often than not.

And sometimes she did.

Maybe KD would help her settle down. Maybe KD would slow her down. It wouldn't hurt. She was, she had to admit, lonelier than she had expected in this life on the road.

Going back home had shown her that.

A man passed her wearing tight black leather pants with their ankles tucked inside cowboy boots, a muscle t-shirt and a derby. She had her palmtop open before she knew it and was recording. It didn't hurt to work. Not while she was waiting.

Not when Dr. Doom said it could take all day.

After she paid the dapper cowboy, she watched the street. It had been weeks since she'd been this far east in Manhattan. Fresh pickings of a kind she hadn't seen in a while. Fresh and bright. Something was changing here—an influx from somewhere, bringing, as they always did, new trends, new innovators, new ways to be original.

With Steffie around, they wouldn't be original for long.

She saw and rejected a woman with long green hair and a yellow rain slicker tied over her breasts, her tattooed stomach bare, and her hips barely covered in a matching yellow skirt. She hesitated over a man in the traditional garb of Scotland, complete with kilt. She had never seen such a thing outside of history shots. But it was too by-the-book, and that made it retro but unoriginal. Real retro took the style and updated it to the moment.

She had just finished catching her second big strike—a woman in white satin, a simple flowing dress that flared at the hips and crossed over her breasts. The back was cut all the way down to her buttocks, and in her hair she wore a matching white ribbon. The look was cool, casual, and completely unself-conscious—when Dr. Doom opened his door.

Actually, Dr. Doom didn't. His assistant did. He saw her flip a plastic at the satin woman, and looked away as if he had witnessed a drug deal.

"We're ready for you," he said.

* * *

The lights were still bright in that sterile room, but the smell was different. The air was fresher as if each molecule had been personally scrubbed. A woman lay on the makeshift bed, a sheet pulled up to her chin. She was as tall as Steffie, and nearly as thin.

The assistant put his hand on her shoulder. "Don't be shocked," he said.

How could Steffie be shocked? The operation was successful. Her older sister looked older, for the first time since Steffie turned three.

Steffie walked up to KD and paused, her heart making a sudden lurch. This was what he was talking about. Not KD's size, but her face.

The skin was lumpy and mottled, broken as if it had tried to go through puberty in the space of a single afternoon. Which, she supposed, it had. KD's nose was truncated, her eyes suddenly small and piggy. Lines formed around her mouth, making it look sad and sour.

She was asleep.

Mercifully.

She didn't have to see Steffie's reaction.

"It's a side effect." The voice belonged to Dr. Doom. She hadn't seen him when she had come in, but he had been there, against the wall, gauging her reaction. "The problem is all her organs look like that. The damage is as obvious and as hard to repair."

"This is why the government shut you down," Steffie whispered.

"Yes," he said. "I can keep them alive, I can make them grow up, but I can't make them pretty. And people who do this to their kids expect pretty."

"How long does she have?" Steffie whispered.

"Years," he said. "And then, one day, something will shut down. But it was bound to happen. Her life span was truncated the moment she took those hormones."

Steffie was shaking. She sat on the bed, and took KD's hand. It was long and slender, the fingers curved inward, just like Steffie's. Only unlike Steffie's the skin on KD's hands was red and cracked, angry-looking, as if she'd kept them in hot water for days.

"She looks like this all over?" Steffie asked.

"Yes," he said.

Her mouth was dry. He was trying to extort more money from her.

It was working.

"Plastic surgery—"

"Isn't an option. The damage is cellular, and skin sloughs off, regrowing itself, regrowing the damage."

"But you work on the cellular level," Steffie said.

"And this is the best I've been able to do." His eyes were intense in his hangdog face. "I wouldn't leave her like this if I had a choice. Believe me."

"She's not going to be happy," Steffie said softly.

"She's alive," Dr. Doom said. "She's an adult. She'll be happy."

Steffie clutched her sister's hand tightly in her own. "I hope you're right," she said.

The assistant gave her a blanket and a pillow, and rolled out a small cot for her. Steffie spent the night on it, her sleep shallow, any little noise waking her up. She kept expecting KD to return to consciousness, but she didn't. She had a lot to recover from, Dr. Doom explained, and she needed the rest.

He could have awakened KD at any point that night or the following day, but he did not. He let her sleep. He let her heal. Steffie had no choice but to sleep, and to brood.

She didn't want to leave KD's side, didn't want her sister—her frail older sister—to awaken alone and frightened. Steffie kept telling herself she would do this for anyone, but she knew the very thought was a lie.

She wouldn't do this for anyone.

She was surprising herself by doing it for KD. She didn't know if it was residual guilt, or if there was actually affection buried beneath all the anger, all the hurt, all the past.

When she did sleep, though, she dreamed of KD the little girl, when KD had truly been a little girl, and remembered all the times they laughed, all the days they huddled in each other's rooms, playing and enjoying each other's company.

Before Steffie got bigger. And KD didn't.

Now KD was big, but still flawed, and perhaps that was the other reason Steffie stayed. KD had hoped for a normal life.

And she would never have one.

On the morning of the second day, KD stirred. Steffie climbed off her cot and went to KD's side, suddenly conscious of the fact that she hadn't showered or changed clothes since she brought KD in.

KD's eyes fluttered, and a door opened beside her. Dr. Doom entered. He had probably been monitoring her from his private room.

KD's eyes opened. She looked at Dr. Doom, then at Steffie. "It worked?" she whispered. Her voice was a raspy croak but it was a deep raspy croak, the kind of woman's voice that made an alto sound as if she were singing first soprano. When KD realized it had come out of her, she giggled, a typical KD giggle, only deeper.

"I guess it did," she said, sitting up.

Dr. Doom was standing near Steffie. He put his hand on KD's shoulder. "There's a few things you should know," he said.

KD's gaze went from him to Steffie. Steffie did not smile, on purpose. KD frowned slightly.

"Look at your hands," Steffie said.

KD did. The frown grew deeper. She stroked the back of the left with the long fingers of the right, then turned her left hand over as if it belonged to a stranger.

"The skin condition is permanent," Dr. Doom said. "And disfiguring. We can't do anything about it."

"How tall am I?" KD asked.

Dr. Doom took a deep breath, then smiled a little. The question shocked Steffie. "I don't know without you standing," he said. "I would guess about five feet, seven inches."

"Five-seven," KD said. She raised her strange small eyes to Steffie. The eyes, even though they were small, still had KD in them. "I'm taller than you."

"Yes," Steffie said.

"I've never been taller than you."

"KD," Steffie said. "The skin—"

"Is disfiguring, yes, I know," KD said. "But it won't interfere with my life, will it?"

That last she addressed to Dr. Doom.

"People will stare at you. They will notice. They will not be kind."

KD shrugged. "That's my whole life," she said. "What else?"

"Your other organs are as damaged. You may not live a normal life span."

KD grinned. "I come back from the jaws of death an adult and you're worried about whether I'll live to ninety? I'm just glad I have tomorrow."

Steffie felt a strange tension in her shoulders. She had expected anger, screaming, tears, but she had never expected this calm acceptance, never figured that KD would take it all in stride.

"You knew," Steffie said. "You knew this was going to happen."

KD looked at her blankly, as if she couldn't understand the emotion that threaded through Steffie's voice. "I told you I read everything. And I had a long time to think about it. What would you rather have? Your freedom, your adulthood, or a pretty face?

I had a pretty face for a long, long time. It didn't get me anywhere."

All that worry. All that agonizing. And KD was more prepared than Steffie gave her credit for. Steffie never really had trusted KD, never really had believed that there was an adult mind inside that child's body. KD played to everyone's prejudices so well.

"So, when can I go free?" KD asked Dr. Doom.

"As soon as we do a few tests," he said.

The tests took four hours. Steffie had to wait in a room she had not seen before while they were underway. When they were over, she went back into the room where she had slept and worried and stayed longer than any other place in New York.

The assistant had KD's new identification tray. Steffie looked it over, and realized that it not only looked authentic; it was authentic. The assistant had used KD's real birth records and put the factual information along with her vital statistics—height, weight, scars and distinguishing marks, and a hologram of her actual appearance. Adult identification, for a woman who had been on the Earth longer than Steffie had.

KD was sitting on the bed when Steffie entered, a series of chip monitors still attached to her left arm.

"We're nearly done," Dr. Doom said, and he sounded cheerful.

"Can we talk while you work?"

"Certainly," he said. "You should be happy to know she's turned out well. I expect great things of her."

KD smiled at him—the KD smile on that ravaged face.

"KD," Steffie said. "When we leave here, we need to deal with Mom and Dad. I could book you—"

"No," KD said. The smile left her face. It was suddenly blank. "I don't want to see them."

"But they'll want to know—"

"You tell them."

"All right," Steffie said, feeling out of her depth. KD was speaking with an anger foreign to Steffie. KD had always had anger, but not force behind it.

Not the force of a grown woman.

"We can decide that after we find a place," Steffie said. "I know a few apartments not far from here. They're large and not too expensive, and we'll each have our own entrances—"

"No," KD said again. Her small eyes narrowed. "You don't get it, Steffie. I'm done with all of you. I'm an adult now. I can do this on my own."

"I know," Steffie said. "But I thought—"

"You thought I'd need some protection in the big city. You thought I'd need to learn how to live. Well, I don't," KD said. She looked up at Dr. Doom. "We don't need her anymore, do we?"

He glanced at Steffie. His expression was apologetic. "No," he said to KD. "You're an adult now. Legally. You can sign everything."

"Then that's it," KD said. "I'm sorry, Steffie. I know this was an inconvenience."

Steffie froze. What was KD doing? "Yeah," she said. "Yeah it was."

"Well, thanks," KD said. "I do appreciate it."

"That's obvious," Steffie snapped. Her initial feeling had been right. She had been manipulated.

Again.

KD had not been able to get anyone else to bring her to Dr. Doom.

She made Steffie.

She manipulated Steffie.

Masterfully.

KD pursed her lips. "There's no need to get upset. You've been moving on with your life a long time now. Just move past this one."

Steffie stared at her. It was an apt description. She had been moving, constantly moving, and mostly because of KD. And when she finally stopped, KD didn't want her. Didn't need her anymore.

If she actually had needed Steffie, in the first place. Or if any adult would have done just as well.

"What do I tell Mom and Dad?" Steffie asked.

"Tell them I'm dead." KD was watching her out of that mockery of a face, the cracked and damaged skin twisting as she raised her eyebrows in typical KD you'd-better-believe-me fashion.

"I can't do that," Steffie said.

KD shrugged. "Then they'll always wonder."

"KD, you should go back there. Or call them. Or something. You owe them that much." Steffie couldn't believe she was arguing for her parents. She couldn't believe that KD had put her in that position. She couldn't believe that anyone could put her in that position.

"Owe them?" KD's voice was unusually soft. Dr. Doom had stepped away from her slightly. The assistant was standing beside the door, holding Steffie's pouch. "I *owe* them? For what? Holding me prisoner all these years? Do you know what it's like, having an adult brain and not being allowed to use it? Do you know how many times I ran away, only to be returned to them like a lost puppy? Do you know how many times I begged to be let out of that house? No, Steffie. I don't owe them anything."

Steffie swallowed. She saw the hints around her, the signals from Dr. Doom and his assistant that she should leave.

She chose to ignore them.

"They loved you, in their own way."

"They loved a beautiful three-year-old doll they called KD because the name they had originally given her—before they decided to alter her—didn't suit a child." KD looked at her identification, then grinned at Dr. Doom.

"At least you got the name right," she said to him.

Steffie didn't have to look. She knew.

Kalianna Danita.

KD was right. The name was pretentious for a child, but it was suited to a woman, particularly a woman whose face had character and whose spirit matched.

"KD," Steffie said. "I've been on my own for a long time. At least let me help you start out."

"So that you can take the first opportunity to contact Mom and Dad?" KD shook her head. "Sorry, Steffie."

"KD," Steffie said, knowing she was losing this, but having to try. "I won't contact them. It's just not easy out there. No matter what you think. No matter what you know."

KD's face went blank. "And you're an expert on this?"

"Actually, I am."

"Then maybe I will be too." She crossed her arms, and frowned. KD's frowns had been imposing as a child. They were twice as imposing on her adult face.

"You don't get it, Steffie," she said. "I don't want you around any more than I want Mom and Dad. I'm done with the family. I've done my time. I'm finished now."

"KD," Steffie said. "You're never done."

"You were," KD said.

"Until you brought me back."

"You thought I was dying."

Steffie shrugged. "You were. I helped."

"We're even." KD tilted her head back slightly. "Now get out."

"KD—"

"Get out."

Steffie stood there for a moment, unable to think. Unable to move. Then the assistant put his hand on her arm.

"Sorry," he said.

She glanced at KD, somehow thinking KD would change her mind, would be different.

But she wasn't even looking at Steffie.

It was as if Steffie were already gone.

Then the assistant tugged on Steffie's arm. She let him show her out.

At the main door, he stopped. "I'm sorry," he said softly. "I've seen them do that before. I think it's part of the process. They've been objects so long, they don't realize when they're treating someone else the same way."

Steffie smiled at him, not really feeling any emotion behind the facial movement. Maybe he was right for other grown-up "children." Maybe. But for KD, it was merely her chance to act as the rest of the family had. To cut all ties, to make her own way.

Only her method had to be more drastic because her life had been so different.

"Do you contact the parents?" Steffie asked, knowing it was a cowardly question.

"No," he said.

She sighed. "I didn't think so," she said, and walked away.

She walked to Central Park. It was, after all, the closest thing she had to a home in the city. She didn't coolhunt on the way; she didn't even look at her surroundings. She could have been followed, she could have been mugged, but she didn't care.

She didn't quite understand what had happened to her, how she had suddenly lost her identity, had become KD's big little sister all over again.

Or maybe that identity never went away. Maybe she had buried it under years of running, years of hunting, years of flopping wherever time and the need took her.

She didn't like the way it had popped back up, the way it had opened her up to feelings like those she hadn't experienced since she was a girl.

Betrayal.

How could she feel betrayed by KD, when all KD had been trying to do was survive?

To have a life like Steffie did.

After all, KD was right.

Steffie had run out on her first.

And it had taken KD a long time to find her.

Was it revenge, then? Was that what KD had done? Or was it

something less conscious, a simple action that had spiraled into something else?

Or maybe it was a combination of both, a simple action that became revenge. Because KD knew, perhaps better than Steffie did, that only a member of the family could have gotten her out of that house.

Steffie managed.

And now KD had her wish.

Steffie walked to her favorite bench and sat down. She had slept more in the last two days than she had slept in a long time, and yet she felt exhausted. Bone deep weary. So tired, she didn't want to hunt. So tired, she couldn't even decide what to do next.

A woman walked by wearing a pale peach tent shirt in a faux paisley pattern, brown gauze pants, and ribbon barrettes pulling her hair from her face. In her arms, she carried a small child wrapped in a blanket.

Steffie froze.

The woman wore boots just like the ones Steffie had on.

Only newer.

Steffie's ribbon barrettes were long gone, and her tent shirt was wrinkled beyond recognition. The brown pants were stained and ripped slightly from their odyssey the past two days.

Only Steffie knew the woman wore the same outfit Steffie did.

She sat still, holding her breath, scanning the park.

She saw a lot of people all going about their own business. None of them were looking at her.

Slowly she let her breath out, and as she did, she saw another young mother carrying a blanket wrapped child. Her ribbon barrettes did not match, nor did she have on the right boots.

Steffie resisted the urge to stand on her bench. She looked, more carefully this time, at the people on the paths, walking through the grass, sitting on the grass. Young couples, babies in carriers, bicyclists—

—and two more young women wearing her outfit, complete with child.

A male version walked past only moments later, the same except that he wore no ribbons in his short hair.

Not early adapters then. The style had been on the market long enough to be mass-produced, long enough to be modified.

Someone had seen her the moment she got off the shuttle with KD, and had coolhunted her. And had shown no class, by not identifying himself, and by not paying her.

She was shaking. It wasn't the lack of money that bothered

her. She had enough money. Nor was it even being coolhunted. It was bound to happen eventually. She had the right attitude, a focus on something else, with the clothes being secondary, but interesting.

No. None of those things disturbed her at all.

It was the lack of understanding.

She had been coolhunted at the most important moment of her life, and the marketing had gotten it all wrong, selling it to parents as a way of looking cool while carrying their child.

For her it had been a matter of life and death.

It had been the central moment of her adulthood. Everything crossed there—her childhood, her feelings about KD, and her future.

More than anything, her future.

She'd been willing to change it all for KD.

Steffie let out a small moan.

What was she going to do? Ignore it all and return to coolhunting, only to get it wrong like the person who had hunted her? How many people had she insulted, how many precious moments had she misunderstood? How much cool had simply been one of life's disasters proceeding in front of her, the trend-setter simply someone who had put on anything from his closet that day because he hadn't had time to think?

How many moments had she touched, and gotten wrong?

She stood, hand to her face. She couldn't go back to coolhunting. Coolhunting was the very thing that led to KD—to KD's imprisonment, to her life, to her rejection of everything she had known. What kind of person would KD have been if she had been allowed to develop normally?

Like Steffie.

"You all right, ma'am?" a woman asked. She was standing some distance away, as if she might catch something from Steffie if she got too close. But the woman had an expression on her face that implied that she had to ask, that she wouldn't have been able to live with herself if she hadn't.

No one had looked at her like that in a long, long time.

"I'm fine," Steffie said, doing her best to look normal, given her filthy clothing, her agitated state. "Really. Thank you."

The woman nodded, obviously not convinced, but not willing to argue. She continued down the path.

Steffie watched her go. What had the woman seen? A disheveled woman who lived on the streets? A woman who had just given her privacy to her sister, only to have the gift rejected?

Or a woman who looked lost, like Steffie felt?

For the first time in her life, she had nothing to run away from. Everything had run away from her.

Not even her mother pretended politeness anymore. When they parted, her mother spoke words of love only to KD.

Steffie groaned again. Her mother expected news of KD, and KD certainly wasn't going to tell her.

Steffie couldn't just e-mail her. She couldn't just say that KD was dead.

And she couldn't ignore it and leave those two people alone together in that house. No matter what they'd done.

Or what she thought they'd done.

Maybe she had been wrong about them, too.

Maybe she hadn't understood their motives any better than she'd understood her own.

She put her hand back to her mouth, knowing her decision was made. She wasn't going to stay in Ann Arbor. She would take an afternoon shuttle there, and an evening shuttle back. And then she would get an apartment on Fifth Avenue with a view of the park.

And invest, maybe, or fashion gamble. She'd be good at that. Better than KD was.

And maybe playing on-line, she might even find KD.

Maybe.

But she doubted it.

To find someone, she had to be looking.

Her hunting days were over.

It was time to look beneath the surfaces to see what lurked in the depths.

And the first place she'd look was the last place anyone would expect her to look. Home.

To see what she had missed.

To see what the place was like without KD.

To take responsibility, for the first time, for her own actions.

She had rescued KD. She had brought change to that house.

Now she had to take it the last step.

Now she had to let her parents know that they could move forward, whether they wanted to or not.

She closed her eyes. Funny how she was always the one bringing change.

And she had finally brought it to herself.

Going Native

"GOD, COULD YOU FIND a duller way to travel?" asks my leggy companion, the luscious Ruth. She has this weekend off, and she insisted on coming with me on my assignment. It'll be fun, she said, and then followed that up with, how can I know what you're doing unless I come along with you on occasion? I listened to the logic of that, and now I find myself trapped in a five-by-six-foot moving room with a woman who finds train travel passé.

Me, I'm afraid that the Amtrak trip up the mountain will be the best part of this assignment. I work for eight on-line editors, and all of them called me last week to ask for an article on the annual TVS convention. Such a uniformity of requests has only happened once before in my career, and that was when a woman that I sat beside in grade school, tormented in middle school, and dated in high school was inaugurated as president of the United States. Suddenly my memoirs had value.

Somehow, I doubt that this essay has the same sort of import.

I also had my doubts about bringing Ruth to kooksville and now, when we're still two hours away from our destination, I know I've made the Wrong Decision. She is lying on the bottom berth, her bare feet against the dirty plastic wall, her skirt pooled around her waist, and she is not thinking of sex.

Neither am I.

"I mean, we've been on this train for hours. How did people travel like this?"

They made love, they ate, they read books. But I do not tell Ruth that. She would see it as a slap, an insult to her great intelligence. In real life, Ruth is a receptionist for a lawyer, but she prefers to call herself a paralegal. She uses legalese, mispronouncing most of it, and pretends that she knows as much as someone who has a law degree.

I've never told her about mine. But then, why should I? It would ruin the sleazy nature of the relationship, the fact that I'm dating her for her deliciously man-made breasts and she's dating me because I know the secrets of the universe.

She believes that's because I'm a journalist. The old-fashioned print kind, even though what we print is done on-line. I'm paid by the download, which is why I'm on this train trip instead of say, investigating the latest bombing in downtown Seattle. No matter how idealistic you start, you soon learn that it's paranoia that sells.

Which is why we're on a train instead of teleporting. There are no teleportation stations in this part of the Cascades. Rumor has it that the first teleportation technician who ventured into this part of Oregon was shot. Whether he lived or died depends on which rumor you believe.

Ruth knew we were heading into no man's land when she decided to come with me, but the closer we get the less I believe she actually *understood* it. I think she thought we'd look at the crazy yokels and then go home.

I think I thought she could handle anything.

Check that. I think I knew, deep down, she was contemplating Marriage, and I wanted to convince her that breaking up was her idea. But that's hindsight. Going in, I was simply concerned about the lack of sex.

"Once," I say, gazing out the window at the snow beside the tracks, "this was the fastest way to travel in the whole world."

"Yeah." She flops an arm over her eyes, missing the deer that stand by a group of trees, staring at us. A nineteenth century vision in the twenty-first. "Sad, isn't it?"

I'm not sure. I'm enough of a romantic to enjoy the view. I'm enough of a romantic to wish that she'd enjoy it with me.

The assignment, if you look at it historically (which is one of the few things that I've retained from law school, a sense of historical perspective), is a perennial: go look at the fringe and report back to the masses. Around the turn of the last century, that meant going to carnivals and fairs to examine the bearded women, the two-headed chickens, and the stillborn fetuses that looked like fish. In my grandfather's day, a reporter on this beat might go to see the mysterious Area 51, thought to be a repository for Unidentified Flying Objects (things so familiar they were known by their acronym UFO) and for the little green men who flew them. Me, I get assigned the annual meeting of the Teleportation Victims Society whose own acronym is TVS, but who is known in newsrooms nationwide as TVSo?. I should've known I was in trouble when I tried to explain this little joke to Ruth and she'd stared at me blankly, not even threatening to smile.

The TVSo?s meet every year in Harbor, Oregon, which used to be a 1990s survivalist camp between Bend and Klamath Falls. The area's only attraction, or so I could glean before I arrived, is that it has no teleportation station, and none is planned. If someone wants to travel in that part of the Cascade Range, they either have to go to Bend, fifty miles to the north, or Klamath Falls, over sixty miles to the south. Then they have to take whatever ground transportation is available, provided, of course, they can get it. Amtrak still serves this part of the country, partly because the sparse population can't justify the teleportation system, and partly because the tracks have existed for nearly two hundred years. It's the only form of public transportation between those two stations, and mostly it's used by the low-income folks who can't afford the cost of speedier travel.

I insisted on taking the train all the way from Seattle, over Ruth's protests, because I wanted my experience at the annual meeting to reflect the experience of all the other TVSo?s. I had secretly hoped I'd meet a few of them on this ride, but Ruth has kept me chained to the room, demanding room service, and not paying for it in the way that I had hoped.

Still I manage to sneak to the club car once, and there I see exactly what I expect, a group of tired, smelly people, most of whom are too drunk to look at the magnificent scenery whizzing past. I realize that, in my new khakis and bomber jacket, I am overdressed and as conspicuous as a rich man in Olympia. No one will talk to me. They barely manage to look at me.

And, for the first time, I worry about how I'll pull this assignment off.

I should say at this stage of article research, I always worry about how I'll pull the assignment off. Even though what I write is dictated into my wrist-top, edited on a larger screen at home, and e-mailed directly to my editor, what I do is really not much different from the work, say, Mark Twain did almost two hundred years ago. He ventured out into places unknown and reported back.

Ernest Hemingway did that, so did Ernie Pyle, and Peter Arnett. The great journalists thrived in times of war. When there is no war—or no war America is interested in—we are stuck with perennials. And no journalist ever became famous by risking his life at a TVSo? convention.

I simply want to go in, find a few things that are amusing, see if I can discover the secret behind the victimology, and return to home base with all parts intact. I know that, by Sunday evening, I will have a story. I'm just not sure if it's the kind of story Hemingway would have dispatched from Spain.

In fact, I know it won't be the moment the train pulls into Harbor, Oregon.

When Ruthie and I get off the train at the small white station nestled against a snow-covered ridge, we are greeted like visiting royalty. I made no secret of my job as a journalist, but it's really Ruthie they want to see. It seems, on the e-slip she sent with her fee, that she listed her employment as she always does.

A paralegal and a journalist. We are a dream couple for the TVSo?s.

I am not the only journalist in this place. Every major television reporter, radio commentator, vid producer, and holotechnician is here to record the loonies in action. I am one of the few print people, and the only one with enough awards to make me semi-famous. Every TVSo? wants to tell me his story, to introduce me to little Jonnie or Suzy or Uncle Billy, and to show me what makes them different.

When I get off the train, I realize I am not ready for this. The grasping hands, the slightly desperate gaze. I insist on going to the hotel before meeting people, and Ruth gives me her I-can't-believe-you're-doing-this look. That's when I realize she's not upset about the location or the people. She's upset that I want to leave them. She not only relishes the attention, she believes she can give these people advice. She doesn't realize how dangerous the situation can be. She's with the only people in the world who might take her seriously. I grip her arm and follow our host to the Compound, our hotel.

The Compound was the former survivalists' camp, and looks it. The outbuildings are made of wood hammered together by people who clearly didn't know what they were doing. The main building, where the restaurant and gift shop reside, was once a ranch-style house, built in the mid-twentieth century, complete with front-facing garage. The building had been added onto, once during its survivalist camp days—that was evident by the concrete bunker in the back—and once by the hotel, the brass and wood facade that tried to make everything upscale.

Our room isn't really a room. It was cabin Number 8. A plaque on the door tells us that it had once been used by the house's original owners as a storage shed, and was remodeled into a cabin when the camp started in the early 1980s. The plaque tells us proudly that eight people lived in this space; I'm wondering how Ruth and I will manage for a weekend.

The room is square, with an area carved out for a bathroom with an ancient shower and plastic tub. The sink has motion detectors instead of computer controls, and the toilet actually has a handle for flushing. Ruth is charmed, but I wonder if that will last into the middle of the night, when one of us stumbles in there and initiates the gurgle and grunt of the ancient plumbing.

We unpack, and then Ruth wants to reenter the fray. I'm more interested in checking out the dining facilities. The reconstituted chicken I had on the train didn't last me long.

Outside, we see several blue and white signs, pointing to various cabins. Most signs are hand-lettered and made specifically for the conference: Registration is to our left; Legal Advice is to our right; and Testimonials is straight ahead. Other signs show us the way to improve our Education, covering everything from Technological Secrets to the History of Transportation. Many of these, I know, are on-going programs, and I will check them out through the weekend. It's the guest speakers I am most interested in, and those are going to be the hardest events to see.

In the registration line I learn that the TVSo?s aren't all low-income poorly educated folks like the research had led me to expect. The man in front of me is a doctor from Philadelphia who has documentation on "differences" and was willing to call it up on his wrist-top right there in the frigid Oregon mud. The slender, pretty woman behind me is a reasonably well-known vid personality whose career went into a decline, she says, after she teleported sixty-five times in one month. I talk to both of them at some length. Ruth has left me alone in line while she went on to the lodge for drinks.

She has been gone a long time.

I draw the same sort of crowd I drew at the train station. I am uncomfortable, used to being the observer, not the observed. Everyone wants to tell me a story; everyone wants me to know how teleportation changes people, how it creates differences where there were none before.

Some of the stories are just silly, like the vid personality's. She claims she lost a little bit of charisma each time she teleported from one place to another. Some are strange, like the woman who has me examine holograms of her now-estranged husband, a man whose eye color changed in the space of one afternoon from green to brown.

The rest are merely sad. Many are from people who claim that their spouses are no longer the same people they married, and they blame use of public teleportation. Others show evidence of medical conditions they claim were caused by teleporting, and still some have tales of close loved ones who died soon after traveling in a teleportation device.

I have read the literature; I am familiar with all variations on these stories and more. I even know their origins.

I ask the eye color woman why she believes her husband's eyes were the only thing to change.

"I didn't say they were the only thing, now did I?" she says angrily.

I turn away, afraid to follow up.

The first big break-through in teleportation occurred in the late 1990s when a team of Austrian scientists successfully completed a transfer on the sub-atomic level. The physics of the break-through was too complex to explain to the layman in the popular newspapers of the day, so many journalists attempted (unsuccessfully) to put the discovery in layman's terms.

I have tried to hunt down the origin of the example used for the laymen and have been, to date, unsuccessful. I suspect either one of the scientists got exasperated with the journalists' stupid questions and used the example to explain, poorly, what was going on, or a journalist attempted to translate what he thought he understood into language that he thought other people could understand.

Their experiment, said the news organizations of the day, was as if the scientists had taken a red ball in one room, made it disappear, and then reappear in another room—although what was teleported was not the ball itself, but the *quality* of redness which was then transferred onto another ball.

It is not what we experience. We experience the teleportation first imagined in pulp fiction stories of over a hundred years ago. Our bodies literally disassemble in one location, are transferred to another location, and are then reassembled. There are documented cases of malfunctions, most dating from the early days of the technology and almost all of them having to do with apes who arrived dead. These deaths were not pretty or simple: they had to do with parts being reassembled in the wrong order, rather like taking a puzzle apart, then trying to put it together by placing all the corners in the middle. Those details were resolved long before any human being stepped onto a teleportation pad. The things we must worry about are simpler: power failures and computer malfunctions, both of which can lose us mid-transfer. This problem is the greatest in Third World countries, in devices built out of scrap metal, most likely, by the operator's Uncle Ralph. Teleportation is not sanctioned to those countries, or is done purely at the user's own risk. Here and in "approved" countries, every device is scrutinized, overhauled, and replaced more often than anything else in our technologically advanced society.

This is what the literature tells me. It is what exists in all published reports, the meetings before Congress, and in several teleportation companies' legal databases. I know there can be problems—we all do. The problems are called "acceptable risks," something we all assume when we step on a teleportation pad, or even when we walk out our front door. What varies from person to person is how acceptable some risks are.

It is the idea that we can be disassembled and reassembled that unnerves people the most. A large number of people (actual estimates vary, depending on the reporting agency) refuse to use teleportation, allowing other forms of mass transit to remain in business. Most of these people are not TVSo?s. They simply don't like the idea of being taken apart and put back together without it being necessary, and are not willing to sacrifice their original unity for the sake of instantaneous travel.

Others cannot imagine traveling any other way. Frequent teleporters receive a discount on each trip. "Frequent" is defined in the industry as anyone making more than ten trips per day. I have only hit the ten-trips-in-one-day milestone once, and it left me feeling disoriented and unnerved—not, I hasten to add, because I was disassembled so many times, but because, after five different teleportation stations, I lost track of my surroundings. Later I learned that frequent travelers set their wrist-top to remind them of their location and their purpose for being there upon arrival.

I have read all the literature, examined all the records, and while I still feel a twinge of nerves when I step on the platform, I prefer the instantaneous shift, the delight at having been in Manhattan one moment and Rome the next. It is not different, my grandmother once told me, than that frisson of fear she used to feel whenever an airplane's wheels left the ground or whenever a train went over a particularly high and narrow bridge.

It is human nature to worry about the accidental, the unexpected, the unknown. It is also human nature to magnify those things into problems so strange as to be somehow plausible.

The TVSo?s have three banquets at their weekend meeting, and I have bought tickets to all three. Ruth did not want to eat at the banquets. In fact, she soon made it clear that she did not want to spend time with me. She says my attitude is too cynical, my remarks too cutting. She is right. I am already thinking in the tone I've decided to take for this article, a tone that my brain established while part of it tried to concentrate on the seriousness of the vid personality's loss of charisma.

The first banquet is on Friday night, and there I am happily surprised. The food is excellent. It is free-range chicken, brought in from a nearby ranch, local vegetables grown and stored here, marinated in local wine, mixed with spices grown in the chef's own herb garden.

Nothing was shipped in: no risk of teleportation tainting the food. And somehow it does seem fresher. Or perhaps the chef, a world-renown man who refused to allow me to use his name in this article, has simply lived up to his spectacular reputation.

The speaker that night is a transportation historian who is, believe it or not, duller than he sounds. He reads his speech off the TelePrompTer modification in his contact lenses, probably much as he does in class, which forces him to stare straight ahead. That, combined with his monotone, makes him seem as if he's teleported one too many times.

The diners at my table, which is toward the back, immediately deduce the problem and begin whispering, as I imagine his students often do. We introduce ourselves and tell each other why we're here.

The woman to my immediate left looks like a Hollywood grandmother, which is to say that she's round, gray-haired and jolly. She confides that she went to see her grandchildren on her only teleportation trip, and instead of arriving in Pittsburgh as planned, she arrived in Philadelphia. The teleportation operators claim she simply told them she was going to Philly, but she claims that they punched in the wrong destination. I take mental notes, knowing that what is at stake here is more than a simple trip. She lives on a fixed income and she scrimped to afford the teleport. She could not afford to then go from Philly to Pittsburgh and back home. She missed a trip, and probably several meals, for that one abortive visit.

This is a problem I can get behind. It is not magic woo-woo incantations in which she claims that she suddenly ballooned in size because her protons expanded or that she got skin cancer that should have belonged to someone else. This is the kind of operator error we all worry about. I have had nightmares about getting on a teleporter in Portland and ending up in Beijing.

The woman next to her confides that there is a lawyer in the legal section who is trying to get enough contacts to initiate a class action suit for just that sort of problem. The grandmother thanks her, and then asks her, whispering politely of course, why she's here. The woman, who is in her mid-forties, has the prettiest lavender hair I've ever seen. She flushes a nice shade of pink that somehow complements the lavender and admits that she would rather not say.

I am beginning to think I've hit a lucky table. Imagine someone who has come to a TVSo? convention who is unwilling to admit why she has come. It is almost antithetical to the purpose of the conference.

I make a mental note to pull her aside later, then ask the man to my right why he has come. "Reporter," he says tersely, not whispering. "Just like you."

He gets shushed by the people at the table behind him, who, believe it or not, are engrossed in the teacher's speech. At that point, I surface briefly, realize the man has droned on for thirty minutes and hasn't yet reached the invention of the automobile. I signal a waiter for more coffee.

The woman to the reporter's right bursts into tears when asked why she's here, and we get shushed again. I actually don't mind because I get an odd sense that the tears are fake. Still, we dutifully lean forward after she dries her eyes with her linen napkin.

"My baby," she whispers, and stifles a sob. The entire table behind us glares at us with angry eyes. We glare back, then lean as close as we can.

"My baby," she says again, "was a boy when he went into the device."

Suddenly I don't want to hear anymore, and neither, it seems, does anyone else. The reporter hands her another napkin, and makes sympathetic noises, but as quickly as he politely can, he rises and makes his way to the men's room.

Ten minutes later, when he has not returned and the speaker is rhapsodizing about the uses of airplanes in World War I, I excuse myself. The corridor outside is empty, but I find a new convention going on at the bar.

"I don't know why they invite him back," says one woman to a gale of laughter. It seems that this is the fifth year the historian has spoken on Friday night, and this year he is actually *more* interesting than he has ever been.

One of the conference organizers overhears, and says rather stiffly, "We invite him so that you all have an historical overview of the problems we face."

"Oh," the laughing woman says, "but don't you think that teleportation is a little different than, say, a Model T?"

"No," the organizer says, and I realize that this is one of those dangerous people to whom the phrase "sense of humor" has no meaning at all, "it is all a manifestation of our need to make the world smaller. Once everyone thought that instantaneous travel would solve all our ills. They didn't realize that it would cause more problems than it solved."

"Do you believe," one woman asks, "that everyone who has been in a teleportation device is still human?"

Not even the conference organizer answers that question. It is too touchy. Most of the people here are here because they have been in a teleportation device. If the woman's right, that would mean none of us are human. I don't believe that. I believe we're very human, although the more I see, the more I wonder what side of humanity we actually belong to.

The next morning, I wander over to Legal, and listen to lawyers pontificate on ways to collect damages from teleportation companies. I hear the familiar litany of successful lawsuits—there aren't many, and most are nuisance cases much like the grandmother's of the night before—but the audience is attentive and asks polite questions.

In the afternoon, I poke my head into Education, and see the historian. I don't run from there, although I'm tempted. I walk slowly, pretending I had ventured into that area by mistake.

Ruth is nowhere to be seen. She did show up in our room the night before, but long after I was asleep, and I thought I smelled brandy, but by that point I didn't really care. I wonder idly who she has found to entertain herself with and how she can use him to further her career. The thought, though accurate, is uncharitable, and I then wonder when I stopped thinking with fondness of Ruth's tendency to exaggerate and began to be annoyed by them. Probably around the point when her manufactured breasts became her most fascinating feature.

That night's speaker is an expert in teleportation technology and I am assured by almost everyone who's been here before that he makes the historian look glib. I am sorry to give up the free-range chicken, but I cannot bear another two hours trapped in those uncomfortable wooden banquet chairs.

I go into the restaurant, where I've had two delicious breakfasts, and cast about for a table. It seems to have a lot of patrons, considering there is a banquet going on in the next room.

Ruth is at a table near the window. Even though it is dark, I can make out the ghostly shape of the nearby mountain, snow-covered and shiny. She waves me over.

She is sitting with the lawyers. They have asked that no other tables be filled around them, and so far the restaurant is able to comply. Ruth, it seems, has been spending her time with the entire legal wing of this conference and learning "a whole heckuva lot."

I sit down, and listen for a while. This seems like an informal version of the panel I had attended in the morning. I order a steak, and do not ask if it was shipped in or slaughtered locally, for which I am teased unmercifully, and then one of the attorneys, an overweight vegetarian who consumes way too much wine during the evening, informs me of the many ways that beef could kill me. Since I have heard this lecture before, I add a few insights of my own, all the while chomping heartily on my dinner.

Finally they ask me why I'm here, and I tell them that I'm a paid observer of human nature.

"He's a journalist," Ruth says, breaking my cover.

They eye me as if *I'm* the slimy species and I explain that I'm a practitioner of New Journalism almost a century after New Journalism was introduced. It is my way of gaining legitimacy among the illegitimate: pretend to a literary value that I don't really have.

The New Journalism comment seems to have silenced them, so to break the ice—and to make my dinner worthwhile—I ask them what they really think about teleportation technology.

"It makes lawyers rich!" one of them said and the others laugh. But I press them, and finally a dark-suited man next to Ruth says, "I used to laugh at these folks and then questions started coming up, questions I couldn't get an answer to."

One of the female attorneys nods, and still another, the overweight vegetarian, says, "Yeah, like why is there a ban on kids under the age of three taking teleportation?"

"It's not a firm ban," a New York lawyer says. "You can get around it with a doctor's permission."

"Yeah," the vegetarian says. "Why a doctor? And what does he give permission for?"

"I've never seen any instances of babies traveling. They don't allow it, with or without the doctor," the woman says.

"But I met a woman who says her baby—" I start and they all shake their heads sadly, silencing me.

"She's here every year," the vegetarian says. "I checked the story out. She doesn't have a kid. I don't even think she's female."

They chuckle again, and the joviality is back. No matter how I push them, I can't learn what the other questions are. The vegetarian promises to tell me if I come to the bar later. I do, and he's passed out in a pile of corn chips. I vow to try and find him the following day.

The next morning, as the speakers are setting up, I go to the Technological Secrets area. It's in a wide auditorium with holographic capabilities. My mind boggles just at the thought of seeing strange machinery in life-size and 3-D.

It takes me a moment to find a speaker who'll talk to me, who doesn't try to get me to wait until his presentation. I tell him about the lawyers' collective unease about the baby ban.

"You ask the teleportation stations they'll tell you it's because babies are too fragile for most kinds of travel. Like they'll ban an infant from a jet." The guy I'm talking to is six feet tall and has a honking nasal voice. I'm glad I elected not to stay for his presentation, even though he seems nice enough. "But it's really because of the stress to the body."

"I thought there is no stress."

He looks at me as if I'm the dumbest thing he's seen at this conference, and given what I've seen, I'm almost insulted. He holds up a glass of water. "You can't teleport crystal either," he says. "Sometimes it shatters. And it shouldn't. I mean, they perfected this at the subatomic level, or so they say."

"You don't think they did?"

"Between you, me, and the wall," he says, "I know they perfected it. The problem is that they don't use the right equipment to teleport people. It's like building a house. We can build a damn fine house with everything correct. But we hire contractors who want to make as much money as possible, and they do it—have done it—since time immemorial by using inferior parts and charging the same as they would for good parts. I try to tell the lawyers that, but it's not glamorous, and it's damned hard to prove. They tell me they'll help me when I can show damage caused by inferior parts. I can show damage. I just can't make a credible link."

Later that day, I check his statements with a few other technology wonks. They agree that the problem with public teleportation is that it's *public*. The system used by the president and other heads of state is state of the art, so protected that nothing can go wrong. The system used by the rest of us, well, these guys would have us all believe it's held together by spit and glue and pieces manufactured just after the turn of the century.

It makes me think of all those bans on teleportation travel to third world countries. If our technology is bad, what is the technology like that was hammered together by someone's Uncle Ralph? The very idea raises images of those poor puzzlebox monkeys with the corners where their middle should be.

Of course when I get back home, and call the various teleportation manufacturers, they all give me the company line and swear teleportation is the safest form of transportation since walking. Even that can go wrong, I say. Think of potholes. Think of missteps, twisted ankles and tripping over small children. But the manufacturers don't find me funny. When I get belligerent, forgetting, for a moment, that this is supposed to be a puff piece and not investigative reporting, they transfer me to their legal departments who remind me of libel laws and how careful I need to be in questioning their companies.

The free-range chicken is gone by the third banquet, but the speaker is delightful. He's a comedian just starting out, and he proves to me that the TVSo?s have a sense of humor, since most of his jokes are aimed at them, and they laugh uproariously. I don't. I feel vaguely embarrassed, mostly because I know I would have laughed if I'd been watching this guy in any other setting but this one.

As I head out, I look for Ruth. She's still surrounded by her lawyers, and when she sees me, she waves me over. She puts a hand on the overweight vegetarian's arm and informs me that he has hired her as a paralegal. I pull her aside, remind her that jobs aren't always that easy to come by and that she'd better check his credentials. She frowns at me, asks me if I think she's dumb or something—a question which I decline to answer—and then stalks off. I gather, from that whole exchange, that she's not taking the train home, and I turn out to be right. My wish has been granted. She has forgotten thoughts of Marriage and believes that our break-up is her idea. I find that I regret the whole plan, not because I wanted to marry her, but because I had hoped that I would at least get to try all parts of train travel, from meal to sleep to sex. We had neglected sex on the way there, and I was hoping for a bit on the way home.

Instead, I spend the next week finding a way to ship her clothes cheaply without using teleportation technology, since the vegetarian likes to keep his office "pure."

I am beginning to understand the sentiment. My moment of hesitation as I step on the teleportation platform in Bend—I see no point in train travel all the way to Seattle if I'm not going to be able to have nookie in transit—lasts nearly three minutes, and customers behind me get angry. But I keep thinking of those banned babies, and Uncle Ralph, and inferior grade equipment, and the way that the sheet rock in my condo flakes like someone's untended dandruff, and I find myself more and more reluctant to travel in that instantaneous sort of way. After all, why am I in such a hurry? I'm a journalist, for god's sake, a man who makes his living off observing, and observation is something that can't be rushed. I am proud of my observation skills, and proud of my capability for contemplation that makes them possible.

But what I've been observing since I got back is my own reflection in the mirror. There's a line down one side of my face, an instant wrinkle that really doesn't look like a laugh line or something that would naturally occur as I age. It looks more like a fold, or a crease, something incorrectly ironed in, as if a section of me was miscut and hemmed wrong.

I never noticed the wrinkle before getting on that teleportation station in Bend. I have been obsessed with it since. And I think, I really think, that my obsession is a product of the TVSo? convention, but not for the reason that you'd think. It's not that I suddenly believe the teleporter has given me a new wrinkle. It's just that I find the idea of a wrinkle induced from the outside better than the idea that I'm growing older. It's easier to believe in the fiction. It's nicer.

It takes the responsibility for that particular line off me.

Or at least, that's what I tell myself. Because I do need to teleport on occasion for my job. Journalists observe, yes. But they must observe in the right places. And when my editor tells me to get to London yesterday, I do the next best thing. I get there two minutes from now, new wrinkles be damned.

But I find that I do examine mirrors more, and I wonder, when I think something particularly cruel, like most of my thoughts about Ruth lately, if I've become less than human. Is humanity something we can lose, little bit by little bit, like the vid personality and her charisma? And if so, how can we tell it's gone? Is it replaced by paranoia, by worry, in equal degrees? And am I, in worrying about this, showing signs of latent TVso?ism?

I don't know. But I do suspect that my recent desire to take the train to the far reaches of the United States has less to do with my unfulfilled sexual fantasy than it does with my desire to avoid a technology that I may have learned to fear. Then I remind myself of the history of this form of paranoia; I know that being a reporter from the fringe requires an ability to cross over into that land and appear to be a native. I'm simply afraid I've taken it too far. Going native requires residency in kooksville, and while it only takes an instant to reach that particular destination, it takes years and expensive psychotherapy to get out.

When I turned in this essay, I thought of asking for a bonus, a sort of combat pay to compensate for the wrinkle, for the increased harassment as I take an extra minute of other people's time while I hesitate before stepping on a teleportation platform.

But my editor vid-conferenced with me this morning, wanting to discuss what he calls "proper compensation." My article, he says—(this thing you are currently reading, without this coda)—has given him an idea. Teleportation has overtaken other forms of transportation so much that his younger readers have probably never flown in a plane or driven a car. He wants me to do these things, and report back about my experiences, as if I have gone to yet another frontier, even if it is a part of the past.

He asks what I want to do first, and then reminds me this will be on the magazine's expense.

"A ticket on the Orient Express," I say.

"Ah, he says. "You'll title it 'Strangers on a Train'?"

I'm thinking not of Patricia Highsmith and Alfred Hitchcock, but of luscious, willing blonds with breasts the size of helium balloons and the ca-thunk, ca-thunk of the wheels on a track suggesting a rhythm that no teleportation device can hope to match.

"I hope so," I say, and realize this is the kind of fringe I like. "I certainly hope so."

Millennium Babies

TWO WEEKS INTO THE second semester, she got the message. It had been sent to her house system, and was coded to her real name, Brooke Delacroix, not Brooke Cross, the name she had used since she was eighteen. At first she didn't want to open it, thinking it might be another legal conundrum from her mother, so she let the house monitor in the kitchen blink while she prepared dinner.

She made a hearty dinner, and poured herself a glass of rosé, before settling down in front of the living room fireplace. The fireplace was the reason she bought this house. She had fallen in love with the idea that she could sit on cold winter nights under a pile of blankets, a real fire burning nearby, and read the ancient paperbacks she found in Madison's antique stores. She read a lot of current work on her e-book, especially research for the classes she taught at the university, but she loved to read novels in their paper form, careful not to tear the brittle pages, feeling the weight of bound paper in her hands.

She had added bookshelves to the house's dining room for her paper novels, and she had made a few other improvements as well. But she tried to keep the house's character. It was a hundred and fifty years old, built when this part of Wisconsin had been nothing but family farms. The farmland was gone now, divided into five-acre plots, but the privacy remained. She loved being out here, in the country, more than anything else. Even though the university provided her job, the house was her world.

The novel she held was a thin volume, and a favorite—*The Great Gatsby* by F. Scott Fitzgerald—but on this night, the book didn't hold her interest. Finally she gave up. If she didn't hear the damn message, she would be haunted by her mother all night.

Brooke left the glass of wine and the book on the end table, her blankets curled at the edge of the couch, and made her way back to the kitchen. She could have had House play an audio-only version of the message in the living room, but she wanted to see her mother's face, to know how serious it was this time.

The monitor was on the west wall beside the microwave. The previous owners—a charming elderly couple—had kept a small television in that spot. On nights like this, Brooke thought the monitor was no improvement.

She stood in front of it, arms crossed, sighed, and said, "House, play message."

The blinking icon disappeared from the screen. A digital voice she did not recognize said, "This message is keyed for Brooke Delacroix only. It will not be played without certification that no one else is in the room."

She stood. If this was from her mother, her tactics had changed. This sounded official. Brooke made sure she was visible to the built-in camera.

"I'm Brooke," she said, "and I'm alone."

"You're willing to certify this?" the strange voice asked her.

"Yes," she said.

"Stand-by for message."

The screen turned black. She rubbed her hands together. Goosebumps were crawling across her skin. Who would send her an official message?

"This is coded for Brooke Delacroix," a new digital voice said. "Personal identification number . . ."

As the voice rattled off the number, she clenched her fist. Maybe something had happened to her mother. Brooke was, after all, the only next of kin.

"This is Brooke Delacroix," she said. "How many more security protocols do we have here?"

"Five," House said.

She felt her shoulders relax as she heard the familiar voice.

"Go around them. I don't have the time."

"All right," House said. "Stand-by."

She was standing by. Now she wished she had brought her glass of wine into the kitchen. For the first time, she felt as if she needed it.

"Ms. Delacroix?" A male voice spoke, and as it did, the monitor filled with an image. A middle-aged man with dark hair and dark eyes stared at a point just beyond her. He had the look of an intellectual, an aesthetic, someone who spent too much time in artificial light. He also looked vaguely familiar. "Forgive my rudeness. I know you go by Cross now, but I wanted to make certain that you are the woman I'm searching for. I'm looking for Brooke Delacroix, born 12:05 A.M., January first in the year 2000 in Detroit, Michigan."

Another safety protocol. What was this?

"That's me," Brooke said.

The screen blinked slightly, apparently as her answer was fed into some sort of program. He must have recorded various messages for various answers. She knew she wasn't speaking to him live.

"We are actually colleagues, Ms. Cross. I'm Eldon Franke . . ."

Of course. That was why he looked familiar. The Human Potential Guru who had gotten all the press. He was a legitimate scientist whose most recent tome became a pop culture bestseller. Franke rehashed the nature versus nurture arguments in personality development, mixed in some sociology and some well-documented advice for improving the lot nature/nurture gave people, and somehow the book hit.

She had read it, and had been impressed with the interdisciplinary methods he had used— and the credit he had given to his colleagues.

". . . have a new grant, quite a large one actually, which startled even me. With that and the proceeds from the last book, I'm able to undertake the kind of study I've always wanted to do."

She kept her hands folded and watched him. His eyes were bright, intense. She remembered seeing him at faculty parties, but she had never spoken to him. She didn't speak to many people voluntarily, especially during social occasions. She had learned, from her earliest days, the value of keeping to herself.

"I will be bringing in subjects from around the country," he was saying. "I had hoped to go around the world, but that makes this study too large even for me. As it is, I'll be working with over three hundred subjects from all over the United States. I didn't expect to find one in my own back yard."

A subject. She felt her breath catch in her throat. She had thought he was approaching her as an equal.

"I know from published reports that you dislike talking about your status as a Millennium Baby, but—"

"Off," she said to House. Franke's image froze on the screen.

"I'm sorry," House said. "This message is designed to be played in its entirety."

"So go around it," she said, "and shut the damn thing off."

"The message program is too sophisticated for my systems," House said.

Brooke cursed. The son of a bitch knew she'd try to shut him down. "How long is it?"

"You have heard a third of the message."

Brooke sighed. "All right. Continue."

The image became mobile again. "—I hope you hear me out. My work, as you may or may not know, is with human potential. I plan to build on my earlier research, but I lacked the right kind of study group. Many scientists of all stripes have studied generations, and assumed that because people were born in the same year, they had the same hopes, aspirations, and dreams. I do not believe that is so. The human creature is too diverse—"

"Get to the point," Brooke said, sitting on a wooden kitchen chair.

"—so in my quest for the right group, I stumbled on thirty-year-old articles about Millennium Babies, and I realized that the subset of your generation, born on January first of the year 2000, actually have similar beginnings."

"No, we don't," Brooke said.

"Thus you give me a chance to focus this study. I will use the raw data to continue my overall work, but this study will focus on what it is that makes human beings succeed or fail—"

"Screw you," Brooke said and walked out of the kitchen. Behind her, Franke's voice stopped.

"Do you want me to transfer audio to the living room?" House asked.

"No," Brooke said. "Let him ramble on. I'm done listening."

The fire crackled in the fireplace, her wine had warmed to room temperature, bringing out a different bouquet, and her blankets looked comfortable. She sank into them. Franke's voice droned on in the kitchen, and she ordered House to play Bach to cover him.

But her favorite Brandenburg Concerto couldn't wipe Franke's voice from her mind. Studying Millennium Babies. Brooke closed her eyes. She wondered what her mother would think of that.

Three days later, Brooke was in her office, trying to assemble her lecture for her new survey class. This one was on the two World Wars. The University of Wisconsin still believed that a teacher should stand in front of students, even for the large lecture courses, instead of delivering canned lectures that could be downloaded. Most professors saw surveys as too much wasted work, but she actually enjoyed it. She liked standing before a large room delivering a lecture.

But now she was getting past the introductory remarks and into the areas she wasn't that familiar with. She didn't believe in regurgitating the textbooks, so she was boning up on World War I. She had forgotten that its causes were so complex, its results so far reaching, especially in Europe. Sometimes she just found herself reading, lost in the past.

Her office was small and narrow, with barely enough room for her desk. Because she was new, she was assigned to Bascom Hall at the top of Bascom Hill, a building that had been around for most of the university's history. The Hall's historic walls didn't accommodate new technology, so the university made certain she had a fancy desk with a built-in screen. The problem with that was that when she did extensive research, as she was doing now, she had to look down. She often downloaded information to her palmtop or worked at home. Working in her office, in the thin light provided by the ancient fluorescents and the dirty meshed window, gave her a headache.

But she was nearly done. Tomorrow, she would take the students from the horrors of trench warfare to the first steps toward U.S. involvement. The bulk of the lecture, though, would focus on isolationism—a potent force in both world wars.

A knock on her door brought her to the twenty-first century. She rubbed the bridge of her nose impatiently. She wasn't holding office hours. She hated it when students failed to read the signs.

"Yes?" she asked.

"Professor Cross?"

"Yes?"

"May I have a moment of your time?"

The voice was male and didn't sound terribly young, but many of her students were older.

"A moment," she said, using her desktop to unlock the door. "I'm not having office hours."

The knob turned and a man came inside. He wasn't very tall, and he was thin—a runner's build. It wasn't until he turned toward her, though, that she let out a groan.

"Professor Franke."

He held up a hand. "I'm sorry to disturb you—"

"You should be," she said. "I purposely didn't answer your message."

"I figured. Please. Just give me a few moments."

She shook her head. "I'm not interested in being the subject of any study. I don't have time."

"Is it the time? Or is it the fact that the study has to do with Millennium Babies?" His look was sharp.

"Both."

"I can promise you that you'll be well compensated. And if you'll just listen to me for a moment, you might reconsider—"

"Professor Franke," she said, "I'm not interested."

"But you're a key to the study."

"Why?" she asked. "Because of my mother's lawsuits?"

"Yes," he said.

She felt the air leave her body. She had to remind herself to breathe. The feeling was familiar. It had always been familiar. Whenever anyone talked about Millennium Babies, she had this feeling in her stomach.

Millennium Babies. No one had expected the craze, but it had become apparent by March of 1999. Prospective parents were timing the conception of their children as part of a race to see if their child could be the first born in 2000—the New Millennium, as the pundits of the day inaccurately called it. There was a more-or-less informal international contest, but in the United States, the competition was quite heavy. There were other races in every developed country, and in every city. And in most of those places, the winning parent got a lot of money, and a lot of products, and some, those with the cutest babies, or the pushiest parents, got endorsements as well.

"Oh, goodie," Brooke said, filling her voice with all the sarcasm she could muster. "My mother was upset that I didn't get exploited enough as a child so you're here to fill the gap."

His back straightened. "It's not like that."

"Really? How is it then?" She regretted the words the moment she spoke them. She was giving Franke the opening he wanted.

"We've chosen our candidates with care," he said. "We are not taking babies born randomly on January first of 2000. We're taking children whose birth was planned, whose parents made public statements about the birth, and whose parents hoped to get a piece of the pie."

"Wonderful," she said. "You're studying children with dysfunctional families."

"Are we?" he asked.

"Well, if you study me, you are," she said and stood. "Now, I'd like it if you leave."

"You haven't let me finish."

"Why should I?"

"Because this study might help you, Professor Cross."

"I'm doing fine without your help."

"But you never talk about your Millennium Baby status."

"And how often do you discuss the day you were born, Professor?"

"My birthday is rather unremarkable," he said. "Unlike yours."

She crossed her arms. "Get out."

"Remember that I study human potential," he said. "And you all have the same beginnings. All of you come from parents who had the same goal—parents who were driven to achieve something unusual."

"Parents who were greedy," she said.

"Some of them," he said. "And some of them planned to have children anyway, and thought it might be fun to try to join the contest."

"I don't see how our beginnings are relevant."

He smiled, and she cursed under her breath. As long as she talked to him, as long as she asked thinly veiled questions, he had her and they both knew it.

"In the past forty years, studies of identical twins raised apart have shown that at least fifty percent of a person's disposition is apparent at birth. Which means that no matter how you're raised, if you were a happy baby, you have a greater than fifty percent chance of being a happy adult. The remaining factors are probably environmental. Are you familiar with DNA mapping?"

"You're not answering my question," she said.

"I'm trying to," he said. "Listen to me for a few moments, and then kick me out of your office."

She wouldn't get rid of him otherwise. She slowly sat in her chair.

"Are you familiar with DNA mapping?" he repeated.

"A little," she said.

"Good." He leaned back in his chair and templed his fingers. "We haven't located a happiness gene or an unhappiness gene. We're not sure what it is about the physical make-up that makes these things work. But we do know that it has something to do with serotonin levels."

"Get to the part about Millennium Babies," she said.

He smiled. "I am. My last book was partly based on the happiness/unhappiness model, but I believe that's too simplistic. Human beings are complex creatures. And as I grow older, I see a lot of lost potential. Some of us were raised to fail, and some were raised to succeed. Some of those raised to succeed have failed, and some who were raised to fail have succeeded. So clearly it isn't all environment."

"Unless some were reacting against their environment," she said, hearing the sullenness in her tone, a sullenness she hadn't used since she last spoke to her mother five years before.

"That's one option," he said, sounding brighter. He must have taken her statement for interest. "But one of the things I learned while working on human potential is that drive is like happiness. Some children are born driven. They walk sooner than others. They learn faster. They adapt faster. They achieve more, from the moment they take their first breath."

"I don't really believe that our entire personalities are formed at birth," she said. "Or that our destinies are written before we're conceived."

"None of us do," he said. "If we did, we wouldn't have a reason to get out of bed in the morning. But we do acknowledge that we're all given traits and talents that are different from each other. Some of us have blue eyes. Some of us can hit golf balls with a power and accuracy that others only dream of. Some of us have perfect pitch, right?"

"Of course," she snapped.

"So it only stands to reason that some of us are born with more happiness than others, and some are born with more drive than others. If you consider those intangibles to be as real as, say, musical talent."

His argument had a certain logic, but she didn't want to agree with him on anything. She wanted him out of her office.

"But," he said. "Those with the most musical talent aren't always the ones on stage at Carnegie Hall. There are other factors, environmental factors. A child who grows up without hearing music might never know how to make music, right?"

"I don't know," she said.

"Likewise," he said, "if that musically inclined child had parents to whom music was important, the child might hear music all the time. From the moment that child is born, that child is familiar with music and has an edge on the child who hasn't heard a note."

She started tapping her fingers.

He glanced at them and leaned forward. "As I said in my message, this study focuses on success and failure. To my knowledge, there has never before been a group of children conceived nationwide with the same specific goal in mind."

Her mouth was dry. Her fingers had stopped moving.

"You Millennium Babies share several traits in common. Your parents conceived you at the same time. Your parents had similar goals and desires for you. You came out of the womb and instantly you were branded a success or a failure, at least for this one goal."

"So," she said, keeping her voice cold. "Are you going to deal with all those children who were abandoned by their parents when they discovered they didn't win?"

"Yes," he said.

The quiet sureness of his response startled her. He spread his hands as if in explanation. "Their parents gave up on them," he said. "Right from the start. Those babies are perhaps the purest subjects of the study. They were clearly conceived only with the race in mind."

"And you want me because I'm the most spectacular failure of the group." Her voice was cold, even though she had to clasp her hands together to keep them from trembling.

"I don't consider you a failure, Professor Cross," he said. 'You're well respected in your profession. You're on a tenure track at a prestigious university—"

"I meant as a Millennium Baby. I'm the public failure. When people think of baby contests, the winners never come to mind. I do."

He sighed. "That's part of it. Part of it is your mother's attitude. In some ways, she's the most obsessed parent, at least that we can point to."

Brooke winced.

"I'd like to have you in this study," he said. "The winners will be. It would be nice to have you represented as well."

"So that you can get rich off this book, and I'll be disgraced yet again," she said.

"Maybe," he said. "Or maybe you'll get validated."

Her shoulders were so tight that it hurt to move her head. " 'Validated.' Such a nice psychiatrist's word. Making me feel better will salve your conscience while you get rich."

"You seem obsessed with money," he said.

"Shouldn't I be?" she asked. "With my mother?"

He stared at her for a long moment.

Finally, she shook her head. "It's not the money. I just don't want to be exploited anymore. For any reason."

He nodded. Then he folded his hands across his stomach and squinched up his face, as if he were thinking. Finally, he said, "Look, here's how it is. I'm a scientist. You're a member of a group that interests me and will be useful in my research. If I were researching thirty-year-old history professors who happened to be on a tenure track, I'd probably interview you as well. Or professional women who lived in Wisconsin. Or—"

"Would you?" she asked. "Would you come to me, really?"

He nodded. "It's policy to check who's available for study at the university before going outside of it."

She sighed. He had a point. "A book on Millennium Babies will sell well. They all do. And you'll get interviews, and you'll become famous."

"The study uses Millennium Babies," he said, "but anything I publish will be about success and failure, not a pop psychology book about people born on January first."

"You can swear to that?" she asked.

"I'll do it in our agreement," he said.

She closed her eyes. She couldn't believe he was talking her into this.

Apparently he didn't think he had, for he continued. "You'll be compensated for your time and your travel expenses. We can't promise a lot, but we do promise that we won't abuse your assistance."

She opened her eyes. That intensity was back in his face. It didn't unnerve her. In fact, it reassured her. She would rather have him passionate about the study than anything else.

"All right," she said. "What do I have to do?"

First she signed waivers. She had all of them checked out by her lawyer—the fact that she even had a lawyer was yet another legacy from her mother—and he said that they were fine, even liberal. Then he tried to talk her out of the study, worried more as a friend, he said, even though he had never been her friend before.

"You've been trying to get away from all of this. Now you're opening it back up? That can't be good for you."

But she wasn't sure what was good for her anymore. She had tried not thinking about it. Maybe focussing on herself, on what happened to her from the moment she was born, was better.

She didn't know, and she didn't ask. The final agreement she signed was personalized—it guaranteed her access to her file, a copy of the completed study, and promised that any study her information was used in would concern success and failure only, and would not be marketed as a Millennium Baby product. Her lawyer asked for a few changes, but very few, considering how opposed he was to this project. She was content with the concessions Professor Franke made for her, including the one which allowed her to leave after the first two months.

But the first two months were grueling, in their own way. She had to carve time out of an already full schedule for a complete physical, which included DNA sampling. This had been a major sticking point for her lawyer—that her DNA and her genetic history would not be made available to anyone else—and he had actually gotten Franke to sign forms that attested to that fact. The sampling, for all its trouble, was relatively painless. A few strands of hair, some skin scrapings, and two vials of blood, and she was done.

The psychological exams took the longest. Most of them required the presence of the psychiatric research member of the team, a dour woman who barely spoke to Brooke when she came in. The woman watched while Brooke used a computer to take tests: a Rorschach, a Minnesota Multiphasic Personality Interview, a Thematic Apperception Test, and a dozen others whose names she just as quickly forgot. One of them was a standard IQ test. Another a specialized test designed by Franke's team for his previous experiment. All of them felt like games to Brooke, and all of them took over an hour each to complete.

Her most frustrating time, though, was with the sociologist, a well-meaning man named Meyer. He wanted to correlate her experiences with the experiences of others, and put them in the context of the society at the time. He'd ask questions, though, and she'd correct them—feeling that his knowledge of modern history was poor. Finally she complained to Franke, who smiled, and told her that her perceptions and the researchers' didn't have to match. What was important to them wasn't what was true for the society, but what was true for *her*. She wanted to argue, but it wasn't her study, and she decided she was placing too much energy into all of it.

Through it all, she had weekly appointments with a psychologist who asked her questions she didn't want to think about. *How has being a Millennium Baby influenced your outlook on life? What's your first memory? What do you think of your mother?*

Brooke couldn't answer the first. The second question was easy. Her first memory was of television lights blinding her, creating prisms, and her chubby baby fingers reaching for them, only to be caught and held by her mother's cold hand.

Brooke declined to answer the third question, but the psychologist asked it at every single meeting. And after every single meeting, Brooke went home and cried.

She gave a mid-term exam in her World Wars class, the first time she had ever done so in a survey class. But she decided to see how effective she was being, since her concentration was more on her own past than the one she was supposed to be teaching.

Her graduate assistants complained about it, especially when they looked at the exam itself. It consisted of a single question: *Write an essay exploring the influences, if any, the First World War had on the Second. If you believe there were no influences, defend that position.*

Her assistants tried to talk her into a simple true/false/multiple choice exam, and she had glared at them. "I don't want to give a test that can be graded by computer," she said. "I want to see a handwritten exam, and I want to know what these kids have learned." And because she wanted to know that—not because of her assistants' complaints (as she made very clear)—she took twenty of the exams to grade herself.

But before she started, she had a meeting in Franke's office. He had called her.

Franke's office was in a part of the campus she didn't get to very often. A winding road took her past Washburn Observatory on a bluff overlooking Lake Mendota, and into a grove of young trees. The parking area was large and filled with small electric and energy efficient cars. She walked up the brick sidewalk. Unlike the sidewalks around the rest of the city, this one didn't have the melting piles of dirty snow that were reminders of the long hard winter. Instead, tulips and irises poked out of the brown dirt lining the walk.

The building was an old Victorian style house, rather large for its day. The only visible signs of a remodel (besides the pristine condition of the paint and roof) were the security system outside, and the heat pump near the driveway.

Clearly this was a faculty-only building; no classes were held here. She turned the authentic glass doorknob and stepped into a narrow foyer. A small electronic screen floated in the center of the room. The screen moved toward her.

"I'm here to see Dr. Franke," she said.

"Second floor," the digital voice responded. "He is expecting you."

She sighed softly and mounted the stairs. With the exception of the electronics, everything in the hall reflected the period. Even the stairs weren't carpeted, but were covered instead in an old-fashioned runner, tacked on the sides, with a long gold carpet holder pushed against the back of the step.

The stairs ended in a long narrow hallway, illuminated by electric lights done up to resemble gaslights. Only one door stood open. She knocked on it, then, without waiting for an invitation, went in.

The office wasn't like hers. This office was a suite, with a main area and a private room to the side. A leather couch was pushed against the window, and two matching leather chairs flanked it. Teak tables provided the accents, with round gold table lamps the only flourish.

Professor Franke stood in the door to the private area. He looked at her examining his office.

"Impressive," she said.

He shrugged. "The university likes researchers, especially those who add to its prestige."

She knew that. She had published her thesis, and it had received some acclaim in academic circles, which was why she was as far ahead as she was. But very few historians became famous for their research. She doubted she would ever achieve this sort of success.

"Would you like a seat?" Franke asked.

She sat on one of the leather chairs. It was soft, and molded around her. "I didn't think you'd need to interview every subject to see if they wanted to continue," she said.

"Every subject isn't you." He sat across from her. His hair was slightly mussed as if he had been running his fingers through it, and he had a coffee stain above the breastpocket of his white shirt. "We had agreements."

She nodded.

"I will tell you some of what we have learned," he said. "It's preliminary, of course."

"Of course." She sounded calmer than she felt. Her heart was pounding.

"We've found three interesting things. The first is that all Millennium Babies in this study walked earlier than the norm, and spoke earlier as well. Since most were firstborns, this is unusual. Firstborns usually speak *later* than the norm because their every need is catered to. They don't need to speak right away, and when they do, they usually speak in full sentences."

"Meaning?"

"I hesitate to say for certain, but it might be indicative of great drive. Stemming, I believe, from the fact that the parents were driven." His eyes were sparkling. His enthusiasm for his work was catching. She found herself leaning forward like a student in her favorite class. "We're also finding genetic markers in the very areas we were looking for. And some interesting biochemical indications that may help us isolate the biological aspect of this."

"You're moving fast," she said.

He nodded. "That's what's nice about having a good team."

And a lot of subjects, she thought. Not to mention building on earlier research.

"We've also found that there is direct correlation between a child's winning or losing the millennium race and her perception of herself as a success or failure, independent of external evidence."

Her mouth was dry. "Meaning?"

"No matter how successful they are, the majority of Millennium Babies—at least the ones we chose for this study, the ones whose parents conceived them only as part of the race—perceive themselves as failures."

"Including me," she said.

He nodded. The movement was slight, and it was gentle.

"Why?" she asked.

"That's the thing we can only speculate at. At least at this moment." He wasn't telling her everything. But then, the study wasn't done. He tilted his head slightly. "Are you willing to go to phase two of the study?"

"If I say no, will you tell me what else you've discovered?" she asked.

"That's our agreement." He paused and then added, "I would really like it if you continued."

Brooke smiled. "That much is obvious."

He smiled too, and then looked down. "This last part is nothing like the first. You won't have test after test. It's only going to last for a few days. Can you do that?"

Some of the tension left her shoulders. She could do a few days. But that was it. "All right," she said.

"Good." He smiled at her, and she braced herself. There was more. "I'll put you down for the next segment. It doesn't start until Memorial Day. I have to ask you to stay in town, and set aside that weekend."

She had no plans. She usually stayed in town on Memorial Day weekend. Madison emptied out, the students going home, and the city became a small town—one she dearly loved.

She nodded.

He waited a moment, his gaze darting downward, and then meeting hers again. "There's one more thing."

This was why he had called her here. This was why she needed to see him in person.

"I was wondering if your mother ever told you who your father is. It would help our study if we knew something about both parents."

Brooke threaded her hands together willing herself to remain calm. This had been a sensitive issue her entire life. "No," she said. "My mother has no idea who my father is. She went to a sperm bank."

Franke frowned. "I just figured, since your mother seemed so meticulous about everything else, she would have researched your father as well."

"She did," Brooke said. "He was a physicist, very well known, apparently. It was one of those sperm banks that specialized in famous or successful people. And my mother did check that out."

Your father must not have been as wonderful as they said he was. Look at you. It had to come from somewhere.

"Do you know the name of the bank?"

"No."

Franke sighed. "I guess we have all that we can, then."

She hated the disapproval in his tone. "Surely others in this study only have one parent."

"Yes," he said. "There's a subset of you. I was just hoping—"

"Anything to make the study complete," she said sarcastically.
"Not anything," he said. "You can trust me on that."

Brooke didn't hear from Professor Franke again for nearly a month, and then only in the form of a message, delivered to House, giving her the exact times, dates, and places of the Memorial Day meetings. She forgot about the study except when she saw it on her calendar.

The semester was winding down. The mid-term in her World Wars class showed her two things: that she had an affinity for the topic which she was sharing with the students; and that at least two of her graduate assistants had a strong aversion to work. She lectured both assistants, spoke to the chair of the department about teaching the survey class next semester, and continued on with the lectures, focusing on them as if she were the graduate student instead of the professor.

By late April, she had her final exam written—a long cumbersome thing, a mixture of true/false/multiple choice for the assistants, and two essay questions for her. She was thinking of a paper herself—one on the way those wars still echoed through the generations—and she was trying to decide if she wanted the summer to work on it or to teach as she usually did.

The last Saturday in April was unusually balmy, in the seventies without much humidity, promising a beautiful summer ahead. The lilac bush near her kitchen window had bloomed. The birds had returned, and her azaleas were blossoming as well. She was in the garage, digging for a lawn chair that she was convinced she still had when she heard the hum of an electric car.

She came out of the garage, dusty and streaked with grime. A green car pulled into her driveway, next to the ancient pick-up she used for hauling.

Something warned her right from the start. A glimpse, perhaps, or a movement. Her stomach flipped over, and she had to swallow sudden nausea. She had left her personal phone inside—it was too nice to be connected to the world today—and she had never gotten the garage hooked into House's computer because she hadn't seen the need for the expense.

Still, as the car shuddered to a stop, she glanced at the screen door, wondering if she could make it in time. But the car's door was already opening, and in this kind of stand-off, fake courage was better than obvious panic.

Her mother stepped out. She was a slender woman. She wore

blue jeans and a pale peach summer sweater that accented her silver and gold hair. The hair was new, and had the look of permanence. Apparently her mother had finally decided to settle on a color. She wore gold bangles, and a matching necklace, but her ears were bare.

"I have a restraining order against you," Brooke said, struggling to keep her voice level. "You are not supposed to be here."

"I'm not the one who broke the order." Her mother's voice was smooth and seductive. Her courtroom voice. She had won a lot of cases with that melodious warmth. It didn't seem too strident. It just seemed sure.

"I sure as hell didn't want contact with you," Brooke said.

"No? Is that why your university contacted me?"

Brooke's heart was pounding so hard she wondered if her mother could hear it. "Who contacted you?"

"A Professor Franke, for some study. Something to do with DNA samples. I was to send them through my doctor, but you know I wouldn't do such a thing with anything that delicate."

Son of a bitch. Brooke hadn't known they were going to try something like that. She didn't remember any mention of it, nothing in the forms.

"I have nothing to do with that," Brooke said.

"It seems you're in some study. That seems like involvement to me," her mother said.

"Not the kind that gets you around a restraining order. Now get the hell off my property."

"Brooke, honey," her mother said, taking a step toward her. "I think you and I should discuss this—"

"There's nothing to discuss," Brooke said. "I want you to stay away from me."

"That's silly." Her mother took another step forward. "We should be able to settle this, Brooke. Like adults. I'm your mother—"

"That's not my fault," Brooke snapped. She glanced at the screen door again.

"A restraining order is for people who threaten your life. I've never hurt you, Brooke."

"There's a judge in Dane County who disagrees, Mother."

"Because you were so hysterical," her mother said. "We've had a good run of it, you and I."

Brooke felt the color drain from her face. "How's that, Mother? The family that sues together stays together?"

"Brooke, we have been denied what's rightfully ours. We—"

"It never said in any of those contests that a child had to be born by natural means. You misunderstood, Mother. Or you tried to be even more perfect than anyone else. So what if I'm the first vaginal birth of the new millennium. So what? It was thirty years ago. Let it go."

"The first baby received enough in endorsements to pay for a college education and to have a trust fund—"

"And you've racked up enough in legal fees that you could have done the same." Brooke rubbed her hands over her arms. The day had grown colder.

"No, honey," her mother said in that patronizing tone that Brooke hated. "I handled my own case. There were no fees."

It was like arguing with a wall. "I have made it really, really clear that I never wanted to see you again," Brooke said. "So why do you keep hounding me? You don't even like me."

"Of course I like you, Brooke. You're my daughter."

"I don't like you," Brooke said.

"We're flesh and blood," her mother said softly. "We owe it to each other to be there for each other."

"Maybe you should have remembered that when I was growing up. I was a child, Mother, not a trophy. You saw me as a means to an end, an end you now think you got cheated out of. Sometimes you blame me for that—I was too big, I didn't come out fast enough, I was breach—and sometimes you blame the contest people for not discounting all those 'artificial methods' of birth, but you never, ever blame yourself. For anything."

"Brooke," her mother said, and took another step forward.

Brooke held up her hand. "Did you ever think, Mother, that it's your fault we missed the brass ring? Maybe you should have pushed harder. Maybe you should have had a C-section. Or maybe you shouldn't have gotten pregnant at all."

"Brooke!"

"You weren't fit to be a parent. That's what the judge decided. You're right. You never hit me. You didn't have to. You told me how worthless I was from the moment I could hear. All that anger you felt about losing you directed at me. Because, until I was born, you never lost anything."

Her mother shook her head slightly. "I never meant that. When I would say that, I meant—"

"See? You're so good at taking credit for anything that goes well, and so bad at taking it when something doesn't."

"I still don't see why you're so angry at me," her mother said.

This time, it was Brooke's turn to take a step forward. "You don't? You don't remember that last official letter? The one cited in my restraining order?"

"You have never understood the difference between a legal argument and the real issues."

"Apparently the judge is just as stupid about legal arguments as I am, Mother." Brooke was shaking. "He believed it when you said that I was brought into this world simply to win that contest, and by rights, the state should be responsible for my care, not you."

"It was a lawsuit, Brooke. I had an argument to make."

"Maybe you can justify it that way, but I can't. I know the truth when I hear it. And so does the rest of the world." Brooke swallowed. Her throat was so tight it hurt. "Now get out of here."

"Brooke, I—"

"I mean it, Mother. Or I will call the police."

"Do you want me at least to do the DNA work?"

"I don't give a damn what you do, so long as I never see you again."

Her mother sighed. "Other children forgive their parents for mistakes they made in raising them."

"Was your attitude a mistake, Mother? Have you reformed? Or do you still have lawsuits out there? Are you still trying to collect on a thirty-year-old dream?"

Her mother shook her head and went back to the car. Brooke knew that posture. It meant that Brooke was being unreasonable. Brooke was impossible to argue with. Brooke was the burden.

"Some day," her mother said. "You'll regret how you treated me."

"Why?" Brooke asked. "You don't seem to regret how you treated me."

"Oh, I regret it, Brooke. If I had known it would have made you so bitter toward me, I never would have talked to you about our problems. I would have handled them alone."

Brooke clenched a fist and then unclenched it. She made herself take a deep breath and, instead of pointing out to her mother that she had done it again—she had blamed Brooke—Brooke said, "I'm calling the police now," and started toward the house.

"There's no need," her mother said. "I'm going. I'm just sorry—"

And the rest of her words got lost in the bang of the screen door.

* * *

An hour later, Brooke found herself outside Professor Franke's office. She ignored the small electronic screen that floated ahead of her, bleating that she didn't have an appointment and she wasn't welcome in the building. It was a dumb little machine; when she had asked if Professor Franke was in, it had told her he was. A good human secretary would have lied.

Apparently the system had already contacted Franke for he stood in his door, waiting for her, a smile on his face even though his eyes were wary.

"Everything all right, Professor Cross?"

"I never gave you permission to contact my mother," she said as she came up the stairs.

"Your mother?"

"She came to my house today, claiming I'd nullified my restraining order by contacting her. She said you asked her for DNA samples."

"Come into my office," he said.

Brooke walked past him and heard him close the door. "We did contact her, as we did all the parents, for DNA samples. We were explicit in expressing our needs as part of the study, and that they had every right to refuse if they wanted. In no way did we ask her to come here or to tell her that you asked us to contact her."

"She says it came from me and she knew I was involved in the study."

"Of course," he said. "One of the waivers you signed gave us permission to examine your genetic heritage. That includes parents, grandparents, living relatives if necessary. Your attorney didn't object."

Her attorney was good, but not that good. He probably hadn't known what that all entailed.

"I want you to send a letter, through your attorney or the university's counsel, stating that I in no way asked you to contact her and that you did it of your own volition."

"Do you want me to apologize?" he asked.

"To me or to her?" she asked.

He drew in his breath sharply and she realized for the first time that she had knocked him off balance.

"I meant to her," he said, "but I guess I owe you an apology too."

Brooke stared at him for a moment. No one had said that to her before.

"Look," he said, apparently not understanding her silence. "I should have thought it through when your mother said she didn't allow such confidential information to be sent to people she didn't know. I thought that was a refusal."

"For anyone else it would have been," Brooke said. "But not for my mother."

"She's an interesting woman."

"From the outside," Brooke said.

He nodded as if he understood. "For the record, I didn't mean to cause you trouble. I'm sorry I didn't warn you."

"It's all right," Brooke said. "Just don't let it happen again."

Except for receiving a copy of the official letter Franke sent to her mother, Brooke didn't think about the study again until Memorial Day weekend. The semester was over. Most of her students successfully answered the question on her World Wars final: *Explain the influence World War I had on World War II.*

One student actually called World War I the mother of World War II. The phrase stopped Brooke as she read, made her shudder, and hoped that not every monstrous mother begot an even more monstrous child.

Professor Franke sent instructions for Memorial Day weekend with the official letter. He asked her to set aside time from mid-afternoon on Friday to late evening on Monday. She was to report to TheaterPlace, a restaurant and bar on the west side of town.

She'd been to the restaurant before. It was a novelty spot in what had once been a four-plex movie palace. The restaurant was in the very center, with huge meeting rooms off to the sides. The builders had called it a gathering place for organizations too small to hold conventions. Still, it had everything—the large restaurant, the bar, places for presentations, places for seminars, places for quiet get-togethers. There were three smaller restaurants in what had once been the projection booths—restaurants that barely seated twenty. One of the larger rooms even showed live theater once a month.

Cars were no longer allowed in this part of town, thanks to a Green referendum three years before. Someone had tried to make exception for electric vehicles but that hadn't worked either as the traffic cops said it would be too hard to patrol. Instead, the light rail made several stops, and some enterprising entrepreneur had built underground tunnels to connect all of the buildings. Many people Brooke knew preferred to shop here in the winter; it kept them out of the freezing cold. But she found the necessity of taking the light rail annoying. She would have preferred her own car so that she could leave on her own schedule.

She walked from the light rail stop near the refurbished mall to TheaterPlace. On the outside, it still looked like a four-plex: the raised roof, the warehouse shape. Only up close did it become apparent that TheaterPlace had been completely gutted and remodeled, right down to the smoke glass that had replaced the clear windows.

A sign on the main entrance notified her that TheaterPlace was closed for a private party. She touched the door anyway—knowing the party was theirs—and a scanner instantly identified her.

Welcome, Brooke Cross. You may enter.

She shuddered slightly, knowing that Franke had programmed the scanner to recognize either her fingerprints on the backside of the door or her DNA. She felt like her mother, worried that Franke had too much information.

The door clicked open and she let herself inside. A short dark-haired woman she had never seen before hurried to her side.

"Professor Cross," the woman said. "Welcome."

"Thanks," Brooke said.

"Just a few rules before we get started," the woman said. "This is the last time we'll be using names today. We ask you not to tell anyone who you are by name, although you may tell them anything else you wish about yourself. Please identify yourself using this number only."

She handed Brooke a stick-on badge with the number 333 printed in bold black numbers.

"Then what?" Brooke asked.

"Wait for Professor Franke to make his announcement. You're in the Indiana Jones room, by the way."

"Thanks," Brooke said. She stuck the label to her white blouse and made her way down the hall. All of the rooms were named after characters from famous movies, and the décor in all of them except the restaurants was the same: movie posters on the wall, soft golden lighting, and a thin light blue carpet. The furniture moved according to the function. She had been in the Jones room before for a faculty party honoring some distinguished professor from Beijing, but she doubted the room would be the same.

The double doors were open and, inside, she heard the sound of soft conversation. She stopped just outside the door and surveyed the room.

The lights were up—not soft and golden at all—but full daylight, so that everyone's faces were visible. The Jones room was one of the largest—the only theater, apparently, whose dimensions had been left intact. It seemed about half full.

There were tables lining the wall, with various kinds of foods and beverages, small plates to hold everything, and silverware glimmering in the brightness. People stood in various clusters. There were no chairs, no furniture groupings, and Brooke knew that was on purpose. Small floating serving trays hovered near each group. Whenever someone set an empty glass on one, the tray would float through an opening in the wall, and another tray would take its place.

Something about the groupings made her nervous, and it wasn't the lack of chairs or the fact that she didn't know anyone. She stared for a moment, trying to figure out what had caught her attention.

No one looked the same; they were fat and thin, tall and short. They had long hair and beards, no hair, and dyed hair. They were white, black, Asian and Hispanic, or they were multiracial, with no features that marked them as part of any particular ethnic group. They were incredibly diverse—but none of them were elderly or underage. None of them had wrinkles, except for a few laugh lines, and none of them seemed younger than twenty.

They were about the same age. She would guess they *were* the same age—the exact same age as she was. It was a gathering of Franke's subjects for this study: all of them born January 1, 2000. All of them thirty years and 147 days old.

She shuddered. No wonder Franke was worried about this second half of the study. Most studies of this nature didn't allow the participants to get to know each other. She wondered what discipline he was dabbling in now, what sort of results he was expecting.

A man stopped beside her just outside the door. He was wearing a denim shirt, a bolo tie, and tight blue jeans. His long blond hair—naturally sunstreaked—brushed against his collar. He had a tan—something she had rarely seen in her lifetime—and it made his skin a burnished gold. He had letters on his name badge: DKGHY.

"Hi," he said. His voice was deep with a Southern twang. "I guess we just go in, huh?"

"I've been steeling myself for it," she said.

He smiled. "Feels like they took away my armor when they

took my name. I'm not sure if I'm supposed to say, 'Hi, I'm DKG—whatever-the-hell the rest of those letters are.' Or if I'm not supposed to say anything at all."

"Well, I don't want to be called 333."

"Can't say as I blame you." He grinned. "How about I call you Tre, and you can call me—oh, hell, I don't know—"

"De," she said. "I'll call you De."

"Nice to meet you, Tre," he said, holding out his hand.

She took it. His fingers were warm. "Nice to meet you, De."

"Where do y'all hail from?"

"Right here," she said.

"You're kiddin'? No travel expenses, huh?"

"And no hotel rooms."

He grinned. "Sometimes hotel rooms can be nice, especially when you don't get to see the inside of them very often."

"I suppose." She smiled at him. He was making this easier than she expected. "Where're you from?"

"Originally Galveston. But I've been in L'siana a long time now."

"New Orleans?"

"Just outside."

"Some city you got there."

"Yeah, but we ain't got a place like this." He looked around. "Want to go in?"

"Now I do," she said.

They walked side-by-side as if they were a couple who had been together most of their lives. Neither of them looked at the food, although he snatched two bottles of sparkling water off one of the tables, and handed one to her. She opened it, glad to have something to carry.

A few more people came in the doors. She and De went farther into the room. Bits of conversation floated by her:

". . . never really got over it . . ."

". . . worked for the past five years as a dental hygienist . . ."

". . . my father wanted to take us out of the country, but . . ."

Then there was a slight bonging sound, and the conversation halted. Franke stood in the very front of the room, where the theater screen used to be. He was easy to see because the floor slanted downward slightly. He held up his hands, and in a moment there was complete silence.

"I want to thank you all for coming." His voice was being amplified. It sounded as if he were talking right next to Brooke instead of half a room away. "Your assignment today is easy. We do not want you sharing names, but you can talk about anything else. We will be providing meals later on in various restaurants—your badge I.D. will be listed on a door—and we will have drinks in the bar after that. We ask that no one leave before midnight, and that you all return at noon tomorrow for the second phase."

"That's it?" someone asked.

"That's it," Franke said. "Enjoy yourselves."

"I have a bad feeling about this, Tre," De said.

"Me, too," Brooke said. "It can't be this simple."

"I don't think it will be."

She sighed. "Well, we signed on for this, so we may as well enjoy it."

He looked at her sideways, his blue eyes bright. "Want to be my date for the day, darlin'?"

"It's always nice to have one friendly face," she said, surprised at how easily she was flirting with him. She never flirted with anyone.

"That it is." He offered her his arm. "Let's see how many of these nice folks are interested in conversation."

"Mingle, huh?" she asked, as she put her hand in the crook of his arm.

"I think that's what we're meant to do." He frowned. "Only god knows, I 'spect it'll all backfire 'fore the weekend's done."

It didn't backfire that night. Brooke had a marvelous dinner in one of the small restaurants with De, a woman from Boston, and two men from California. They shared stories about their lives and their jobs, and only touched in passing on the thing that they had in common. In fact, the only time they discussed it was when De brought it up over dessert.

"What made y'all sign up for this foolishness?" he asked.

"The money," said the man from Los Gatos. He was slender to the point of gauntness, with dark eyes and thinning hair. His shirt had wear marks around the collar and was fraying slightly on the cuffs. "I thought it'd be an easy buck. I didn't expect all the tests."

"Me, either," the woman from Boston said. She was tall and broadshouldered, with muscular arms. During the conversation, she mentioned that she had played professional basketball until she was sidelined with a knee injury. "I haven't had so many tests since I got out of school."

The man from Santa Barbara said nothing, which surprised Brooke. He was a short stubby man with more charm than he had originally appeared to have. He had been the most talkative during dinner—regaling them with stories about his various jobs, and his two children.

"How about you, Tre?" De asked Brooke.

"I wouldn't have done it if I wasn't part of the university," she said, and realized that was true. Professor Franke probably wouldn't have had the time to convince her, and she would have dismissed him out of hand.

"Me," De said, "I jumped at it. Never been asked to do something like this before. Felt it was sort of important, you know. Anything to help the human condition."

"You don't really believe that," Santa Barbara said.

"If you don't believe it," Los Gatos said to Santa Barbara, "why'd you sign up?"

"Free flight to Madison, vacationer's paradise," Santa Barbara said, and they all laughed. But he never did answer the question.

When Brooke got home, she sat on her porch and looked at the stars. The night was warm. The crickets were chirping and she thought she heard a frog answer them from a nearby ditch.

The evening had disturbed her in its simplicity. Like everyone else, she wanted to know what Franke was looking for. The rest of the study had been so directed, and this had been so free form.

Dinner had been nice. Drinks afterward with a different group had been nice as well. But the conversation rarely got deeper than anecdotes and current history. No one discussed the study, and no one discussed the past.

She lost De after dinner, which gave her a chance to meet several other people: a woman from Chicago, twins from Akron, and three friends from Salt Lake City. She'd had a good time, and found people she could converse with—one historian, two history buffs, and a librarian who seemed to know a little bit about everything.

De joined her later in the evening, and walked her to the rail stop. He'd leaned against the plastic shelter and smiled at her. She hadn't met a man as attractive as he was in a long time. Not since college.

"I'd ask you to my hotel," he said, "but I have a feelin' anything we do this weekend, in or out of that strange building, is going to be fodder for scientists."

She smiled. She'd had that feeling too.

"Still," he said, "I got to do one thing."

He leaned in and kissed her. She froze for a moment; she hadn't been kissed in nearly ten years. Then she eased into it, putting her arms around his neck and kissing him back, not wanting to stop, even when he pulled away.

"Hmm," he said. His eyes were closed. He opened them slowly. "I think that's titillatin' enough for the scientists, don't you?"

She almost said no. But she knew better. She didn't want to read about her sex life in Franke's next book.

The rail came down the tracks, gliding silently toward them. "See you tomorrow?" she asked.

"You can bet on it," De said. And there had been promise in his words, promise she wasn't sure she wanted to hear.

She brought her knees onto her lawn chair, and wrapped her arms around them. Part of her wished he was here, and part of her was glad he wasn't. She never let anyone come to her house. She didn't want to share it. She had had enough invasions of privacy in her life to prevent this one.

But she had nearly invited De, a man she didn't really know. Maybe De really wasn't a Millennium Baby. Perhaps a bunch of people weren't. Perhaps that was what the numbers and the letters meant. She had spent much of the evening staring at them, wondering. They appeared to be randomly generated, but that couldn't be. They had to have some purpose.

She shook her head and rested her cheek on her knees. She was taking this much too seriously, like she always took things. And soon she would be done with it. She would have bits of information she hadn't had before, and she would store them into a file in her mind, never to be examined again.

Somehow that thought made her sad. The night was beginning to get chilly. She stood, stretched, and made her way to bed.

The next morning, they met in a different room—the Rose room—named after the character in the twentieth century movie *Titanic*. Brooke hoped that the name wasn't a sign.

There were pastries and coffee on a table against the wall, along with every kind of juice imaginable and lots of fresh fruit, but again, there were no chairs. Brooke's feet hurt from the day before—she usually stood to lecture, but not for several hours—and she hoped she'd get a chance to sit before the day was out.

She was nearly late again, and hurried inside as they closed the doors. The room smelled of fresh air mixed with coffee and sweat. The group had gathered again, the faces vaguely familiar now, even the faces of people she hadn't yet met. The people toward the back who saw her enter, smiled at her or nodded in recognition. It felt like they had all bonded simply by spending an evening in the same room. An evening and the promise of a long weekend.

She shivered. The air conditioning was on high, and the room was cold. It would warm up before the day was out; the sheer number of bodies guaranteed that. But she still wondered if she was dressed warmly enough in her casual lilac blouse and her khaki pants.

"Strange how these places look the same, day or night."

She turned. De was half a step behind her, his long hair loose about his face. He still wore jeans and his fancy boots, but instead of the denim shirt and bolo tie, he wore an understated white open collar shirt that accented his tan. Somehow, she suspected, he seemed more comfortable in this. Had he worn the other as a way of identifying himself or a way of putting others off? She would probably never know.

"The people look different," she said.

"Just a little." He smiled at her. "You look nice."

"And you're flirting."

He shrugged. "I always believe in using my time wisely."

She smiled, and turned as a hush fell over the crowd. Franke had mounted the stage in front. He seemed very small in this place. A few of his assistants stood on either side of him.

"Here it comes," De said.

"What?"

"Whatever it is that's going to make this cocktail party stop." He was staring at Franke too, and his clear blue eyes seemed wary. "I've half a mind to leave now. Want to join me?"

"And do what?"

"Dunno. See the sights?"

It sounded like a good idea. But, as she had said the day before, she had signed up for this, and she didn't break her commitments. And, she had to admit, she was curious.

She bit her lower lip, trying to think of a good way to respond. Apparently she didn't have to.

De sighed. "Didn't think so."

The silence in the room was growing. Franke stared at all of them, rocking slightly on his feet. If Brooke had to guess, she would have thought him very nervous.

"All right," he said. "I have a few announcements. First, we will be serving lunch at 1 P.M. in the main restaurant. Dinner will be at 7 in the same place. You will not have assigned seating. Secondly, after I'm through, you're free to tell each other your names. We've had enough of secrets."

He paused, and this time Brooke felt it, that dread she had seen in De's eyes.

"Finally, I would like everyone with a letter on your name badge to go to the right side of the room, and everyone with a number to go to the left."

People stood for a moment, looking around, waiting for someone to go first. De put a hand on her shoulder. "Here goes nothing," he said. He ran his finger along her collarbone and then walked to the right.

"Come on, folks," Franke said. "It's not hard. Letters to the right. Numbers to the left."

Brooke could still feel De's hand on her skin. She looked in his direction, seeing his blond head towering over the small group of letters who had gathered near the pastries along the far right wall.

She took a deep breath and headed left.

The numbers had gathered near the pastries too, only on the left. She wondered what Franke's researchers would make of that. Los Gatos was there, his hand hovering between the cinnamon rolls and the donuts as if he couldn't decide. So was one of the twins from Akron, and the woman from Boston. Brooke joined them.

"What do you think this is?" Brooke asked.

"A way of identifying us as we run through the maze."

Brooke recognized that voice. She turned and saw Santa Barbara. He shrugged and smiled at her.

She picked up a donut hole and ate it, then made herself a cup of tea while she waited for the room to settle.

It finally did. There was an empty space in the center of the carpet, a space so wide it seemed like an ocean to her.

"Good," Franke said. "Now I'm going to tell you what the badges mean."

There was a slight murmuring as the groups took that in. Boston, Santa Barbara, and Los Gatos flanked Brooke. Her dinner group, minus De.

"Those of you with letters are real Millennium Babies."

Brooke felt a protest rise in her throat. She was born on January 1, 2000. She was a Millennium Baby.

"You were all chosen as such by your state or your country or your city. Your parents received endorsements or awards or newspaper coverage. Those of you with numbers . . ."

"Are fucking losers," Los Gatos mumbled under his breath.

". . . were born near midnight on January first, but were too late to receive any prizes. You're here because your parents also received publicity or gave interviews before you were born stating that the purpose behind the pregnancy wasn't to conceive a child, but to conceive a child born a few seconds after midnight on January first of 2000. You were created to be official Millennium Babies, and failed to receive that title."

Franke paused briefly.

"So, feel free to make real introductions, and mingle. The facility is yours for the day. All we ask is that you do not leave until we tell you to."

"That's it?" Boston asked.

"That's enough," Santa Barbara said. "He's just turned us into the haves and the have-nots."

"Son of a bitch," Los Gatos said.

"We knew that the winners were here," Boston said.

"Yeah, but I assumed there'd be only a few of them," Los Gatos said. "Not half the group."

"It makes sense though," Santa Barbara said. "This is a study of success and failure."

Brooke listened to them idly. She was staring at the right side of the room. All her life, she had been programmed to hate those people. She even studied a few of them, looking them up on the net, seeing how many articles were written about them.

She had stopped when she was ten. Her mother had caught her, and told her what happened to the others didn't matter. Brooke and her mother would have made more of the opportunity, if they had just been given their due.

Their due.

De was staring at her from across the empty carpet. That look of dread was still on his face.

"So," Santa Barbara said. "I guess we can use real names now."

"I guess," said Los Gatos. He hitched up his pants, and glanced at Boston.

She shrugged. "I'm Julie Hunt. I was born at 12:15 Eastern Standard Time in . . ."

Brooke stopped listening. She didn't want to know about the failures. She knew how it felt to be part of their group. But she didn't know what it was like to be with the winners.

She wiped her damp hands on her pants and crossed the empty carpet. De watched her come. In fact the entire room watched her passage as if she were Moses parting the Red Sea.

The successes weren't talking to each other. They were staring at her.

When she was a few feet away from him, he reached out and pulled her to his side, as if she were in some sort of danger and he needed to recognize her.

"Comin' to the enemy?" he asked, and there was some amusement in his tone. "Or'd they give you a number when you shoulda had a letter?"

The lie would have been so easy. But then she would have had to lie about everything, and that wouldn't work. "No," she said. "I was born at 12:05 A.M. in Detroit, Michigan."

One of the women toward the back looked at her sharply. Anyone from Michigan might recognize that time. Her mother's lawsuits created more than enough publicity. Out of the corner of her eye, Brooke saw Franke. She could feel his intensity meters away.

"Then how come you made the crossin', darlin'?" De's accent got thicker when he was nervous. She had never noticed that before.

She could have given him the easy answer, that she wanted to be beside him, but it wasn't right. The way the entire group was staring at her, eyes wide, lips slightly parted, breathing shallow. It was as if they were afraid she was going to do something to them. But what could she do? Yell at them for something that was no fault of their own? They were the lucky ones. They'd been born at the right time in the right place.

But because they hadn't earned that luck, they were afraid of her. After all, she had been part of the same contest. Only she had been a few minutes late.

No one had moved. They were waiting for her to respond.

"I guess I came," she said, "because I wanted to know what it was like to be a winner."

"Standing over here won't make you a winner," one of the men said.

She flushed. "I know that. I came to listen to you. To see how you've lived. If that's all right."

"I'm not sure I understand you, darlin'," De said. Only his name wasn't De. She didn't know his name. Maybe she never would.

"You were all born winners. From the first moment. Just like we were losers."

Her voice carried in the large room. She hadn't expected the acoustics to be so good.

"I don't know about everyone else in my group, but my birth-time has affected my entire life. My mother—" Brooke paused. She hadn't meant to discuss her mother "—never let me forget who I was. And I was wondering if any of you experienced that. Or if you felt special because you'd won. Or if you even knew."

Her voice trailed off at the end. She couldn't imagine not knowing. A life of blissful ignorance. If she hadn't known, she might have gone on to great things. She might have reached farther, tried harder. She might have expected success with every endeavor, instead of being surprised at it.

They were staring at her as if she were speaking Greek. Maybe she was.

"I don't know why it matters," a man said beside her. "It was just a silly little contest."

"I hadn't even remembered it," a woman said, "until Dr. Franke's people contacted me."

Brooke felt something catch in her throat. "Was it like that for all of you?"

"Of course not," De said. "I got interviewed every New Year's like clockwork. What's it like five years into the millennium? Ten? Twenty? That's one of the reasons I moved to L'siana. I'm not much for attention, 'specially the kind I don't deserve."

"Money was nice," one of the women said. "It got me to college."

Another woman shook her head. "My folks spent it all."

More people from the left were moving across the divide, as if they were drawn to the conversation.

"So'd mine," said one of the men.

"There wasn't any money with mine. Just got my picture in the newspaper. Still have that on my wall," another man said.

Brooke felt someone bump her from behind. Los Gatos had joined her. So had Santa Barbara and Boston—um, Julie.

"Why'd this contest make such a difference to you?" one of the letter women asked. She was staring at Brooke.

"It didn't," Brooke said after a moment. "It mattered to my mother. She lost."

"Hell," De said. "People lose. That's part of living."

Brooke looked at him. There was a slight frown mark between his eyes. He didn't understand either. He didn't know what it was like being outside, with his face pressed against the glass.

"Three weeks after I was born," Los Gatos said, "My parents

dumped me with a friend of theirs, saying they weren't ready for a baby. I never saw them. I don't even know what they look like."

"My parents said they couldn't afford me," Santa Barbara said. "They were planning on some prize money."

"They abandoned you too?" the woman asked.

"No," he said. "They just made it clear they didn't appreciate the financial burden. If they'd won, I wouldn't've been a problem."

"Sure you would have," De said. "They just would've blamed their problems on something else."

"It's not that simple," Brooke said. Her entire body was sweating despite the chill in the room. "It was a contest, a race. A lot of people didn't look beyond that. There were news articles about abandoned and abused babies, and there were a disproportionate number born in December, January, and February of 2000, because parents wanted to split some of the glory."

"You can't tell me," De said, "that something as insignificant as the time we were born determines our future."

"It does," Brooke said, "if we're brought up to believe it does."

"That bear out, Professor Franke?" De said.

Brooke turned. The professor was standing close to them, listening, looking both bemused and perplexed. Apparently he had expected some kind of reaction, but probably not this one.

"That's what I'm trying to determine," Franke said.

"And I'm askin' you if you determined it," De said.

Franke glanced at one of his assistants. The assistant shrugged. The entire room full of people was crowded around Franke, and was silent for the second time that day.

"This part of the study is experimental," he said. "I'm not sure if answering you will corrupt it."

"But you want to answer me," De said.

Franke smiled. "Yes, I do."

"It's an experiment," Brooke said. "You can always throw this part out. You might have done that anyway. Isn't that what you told me? Or at least implied?"

Franke glanced from her to De. Then Franke straightened his shoulders, as if the gesture made him stronger. "I believe that Brooke is right. My studies have convinced me that something becomes important to a child's development because that child is told that something is important."

"So us losers will remain losers the rest of our lives," Los Gatos said.

Franke shook his head. "That is not my conclusion. I believe that when something becomes important, you chose how to react to it." His voice got louder as he spoke. His professor's voice. "Some of you wearing letters have not done as well as expected. You've rebelled against those expectations and worked at proving you are not as good as you were told you were."

A flush colored De's tan cheeks.

"Others lived up to the expectations and a few of you, a very small few, exceeded them. But—" Franke paused dramatically. "Those of you who wear numbers are financially more successful as a group than your lettered peers. You strive harder because you feel you have something to overcome."

Brooke felt Los Gatos shift behind her.

"I think it goes back to the parameters of the study," Franke said. "Your parents—all of your parents—wanted to improve their lot. They all had drive, therefore most of you have drive. We've found a biological correlation."

"Really? Wow," Santa Barbara said.

"But there's more than biology at work here."

"I'd hope so," De said. "I'd hate to think you can determine who I am by reading my genes."

Franke gave him a small smile. "Your parents," Franke said, "all chose a contest as the method of improving their lives. A lottery, if you will. And most of them failed to win. Or if they succeeded, they discovered Easy Street wasn't so easy after all. You numbered folk have realized that luck is overrated. The only thing you can trust is work you do yourselves."

"And what about those of us with letters?" one of the twins from Akron asked.

"You learned a different lesson. Most of you learned that luck is what you make of it. You might win the lottery, but that doesn't make you or your family any happier than before." Franke looked at Brooke. "There were a lot of studies, some of them prompted by your mother, that showed how many unsuccessful Millennium Babies were abandoned or mistreated. But the successful ones had similar problems. Only no one wanted to lose the golden goose as long as it was still golden. Many of those abandonments were emotional, not physical. People became parents to become rich or famous, not because they wanted children."

"Sounds like you should be studying our parents," Los Gatos said.

Franke grinned. "Now you have my next book."

And the group laughed.

"Feel free to enjoy the rest of the day," Franke said. "Over the rest of the weekend, I'll be talking to individuals among you, wrapping things up. I want to thank you for your time and participation."

"That's it?" De asked.

"When you leave here tonight, if I haven't spoken to you," Franke said. "That's it."

His words were met with a momentary silence. Then he started to make his way through the group. Some people stopped him. Brooke didn't. She turned away, not sure how to feel.

She wasn't as successful as she wanted to be, but she was better off than her mother had said she would be. Brooke had her own house, a good job, interests that meant something to her.

But she was as alone as her mother was. In that, at least, they were the same.

"So," De said. "Is your life profoundly different thanks to this study?"

The question had a mixed tone. Half sarcasm, half serious. He seemed to be waiting for her answer.

"What's your name?" she asked.

"Adam," he said, wincing. "Adam Lassiter."

"The first man."

"If I'd missed my birth time, I'd have been named Zeb." He smiled as he said that, but his eyes didn't twinkle.

"I'm Brooke Cross." She waited, wondering if he'd guess at the name, despite the change. He didn't. Or if he did, he didn't say anything.

"You didn't answer my question," he said.

She looked at the room, at all the people in it, most engaged in private conversations now, hands moving, gazes serious as they compared and contrasted their experiences, trying to see if they agreed with Professor Franke.

"When I was a little girl," she said. "We lived in a small white house, maybe 1200 square feet. A starter, my mother called it, because that was all she could afford. And to me, that house was the world. My mother's world."

"What kind of world was that?" he asked.

She shook her head. How to explain it? But he had asked, and she had to try.

"A world where she did everything right and failed, and everyone else cheated and somehow succeeded. If she'd had the same kind of breaks your parents had, she believed she would have done better than they did. If she hadn't had a child like me, one who was chronically late, her life would have been better."

He was watching her. The crease between his eyes grew deeper.

Her heart was pounding, but she made herself continue. "A few years ago, when I was looking for my own home, I saw dozens and dozens of houses, and somewhere I realized that to the people living in them, those houses were the world."

"So each block has dozens of tiny worlds," he said.

She smiled at him. "Yeah."

"I still don't see how that relates."

She looked at him, then at the room. The other conversations were continuing, as serious as hers was with him. "You asked me if this study changed my life. I can't answer that. I can say, though, that it made me realize one thing."

His gaze was as intense as Franke's.

"It made me realize that even though I had moved out of that house, I hadn't left my mother's world."

He studied her for a moment longer, then said, "Sounds like a hell of a realization."

"Maybe," she said. "It depends on what I do with it."

He laughed. "Thus proving Franke's point."

She flushed. She hadn't realized she had done so, but she had. He leaned toward her.

"You know, Brooke," Adam said softly, "I like women who are chronically late. It balances my habitual timeliness. How's about we have lunch and talk about our histories. Not just the day we were born, but other things, like what we do and where we live and who we are."

She almost refused. He was from Louisiana, and she was from Wisconsin. This friendship—if that's all it was—could go nowhere.

But it was that attitude which had limited her all along. She had been driven, as Franke said, to succeed materially and professionally on her own merits. But she had never tried to succeed socially.

She had never wanted to before.

"And," she said, "you get to tell me what you learned from this study."

"Assumin'," he said with a grin, "that I'm the kinda man who can learn anything a'tall."

"Assuming that," she said and slipped her hand in his. It felt good to touch someone else, even if it was only for a brief time. It felt good.

It felt different.

It felt right.

Harvest

1

TIME TO PLANT TEARS, said the almanac, and so Kerry took the bucket she had carefully stored away at the back of the cupboard and went into the darkened bedroom. She took out each tear—perfectly formed, perfectly remembered, perfectly stored—cupped her hand around it so that the light from the hallway wouldn't catch the drop, and gently, ever so gently, tucked each tear in the fertile heart of the sleeping child.

2

Steam beaded the wallpaper. Amanda shut off the burner and moved the whistling teakettle. The morning was cold and gray. She felt chilled even though it was the beginning of summer. She set a tea bag in the mug Daniel had given her for her thirtieth birthday, and poured the water. Steam rose, fogging her glasses. She took them off, leaving the world a blur of greens and grays, grabbed a towel, and wiped the lenses. When she put her glasses back on, she saw that the tea bag had already stained the liquid brown.

She picked up the mug, happy for its warmth against her cold hands. Then she leaned against the refrigerator and sighed. She hated mornings like this. A stack of orders waited for her in her workroom, and she barely had enough energy to make a cup of tea. Part of the problem was the grayness. It oppressed her, brought out buried aches and pains. How could she sew when her hands were tight with cold, when the artificial light clashed with the darkness of a cloudy morning, making her stitches nearly impossible to see?

She made herself cross the living room into the workroom. Half-finished clothes lined the walls. The dress for Missy Anderson's wedding, still lacking a hem; the shirt for Carleton Meyer with the intricate hand-stitching undone; the pile of fabric that should already have been skirts for the high school's swing choir —all faced her like an accusation. The problem was the quilt that lay half-finished on the cluttered deacon's bench, the quilt that Amanda wanted to give Grandmother Kerry on her birthday only a week away.

Quilts were Amanda's specialty, but no one wanted quilts anymore. It was easier and cheaper to buy mass-produced things at the department stores down at the mall. Custom-made quilts were a luxury, like custom-made clothes, but for some reason people were willing to spend the money on a dress that they would use once rather than on a quilt that would cover their bed for the next fifty years.

Amanda looked at the projects hanging on the wall, and then at the others stacked in her workbasket. She set her teacup down on the end table covered with pins and patterns, then grabbed the stack of swing choir skirts. They would take her half a day if she set her mind to the work.

She moved her worktable over, picked up the bolt of fabric, and laid it on the floor. The dark green velvet seemed ostentatious for a high school group, but they had chosen it. She smoothed out the first segment, measured to see if she had the correct amount, and cut off the end of the fabric. Then she grabbed the pattern and pulled the tightly wrapped tissue pieces out of their paper folder.

Carefully, Amanda smoothed the tissue over the material. The thin paper crinkled as she worked. She checked naps and widths, making sure that everything lined up properly, so that the skirt would be as beautiful as possible. Then she pinned the tissue to the velvet, shoving the slender silver pins in with a force unnecessary to her task. She pinched the fabric tightly, and shoved. The third pin went straight through both layers of velvet, shot across the tissue, and dug deep into the index finger of her left hand.

Amanda stared at the pin jutting out of her finger. Then the pain announced itself in a hard, burning jab. She pulled her finger away, squeezed the injured area, and watched the blood well into a tiny, tear-shaped drop. She put the fingertip in her mouth. It tasted of salt and iron.

A small smear of blood stained the green velvet. Tears rose in her eyes. She couldn't do anything right. She knew that she had to move quickly to make sure that the bloodstain wouldn't be permanent, but she remained still, sitting like a child, one finger in her mouth, and knees tucked under her body until her tears slowly slid back into the tear ducts where they belonged.

3

The clock in the dining room chimed midnight as Daniel unlocked the door and stepped in. The house felt heavy and oppressive in the dark. He flicked on the switch, and the soft lights scattered across the room, leaving corners filled with shadows. Amanda's tea mug sat on the floor beside the couch. A book, face down, leaned against the mug. A pillow, still bearing Amanda's headprint, had been crushed into the corner of the couch, and on the other end, a quilt had been thrown messily back.

He felt a twinge of guilt. Amanda had waited up for him and then, when she could wait no longer, had stumbled off to bed. He knew how he would find her, curled up like a child, fist against her face, hair sprawled against the pillow. He sighed. He lost track of time so easily, forgetting that she was here, waiting for him. And he found things that made it easy to forget. He hadn't needed that drink after work with Rich. Or to meet Margot for dinner. They could have discussed the Johnson account at the office, with a desk between them, instead of sitting hip to hip in Harper's while soft jazz echoed in the background.

Daniel left Amanda's mess—he had long ago stopped picking up after her—and went into the kitchen. She had left the light above the stove on for him, like she always did.

On the wall beside the teakettle, water beaded. As he watched, one droplet slowly ran down and fell onto the oven's smooth metal surface. She had to stop facing that kettle toward the wall. The steam would ruin the wallpaper. He grabbed a paper towel and wiped the water away. Then he shut off the stove light and headed to bed.

The bedroom was dim, but not completely dark. Amanda had left the bathroom light on as well, and it fell softly across the bed, illuminating her slender form. She was curled up on her right side, one hand stretched across his pillow. The quilt had fallen off her shoulder, revealing soft skin and one well-formed breast.

He grabbed the knot of his tie, slipped it down, and slid the tie from his neck. Then he took off his clothes and carefully folded them, setting them on the rocking chair beneath the shaded windows. As he crawled into bed, he picked up her hand and ran it down his body, setting it on his groin so that as she awakened she could feel his arousal.

"Amanda," he said softly.

She stirred. He caressed her, touched every part of her, and then slipped inside of her. She didn't wake up until her first orgasm and then she cried, "Daniel!" as if he had surprised her. He buried his face in her shoulder, smelling the musky scent of her. He grabbed her waist, rolled over onto his side, holding them together so that they faced each other and let sleep drift through his body. The bathroom light shone in his eyes, but he didn't care. Amanda stirred, awake now, and he thought he felt a shudder run through her, like a sob. But when he reached up to touch her cheek, the skin was smooth, soft, and dry.

4

Amanda set the tea tray down on the coffee table. She picked up the porcelain teapot and poured. The thin liquid filled the fragile cup. Carefully, she handed the cup to her grandmother, then poured another cup. Kerry seemed frail and tired that morning, but as strong as ever. She wore a dainty summer dress of pale pink and kept her lacy off-white shawl about her shoulders.

Amanda sighed and settled back into the armchair. The rain pattered outside, dousing everything in grayness. Kerry reached over and wiped a bead of water from the teapot. Since she had arrived, she had wiped water off the wall in the kitchen, the bathroom, even the foyer where the swing choir skirts hung, waiting for the director to pick them up.

"I don't know what it is, Grandma," Amanda said. "I think it's the rain causing the dampness in the house."

Kerry shook her head. "The house is well-sealed," she said. "It's time you had children, Amanda."

Amanda looked up sharply. The non sequitur surprised her.

Kerry had never said a word about children before. "I don't have time for children."

"You need them." Kerry set down her teacup. She squirmed uncomfortably, wiped another water bead off the wall, and frowned. "I can't sit here any longer. I have to go home, Amanda."

Amanda set her own teacup down, feeling a sense of panic build in the pit of her stomach. Her grandmother was in her eighties. Perhaps something had happened to her to make her so vague, something Amanda hadn't known about. "You all right, Grandma?"

Kerry leaned heavily on her cane as she got to her feet. "I'll be fine once I get home. You just remember what I said."

Amanda grabbed a sweater, wrapped it around her shoulders, and walked her grandmother to the door. Though it had stopped raining, Amanda asked, "You going to be okay walking home, Grandma?"

Kerry nodded. "It is only a block, Amanda. I haven't fallen apart yet."

Amanda smiled. Her grandmother was feisty even when she was vague. Amanda went out onto the porch and watched as Kerry made her way down the sidewalk. Two houses down, she stopped, turned, and look at Amanda. "You'll have my birthday?"

"I won't miss it," Amanda said. Her grandmother kept walking, slowly, toward her own home. Amanda frowned. The discussion had bothered her. For the first time, her grandmother had seemed unfocused, slightly out of touch. But she was getting older. And in some ways, loss was inevitable. Or at least, that was what Daniel would say.

Daniel. Amanda grabbed the porch door and let herself back inside. He had left before she was up that morning. She rarely saw him anymore. Supposedly they spent weekends together, but he usually went off to play golf with clients or back to the office to work. He was a workaholic, a man who barely had time enough for his own wife. And her grandmother wanted Amanda to have children with him. Children were a partnership, a joint gift that a couple gave each other. If she had children now, she would merely be taking, for herself.

5

Kerry closed the door. Her house smelled like flowers and lemon furniture polish, not damp like Amanda's had. All the water on the walls, threatening to break through, and Amanda living there, working there, every day. Kerry made her way to the book on the shelf beside the stove. She picked it up, rubbing her hands across its worn leather cover before thumbing past the ripped and stained pages to the last page with writing on it, the page that had been blank the day before. She knew what she would find.

Time to plant tears, the almanac said.

Kerry closed the almanac and set it back on the shelf. Then she stared at the cupboard where her bucket was hidden, had been hidden for thirty years since Amanda's mother had used it months before her death. The bucket was dry and empty. Poor Amanda, Kerry thought as a wave of guilt twisted through her stomach. In some ways it was already too late. Amanda didn't want children, that was clear, and if she didn't have any, the water would burst through the walls and engulf her. Amanda would drown beneath the weight of her family's accumulated sorrows.

Kerry remembered her own grandmother explaining the process. *Children are stronger. They can carry the pain with ease—and pass it on when the pain grows too much for them.*

It sounded so simple, except when someone wanted to take the pain back. Kerry was old. She could die and take all those hurts with her. But she knew that she could never reclaim her gift of tears; her grandmother had told her that it was impossible.

So she would take the only other solution, the only other way she could help her beloved Amanda, even though it would cost them some of their family heritage. Kerry opened the almanac to the first page and ran down the list of names until she found Steiger's. Steiger would hold the water at bay until Amanda decided to have children. He had done it before.

6

Amanda was finishing the hand stitching on Carleton Meyer's shirt while the radio blared a talk show. The topic, apparently planned weeks in advance, was how to keep cool in the summer heat. Callers reminded the poor host that the only heat they had felt so far had been from furnaces running to protect them from the chill outdoor damp.

The shirt was lovely. The stitching gave it an elegant, western look that would accent Carleton's appearance rather than detract from it. Three new projects sat on her worktable, waiting for her to start them. And the quilt pieces still lay on the deacon's bench, silently reproaching her. Her grandmother's birthday was only two days away. Amanda had nothing else to give her.

A firm rap on the front door brought her attention away from the shirt. A woman's voice echoed from the radio, suggesting dry ice in the bathtub as the best cure for the summer doldrums. Amanda gripped the ribbed dial and turned off the radio as she walked to the entrance.

The man standing on her porch was not a client. She could tell that immediately. He wore sturdy Levi's and a workshirt under his rain gear. Water dripped from the brim of his hat onto the dry concrete under the overhang. She pulled open the door and adopted her best anti-salesman pose.

"Name's Steiger, ma'am." He handed her his business card. "I do house care. Been going door to door in this wet weather, asking folks if they're having troubles with mildew and damp."

Amanda frowned. She saw his truck parked near the curb. It was large and white, with STEIGER's painted in blue along the cab. Underneath was a phone number and a slogan: SPECIALIZING IN LOST DREAMS AND MEMORIES. She glanced down at the card. The same phrase ran along the bottom. She pointed to it.

"What's that mean?"

Steiger grinned. He had a solid face, rather ordinary. She thought that if she had to describe it to Daniel, she would say Steiger had no distinguishing features. "Lost dreams and memories," he repeated and then shrugged. "Just personal fancy, ma'am. I like to think houses are part of their people. When they first buy the place, it's a dream come true. Then it becomes a headache filled with memories. Me, I try to turn it back into a dream again."

The idea pleased her. She felt a slight release as she stepped away from the door. "I have water dripping down my walls, Mr. Steiger. What would you charge to fix that?"

"Depends on the problem, ma'am." He shook the water out of his coat, removed his hat, and walked in. Then he hung everything on the coat-tree near the door, careful to move the tree so that the rainwater dripped onto the tile entry instead of the carpet. "Let's take a look."

She led him into the kitchen where water still beaded near the stove. She had turned the teapot that morning so that the steam exploded against empty air, but the beading remained. He examined the water as closely as a jeweler examined a diamond. Then he let out air gently. "You need my services, ma'am."

"What will you do?"

"First, I'll clean up the water. Then I'll see what I can do to dam it up."

"How much will it cost?" Amanda clutched her hands tightly together. She felt tense.

He continued to stare at the water. "Seventy-five dollars."

"Per hour?"

He shook his head. "Just seventy-five dollars."

No wonder he was going door to door; he couldn't make any money at the prices he charged. "I'll pay you by the hour," Amanda said.

He looked at her. His eyes were dry and inwardly focused, like the eyes of a person who had been reading for hours. "You're very kind, ma'am. But all I charge is seventy-five dollars. Feels like I'm cheating you at that rate."

Amanda wasn't going to argue with him. She ran a hand through her hair. "Will it take you long?"

"A few hours, at most. You have this anywhere else?"

"In the bathroom." A memory touched her mind, a small one, of waking up alone. "And I think some are starting on the ceiling in the bedroom."

He nodded, as if he had expected her to say that. "Don't worry, ma'am. I'll take care of it for you. You just go back to whatever it was you were doing, and leave the rest to me."

Amanda returned to her office as he ran to his truck. Carleton's shirt lay crumpled where she left it, needle still piercing the fabric. She started to flick on the radio, but stopped. Her hand went to the quilt, and this time, she didn't stop.

7

Daniel couldn't explain why he was driving home in the middle of the day, but when he arrived and saw the unusual truck parked outside, he knew that his sixth sense had been working overtime. Amanda had gotten in trouble. He could feel it.

He opened the door and stepped into the house. It was quiet. The damp smell he had been noticing over the past month was barely there. A raincoat and hat he didn't recognize hung on the coat-tree by the door. A light trailed down the hallway from the sewing room. The bedroom was dark, but he heard rustlings coming from it and suddenly felt ill.

He had been neglecting Amanda this past year, and she had not complained. He had never thought that she would see someone else, that slowly she was replacing him as the center of her life. His breathing became shallow as he walked. He rounded the corner into the bedroom door, expecting to find Amanda as only he had seen her, cheeks flushed with passion, eyes bright, hair flowing across her well-formed, naked body. Instead, he found a man he had never seen before scraping the ceiling.

"What the hell are you doing?" Daniel demanded.

The man stopped working. He took the little vial he had been holding in his hand and shoved it in his pocket. "I'm done," he said as he stepped off the stool he had been standing on.

"Let me see what you have there," Daniel said. He knew that the man had taken something valuable, could feel it in his bones.

"Sorry," the man said. "I contracted this work with your wife."

Daniel turned. "Amanda!"

She came out of the sewing room into the hall. Her expression was sleep-blurry, and her hair was mussed. In her right hand, she clutched an oval-shaped quilt piece. "I didn't know you were home," she said.

"Damn right. What is this man doing here?"

Amanda smiled. "He's cleaning out the water."

"He's been stealing from us." Daniel could feel it as firmly as he had felt the impulse to come home. The man had been stealing. Valuable things. Family heirlooms. Things passed from generation to generation.

Amanda shook her head. "Don't be silly, Daniel. There's nothing to steal."

"I want him out of here," Daniel said. "Now!"

The man opened his hands, bowed slightly at Daniel, but spoke to Amanda. "I'm sorry," he said. "It's nearly finished."

"Let me walk you to the door." Amanda walked beside the man. Daniel followed, feeling angry, betrayed, as if she had dismissed him and sided with the thief. She picked up her purse from the bench near the door and handed the man some money.

"Amanda!" Daniel cried. "The man has been stealing."

"Thank you," she said without a glance at Daniel.

The man took the money, stuffed it in his shirt pocket, then put on his rain gear. "You are too kind for this," he said. "I wish you the best, Amanda."

He walked out into the rain. Daniel leaned out the door and memorized the license off the truck. Then he went to the phone.

"What are you doing?" Amanda asked.

"Calling the cops." Daniel pushed the buttons, dialing as fast as he could. "He was robbing from us. And you paid him."

Amanda reached over, took the receiver from his hand, and hung it up. "It was my money. And he wasn't stealing. He was cleaning. Tell me what he took."

Family heirlooms. Treasures passed from generation to generation. "I don't know," Daniel said slowly. "But I could feel something—"

"You don't feel," Amanda snapped. She walked down the hall to the sewing room and closed the door. Daniel stood in the darkened hallway. She had rebuked him, turning his words to another meaning. For the first time with Amanda, he felt unsure of himself and a little frightened.

8

Amanda sat on the deacon's bench. While Steiger had been there, she had nearly finished the quilt. She wished he had stayed, had been able to finish the job. Somehow, now, she felt that the burden was on her. Her eyes were tired and her back ached. She hadn't meant to snap at Daniel, but he was so self-important. He had offended her and, she realized, it had not been the first time. He always assumed she would be there, but he treated her as if she were replaceable, as if she didn't matter. A tear formed in her eye and rolled down her cheek. She shivered as the warm drop traced her jawbone and settled on her chin. It had been a long time since she cried. She couldn't remember the last time.

Carleton's shirt still lay crumpled on the floor. An accusation. Shirts made money. Quilts did not. She picked up the shirt and stroked its fine handwork. Only an hour's work left on that versus an evening with the quilt. She sighed, thinking that if she still had energy when she finished the shirt, she would work on the quilt.

She could hear Daniel slamming about in the kitchen, trying to call attention to himself with the noise he was making. This time she would not go and try to calm him. This time she would take care of herself.

The shirt felt heavy in her hands. Carleton could wait an extra day for the shirt. She wanted to work on the quilt. No project had ever absorbed her like that one. She took the thick material and ran it across her lap. The tear dripped from her chin into the fabric. A round moisture stain appeared for a moment, and then faded. Amanda squeezed the material. It felt thicker where the tear had landed, but not wet. She nodded, feeling her eyes overflow. Slowly, she stitched and ignored the tears as they fell.

9

The presents sat at Kerry's feet like obedient schoolchildren. Conversation hummed around her. Aunts, cousins, second cousins, friends all filled Amanda's living room. But Kerry didn't watch them. She watched Amanda flow through the crowd with a grace the girl had never had before. Amanda poured herself a glass of punch, then came and sat beside Kerry.

"You're not socializing," Amanda said.

"I've been watching you." Kerry took her granddaughter's dry hand into her own. "You're not pregnant, are you? You have that glow."

Amanda shook her head and lowered her gaze, but not before Kerry saw what was in it. No children. Not then. Not ever—at least, with Daniel. "I want to talk to you, Grandma, but not today."

Kerry nodded. She didn't want to hear it today. At least Steiger had helped, a little.

Amanda reached down and grabbed the largest box. It was wrapped in silver paper and tied with a large red bow. "It's from me, Grandma. Open it."

Kerry took the package and set it on her lap. It felt heavy and oppressive. Her hands shook as she reached for the red bow. Slowly she untied it, then slipped her fingers through the cool paper. As she pulled off the lid, her heart thudded against her chest.

"It's a quilt, Grandma," Amanda said. "I made it for you."

But Kerry didn't have to hear the words. She knew that the quilt was hers. She recognized the tears woven into every stitch. She touched the first and saw the day her father died, that stark, cold gray day when her father's face had matched the sky. And the next tear—the day Thomas first hit her. Married only a month and already he had drawn blood. And older tears, memories that weren't hers, but that she had carried for years until she had harvested them along with her own crop and planted the seeds with the next generation. She had thought of taking them, but she had never realized that a child could give them back.

The gift had been given, the seeds planted. But there would never be another harvest.

"Is it okay, Grandma?" Amanda sounded worried. "I thought you would like it."

Kerry looked up and saw that her granddaughter was happy for the first time. "I love you, child," Kerry said, hugging the quilt tightly to her chest.

—with thanks to poet Elizabeth Bishop

Strange Creatures

DAN RETSLER SAT on the hull of a half-submerged boat, the mud thick around his thigh-high fishing waders. In his right hand, he held an industrial quality flashlight; in his left a pocketknife. He was filthy and wet and exhausted. Night was coming and there was still hours of work to do, buildings to search, items to move. He had managed to send the warning out early enough to evacuate most of the homes along the river, but the destruction was still heart-rending, the loss almost unimaginable.

The trailers were the worst. The water had knocked them about like Tonka Toys, ripping them in half, crushing them, scattering them all over the low-lying valley as if they weighed little more than matchsticks.

They were worth about that much now.

He ran a hand through his hair, feeling the thick silt that seemed to have become a part of him. The foul stench of the mud might never come out of his nostrils.

The river looked so tame now, a narrow trickle through the valley. He had seen the Dee flood before: once after a particularly wet December, and during the 1996 February storms, dubbed The Storm of the Century by commentators who felt it was pretty safe to apply that label when the century was nearly done. But he had never seen anything like this, so sudden, so furious, and so severe.

The Dee was a tidal river which opened into Hoover Bay just south of Whale Rock. High tides and too much rain often caused the Dee to flood her banks, but the floods were low and fairly predictable. Until 1996, no water had ever touched the trailer park, dubbed Hoover Village by some wag, and, until that morning, had never touched the highway winding its way along the valley and into the Coastal Mountain Range.

The sun was going down, turning the sky a brilliant orange and red, with shades of deep blue where the clouds appeared. The Pacific reflected the colors. Retsler stared at it, knowing that any other day, he would have stopped, appreciated the beautiful sunset, and called someone else's attention to it.

A hand touched his shoulder. He looked up, saw the coroner, Hamilton Denne, standing beside him. Denne had a streak of river mud on the left side of his face, and his blond hair was spiked with dirt. His silk suit had splotches and watermarks, and his Gucci loafers were ruined.

Denne's wife would probably have a fit—she came from one of Oregon's richest families, and despised the fact that Denne still insisted on doing his job even though they didn't need the money. If anyone asked her what Denne did, she would tell them he was a doctor, or if they pushed, a pathologist. She never admitted to the fact that he worked best with corpses. He was able to keep the secret because the coroner's position was an appointed one in Seavy County, and no one ever printed his name in the papers.

In his left hand, Denne balanced a clean McDonald's bag and a cardboard tray with two styrofoam cups of coffee. He nodded toward the sunset. "This looks like the best seat in the house. Mind if I share it? I'll pay my way with food."

Retsler didn't reply. Any other time, he would have bantered back, said something about bribing a public official, or teased Denne about whether or not he could have afforded the food. But Retsler didn't feel like banter. He didn't feel like company either, although he didn't say so.

Denne handed him the coffee tray, then sat beside him. Retsler took out a cup and wrapped his hand around it, letting the warmth sink through him.

"Didn't know what you liked, so I got everything," Denne said. "Whopper, Fish something or other, Biggie Fry—"

"Whopper's from Burger King," Retsler said.

"Well, you know me," Denne said. "It was my first time at a drive-through window. The wonders of technology."

Retsler was too exhausted to smile. He knew it wasn't Denne's first time in a fast-food joint, since he'd dragged Denne to them countless times. Denne always protested, and then ate like a thirteen-year-old at a basketball game.

Denne was holding the bag open. Retsler reached inside, and pulled out a Big Mac and fries. The smell of grease and sugar made his stomach cramp, but he knew he had to eat. He pulled the wrapper back and took a bite, tasting mustard, catsup, pickles and mayonnaise long before he got to the meat.

With the lining of his silk suit, Denne wiped mud off the boat's aluminum hull. Then he set the bag down, and rooted inside of it, pulling out a Filet-O-Fish. Denne had a penchant for the things, which Retsler always found odd, considering they lived in a place where they could get the freshest fish in the world.

"At the Club," Denne said, peeling the wrapper from his fish sandwich. He was referring to the Club at Glen Ellyn Cove, Whale Rock's gated community. "They have old maps of this coastline, some dating from the turn of the century. The last century."

Half of Retsler's Big Mac was gone. He was hungrier than he thought. He took a sip of coffee, waiting for Denne to finish. It was always easier to ignore Denne when the man was talking.

"Up until 1925 or so, this river wasn't the Dee at all. It was the Devil's River."

That didn't surprise Retsler. The Devil, in his opinion, had once dwelt on the Oregon Coast, eventually leaving behind his Punchbowl, his Churn, and oddly, his Elbow.

"When folks decided they wanted to bring tourism into Whale Rock, they shortened the name of the river." Denne took a bite of the sandwich and talked while he chewed. "Know why it was called the Devil's River?"

"Sea monster?" Retsler said. The food must have helped him feel slightly better. He answered Denne this time.

"No," Denne said. "That's Lincoln City. Devil's Lake."

Retsler wadded up the sandwich wrapper, and shoved it in the bag. He sipped his coffee. It was black and burned. He drank it anyway.

"They called it Devil's River," Denne said, "because it flooded unexpectedly fourteen times between 1899 and 1919. On clear nights, they said, the river would rise and fill the valley until this place looked like a lake."

In the distance, cars swooshed across the Dee River Bridge, oblivious to the destruction hundreds of feet below them. The sun was gone now, leaving traces of orange against the night sky.

"You're saying this is not my fault," Retsler said.

"Acts of God happen," Denne said.

Retsler drained the styrofoam cup. "You don't believe that."

"Of course I do."

Retsler turned to him. "Hamilton, you and I've seen some strange things in Whale Rock."

Denne's eyes were hidden by the growing darkness. "It was a freak storm."

"You've never lied to me before, Hamilton. Don't start now." Retsler stood, grabbed his flashlight, and flicked it on. The beam made the mud glisten. "Thanks for the comfort food."

Denne had his elbows on his knees, his right hand holding the cup from the lip. "Dan," he said. "You didn't start this thing."

Retsler paused, wondering why that didn't make him feel better. Then he said, "And I didn't end it, either."

It began a few days earlier, on the first day of the new year. Retsler answered the call about a suspicious smell on the beach.

The woman who had obviously made the call sat in the loose sand near the concrete cinderblocks lining the beach access. Her black hair flowed down her back. The constant ocean breeze stirred a few strands, but she didn't seem to notice. Her legs were spread in front of her, her toes buried in the sand. She wore a light jacket despite the day's chill. Retsler had a sense that she had been crying, but she wasn't now. Instead, she was staring out to sea, as if the frothy brown surface—filled with dirt from the rainstorms of the last few days—held the answers to questions he hadn't even heard yet.

Retsler stood on the concrete slab above the beach access and watched her for a moment. She didn't seem to know she was being observed. Cool mist pelted his face. The moisture felt good. He hadn't gotten much sleep last night: fifteen drunk and disorderlies; dozens of drunk driving stops; illegal fireworks on the beach. By the time he had turned in, about 4 A.M., he was praying that the Y2K bug would hit on Christmas so that no one could travel to the coast for New Year's Eve. Vain hope, he knew, but it was the only one he had.

He walked down the sand-covered ramp. Driftwood littered the beach, a testament to the rough surf of the last month. The air stank of charred wood and something else, something he didn't want to think about.

When he reached her, he crouched. "Maria Selvado?"

She raised luminous brown eyes to his. Her eyes were so dark they seemed to have no pupils. The whites were stunningly clear. There was moisture on her lower lashes, but he couldn't tell if it was from the mist or from tears. "Yes?"

"I'm Dan Retsler. I'm the chief of police here in Whale Rock." As if that meant something. He ran a department of ten, double what they'd had two years ago. Whale Rock was big enough to keep them busy, but not big enough to pay the salaries of more officers.

"Thanks for coming. I didn't know who to call."

Probably Fish and Game, he thought. Or the State Department of Natural Resources. Half a dozen agencies probably had jurisdiction over this one.

"Where?"

She waved a hand toward the surf. "That one."

He followed her gaze. The remains of a bonfire, piled high on a dune. He swallowed hard, thankful that he hadn't partied the night before, and stood.

The stench was intermittent, whenever the breeze happened to blow in his direction. Otherwise, he smelled only the salty ocean freshness and knew it could lull him into thinking nothing was wrong.

He slogged through deep sand as he walked up the dune, then crossed to a driftwood log the color of long abandoned houses. On the other side of the log was a pile of charred wood half covered in sand, and about two dozen beer cans, scattered in a semi circle. The odor was strong here, and mixed with the smell of Budweiser and old vomit.

The carcass lay half in the fire, flesh burned and bubbled, but still recognizable by shape: a seal pup, skinned. Bile rose in his throat and he swallowed it down, reminding himself that he had seen worse and not too long ago: the cats in the bag by the river; the dog the vet said had been tortured for days; the horse, still alive, and half crazed by knife wounds all along its flank.

Retsler had read the studies, taken classes, knew the psychiatric lingo. Serial killers started like this—usually as teenagers, practicing on bigger or more difficult targets, needing a greater thrill each time to duplicate that same sick feeling of pleasure.

Seal pups. Jesus.

He looked away, stared at the ocean just as the woman had been doing. The sun peeked through a break in the clouds, falling on the white caps, adding a golden hue to the ocean's brown and blue surface. He reached into his pocket and pulled out his cell phone, flipping it open and hitting his speed dial.

After two rings, he got an answer. "Hamilton," he said, "sorry to disturb your holiday, but I've got something I need you to see."

The woman chose to wait beside him. When he told her he could take her statement, if she wanted, and then she could go, she shook her head. She seemed to think her actions warranted an explanation because, after a few moments, she told him that she worked at the Hatfield Marine Science Center in Newport. Her specialty was seals.

Denne saved him from answering. Retsler heard the rumble of Denne's rusted Ford truck, the one he'd bought in November against his wife's wishes, because he was tired, he said, of showing up at crime scenes in his silver Mercedes. Not that there were that many murders in Seavy County, which was Denne's jurisdiction. But Denne had an eye for detail and a knowledge of the obscure that made him useful to all the police departments in the county. For a job that was supposed to be part-time, a job that should have taken very little of his precious social time, it seemed to be a major preoccupation for him, one that was growing more and more of late.

The door slammed and Denne made his way down the beach. Retsler led him to the carcass, and watched as Denne's face went white.

"This is how someone chose to ring in the New Year?" he asked.

Retsler stuck his hands in the back pockets of his jeans. "I want you to treat this like a human murder scene. And then we'll—"

"Compare it to that dog, I know." Denne glanced at the ocean, then at the bonfire. "They wanted us to find this. It's above the high water line."

"Or maybe they were just careless," Retsler said. "That's a lot of beer."

"Looks like it was some party," Denne said. "I'll bet there're one or two people who aren't happy about how it ended."

"Thought of that," Retsler said.

"You know you'll have to call the State. These pups are protected. Hell, you could get slapped with a gigantic fine if you move a live one. I have no idea what happens if you kill one."

"It's the same thing," Retsler said. Tourists came across seal pups alone on the beach all the time, then picked "the poor things" up and hauled them to a vet, thinking they were orphans. The act of kindness always doomed the pup, whose mother had left it on the beach on purpose and would have been back for it. Very few pups were ever safely returned to the wild; most died after being separated from the mother.

"It's not quite the same," Denne said, and went to work.

After he'd collected the beer cans and all the other evidence he could find, Retsler offered to drive Maria Selvado back to Newport, but she refused. She said she was staying in Whale Rock for her work. She had told him, as if it were more a threat than a promise, that she would stop by his office on Monday to find out how his work was progressing.

He had left Denne to the mess, and had driven back to the station. It was in the center of downtown, with a display window that overlooked Highway 101. The station had once been prime retail space, but Retsler's predecessor had demanded, and received, the building because, he said, most crimes were committed just outside its doors.

That was true enough. On most days, the police log was something Jay Leno might read as a joke: two people pulled over for running red lights; SLOW CHILDREN sign vandalized (for the eighth time) on South Jetty Road; lost puppy found before Safeway store, identified and returned to owner.

It was the other days that were difficult: the spur-of-the-moment kidnapping outside the local Dairy Queen; the gang war, featuring rival gangs imported from Portland, on the Fourth of July; the drownings, search-and-rescue operations, all caused by the stupid things tourists did on the beach. If someone asked him how hard his job could get, those were the things he mentioned. He never brought up Whale Rock's secret side.

Denne was familiar with it, and Retsler's dispatch, Lucy Wexel, was a firm believer that there was some sort of vortex here that brought out the magic in the world. Retsler's introduction had come two years ago when intact and seemingly recently deceased bodies appeared on the beach, all from the same sixty-year-old shipwreck. Then there were the three so-called women who seduced people to their deaths in the sea; Retsler had seen them, and narrowly escaped. Denne called them mermaids, but they weren't. They were sirens, perhaps, or sea hags, and they were something Retsler never ever talked about.

Eddie was working dispatch today, with Retsler on call. New Year's Eve was always a nightmare, but New Year's Day was usually as quiet as a church—people were either too hungover or too tired to get out of the house. Even though the sun was peaking through the clouds, the beach was empty, something Retsler was grateful for.

Eddie was sitting with his feet on Lucy's desk, a *Car and Driver* magazine on his lap, and three Hershey's candy wrappers littering the floor around him. When Retsler entered, Eddie sat up, and immediately started cleaning.

"Sorry, boss. Didn't expect you."

Retsler waved a hand. "You're fine."

"Figure out what died on the beach?" Eddie, of course, had taken Selvado's call.

"Seal pup. Skinned and burned."

"Je-Zus." Eddie whistled, then shook his head. He'd seen a lot of the strange things around Whale Rock as well, but they never ceased to surprise him either. "What the hell would anyone do that for?"

"Kicks, it looks like." He took one of Eddie's candy bars. "Mind?"

Eddie shook his head.

"Do me a favor. Look through the files, see if you can find more animal killings, anything that predates that spate of them we had last year."

"You got it."

"And do a location map for me too, would you?"

"Sure." Eddie actually looked relieved. He was usually patrolling because he liked to be busy. He wasn't suited for dispatch.

Retsler went through the open door into his tiny office. He didn't pull the blinds on the glass windows—another feature left over from the retail days—but he sat hard at his desk. Incident reports from the night before littered the left corner. He stared at them for a moment, as if they were the enemy, then he frowned.

He might find something in them as well.

He slid them over to the center of his desk, and began to scan. He had to sign off on them anyway—a departmental policy as old as Whale Rock and one he saw no need to change—and he may as well do so now while he was waiting for Denne. Retsler had a few incident reports of his own to file from the night before, as well as the one this afternoon, but he wasn't ready to put anything down on paper just yet.

Fifteen reports later, almost all of them drunk and disorderlies, almost all of them depressing in their sameness, Retsler stood and stretched his cramping hand.

"Hey!" Eddie said from the front. "Got something weird."

Retsler left his desk and walked to the dispatch area. Eddie had files scattered around him—both of them would pay dearly for that when Lucy came in on Monday morning—and at the center of it all, a map of Whale Rock. There were multicolored dots all over the village. Retsler had forgotten how good Eddie was at details. Usually he didn't have to focus on them when he was on the street.

"I used red for this year," Eddie said. "I mean, last year. You know, '98. Green's for '97, and blue's for '96. I put the seal pup in last year's because the poor thing probably died before sundown."

"How do you figure?" Retsler asked.

"It takes a lot of work to skin an animal, don't care how good you are at it. It's harder if you can't see too good."

"They had a bonfire."

"And found a seal pup at night? I don't think so."

He had a good point. Retsler made a mental note of it. He leaned over the map and saw, while there were a few dots all over the city, the biggest concentration of them was around Hoover Bay.

"That's odd," Retsler said.

"That's what I thought," Eddie said, pointing to them. "And they're mostly from the last year or so. The rest're what you'd expect, and if I'd had time, I'd've marked 'em by month too. Outside the bay, most of the animals died between May and September."

"Tourists."

"Sicko, psycho kids, probably brought to the beach because there's nothing for them to tear up, or so the parents think."

That was one of the things Retsler hated the most about summer, the teenagers who invaded from other towns. After they saw the single movie playing at the Bijou, shopped at all the stores, and found out that the casino just outside of town really did enforce its eighteen and above rule, they turned to vandalism or small acts of terror to take up their time.

"What about the others?" Retsler asked.

"Late '96, spaced about a month apart. Been escalating since

October. That dog you found tied to the river piling was only two weeks ago, and the cats a week before that."

"You forgot the horse," Retsler said.

"Horse?"

"You know, Drayton's new mare, the one they'd bought their daughter for Christmas."

"Oh, yeah," Eddie said, and grimaced in distaste. "It's not down here as a killing."

"It should have been," Retsler said. "The vet had to put her down." The little girl had been heartbroken, and convinced, somehow, that it was her fault. The parents had promised her a new horse, but she had refused, saying she couldn't be sure it would be safe. The parents had looked at Retsler then, perhaps wanting him to reassure her, but he said nothing. He wasn't sure the family would be safe on hillside retreat, with its two-mile long road and 360 degree view of the ocean and the river. He'd thought the horse incident particularly cruel and had thought perhaps it had been directed at the Draytons.

Now he wasn't so sure. They lived awfully close to Hoover Bay, and a horse wasn't a dog or a seal pup. Horses had an amazing amount of strength.

Had the horse been the killer's attempt to ratchet up the pleasure, only to be thwarted? Maybe that's why the killer went after something like a seal pup, something so helpless and vulnerable and cute that it would be easy to kill.

A shiver ran through Retsler. He didn't like what was loose in his little town.

Denne showed up three hours later. He was wearing a Harvard sweatshirt over a pair of chinos. His deck shoes were mottled and ruined, and he wore no socks. Retsler had seen the outfit before. It was the one Denne kept at his office and used only when something at a crime scene made him leave his regular clothes behind.

Denne's blond hair was ruffled and his mouth a thin line. He pulled open the door, nodded to Eddie, and then came into Retsler's office without knocking.

Retsler had just finished going through the reports. Nothing from the area of the beach where they had found the seal pup. He would have expected something to come from the nearby hotels, perhaps, someone seeing the skinning of the pup or getting upset by the conduct of the beer drinkers. He was surprised no one had complained about the smell until that afternoon.

Denne sat in the chair before Retsler's desk. Even though he was wearing his grubbiest clothes, Denne's pants still had a crease, and his sweatshirt looked pressed.

"If you can call two a pattern," Denne said without preamble. "We've got one."

"Looks like a different m.o. to me," Retsler said. He'd had all afternoon to think about it. "Dog tortured to death, left on a stake beneath the Dee River Bridge. Pup's skinned and burned on the beach. All those beer cans. I'm thinking a bunch of drunk kids got carried away—"

"Whoever skinned that pup was an expert," Denne said. "The flesh was clean in the unburned areas. And the pup bled. It was alive, at least for part of it. But that isn't the clincher."

Retsler folded his hands over the report. He hadn't wanted to hear that the pup was alive. He hated some of the things this profession made him think about.

"The clincher is the knife itself. It's one of those thin serrated knives, made especially for that sort of work. Around here, folks usually use knives like that on deer or elk. It's got a slight nick in the blade. It leaves an identifiable mark. The dog and the pup had it. If I'd thought to keep those cats, I bet they'd have had it too."

Retsler sighed. Apparently Denne took that for disappointment because he added, "If I were dealing with human deaths here, I could make a case for a serial killer based on the knife evidence alone."

"What else have you got?"

"Some fibers. A pretty good print, in blood, on the body itself."

"Good," Retsler said. "That's a start. With that, and the cans, we might be able to find something."

"Hope so." Denne stood, then paused as if he had a thought. "There's one more thing. It may be nothing, or it might be everything."

"What?" Retsler asked.

"Did you find the pelt?"

Retsler shook his head. "I assumed it got burned."

"No. There was no fur in the fire at all, and they were too far from the water line for it to have been swept away with the tide."

"I'd better get someone to comb the beach, then," Retsler said.

"Yeah," Denne said. "But I don't think you'll find anything."

Retsler met his gaze. "You think our friend is selling the pelts?"

"Probably not. I have a hunch we're dealing with someone young here."

Retsler felt himself go cold. "Trophy hunter."

Denne nodded. "I suspected it with the dog, and I bet, if I looked at your report on the cats, I could find something too."

"The horse's mane," Retsler murmured.

"Hmm?"

"Nothing," Retsler said.

"If you don't find that pelt," Denne said, "I'd bet every dime I've got that our killer still has it."

"Should make it easier to convict someone."

"On what? Animal cruelty?" Denne said. "Seems minor for this kind of offense."

Retsler agreed, but felt the day's frustration fill him. "What am I supposed to charge him with? Prospective serial killing?"

"Wish you could," Denne said.

"We'll get the state involved," Retsler said. "Maybe they'll have ideas."

"They'll think we're a small town with too much time on our hands."

"Maybe they would have with the dog or the horse," Retsler said. "But we're dealing with a seal pup. That makes TV news reporters sit up and beg."

"Think twice before you invite those vultures here," Denne said. "They'll mess up the entire case."

"I'll wait," Retsler said, "until I have something that'll stick."

Denne nodded. "I'll give you all the help I can."

Retsler smiled. "You've already given me plenty."

The weekend wasn't as calm as Retsler would have liked. Two major accidents on 101 backed up traffic for hours, and caused several more citations. A suspicious fire downtown in one of Whale Rock's failing seasonal businesses had Retsler calling in a state arson team. A Saturday night bar fight got out of control and spilled into the street, forcing Retsler to call his entire team to help quell the violence. He wasn't able to think about seal pups and animal mutilations until he arrived at work at 8 A.M. Monday morning, sleep deprived, bruised, and more thankful than he cared to admit that all the tourists had finally gone home.

Lucy was already at her desk, an unlit cigar in her mouth. She had curly gray hair and a military manner that her grandmotherly face somehow softened. Retsler had known her since he was a boy, and sometimes she still made him feel like that boy. He really didn't want to cross her.

She had two tall cups from Java Joes on her desk. As he passed, she handed him one. He turned to her in surprise. She had made it clear, when he became chief, that she didn't do windows or coffee.

"What's this for?"

"I figure you haven't gotten no rest since New Year's Eve. Caffeine won't cure it, but it'll cover it up."

He grinned at her. "You're a lifesaver, Lucy."

She frowned. "Don't go ruining my reputation."

"I won't tell a soul."

"Good," she said. Then she leaned back in her chair. "You got a woman in your office."

He glanced over, surprised he had missed it. Maria Selvado was sitting primly in the chair in front of his desk, a vinyl purse clutched to her white sweater. Her coat hung over the back of the chair, and she wore what appeared to be a very cheap pair of boots beneath her faded jeans.

"How long's she been here?"

"Half hour or so. I told her you don't normally come in until ten."

"Lucy!"

Lucy chuckled. "Well, I figured if you got in any earlier than ten, she'd think you were good at your job."

"I am good at my job."

"Just goes to show," Lucy said. Then she raised an eyebrow at him. "And if you let that Eddie dig in my files again, so help me God, I'll pour that coffee down your back."

"Yes, ma'am."

This time it was Retsler who chuckled as he headed to his office. Maria Selvado turned her face toward him. She looked even more exotic in the artificial light. "Chief," she said in greeting.

"Dan," he corrected.

She nodded. He sat behind his desk. She leaned forward, still clutching that purse. "I came for an update."

"I can't tell you much," he said. "We know that the pup's death is part of a pattern, and we are working on that angle. We have some leads—"

"A pattern?" she murmured.

He stopped, frowning. She seemed disturbed by his words. "Yes. There have been other animals killed in the same area—"

"But not other pups."

"Not that we know of."

She let out a small breath. The news seemed to relieve her. "But you have nothing on the killer."

"Not yet."

She raised those liquid eyes to his, and he thought he saw accusation in them. He parted his hands defensively, and then shook his head a little. He didn't have to defend himself to anyone.

But he did say, because he felt she needed to know, "We don't have much of a lab facility here. We've sent several items to the State Crime Lab. We should hear later today."

She bit her lower lip. "You'll keep me informed."

"If I know where I can find you."

"I'm at the Sandcastle."

He shuddered. He couldn't help it. Someone bought the land a year ago, and in that time tore down the old hotel. The new one had the look of the old—once one of the Coast's premiere resorts—and people from all over the world had flocked to it in the last few days of the summer. But he had memories of the Sandcastle, memories of finding intact bodies before it, memories of unusual goings on that dated to his boyhood—talk of ghosts and kelpies and strange creatures that emerged from the sea.

She looked amused. His reaction must have been visible. "They've remodeled," she said. "It's quite nice."

"I have no doubt."

She smiled and stood, her movements fluid and graceful. "Thank you for cooperating with me, Chief."

"You're welcome," he said, and waited for her to leave before he shut his office door.

That night, Lucy chose the dinner spot and, as always, she picked the False Colors. It was a pirate-themed bar just off 101, but more locals went there than tourists. The sea chanties, the fireplace that burned real wood, the ropes and life rings that came from real ships played to the out-of-towners, but most people who came to the coast brought their families. The skull and crossbones that decorated most corners, the human skulls on the mantel, the tales of death and murder framed on the walls were not the best atmosphere for children. So tourists usually came once and never returned, allowing the locals to enjoy the excellent food and the even better bar.

Retsler ordered his usual, a cutely named fish and chips entree that came with a large salad and a double order of bread. He got a Rogue Ale with that, and planned to get a huge dessert, thinking that the combination might allow him to go home and go to sleep at 9 P.M.

Lucy had the fisherman's platter, a meal three times the size of Retsler's, and he knew that by the end of the evening, she would eat all of it. After a few minutes, Eddie joined them.

He was still in uniform, and as he sat down, June, the waitress scurried over. "You know Jeff don't like it when you guys come in your blues," she said in a half whisper.

"What's he going to do, call the cops?" Lucy asked and then smiled, a grandmother with fangs.

"It's just he doesn't think the presence of police adds to the atmosphere."

"He's afraid the real pirates will stop patronizing the place," Lucy said and chuckled.

"It's okay," Eddie said. "I won't do it again. It's just I had to talk to Dan and I didn't have time to change."

"Tell Jeff it's January fourth and the tourists went home, not that they're going to be in here anyway," Dan said. "And tell him he can chase his regulars away if he wants, but this is the slow season and it probably wouldn't be wise."

June bobbed her head. "It wasn't from me, you know. It's just that Jeff—"

"Is delusional." Lucy picked up a crab leg and broke it in half. "We know."

June flushed. "You want something, Eddie?"

"Burger and fries and a diet."

June left and Eddie leaned forward. "I've got a couple of things on that seal pup killing," he said softly, even though there were no other patrons within hearing range. "Okay to tell you here?"

Sometimes Retsler frowned on discussing work at the False Colors. But that was usually in the summer, when the place was packed with first-timers who really didn't need tales of car crashes and children crushed by driftwood logs as an accompaniment to their meals.

Retsler picked up a fry. "Let's hear it."

Any news would be good news. Retsler expected a visit the next morning from Maria Selvado, and he hadn't heard from the crime lab yet. He supposed he could give her some information from Denne's autopsy of the pup, but even someone as involved as Selvado probably didn't want to hear about knife serrations and the fact that the pup had been skinned alive.

Retsler winced at the memory.

"You okay?" Eddie asked.

Retsler nodded. Then the main door opened, and Denne walked in. Retsler looked up. Denne's wife had expressly forbidden him from coming here. She had discovered, through small town gossip probably, that twice before Denne had shown up here to discuss a case, and she had demanded that he not disgrace the family by showing his face in the False Colors again.

Yet there he was, in a charcoal-colored silk suit with a sterling silver pocket watch attached to a fob on the outside. His blond hair had been slicked back, and his aesthetic face looked almost haunted.

"She's pushing him too hard," Lucy murmured. "He's drifting over to the other side."

Retsler started, then considered the evidence: the truck, the clothes Denne had worn home on New Years, and now the appearance at the False Colors. Denne was abandoning his gated community for the peasants who ran this small town.

Eddie sighed. "You want to hear this or not?"

"Let's wait for Hamilton," Retsler said as he waved. Denne smiled—he never quite grinned—and walked down the worn stairs into the main dining area. As he did, he stopped June and ordered, then took the only empty chair at the table.

"Eddie," Retsler said, "was about to tell us news on our seal pup."

"Really?" Denne removed his suitcoat and hung it on the back of the chair.

Then he rolled up the sleeves of his white button-down shirt, revealing muscular forearms. With his left hand, he loosened his tie, and pulled it off. The entire group was watching him with astonishment. Retsler could feel his own mouth open in surprise.

Denne raised his eyebrows. "Don't let me stop you, Eddie."

"Um, yeah." Eddie shot Denne a slightly perplexed look, then said, "I been having conversations all day, casual ones, you know."

Retsler did know. One of the strengths of Whale Rock was its citizens' willingness to discuss anything if approached properly by someone they knew. A glance at the ocean, a mention of the dead pup, and a softly worded query about something related often got a glut of information.

"And I didn't get nothing on anyone selling pelts."

"I called fifteen different departments," Lucy said as she stabbed a scallop with her fork, "and no one in the entire state of Oregon has heard of anyone poaching seals."

"I asked her to. Hope you don't mind, boss," Eddie said.

A year ago, Eddie never would have taken that kind of initiative. "I gave you the legwork of the investigation," Retsler said. "You can divide it up how you want."

June brought a long neck for Eddie and an Alaskan Amber for Denne. Retsler looked at him in surprise, but Denne didn't seem to notice. Lucy did, however, and winked.

"Then what did you need to tell me?" Retsler asked when June left.

"You remember when they tore down the Sandcastle to make way for the new version?"

"A mistake if there ever was one," Denne said. "You do realize the hotel is on the beach."

They all looked at him. Building on the beaches—on the sand—was against the law in Oregon.

"How'd that happen?" Retsler said.

"You know the Planning Commission." Denne took a sip of the amber and looked like a man who had just had the most sublime experience of his life.

"It's a state law," Lucy said.

Denne raised his eyebrows. "The Sandcastle Hotel predates the law. The Commission claimed they couldn't do anything because it grandfathers in."

"How much did Roman Taylor pay them?" Retsler asked.

"Pay them? Kickbacks, in our small town? Impossible." Denne leaned back. "Just a sidebar. Didn't mean to derail you, Eddie."

Eddie grunted, and took a sip out of his long neck. "Anyway," he said, "when they were bulldozing the Sandcastle, they found an open area underneath it. There was all kinds of junk under there, old watches, gold coins, shiny stuff. Some of it wasn't worth much, but some of it was worth a lot, and Taylor said he got it, because he bought the property. Nobody fought him about it and nobody tried to trace it."

"And, not surprisingly, nobody thought to call us," Retsler said.

Eddie nodded, meeting his gaze. "Ain't it amazing how some things just don't make it to our attention until we can't do nothing about them."

"So what do the shiny things have to do with this investigation?" Lucy asked.

"Well, in there was a pile of fur, all sleek and shiny. Turns out it was seal pelts—about twenty of them. Just beautiful things. I guess Taylor's the kind of guy who hangs deer heads on the walls and he was really excited about them pelts. He took them home."

Retsler whistled. "This was what? Last January?"

"Yep," Eddie said. "And that's not all. Various folks have come up asking for them seal pelts, even though the only people who knew about them were the digging crew and Taylor. Taylor won't talk to anybody about them."

"Curiouser and curiouser," Lucy said.

June set down Eddie's hamburger, and placed a double cheeseburger—an item the False Colors proudly called its Gut Blaster—in front of Denne. Retsler couldn't resist.

"Your wife isn't going to be too happy when you come home smelling of hot sauce, jalapeños, and onions."

Denne shrugged. "The woman's got to learn to calm down."

This time, Eddie was the one who raised his eyebrows. He picked up the catsup and proceeded to pour it all over his food. "I got one more thing to tell you about them pelts," he said. "The latest person who's come to inquire about them is Maria Selvado. She's been after Taylor since the first of December, and she's got the Marine Science Center behind her. Guess they're doing some sort of seal study or something, and the pelts would be really useful. They're even offering to pay him. But he won't meet with her. She says she's not leaving until he does."

"Our Miss Selvado gets around," Lucy said.

"Yeah," Eddie said. "She even went up to his house on the Dee. Got real mad when she saw how he's displaying the pelts. Guess he's got them in one of those wall-sized glass cases beside his fireplace. He came to the door and she was yelling something about pins ruining the fur, or something. Anyway, he threw her off the porch, damn near landed her in the river. She hasn't been up there since."

"But there was a break-in," Retsler said.

"Thwarted break-in," Lucy said. "The alarm kicked on with the sirens and all the lights, remember?"

"And tiny footprints, woman-sized, in the mud beside the window on the fireplace side of the house. Passionate woman," Retsler said.

"Mystery woman," Denne said. "She called me, asking if she could have the pup's body when I was through with it, said she wanted it for the Science Center. I offered to drive it over there for her—I mean, who wants a corpse in your car if you can help it?—and she turned me down. That made me suspicious, so I called the Science Center."

"And they'd never heard of her," Lucy said, her eyes sparkling as they always did when the story started getting juicy.

"Oh, they'd heard of her all right. But she hadn't worked for them for six months. Seems that she broke into the Oregon Coast Aquarium last summer, and was going to liberate the seals. Security stopped her before she made it to the outdoor pen, but the Aquarium offered not to press charges—which would have embarrassed the Science Center—if she promised to leave Newport. She did."

"And came here?" Retsler asked. "That seems odd to me. We're not that far from Newport."

Denne nodded. "The Science Center is none too happy that she's still representing herself as part of their staff. Not that she was ever staff-staff anyway. She was one of the student projects, interns or whatever, that they get coming through. But they still don't want their name connected to hers."

"And they have no interest in the seal pelts?" Retsler asked.

"None," Denne said.

Lucy nodded. "Selkies," she said.

All three of them turned to her. She grinned and shrugged. "Come on," she said. "We have no secrets between us. We are talking Whale Rock, aren't we?"

"Silkies?" Eddie asked.

"Selkies," Retsler said. He'd been boning up on his sea-faring lore since the last strange encounter. "They look like seals in the sea, but when they come on shore and shed their skin, they look human."

"Oh, God," Eddie said.

"But don't they usually come looking for love?" Denne asked. "Aren't they supposed to mate with human women, leave them pregnant, and return to the sea?"

"You've been reading too many Celtic stories," Lucy said. "That may have been true hundreds of years ago. But I think Selkies are more sophisticated than that."

"Sophisticated?" Denne placed his chin on the palm of his hand and looked at her. "Do you mean they're sending their children ashore in search of a better education?"

"You may mock me, young man, but think about it. What better way to find out about the things that threaten your people than to study those things?"

Retsler was silent. A lot threatened the seal population, which had been thinning in recent years. Some blamed oil spills farther up the coast, others blamed changes in commercial fishing laws, and still others blamed things like tourists taking pups off the beaches. Whatever the cause, there were fewer seals in the last few years than there had been in a long time.

"That seal pup," Denne said, "was one hundred percent seal. There was nothing magical about it."

"The myths say that the smaller seals—like the common seal—belong entirely to the animal world, but the larger seals, like the gray, the great, and the crested, can be selkie folk." Lucy pushed her plate aside. "How else do you explain the clean, unrotted pelts, found among all that shiny stuff, as Eddie calls it. It was a nest, a place to hide wealth that enabled them to trade in Whale Rock."

Retsler put aside the remains of his fish and chips. "So?" he asked. "We have a bunch of selkies in human form walking around Whale Rock?"

"Or in the sea without their pelts. It's probably hazardous to their health." Lucy shook her head. "A year's a long time."

"What does this have to do with our dead pup?" Denne asked.

"Maybe nothing," Lucy said, "but selkies do have a kinship with seals. They're probably not happy about this."

"You think Maria Selvado is a selkie?" Retsler asked.

"I didn't say that." Lucy sniffed loudly. Of course she hadn't said that. She had implied it, like she often did, and Retsler could ignore her at his own peril.

"Selkies," Denne mused. "I thought selkies were dangerous."

"Only if you're a man in lust," Retsler said.

"No," Lucy said. "They are dangerous, if you kill one."

"What?" Eddie asked, setting down the long neck. "All the other selkies toss their pelts at you?"

"No," Lucy said. "If you kill one, don't get its blood in the ocean."

"Or?" Denne asked.

"Or a storm'll come up the likes of which you've never seen."

Retsler sighed. "Do you actually believe that, Lucy?"

She met his gaze. There was no twinkle in her gray eyes. "I've seen a lot of things, Dan. I don't disbelieve anything."

"But you don't actually believe it."

"Let me put it this way," Lucy said. "That myth is not one I'd want to test."

"The language is plain, Retsler." Roman Taylor was a large man, made to seem even larger by the low ceilings in the second story of his riverside home. He hunched over a rough-hewn log table, made to match the rough edges on the outer walls. The inner walls were smooth and painted white. It was on one of those that the huge case with the pelts gleamed in the morning sunshine. "I bought the Sandcastle Motel and all its contents. The pelts and the treasures in that room around them were inside the Sandcastle. No one disputes that."

Retsler stared at the deed before him. Apparently he stared too long because Taylor shifted from one foot to another.

The language was clear. Taylor did own the pelts and there was nothing Retsler could do about it.

"Maybe you should show this to the city attorney," Taylor said. "Then maybe people'll leave me alone."

"They'll leave you alone now," Retsler said. "Sorry to bother you."

Taylor nodded once at the apology. Then he glanced at the case. "That woman's crazy, you know. If I could find a way to get her out of my motel I would. If you could think of something, I'd be forever in your debt."

"Has she broken any laws, Mr. Taylor?"

"I'd be the first to scream if she did." He walked over to the case. "She says the seals that had these pelts are still alive, and they need them. Isn't that nuts? You can't skin an animal like this and have the animal live."

"Can I see one?" Retsler asked.

Taylor opened the case. The glass swung open, and the scent of fur and an animal musk filled the room. "Come here."

Retsler obliged. The pelts glistened as if they were still wet, but there was a dullness that was starting to appear around their edges.

Taylor picked up a corner of the nearest fur. "See that?" he asked. "Best work I've ever seen. Not a trace of flesh, no knife marks. Just the fur. Isn't it beautiful?"

Beautiful wasn't a word that Retsler would have used, but he nodded anyway.

"Hey, Dad!"

Both men turned. A teenage boy stood in the stairwell, face flushing when he saw Retsler.

"Didn't know you had company," the boy said.

"The chief's just leaving."

The boy grunted. He stood perfectly still as if movement weren't allowed. "Why're you showing him the pelts?"

Something in the question made Retsler look at the boy. The

boy's eyes were bright, almost too bright. And cold. So cold that Retsler felt a chill run through him.

"He'd heard about them, that's all," Taylor said.

"Dad thinks those pelts are the real thing," the boy said, his chin raised in something of a challenge.

Retsler became completely still. "You don't?"

"I think they're fake. I think he should get them checked."

"Why?" Retsler asked.

"Because I don't care how good you are, you can't remove a pelt making a single cut."

"Hmm," Retsler said. "Have you tried?"

"He hunts with me sometimes," Taylor said too fast. "Don't you, Michael?"

"We've never hunted together in our lives. My father never pays attention to me." The boy tilted his head, eyeing Retsler speculatively. "You ever spend New Year's Eve on the beach, Chief?"

Retsler didn't answer. Taylor's face flushed.

"It's amazing what people'll burn—"

"Michael!" Taylor said.

The boy grinned and shrugged, as if he had just been making conversation. "Nice seeing you. *Chief.*"

And then he walked down the stairs. Retsler's entire body had turned numb. He had expected a teenager, but not one that would challenge him. Although he had heard stories about Michael Taylor for the last year. A teacher at the high school had asked how to deal with a boy who seemed to love violence. A female student filed a complaint, only to withdraw it a day later.

Retsler debated for a moment whether or not he should follow, whether or not he should search the boy's room, and then decided the boy wouldn't issue a challenge like that if he expected to get caught. Better to take it slow, build a case the right way. Maybe Retsler could even talk to Taylor, convince him to send the boy to a hospital where he could get help.

"Sorry about that," Taylor was saying. "He's at that age when no adult is worth his time."

Retsler stared at him. Taylor's flush deepened. "You know we found a skinned pup on the beach New Year's Day."

"No," Taylor said. "I hadn't. It's amazing what people will do."

"Isn't it?" Retsler asked. He looked at the case again. "How many of these did you find?"

"Twenty," Taylor said. "And that's how many are there."

Retsler silently counted to himself. Twenty. If the other pelt were here, it was somewhere else. "Maybe I should take a peek at your son's room."

"Not without a warrant," Taylor said.

Retsler nodded. It played out just as he expected. He shrugged, like the boy had, then he thanked Taylor for his time, and left the house.

The river was low here, sixty feet down the bank, and sparkling in the bright sunshine. Taylor had bought the land and built the house the year before he had bought the Sandcastle. Lucy said that Taylor had spent that year getting on the good side of the Planning Commission. Lucy would know.

The pelts were disturbing, the boy more so. But Taylor had a legal right to the pelts, and Retsler would have to work hard to make anything more than a misdemeanor stick on the boy. Taylor had more money than God, which meant that he could afford the biggest lawyers in the country.

Retsler was suddenly walking into the big leagues, and he wasn't even sure he wanted to play the game.

The State Crime Lab could find no match on the fingerprints, nor did they have anything to say about the requests from Whale Rock. They apologized profusely, but perfunctorily, and probably, when they got off the phone, chuckled at the things that passed for important in small towns.

Retsler didn't care. He had other things to check. Lucy had called Seavy County Deeds and Records, and had found the date of Taylor's home purchase. It was one month before the animal mutilations started near Hoover Bay. Now she was checking with the local police department in Taylor's previous home in San Jose, hoping to find another pattern.

It wasn't much, but it was a start. He also had a call in to an old friend at the FBI who might have a few ideas on how to proceed in a case as delicate, and insubstantial, as this one. Animal deaths and mutilations were bad enough, but, truth be told, they weren't what Retsler was really worried about. What worried him the most was the coldness of that boy's eyes, and the possibility—make that the probability—of what the boy would become.

Retsler had all that on his mind as he drove to the Sandcastle. He wasn't sure why he wanted to see Maria Selvado, but he knew he probably should.

Her room was on the top floor of the Sandcastle Motel. Like

all of the rooms, it had double glass doors on the ocean side that opened onto an extra long balcony. When she led Retsler onto it, it made him feel as if he were standing over the water. He supposed, in high tide, that he would be. The balconies hung over the concrete breaker that protected the hotel from high surf—another illegal measure grandfathered in by the Planning Commission. Retsler had hated the look from the ground, but he had to admit that, from the balconies themselves, the view was spectacular.

Selvado had let him in, no questions asked. That she had been in her room on such a beautiful afternoon, neither of them mentioned. The room itself was spectacular. The door opened into a hallway which led to a large bathroom, past a king-sized bedroom, and opened into a well-apportioned sitting room filled with antiques and facing a marble fireplace. The ubiquitous television was hidden in a wall unit that still looked suspiciously out of place. It was also covered with dust.

The ocean breeze had a trace of mist. Selvado raised her face to it as if it gave her life. She was obviously waiting for him to speak.

He cleared his throat. "I spoke to Roman Taylor today about the pelts."

She turned, stunned.

"He showed me the deed. They're clearly his."

"They have nothing to do with him," she said fiercely. "They don't belong to him."

"By law they do."

She bit her lip and turned away. "The law is wrong."

"The law is what we have, Ms. Selvado. It may not be right all the time, it may not make things easy, but it's what we have."

She shook her head. "It's not enough."

He knew that. He leaned on the balcony railing, and dangled his arms over the edge. This next part he did partly because he knew he had made her angry, and he agreed with Taylor: she had to leave Whale Rock. She was too unpredictable. Retsler was afraid she would try to break into Taylor's house again. If she got near that teenage boy, her own life might be in danger.

"I've also learned that you're presenting yourself as an employee of the Marine Science Center, and asking for privileges due to your position."

"I am—"

"You were," he said. "I found out about the dismissal. You're bordering on fraud, Ms. Selvado. I'll look at your actions as a simple misunderstanding right now, but any more of it, and I'll have to inform the Newport police."

She whirled toward him, her liquid eyes full of fire. There was a power to her, like the sea the day before a storm. "You wouldn't."

"I have to, Ms. Selvado."

"Taylor put you up to this."

"No." Retsler sighed. He would give her this next because he had to give her something, and then he would ask her to leave. "I'm dealing with Taylor in my own fashion. I'm trying to make a case against his son. I'm pretty sure the boy is the one who slaughtered that pup."

"Pretty sure?"

He held out his hands. "Meaning I'm convinced the boy's the one we want. I simply have to prove it. So if you'll leave me to my work, maybe I'll be able to help you."

"Bargain the boy's freedom for the pelts?"

"No," Retsler said. "I think the boy's too dangerous for that."

"Then what?"

"I'm not sure yet," he said, and felt the emptiness of his promise. "But I'll do the best I can."

"By asking me to leave town?" she asked.

"It's a start," he said.

"For you perhaps." Then she paused. The ocean was a deep clear blue. The sunshine this early in January was unusual, and welcome. She stared at it as if it gave her an idea. "And maybe for me as well."

The next morning brought a spate of strange calls: boats all over the coastline and up the river had been damaged, not badly enough to ruin them, but enough to prevent anyone from going on the ocean that day. At a dock near Hoover Village, one old fisherman claimed he saw a group of seals nudging a hole in the hull of his boat, then moving to his neighbor's boat at the next mooring. Retsler had to call his entire staff in to meet the workload of examining each and every boat, and Lucy had the volunteer firemen help as well.

Retsler was so busy, he missed what later turned out to be the most important calls of the day.

Hotel patrons of the Sandcastle lit up the emergency lines with a gruesome tale: a dark-haired woman, bleeding from both arms, dove off her balcony into the sea.

When Retsler finally got the page, he knew at once who had died. Maria Selvado. And he had felt a chill. He went over to the Sandcastle, and demanded to be let into her room.

The door was locked from the inside. A bloody knife sat on the back of the toilet. The bathroom floor was covered with blood. The trail led to the balcony. There was only one set of footprints —women's size six, flat footed (no arch) with webs between the toes. They ended at the railing, although there were bloody handprints on the iron, and another splotch of blood on the top of the concrete breaker.

The body below was gone, taken by the rising tide, returned to the sea.

On the fireplace mantel was a note addressed to Retsler. It said, simply: *When the laws of man fail, we rely on the laws of God.* And it was signed with an M.

The storm came an hour later, at high tide. Intense and furious, it concentrated on Hoover Bay, the Dee River, and Whale Rock. The rest of the coast had delicious sun and a perfect January day. In Whale Rock, sustained winds of one hundred miles per hour ripped the roof off a gas station, tore down several signs, and knocked out power to half the town. Waves crossed the concrete breaker and smashed into the Sandcastle Motel, destroying it as if it were made of paper.

Retsler had ordered an emergency evacuation of all low-lying areas, even though the National Weather Service swore that the satellite pictures showed no storm system in the vicinity. He had the radio and TV stations broadcast warnings, ordering everyone to high ground, to places that could survive winds, to places of safety. And because he was trusted, the town listened.

Someone later said that the storm would have caused a lot more destruction if it weren't for Retsler's clear thinking. Later they would call him a hero because he had saved hundreds of lives. That only two were lost in a freak storm, the governor would say, was miraculous. But Retsler knew better. He knew, the moment he saw the blood, how he had failed.

Denne stood, a shadow in the growing darkness. He picked up the McDonald's bag and shoved his styrofoam cup into it. Then he walked around the boat to Retsler.

"You've ruined those clothes," Retsler said, avoiding, knowing that he was avoiding. He shut off his flashlight, listening to the calm ocean in the distance, the gurgle of the river behind him. In the darkness, the cloying stink of the mud was almost overpowering. "The wife'll be mad."

"The wife isn't entitled to an opinion anymore," Denne said. "New Year's resolution."

"You can't stop a woman from having an opinion."

"You can when you move out." Denne turned on his own flashlight. The beam illuminated the mud before them, and the footprints that led up to the Taylor's log house. He put a hand on Retsler's back. "You can't avoid this forever, Danny."

"I'm not sure I want to see this in the dark."

"It won't be any better in the light."

Denne led the way down the path that, twenty-four hours before, had been covered with greenery and winter flowers. He mounted the stairs to the main level.

The windows were gone, the door off its hinges. The water damage was so severe that the rough-hewn logs looked as if they'd been polished smooth.

Denne ducked inside. He shown a light toward the fireplace. It took a moment for Retsler's eyes to adjust. The light was reflecting off the glass on the case. He stepped away from the beam and peered inside.

Roman Taylor had been crammed into the square space, his arms and legs held in place by some wickedly tight knots. It didn't take a degree in forensic medicine to know that the man had been alive when he had been tied down. The water mark was two inches below the ceiling, and there was mud in the bottom of the case.

Mercifully, Denne moved the light. Retsler didn't use his.

"I'll photograph all of this tomorrow," Denne said.

"There's no need," Retsler said. "He drowned."

Denne looked sharply at him.

Retsler shrugged. "Who am I going to charge?"

"You might want to wait until you see the rest." Denne led him down the stairs into the daylight basement. In the corner, someone had stuck a log into the floor. It looked like one of the mooring posts that littered the river. Onto it, Taylor's son Michael —or what was left of him— stared balefully at them.

Retsler swallowed hard to keep down the bile. He recognized the position—recognized everything, in fact, right down to the expression on Michael's face.

The dog. That was how they had found the dog.

Denne raised his flashlight beam. It caught on a knife stuck into the pole. The knife was serrated and used for gutting animals. The handle was ivory, and engraved on it, was this: *Michael Taylor. Happy 13th Birthday. Love, Dad.*

"Is it our knife?" Retsler asked.

"No doubt about it," Denne said.

Retsler closed his eyes. He would have had the proof he needed after all. Damn him for talking to Selvado. Damn him and his worries about a conviction. Damn him, and the lack of respect he had for his own abilities.

"Of course," Denne said slowly, "any good lawyer could make hash of a case based on one single knife."

"Really?" Retsler asked.

"I think so," Denne said. He took one more glance at the body. "And I don't think I was alone in that belief."

"Millions of dollars in damage," Retsler said. "Lives ruined. Two deaths. Because of me and my mouth."

"You didn't start this," Denne said.

"But I should have ended it," Retsler said. He sighed and sloshed his way back to the stairs. "Next time, I trust Lucy."

"Next time?" Denne asked, following him. "Let's hope to God there is no next time."

But there would be, Retsler knew. As long as Whale Rock was here, as long as strange things happened, there would be another clash between the humans and the strange creatures that lived in the sea. He only hoped that the next time, he would try some cooperation, maybe learn how to bend the laws of man, so that no one had to rely on the laws of God.

THE CALIFORNIA PERSPECTIVE: REFLECTIONS ON MT. RUSHMORE

BY

L. EMILIA SUNLAKE

The union of these four presidents carved on the face of the everlasting hills of South Dakota will contribute a distinctly national monument. It will be decidedly American in its conception, in its magnitude, in its meaning, and altogether worthy of our country.

—Calvin Coolidge at the dedication of Mt. Rushmore in 1927

CARS CRAWL ALONG Highway 16. The hot summer sun reflects off shiny bumperstickers, most plastered with the mementos of tourist travel: Sitting Bull Crystal Cave, Wall Drug, and I (heart) anything from terriers to West Virginia. The windows are open, and children lean out, trying to see magic shimmering in the heat visions on the pavement. The locals say the traffic has never been like this, that even in the height of tourist season, the cars can at least go thirty miles an hour. Kenny, the photographer, and I have been sitting in this sticky heat for most of the afternoon, moving forward a foot at a time, sharing a Diet Coke, and hoping the story will be worth the aggravation.

I have never been to the Black Hills before. Until I started writing regularly for the slick magazines, I had never been out of California, and even then my outside assignments were rare. Usually I wrote about things close to home: the history of Simi Valley, for instance, or the relationships between the Watts riot and the Rodney King riot twenty-five years later. When *American Observer* sent me to South Dakota, they asked me to write from a California perspective. What they will get is a white, middle-class, female California perspective. Despite my articles on the cultural diversity of my home state, *American Observer*—published in New York—continues to think that all Californians share the same opinions, beliefs, and outlooks.

Of course, now, sitting in bumper-to-bumper traffic in the dense heat, I feel right at home.

Kenny has brought a lunch—tuna fish—which, in the oppressive air has a rancid two-day dead odor. He eats with apparent gusto, while I sip on soda and try to peer ahead. Kenny says nothing. He is a slender man with long black hair and wide dark eyes. I chose him because he is the best photographer I have ever met, a man who can capture the heart of a moment in a single image. He also rarely speaks, a trait I usually enjoy, but one I have found annoying on this long afternoon as we wait in the trail of cars.

He sees me lean out the window for the fifth time in the last minute. "Why don't you interview some of the tourists?"

I shake my head and he goes back to his sandwich. The tourists aren't the story. The story waits for us at the end of this road, at the end of time.

When I think of Mount Rushmore, I think of Cary Grant clutching the lip of a stone-faced Abraham Lincoln with Eva Marie Saint beside him, looking over her shoulder at the drop below. The movie memory has the soft fake tones of early color or perhaps early colorization—the pale blues that don't exist in the natural world, the red lipstick that is five shades too red. As a child, I wanted to go to the monument and hang off a president myself. As an adult, I disdained tourist traps, and had avoided all of them with amazing ease.

Later, I tell my husband of this, and he corrects me: Cary

Grant was hanging off George Washington's forehead. Kenny disagrees: he believes Grant crawled around Teddy Roosevelt's eyes. A viewing of *North by Northwest* would settle this disagreement, but I saw the movie later, as an adult, and found the special effects not so special, and the events contrived. If Cary Grant hadn't, stupidly, pulled the knife from a dead man's body, there would have been no movie. The dead man, the knife, were an obvious set-up, and Grant's character fell right into the trap.

Appropriate, I think, for a Californian to have a cinematic memory of Mount Rushmore. As I study the history, however, I find it much more compelling, and frighteningly complex.

The Black Hills are as old as any geological formation in North America. They rise out of the flat lands on the Wyoming and Dakota borders, mysterious shadowy hills that are cut out of the dust. The dark pine trees made the hills look black from a distance. The Paha Sapa, or the Black Hills, were the center of the world for the surrounding tribes. They used the streams and lakes hidden by the trees; they hunted game in the wooded areas; and in the summer, the young men went to the sacred points on a four-day vision quest that would shape and focus the rest of their lives.

According to Lakota tribal legend, the hills were a reclining female figure from whose breasts flowed life. The Lakota went to the hills as a child went to its mother's arms.

In 1868, the United States government signed a treaty with the Indians, granting them "absolute and undisturbed use of the Great Sioux Reservation," which included the Black Hills. Terms of the treaty included the line: "No white person or persons shall be permitted to settle upon or occupy any portion of the territory, or without the consent of the Indians to pass through the same."

White persons have been trespassing ever since.

Finally I can stand the smell of tuna no longer. I push the door open on the rental car and stand. My jeans and t-shirt cling to my body—I am not used to humid heat. I walk along the edge of the highway, peering into cars, seeing pale face after pale face. Most of the tourists ignore me, but a few watch hesitantly, as they fear that I am going to pull a gun and leap into their car beside them.

Everyone knows of the troubles in the Black Hills, and most people have brought their families despite the dangers. Miracles only happen once in a lifetime.

I see no one I want to speak to until I pass a red pick-up truck. Its paint is chipped, and the frame is pocked with rust. A Native American woman sits inside, a black braid running down her back. She is dressed as I am, except that sweat does not stain her white t-shirt, and she wears heavy turquoise rings on all of her fingers.

"Excuse me," I say. "Are you heading to Mount Rushmore?"

She looks at me, her eyes hooded and dark. Two little boys sleep in the cab, their bodies propped against each other like puppies. A full jug of bottled water sits at her feet, and on the boys' side of the cab, empty pop cans line up like soldiers. "Yes," she says. Her voice is soft.

I introduce myself and explain my assignment. She does not respond, staring at me as if I am speaking in a foreign tongue. "May I talk with you for a little while?"

"No." Again, she speaks softly, but with a finality that brooks no disagreement.

I thank her for her time, shove my hands in my pockets and walk back to the car. Kenny is standing outside of it, the passenger door open. His camera is draped around his neck, reflecting sunlight, and he holds a plastic garbage bag in his hand. He is picking up litter from the roadside—smashed Pepsi cups and dirt-covered McDonald's bags.

"Lack of respect," he says, when he sees me watching him, "shows itself in little ways."

Lack of respect shows itself in larger ways too: in great stone faces carved on a mother's breast; in broken treaties; in broken bodies bleeding on the snow. The indignities continue into our lifetimes—children ripped from their parents and put into schools that force them to renounce old ways; mysterious killings and harassment arrests; and enforced poverty unheard of even in our inner cities. The stories are frightening and hard to comprehend, partly because they are true. I grasp them only through books—from Dee Brown to Peter Matthiessen, from Charles A. Eastman (Ohiyesa) to Vine Deloria, Jr.—and through film—from documentary to documentary (usually produced by P.C. White men), ending with *Incident at Ogala,* and from fictional accounts (staring non-Natives, of course) from *Little Big Man* to *Thunderheart.*

Some so-called wise person once wrote that women have the capacity to understand all of American society: we have lived in a society dominated by white men, and so had to understand their perspective to survive; we were abused and treated as property within our own homes, having no rights and no recourse under the law, so we understand Blacks, Chicanos, and Native Americans. But I stand on this road, outside a luxury car that I rented with my gold Mastercard, and I do not understand what it is like to be a defeated people, living among the victors, watching them despoil all that I value and all that I believe in.

Instead of empathy, I have white liberal guilt. When I stared across the road into the darkness of that truck cab, I felt the Native American woman's eyes assessing me. My sons sleep in beds with Ninja Turtles decorating the sheets; they wear Nikes and tear holes in their shirts on purpose. They fight over the Nintendo and the remote controls. I buy dolphin-safe tuna, and pay attention to food boycotts, but I shop in a grocery store filled with light and choices. And while I understand that the fruits of my life were purchased with the lives of people I have never met, I tell myself there is nothing I can do to change that. What is past is past.

But the past determines who we are, and it has led to this startling future.

I remember the moment with the clarity my parents have about the Kennedy assassination, the clarity my generation associates with the destruction of the space shuttle Challenger. I was waiting in my husband's Ford Bronco outside the recreation center. The early June day was hot in a California desert sort of way—the dry heat of an oven, heat that prickles but does not invade the skin. My youngest son pulled open the door and crawled in beside me, bringing with him dampness and filling the air with the scents of chlorine and institutional soap. He tossed his wet bathing suit and towel on the floor, fastened his seatbelt and said, "Didja hear? Mount Rushmore disappeared."

I smiled at him, thinking it amazing the way ten-year-old little boy minds worked—I hadn't even realized he knew what Mount Rushmore was—and he frowned at my response.

"No, really," he said, voice squeaking with sincerity. "It did. Turn on the news."

Without waiting for me, he flicked on the radio and scanned to the all-news channel.

". . . not an optical illusion," a female voice was saying. "The site now resembles those early photos, taken around the turn of the century, before the work on the monument began."

Through the hour-long drive home, we heard the story again

and again. No evidence of a bomb, no sign of the remains of the great stone faces. No rubble, nothing. Hollywood experts spoke about the possibilities of an illusion this grand, but all agreed that the faces would be there, behind the illusion, at least available to the sense of touch.

My hands were shaking by the time we pulled into the driveway of our modified ranch home. My son, whose assessment had gone from "pretty neat" to "kinda scary" within the space of the drive (probably from my grim and silent reaction), got out of the car without taking his suit and disappeared into the backyard to consult with his older brother. I took the suit, and went inside, cleaning up by rote as I made my way to the bedroom we used as a library.

The quote I wanted, the quote that had been running through my mind during the entire drive, was there on page 93 of the 1972 Simon and Schuster edition of Richard Erdoes' *Lame Deer: Seeker of Visions:*

> *One man's shrine is another man's cemetery, except that now a few white folks are also getting tired of having to look at this big paperweight curio [Mount Rushmore]. We can't get away from it. You could make a lovely mountain into a great paperweight, but can you make it into a wild, natural mountain again? I don't think you have the know-how for that.*
>
> *—John Fire Lame Deer*

Lame Deer went on to say that white men, who had the ability to fly to the moon, should have the know-how to take the faces off the mountain.

But no one had the ability to take the faces off overnight.

No one.

We finally reach the site around 5 P.M. Kenny has snapped three rolls of film on our approach. He began shooting about sixty miles away, the place where, they tell me, the faces were first visible. I try to envision the shots as he sees them: the open mouths, the shocked expressions. I know Kenny will capture the moment, but I also know he will be unable to capture the thing which holds me.

The sound.

The rumble of low conversation over the soft roar of car engines. The shocked tones, rising and falling like a wave on the open sea.

I see nothing ahead of me except the broad expanse of a

mountain outlined in the distance. I have not seen the faces up close and personal. I cannot tell the difference. But the others can. Pheromones fill the air, and I can almost taste the excitement. It grows as we pull into the over-crowded parking lot, as we walk to the visitor's center that still shows its 1940s roots.

Kenny disappears into the crowd. I walk to the first view station, and stare at a mountain, at a granite surface smooth as water-washed stone. A chill runs along my back. At the base, uniformed people with cameras and surveying equipment check the site. Other uniformed people move along the top of the mount; it appears that they have just pulled someone up on the equivalent of a window-washer's pull cart.

All the faces here are white, black or Asian—non-Native. We passed the Native woman as we drove into the parking lot. Two men, wearing army fatigues and carrying rifles had stopped the truck. She was leaning out of the cab, speaking wearily to them, and Kenny made me slow as we passed. He eavesdropped in his intense way, and then nodded once.

"She will be all right," he said, and nothing more.

The hair on my arms has prickled. TV crews film from the edge of the parking lot. A middle-aged man, his stomach parting the buttons on his short-sleeved white shirt, aims a video camera at the site. I am not a nature lover. Within minutes, I am bored with the changed mountain. Miracle, yes, but now that my eyes have confirmed it, I want to get on with the story.

Inside the visitor's center is an ancient diorama on the building of Mt. Rushmore. The huge sculpted busts of George Washington, Abraham Lincoln, Thomas Jefferson, and Theodore Roosevelt took fourteen years to complete. Gutzon Borglum (Boreglum, how appropriate) designed the monument, which was established in 1925, during our great heedless prosperity, and finished in 1941, after the Crash, the Depression, and at the crest of America's involvement in World War II. The diorama makes only passing mention—in a cheerful "aren't they cute?" 1950s way—to the importance of the Mount to the Native tribes. There is no acknowledgment of the fact that when the monument was being designed, the Lakota had filed a court claim asking for financial compensation for the theft of the Black Hills. A year after the completion of the monument, the courts denied the claim. No acknowledgment of the split between Native peoples that occurred when the case was revived in the 1950s—the split over financial compensation and return of the land itself.

Nor is there any mention of the bloody history of the surrounding area that continued into the 1970s with the American Indian Movement: the death of two FBI agents and an Indian on the Pine Ridge Reservation, the resulting trials, the violence that marked the decade, and the attempted take-over of the Black Hills themselves.

In the true tradition of a conquering force, of an occupying army, all mention of the on-going war has been obliterated.

But not forgotten. The army, with their rifles, are out in force. Several young boys, their lean muscled frames outlined in black t-shirts and fatigue pants, sit at the blond wood tables. Others sit outside, rifles leaning against their chairs. We were not stopped as we entered the parking lot—Kenny claims our trunk is too small to hold a human being—but several others were.

One of the soldiers is getting himself a drink from the overworked waitress behind the counter. I stop beside him. He is only a few years older than my oldest son, and the ferocity of the soldier's clothes make him look even younger. His skin is still pockmarked with acne, his teeth crooked and yellowed from lack of care. Things have not changed from my youth. It is still the children of the poor who receive the orders to die for patriotism, valor, and the American Way.

"A lot of tension here," I say.

He takes his ice tea from the waitress and pours half a cup of sugar into it. "It'd be easier if there weren't no tourists." Then he flushes. "Sorry, lady."

I reassure him that he hasn't offended me, and I explain my purpose.

"We ain't supposed to talk to the press." He shrugs.

"I won't use your name," I say. "And it's for a magazine that won't be published for a month, maybe two months from now."

"Two months anything can happen."

True enough, which is why I have been asked to capture this moment with the vision of an outsider. I know my editor has already asked a white Dakota correspondent to write as well, and she has received confirmation that at least one Native American author will contribute an essay. In this age of cynicism, a miracle is the most important event of our time.

The boy sits at an empty table and pulls out a chair for me. His arms are thick, tanned, and covered with fine white hairs. His fingers are long, slender and ringless, his nails clean. He doesn't look at me as he speaks.

"They sent us up here right when the whole thing started," he said, "and we was told not to let no Indians up here. Some of our guys, they been combing the woods for Indians, making sure that this ain't some kind of front for some special action. I don't like it. The guys are trigger happy, and with all these tourists, I'm afraid that someone's going to do something, and get shot. We ain't going to mean for it to happen. It'll be an accident, but it'll happen just the same."

He drinks his tea in several noisy slurps, tells me a bit about his family—his father, one of the few casualties of the Gulf War; his mother remarried to a foreman of a dying assembly plant in Michigan; his sister, newly married to a career army officer; and himself, his dreams for a real life without a hand-to-mouth income when he leaves the army. He never expected to search cars at the entrance to a National Park, and the miracle makes him nervous.

"I think it's some kind of Indian trick," he says. "You know, a decoy to get us all pumped up and focused here while they attack somewhere else."

This boy, who grew up poor hundreds of miles away, and who probably never gave Native Americans a second thought, is now speaking the language of conquerors, conquerors at the end of an empire, who feel the power slipping through their fingers.

He leaves to return to his post. I speak with a few tourists, but learn nothing interesting. It is as if the Virgin Mary has appeared at Lourdes—everyone wants to be one of the first to experience the miracle. I am half-surprised no one has set up a faith healing station—a bit of granite from the holy mountain, and all ailments will be cured.

The light is turning silver with approaching twilight. My stomach is rumbling, but I do not want one of the hot dogs that has been twirling in the little case all afternoon. The oversized salted pretzels are gone, and the grill is caked with grease. The waitress herself looks faded, her dishwater-blond hair slipping from its bun, her uniform covered with sweat stains and ketchup. I go to find Kenny, but cannot see him in the crowds. Finally I see him, on a path just past the parking lot, sitting beneath a scraggly pine tree, talking with an elderly man.

The elderly man's hair is white and short, but his face has a photogenic cragginess that most WASP photographers find appealing in Native Americans. As I approach, he touches Kenny's arm, then slips down the path and disappears into the growing darkness.

"Who was that?" I ask as I stop in front of Kenny. I am standing over him, looming, and the question feels like an interrogation, as if I am asking for information I do not deserve. Kenny grabs his camera and takes a picture of me. When we view it later, we will see different things: he will see the formation of light and shadow into a tired irritable woman, made more irritable by an occurrence she cannot explain or understand, and I will see the teachers from my childhood enforcing some arbitrary rule on the playground.

When he is finished, he holds out his hand and I pull him to his feet. We walk back to the car in silence, and he never answers my question.

Speculation is rife in Rapid City. The woman at the Super Eight on the Interstate hands out her opinion with the old-fashioned room keys. "They're using some new-fangled technology and trying to scare us," she says, her voice roughened by her six-pack-a-day habit. Wisps of smoke curl around the Mt. Rushmore mugs and the tourist brochures that fill the dark wood lobby. "They know if that monument goes away there's really no reason for folks to stop here."

She never explains who she means by "they." In this room filled with white people, surrounded by mementos of the "Old West," the meaning of "they" is immediately clear.

As it is downtown. The stately old Victorian homes and modified farmhouses attest to this city's roots. Some older buildings still stand in the center of town, dwarfed by newer hotels built to swallow the tourist trade. Usually, the locals tell me, the clientele is mixed here. Some business people show for various conventions and must fraternize with the bikers who have a convention of their own in nearby Sturgis every summer. The tourists are the most visible: with their video cameras and tow-headed children, they visit every sight available from the Geology Museum to the Sioux Indian Museum. We all check our maps and make no comment over roads named after Indian fighters like Philip Sheridan.

In a dusky bar whose owner does not want to be named in this "or any" article, a group of elderly men share a drink before they toddle off to their respective homes. They too have theories, and they're willing to talk with a young female reporter from California.

"You don't remember the seventies," says Terry, a loud-voiced, balding man who lives in a nearby retirement home. "Lots of young reporters like you, honey, and them AIM people, stirring up trouble. There were more guards at Rushmore than before or since. We always thought they'd blow up that monument. They hate it, you know. Say we've defaced—" (and they all laugh at the pun) "—defaced their sacred hills."

"I say they lost the wars fair and square," says Rudy. He and his wife of forty-five years live in a six-bedroom Victorian house on the corner of one of the tree-lined streets. "No sense whining about it. Time they start learning to live like the rest of us."

"Always thought they would bomb that monument." Max, a former lieutenant in the Army, fought "the Japs" at Guadalcanal, a year that marked the highlight of his life. "And now they have."

"There was no bomb," says Jack, a former college professor who still wears tweed blazers with patches on the elbows. "Did you hear any explosion? Did you?"

The others don't answer. It becomes clear they have had this conversation every day since the faces disappeared. We speak a bit more, then I leave in search of other opinions. As I reach the door, Jack catches my arm.

"Young lady," he says, ushering me out into the darkness of the quiet street. "We've been living the Indian wars all our lives. It's hard to ignore when you live beside a prison camp. I'm not apologizing for my friends—but it's hard to live here, to see all that poverty, to know that we—our government—causes that devastation because the Indians—the Natives—want to live their own way. It's a strange prison we've built for them. They can escape if they want to renounce everything they are."

In his voice I hear the thrum of the professor giving a lecture. "What did you teach?" I ask.

He smiles, and in the reflected glare of the bar's neon sign, I see the unlined face of the man he once was. "History," he says. "And I tell you, living here, I have learned that history is not a deep dusty thing of the past, but part of the air we breathe each and every day."

His words send a shiver through me. I thank him for his time and return to my rented car. As I drive to my hotel, I pass the Rushmore Mall—a flat late-'70s creation that has sprawled to encompass other stores. The mall is closing, and hundreds of cars pull away, oblivious to the strangeness that has happened only a few miles outside the city.

By morning, the police, working in cooperation with the FBI, have captured a suspect. But they will not let any of the reporters talk with him, nor will they release his name, his race, or anything else about him. They don't even specify the charges.

"How can they?" asks the reporter for *The New York Times* over an overpriced breakfast of farm-fresh eggs, thick bacon and wheat toast at a local diner. "They don't know what happened to the monument. So they charge him with making the faces disappear? Unauthorized use of magic in an un-American fashion?"

"Who says it's magic?" the CNN correspondent asks.

"You explain it," says the man from the *Wall Street Journal*. "I touched the rock face yesterday. Nothing is carved there. It feels like nothing ever was."

The reporters are spooked, and the explanations they share among themselves have the ring of mysticism. That mysticism does not reach the American people, however. On the air, in the pages of the country's respected newspapers and magazines, the talk revolves around possible technical explanations for the disappearance of the faces. Any whisper of the unexplainable and the show, the interviewee, and the story are whisked off the air.

It is as if we are afraid of things beyond our ken.

In the afternoon, I complain to Kenny that, aside from the woman in the truck and the man he talked to near the monument, I have seen no Natives. The local and national Native organizations have been strangely silent. National spokespeople for the organizations have arrived in Rapid City—only to disappear behind some kind of protective walls. Even people who revel in the limelight have avoided it on this occasion.

"They have no explanations either," Kenny says with such surety that I glare at him. He has been talking with the Natives while I have not.

Finally he shrugs. "They have found a place in the Black Hills that is theirs. They believe something wonderful is about to happen."

"Take me there," I say.

He shakes his head. "I cannot. But I can bring someone to you."

Kenny drives the rental car off the Interstate, down back roads so small as to not be on the map. Old faded signs for now-defunct cafés and secret routes to the Black Hills Caverns give the area a sense of twilight zone mystery. Out here, the towns have names that send chills down my back, names like Mystic and Custer. Kenny leaves me at a roadside café that looks as if it closed when Kennedy was president. The windows are boarded up, but the door swings open to reveal a dusty room filled with rat prints and broken furniture. Someone has removed the grill and the rest of the equipment, leaving gaping holes in the sideboards, but the counter remains, a testament to what might have been a once-thriving business.

There are tables near the gravel parking lot outside. They have been wiped clean, and one bears cup rings that look to be fairly recent. The café may be closed, but the tables are still in use. I wipe off a bench and sit down, a little unnerved that Kenny has left me in this desolate place alone—with only a cellular phone for comfort.

The sun is hot as it rises in the sky, and I am thankful for the bit of shade provided by the building's overhang. No cars pass on this road, and I am beginning to feel as if I have reached the edge of nowhere.

I have brought my laptop, and I spend an hour making notes from the day's conversations, trying to place them in a coherent order so that this essay will make sense. It has become clearer and clearer to me that—unless I have the luck of a fictional detective—I will find no answers before my Monday deadline. I will submit only a series of impressions and guesses based on my own observations of a fleeting moment. I suppose that is why the *American Observer* hired me instead of an investigative reporter, so that I can capture this moment of mystery in my white California way.

Finally I hear the moan of a car engine, and relief loosens the tension in my shoulders. I have not, until this moment, realized how tense the quiet has made me. Sunlight glares off the car's new paint job, and the springs squeak as the wheels catch the potholes that fill the road. Kenny's face is obscured by the windshield, but as the car turns in the parking lot, I recognize his passenger as the elderly man I had seen the day before.

The car stops and I stand. Kenny gets out and leads the elderly man to me. I introduce myself and thank the man for joining us. He nods in recognition but does not give me his name. "I am here as a favor to Little Hawk," he says, nodding at Kenny. "Otherwise I would not speak to you."

Kenny is fiddling with his camera. He looks no different, and yet my vision of him has suddenly changed. We never discussed his past or mine for that matter. In California, a person either proclaims his heritage loudly or receives his privacy. I am definitely not an investigator. I did not know that my cameraman has ties in this part of the Dakotas.

I close my laptop as I sit. The old man sits beside me. Silver mixes with the black hair in his braid. I have seen his face before. Later I will look it up and discover what it looked like when it was young, when he was making the news in the 1970s for his association with AIM.

I open my mouth to ask a question and he raises his hand, shaking his head slightly. Behind us, a bird chirps. A drop of sweat runs down my back.

"I know what you will ask," he says. "You want me to give you the answers. You want to know what is happening, and how we caused it."

My questions are not as blunt as that, but he has the point. I have fallen into the same trap as the locals. I am blaming the Natives because I see no other explanation.

"When he gave his farewell address to the Lakota," the old man said in a ringing voice accustomed to stories, "he said, 'As a child I was taught the Supernatural Powers were powerful and could do strange things. . . . This was taught me by the wise men and the shamans. They taught me that I could gain their favor by being kind to my people and brave before my enemies; by telling the truth and living straight; by fighting for my people and their hunting grounds . . .'

"All my life we have fought, Ms. Sunlake, and we have tried to live the old path. But I was taught as a child that we had been wicked, that we were living in sin, and that we must accept Christ as our Savior, for in Him is the way.

"In Him, my people found death over a hundred years ago, at Wounded Knee. In Him, we have watched our Mother ravaged and our hunting grounds ruined. And I wish I could say that by renouncing Him and His followers we have begun this change. But I cannot."

The bird has stopped chirping. His voice echoes in the silence. Kenny's camera whirs, once, twice, and I think of the old superstition that Crazy Horse and some of the others held, that a camera stole the soul. This old man does not have that fear.

He puts out a hand and touches my arm. His knuckles are large and swollen with age. A twisted white scar runs from his wrist to his elbow. "We have heard that there are many buffalo on the Great Plain, and that the water is receding from Lake Powell. We are together now in the Hills, waiting and following the old traditions. Little Hawk has been asked to join us, but he will not."

I glance at Kenny. He is holding his camera chest high and staring at the old man, tears in his eyes. I look away.

"In our search for answers, we have forgotten that Red Cloud is right," the old man said. "*Taku Wakan* are powerful and can do strange things."

He stands and I stand with him. "But why now?" I ask. "Why not a hundred years ago? Two hundred years ago?"

The look he gives me is sad. I am still asking questions, unwilling to accept.

"Perhaps," he said, "the *Taku Wakan* know that if they wait much longer the People will be gone, and the Earth will belong to madmen." Then he nods at Kenny and they walk to the car.

"I will be back soon," Kenny says. I sit back down and try to write this meeting down in my laptop. What I cannot convey is the sense of unease with which it left me, the feeling that I have missed more than I could ever see.

"Why don't you go with them?" I ask Kenny as we drive back to Rapid City.

For a long time, he does not answer me. He stares straight ahead at the narrow road, the fading white lines illuminated only by the car's headlights. He had come for me just before dark. The mosquitoes had risen in the twilight, and I had felt that the essay and I would die together.

"I cannot believe as they do," he says. "And they need purity of belief."

"I don't understand," I say.

He sighs and pushes a long strand of hair away from his face. "He said we were raised to be ashamed of who we are. I still am. I cringe when they go through the rituals."

"What do you believe is happening at Mount Rushmore?" I keep my voice quiet, so as not to break this, the first thread of confidence he has ever shown in me.

"I'm like you," he says. His hands clutch the top of the wheel, knuckles white. "I don't care what is happening, as long as it provides emotion for my art."

We leave the next morning on a 6 A.M. flight. The plane is nearly empty. The reporters and tourists remain, since no one has any answers yet. The first suspect has been released, and another brought into custody. Specialists in every area from virtual reality to sculpture have flooded the site. Experts on Native Americans posit everything from a bombing to Coyote paying one last, great trick.

I have written everything but this, the final section. My hands shook last night as I typed in my conversation with Kenny. I am paid to observe, paid to learn, paid to be detached—but he is right. So few stories tug my own heartstrings. I won't let this one. I refuse to believe in miracles. I too want to see the experts prove that some odd technology has caused the change in the mountain-side.

Yet as I lean back and try to imagine what that moment will feel like—the moment when I learn that some clever person with a hidden camera has caused the entire mess—I feel a sinking in my stomach. I want to believe in the miracle, and since I cannot, I want to have the chance to believe. I don't want anyone to take that small thing away from me.

Yet the old man's words do not fill me with comfort either. For the future he sees, the future he hopes for, has no place for me or my kind in it. Whatever has happened to the Natives has happened to them, and not to me. Please God, never to me.

The sunlight has a sharp, early morning clarity. As the plane lifts off, its shadow moves like a hawk over the Earth. My gaze follows the shadow, watching it move over buildings and then over the hills. As we pull up into the cloud, I gasp.

For below me, the hills have transformed into a reclining woman, her head tilted back, her knees bent, her breasts firm and high. She watches us until we disappear.

Until we leave the center of the world.

Spirit Guides

LOS ANGELES. City of the Angels.

Kincaid walked down Hollywood Boulevard, his feet stepping on gum-coated stars. Cars whooshed past him, horns honking, tourists gawking. The line outside Graumann's Chinese clutched purses against their sides, held windbreakers tightly over their arms. A hooker leaned against the barred display window of the corner drug store, her make-up so thick it looked like a mask in the hot sun.

The shooting had left him shaken. The crazy had opened up inside a nearby Burger Joint, slaughtering four customers and three teenaged kids behind the counter before three men, passing on the street, rushed inside and grabbed him. Half a dozen shots had gone wild, leaving fist-sized holes in the drywall, shattering picture frames, and making one perfect circle in the center of the cardboard model for a bacon double cheeseburger.

He'd arrived two minutes too late, hearing the call on his police scanner on his way home, but unable to maneuver in traffic. Christ, some of those people who wouldn't let him pass might have had relatives in that Burger Joint. Still and all, he had arrived first to find the killer trussed up in a chair, the men hovering around him, women clutching sobbing children, blood and bodies mixing with French fries on the unswept floor.

A little girl, no more than three, had grabbed his sleeve and pointed at one of the bodies, long slender male and young, wearing a 49ers t-shirt, ripped jeans and Adidas, face a bloody mass of tissue, and said, "Make him better," in a whisper that broke Kincaid's heart. He cuffed the suspect, roped off the area, took names of witnesses before the backup arrived. Three squads, fresh-faced uniformed officers, followed by the swat team, nearly five minutes too late, the forensic team and the ambulances not far behind.

Kincaid had lit a cigarette with shaking fingers and said, "All yours," before taking off into the sun-drenched crowded streets.

He stopped outside the Roosevelt, and peered into the plate glass. His own tennis shoes were stained red, and a long brown streak of drying blood marked his Levi's. The cigarette had burned to a coal between his nicotine-stained fingers, and he tossed it, stamping it out on the star of a celebrity whose name he didn't recognize.

Inside stood potted palms and faded glamour. Pictures of motion picture stars long dead lined the second floor balcony. Within the last ten years, the hotel's management had restored the Roosevelt to its 1920s glory, when it had been the site for the first ever Academy Award celebration. When he first came to L.A., he spent a lot of time in the hotel, imagining the low-cut dresses, the clink of champagne flutes, the scattered applause as the nominees were announced. Searching for a kind of beauty that existed only in celluloid, a product of light and shadows and nothing more.

El Pueblo de Nuestra Señora la Reina de los Angeles de Porciúncula.

The City of Our Lady, Queen of the Angels of Porciuncula.

He knew nothing of the Angels of Porciuncula, did not know why Felipe de Neve in 1781 named the city after them. He suspected it was some kind of prophecy, but he didn't know.

They had been fallen angels.

Of that he was sure.

He sighed, wiped the sweat from his forehead with a grimy hand, then returned to his car, knowing that home and sleep would elude him for one more night.

Lean and spare, Kincaid survived on cigarettes, coffee, chocolate and bourbon. Sometime in the last five years, he had allowed the LAPD to hire him, although he had no formal training. After a few odd run-ins and one overnight jail stay before it became clear that he wasn't anywhere near the crime scene, Kincaid had met Davis, his boss. Davis had the flat gaze of a man who had seen too much, and he knew, from the records and the evidence before him, that Kincaid was too precious to lose. He made Kincaid a plainclothes detective and never assigned him a partner.

Kincaid never told anyone what he did. Most of the cops he worked with never knew. All they cared about was that when Kincaid was on the job, suspects were found, cases were closed, and files were sealed. He worked quietly and he got results.

They didn't need him on this one. The perp was caught at the scene. All he had to do was write his report, then go home, toss the tennies in the trash, soak the Levi's, and wait for another day.

But it wasn't that easy. He sat in his car, an olive-green 1968 Olds with a fading pine-shaped airfreshener hanging from the rearview mirror, long after his colleagues had left. His hands were still shaking, his nostrils still coated with the scent of blood and burgers, his ears clogged with the faint sobs of a pimply-faced boy rocking over the body of a fallen co-worker. The images would stick, along with all of the others. His brain was reaching overload. Had been for a long time. But that little girl's voice, the plea in her tone, had been more than he could bear.

For twenty years he had tried to escape, always ending up in a new town, with new problems. Shootings in Oklahoma parking lots, bombings in Upstate New York, murders in restaurants and shopping malls and suburban family pick-ups. The violence surrounded him, and he was trapped.

Surely this time, they would let him get away.

A hooker knocked on the window of his car. He thought he could smell the sweat and perfume through the rolled-up glass. Her cleavage was mottled, her cheap elastic top revealing the top edge of brown nipple.

He shook his head, then turned the ignition and grabbed the gearshift on the column to take the car out of park. The Olds roared to life, and with it, came the adrenaline rush, hormones tinged with panic. He pulled out of the parking space, past the hooker, down Hollywood Boulevard toward the first freeway intersection he could find.

Kincaid would disappear from the LAPD as mysteriously as he had arrived. He stopped long enough to pick up his clothes, his credit cards, and a hand-painted coffee mug a teenaged girl in Galveston had given him twenty years before, when she mistakenly thought he had saved her life.

He merged into the continuous L.A. rush hour traffic for the last time, radio off, clutching the wheel in white-knuckled tightness. He would go to Big Bear, up in the mountains, where there were no people, no crimes, nothing except himself and the wilderness.

He drove away from the angels.

Or so he hoped.

Kincaid drove until he realized he was on the road to Las Vegas. He pulled the Olds over, put on his hazards and bowed his head, unwilling to go any farther. But he knew, even if he didn't drive there, he would wake up in Vegas, his car in the lot outside. It had happened before.

He didn't remember taking the wrong turn, but he wasn't supposed to remember. They were just telling him that his work wasn't done, the work they had forced him to do ever since he was a young boy.

With a quick, vicious movement, he got out of the Olds and shook his fist at the star-filled desert sky. "I can't take it anymore, do you hear me?"

But no shape flew across the moon, no angel wings brushed his cheek, no reply filled his heart. He could turn around, but the roads he drove would only lead him back to Los Angeles, back to people, back to murders in which little girls stood in pools of blood. He knew what Los Angeles was like. Maybe they would allow him a few days rest in Vegas.

Las Vegas, the fertile plains, originally founded in the late 1700s like L.A., only the settlement didn't become permanent until 1905 when the first lots were sold (and nearly flooded out five years later). He thought maybe the city's youth and brashness would be a tonic, but even as he drove into town, he felt the blood beneath the surface. Despair and hopelessness had come to every place in America. Only here it mingled with the cajing-jing of slot machines and the smell of money.

He wanted to stay in the MGM Grand, but the Olds wouldn't drive through the lot. He settled on a cheap tumbledown hotel on the far side of the strip, complete with chenille bedspreads and rattling window air conditioners that dripped water on the thin brown indoor-outdoor carpet. There he slept in the protective dark of the black-out curtains, and dreamed:

Angels floated above him, wings so long the tips brushed his face. As he watched, they tucked their wings around themselves and plummeted, eagle-like, to the ground below, banking when the concrete of a major superhighway rose in front of them. He was on the bed, watching, helpless, knowing that each time the long white tailfeathers touched the Earth, violence erupted somewhere it had never been before.

He started awake, coughing the deep racking cough of a three-pack-a-day man. His tongue was thick and tasted of bad coffee and nicotine. He reached for the end table, clicking on the brown glass bubble lamp, then grabbed his lighter and a cigarette from the pack resting on top of the cut-glass ashtray. His hands were still shaking, and the room was quiet except for his labored breathing. Only in the silence did he realize that his dream had been accompanied by the sound of the pimply-faced boy, sobbing.

It happened just before dawn. A woman's scream, outside, cut off in mid-thrum, followed by a sickening thud and footsteps. He had known it would, the minute the car had refused to enter the Grand's parking lot. And he had to respond, whether it was his choice or not.

Kincaid paused long enough to pull on his pants, checking to make sure his wallet was in the back pocket. Then he grabbed his key and let himself out of the room.

His window overlooked the pool, a liver-shaped thing built in the late fifties of blue tile. The management left the terrace lights on all night, and Kincaid used those to guide him across the interior courtyard. In the half-light, he saw another shape running toward the pool, a pear-shaped man dressed in the too-tight uniform of a national rent-a-cop service. The air smelled of chlorine and the desert heat was still heavy despite the early morning hour. Leaves and dead bugs floated in the water, and the surrounding patio furniture was so dirty it took a moment for Kincaid to realize it was supposed to be white.

The rent-a-cop had already arrived on the scene, his pasty skin turning green as he looked down. Kincaid came up behind him, stopped, and stared.

The body was crumpled behind the removable diving board. One look at her blood-stained face, swollen and bruised neck, her chipped and broken fingernails and he knew.

All of it.

"I'd better call this in," the rent-a-cop said, and Kincaid shook his head, knowing that if he were alone with the body, he would end up spending the next few days in a Las Vegas lock-up.

"No, let me." He went back to his room, packed his meager

possessions and set them by the door. Then he called 911 and reported the murder, slipping on a shirt before going back outside.

The rent-a-cop was wiping his mouth with the back of his hand. The air smelled of vomit. Kincaid said nothing. Together they waited for the Nevada authorities to show: a skinny plainclothes detective whose eyes were red-rimmed from lack of sleep and his female partner, busty and official in regulation blue.

While the partner radioed in, the rent-a-cop told his version: that he had been making his rounds and heard a couple arguing poolside. He was watching from the window when the man backhanded the woman, and then took off through the casino. The woman didn't get up, and the cop decided to check on her instead of chasing the guy. Kincaid had shown up a minute or two later from his room in the hotel.

The plainclothes man turned his flat gaze on Kincaid. Kincaid flashed his LAPD badge, then told the plainclothes man that the killer's name was Luther Hardy, that he'd killed her because her anger was the last straw in a day that had seen him lose most of their $10,000 savings on the Mirage's roulette table. Even as the men spoke, Hardy was sitting at the only open craps table in Circus Circus, betting $25 chips on the come line.

Then Kincaid waited for the disbelief, but the plainclothesman nodded, thanked him, rounded up the female partner and headed toward Circus Circus, leaving Kincaid, not the rent-a-cop, to guard the scene. Kincaid rubbed his nose with his thumb and forefinger, trying to stop a building headache, feeling the rent-a-cop's scrutiny. Kincaid could always pick them, the ones who had seen everything, the ones who had learned through hard experience and crazy knocks to check any lead that came their way. Like Davis. Only Kincaid was new to this plainclothesman, so there would be a hundred questions when they returned.

Questions Kincaid was too tired to answer.

He told the rent-a-cop his room number, then staggered back, picked up his things and checked out, figuring he would be halfway to Phoenix before they discovered he was gone for good. They would call LAPD, and Davis would realize that Kincaid had finally left, and would probably light a candle for him later that evening because he would know that Kincaid's singular talent was still controlling his life.

Like a hick tourist, Kincaid stopped on the Hoover Dam. At 8 A.M., he stood on the miraculous concrete structure, staring at the raging blue of the Colorado below. An angel fluttered past him, then wrapped its wings around its torso and dove like a gull after prey. It disappeared in the glare of the sunlight against the water, and he strained, hoping and fearing he'd catch a glimpse as the angel rose, dripping, from the water.

The glimpses had haunted him since he was thirteen. He'd been in St. Patrick's Cathedral with his mother, and one of the stained glass angels left her window, floated through the air, and kissed him before alighting on the pulpit to tickle the visiting priest during Mass. The priest hadn't noticed the feathers brush his face and neck, but he had died the next day in a mugging outside the subway station at Sixty-third and Lexington.

Kincaid hadn't seen the mugging, but his train had arrived only a few seconds after the priest died.

Years later, Kincaid finally thought to wonder why he hadn't died from the angel's kiss. And, although he still didn't have the answer, he knew that his second sight came from that morning. All he needed to do was look at a body to know who had driven the spirit from it, and why. The snapshots remained in his mind in all their horror, surrounded by faces frozen in agony, each shot a sharp moment of pain that pierced a hole in his increasingly fragile soul.

As a young man, he believed he could stop the pain, that he had been given the gift so that he could end the horrors. He would ride out, like St. George, and defeat the dragon that had terrified the village. But these terrors were as old as time itself, and instead of stopping them, Kincaid could only observe them, and report what his inner eye had seen. He had thought, as he grew older, that using his skills to imprison the perpetrators would help, but the deaths continued, more each year, and the little girl in the Burger Joint had provided the final straw.

Make him better.

Kincaid didn't have that kind of magic.

The angel flew out of the wide crevice, past the canyon walls, its tail feathers dripping just as Kincaid had feared. Somewhere within a two hundred mile radius, someone would die violently because an angel had brushed the Earth. Kincaid hunched himself against the bright morning, then turned and walked along the rock-strewn highway to his car. When he got inside, he kept the radio off so that the news of the atrocity would not hit him when it happened.

But the silence wouldn't keep him ignorant forever. He would turn on the TV in a hotel, or pass a row of newspapers outside a restaurant, and the information would present itself to him, as clearly and brightly as it always had, as if it were his responsibility, subject to his control.

The car led him into Phoenix. From the freeway, the city was a row of concrete lanes, marred by machine-painted lines. From the sidestreets, it had well manicured lawns and tidy houses, too many strip restaurants and the ubiquitous mall. He was having a chimichanga in a neighborhood Garcia's when he watched the local news and realized that he might not hear of an atrocity after all. He finished the meal and left before the national news aired.

He was still in Phoenix at midnight, and had not yet found a hotel. He didn't want to sleep, didn't want to be led to the next place where someone would die. He was sitting alone at a small table in a high-class strip joint, sipping bourbon that actually had a smooth bite instead of the cheap stuff he normally got. The strippers were legion, all young, with tits high and firm and asses to match. Some had long lean legs and others were all torso. But none approached him, as if a sign were flashing above him, warning the women away. He drank until he could feel it—he didn't know how many drinks that was anymore—and was startled that no one noticed him getting tight.

Even drunk, he couldn't relax, couldn't laugh. Enjoyment had leached out of him, decades ago.

When the angel appeared in front of him, he thought it was another stripper, taller than most, wrapped in gossamer wings. Then it unfolded the wings and extended them, gently, as if it were doing a slow-motion fan dance, and he realized that its face had no features, and its body was fat and nippleless like a butterfly.

He raised his glass to it. "You gonna kiss me again?" His thoughts had seemed clear, but the words came out slurred.

The angel said nothing—it probably couldn't speak since it had no mouth. It merely took the drink from him, and set the glass on the table. Then it grabbed his hand, pulled him to his feet, and led him from the room like a recalcitrant child. He vaguely wondered how he looked, stumbling alone through the maze of people, his right arm outstretched.

When the fresh air hit him, the bourbon backed up in his throat like bile. He staggered away from the beefy valets, and threw up behind the potted cactus, the angel standing beside him, still as a statue. After a moment, he stood up and wiped his mouth with the crumpled handkerchief he kept folded in his back pocket. He still felt drunk, but not as bloated.

Then the angel scooped him in its arms. Its body was soft and cold as if it contained no life at all. It cradled him like a baby, and they flew up until the city became a blaze of lights.

The wind ruffled his hair and woke him even more. He felt strangely calm, and he attributed that to the alcohol. Just as he was getting used to the oddness, the angel wrapped its wings around them and plummeted toward the ground.

They were moving so fast, he could feel the force of the air like a slap in his face. He was screaming—he could feel it, ripping at his throat—but he could hear nothing. They hurtled over the interstate. The cars were the size of ants before the angel extended its wings to ease their landing.

The angel tilted them upright, and they touched down in an empty glass-strewn parking lot that led to an insurance office whose door was surrounded by yellow police tape. He recognized the site from the local newscast he had caught in Garcia's: since eight that morning, the insurance office had been the location of a hostage situation. A husband had decided to terrorize his wife who worked inside and, although shots had been fired, no one had been injured.

He stared at the building, felt the terror radiate from its walls as if it was a furnace. The insurance company was an old one: the gold lettering on the hand-painted window was chipped, and inside, he could barely make out the shape of an overturned chair. He turned to ask the angel why it had brought him there, when he realized it was gone.

Kincaid stood in the parking lot for a moment, one hand wrapped around his stomach, the other holding his throbbing head. They had flown for miles. He still had his wallet, but had no idea where he was or how he would find a pay phone.

And he didn't know what the angel had wanted from him.

He sighed and walked across the parking lot. The broken glass crunched beneath his shoes. His mouth was dry. The police tape looked too yellow in the glare of the streetlight. He stood on the stoop and peered inside, half hearing the voices from earlier in the day, the shouts from the police bullhorn, the low tense voice of the wife, the terse clipped tones of her husband. About noon he had gone outside to smoke a cigarette—his wife hated smoke—and had shot a stray dog to ward off the policeman who had been sneaking up behind him.

Kincaid could smell the death. He followed his nose to the side of the building. There, among the gravel and the spindly flowerless rose bushes, lay the dog on its side. It was scrawny and its coat was mottled. Its tongue protruded just a bit from its open mouth. Its glassy eyes seemed to follow Kincaid, and he wondered how the news had missed this, the sympathy story amidst all the horror.

The stations in L.A. would have covered it.

Poor dog. A stray in life, unremembered in death. Just standing over it, he could see the last moments—the enticing smell of food from the police cars suddenly mingled with the scent of human fear, the glittery eyes of the male human and then pain, sharp, deep, and complete.

Kincaid crouched beside it. In all his years, he had never touched a dead thing, never felt the cold lifeless body, never totally understood how a body could live and then not live within the same instant. In the past he had left the dead for someone else to clean up, but here no one would. The dog would rot in this site of trauma and near-human tragedy, and no one would take the care to bury the dead.

Perhaps that was why the angel brought him, to show him that there had been carnage after all.

He didn't know how to bury it. All he had were his hands. But he touched the soft soil of the rose garden, his wrist brushing the dog's tail as he did so.

The dog coughed and struggled to sit up.

Kincaid backed away so quickly he nearly fell. The dog choked, then coughed again, spraying blood all over the bushes, the gravel, and the concrete. It looked at him with a mixture of fear and pain.

"Jesus," Kincaid muttered.

He pushed himself forward, then grabbed the dog's shoulders. Its labored breathing eased and its tail thumped slightly against the ground. Something clattered against the pavement, and he saw the bullet, rolling away. The dog stood, whimpered, licked his hand, and then trotted off to fill its empty stomach.

Kincaid sat down in the glass and gravel, staring at his blood-covered hands.

Phoenix.

A creature of myth that rose from its own ashes to live again.

He had been such a fool.

All those years. All those lives.

Such a fool.

He looked up at the star-filled desert sky. The angel that had brought him hovered over him like a teacher waiting to see if the student understood the lecture. He couldn't relive his life, but maybe, just maybe, he could help one little girl who had spoken with the voice of angels.

Make him better.

"Take me back to Los Angeles," he said to the angel. "To the people who died yesterday."

And in a heartbeat, he was back in the Burger Joint. The killer, an overweight acne-scarred man with empty eyes, was tied to a chair near the window, a group of men milling nervously around him, the gun leaning against the wall behind them. All the children were crying, their parents pressing the tiny faces against shoulders, trying to block the sight. The air smelled of burgers and fresh blood.

A little girl, no more than three, grabbed Kincaid's sleeve and pointed at one of the bodies, long slender male and young, wearing a 49ers t-shirt, ripped jeans and Adidas, face a bloody mass of tissue, and said, "Make him better," in a whisper that broke Kincaid's heart.

Kincaid crouched, hands shaking, wishing desperately for a cigarette, and grabbed the body by the arm. Air whistled from the lungs, and the blood bubbled in the remains of the face. As Kincaid watched, the face returned, the blood disappeared, and a young man was staring at him with fear-filled eyes.

"You all right, friend?" Kincaid asked.

The man nodded and the little girl flung herself in his arms.

"Jesus," someone said behind him.

Kincaid shook his head. "It's amazing how bad injuries can look when someone's covered with blood."

He didn't wait for the response, just went to the next body and the next, his need for a cigarette decreasing with touch, the blood drying as if it had never been. When he got behind the counter, he gently pushed aside the pimply-faced boy sobbing over the dead co-worker, and then he paused.

If he reversed this one, they would have nothing to indict the killer on.

The boy's breath hitched as he watched Kincaid. Kincaid turned and looked over his shoulder at the killer tied to the chair near the entrance. Holes the size of fists marred the drywall and made one perfect circle in the center of the cardboard model for a bacon double cheeseburger. It would be enough.

He grabbed the body's shoulders, feeling the grease of the uniform beneath his fingers. The spirit slid back in as if it had never left, and the wounds sealed themselves as they would on a videotape run backwards.

All those years. All those wasted years.

"How did you do that?" the pimply-faced boy asked, his face shiny with tears.

"He was only stunned," Kincaid said.

When he was done, he went outside to find the backup team interviewing witnesses, the ambulances just arriving, five minutes too late.

"All yours," he said, before taking off into the sun-drenched crowded streets.

Now he had to keep moving. No jobs with police departments, no comfortable apartments. He had to stay one step ahead of a victim's shock, one step ahead of the press who would someday catch wind of his ability. He couldn't let them corner him, because the power was not his to control.

He was still trapped.

He stopped outside the Roosevelt, lit a cigarette, and peered into the plate glass. His own tennis shoes were stained red, and a long brown streak of drying blood marked his Levi's. The cigarette had burned to a coal between his nicotine-stained fingers before he had a chance to take a drag, and he tossed it, stamping it out on the star of a celebrity whose name he didn't recognize.

All those years and he never knew. The kiss made some kind of cosmic sense. Even Satan, the head of the fallen angels, was once beloved of God. Even Satan must have felt remorse at the pain he caused. He would never be accepted back into the fold, but he might use his powers to repair some of the pain he caused. Only he wouldn't be able to alone, for each time he touched the Earth, he would cause another death. What better to do, then, but to give healing power to a child, who would learn and grow into the role.

Kincaid's hands were still shaking. The blood had crusted beneath his fingernails.

"I never asked for this!" he shouted, and people didn't even turn as they passed on the street. Shouting crazies were common in Hollywood. He held his hands to the sky. "I never asked for this!"

Above him, angels flew like eagles, soaring and dipping and diving, never coming close enough to endanger the Earth. Their featureless faces radiated a kind of joy. And, although he would never admit it, he felt that joy too.

Although he would not slay the dragon, he wouldn't have to live with its carnage either. Finally, at last, he could make some kind of difference. He let his hands fall to his side, and wondered if the Roosevelt would shirk at letting him wash the blood off inside. He was about to ask when a stray dog pushed its muzzle against his thigh.

"Ah, hell," he said, looking down and recognizing the mottled fur, the wary yet trusting eyes. He glanced up, saw one angel hovering. A gift then, for finally understanding. He touched the dog on the back of its neck, and led it to the Olds. The dog jumped inside as if it knew the car. Kincaid sat for a moment, resting his shaking hands against the steering column.

A hooker knocked on the window. He thought he could smell the sweat and perfume through the rolled-up glass. Her cleavage was mottled, her cheap elastic top revealing the top edge of brown nipple.

He shook his head, then turned the ignition and grabbed the gearshift on the column to take the car out of park. The dog barked once, and he grinned at it, before driving home to get his things. This time he wouldn't try Big Bear. This time he would go wherever the spirit led him.

Burial Detail

A PHOTOGRAPHER'S WAGON SETS at the edge a this field. His horse nuzzles the dry ground while the photographer—a white man—roots in the back, pullin out stuff like a man sittin up camp. I stand in fronta my full litter and watch—anythin for a break. Behind me, Dawson says sumpin loud enough for me ta hear, but too low for me ta catch the words. I don't miss the meanin. He thinks I don't work hard enough.

Maybe not. I ain't supposed ta be here. Battlegrounds is dangerous for a man like me, even battlegrounds ten months old. But I need the money and the U.S. government is payin more than I'd make anywhere else. Luce is pregnant, and times is so different now. Different than they was a month ago. If we kin get out a Virginia, we kin live a real life. A real life—that's worth touchin the souls a the dead.

The white man, he gets out a the wagon, draggin a long three legged black stand. He ain't that tall, kinda skinny, with a big black beard and stringy hair. His coat's too warm for the day, even though the air's got a bite. He'll be bakin before the afternoon's out. April in Virginia's a bad mix a hot and cold; mornins like ta freeze your hands and afternoons sometimes make you sweat. I ain't got many clothes but I wear my oldest pants, a heavy shirt

I kin pull off if I gotta, and a stockin cap that folds over my brow. Last night, I searched our place for gloves, but we ain't got none, or at least none Luce'll let me dirty so I got ta do this work with my bare hands. So far I ain't touched nothin but cloth. Cloth was bad enough.

As I think on that, I wipe my palms on the thick cotton a my pants. Corpses ten months dead ain't quite skeletons yet. They got bits a skin hangin off the bones, and some lumpish stuff in the skull. The clothes is still on em, hangin rag-like now, with the stench a death still clingin. Mosta these white boys been layin in the Virginia sun since last June. A few been claimed by family—mostly Rebs who lived nearby—but the rest, their families been told they was lost or died "valiantly" or was buried by comrades.

Guess I count as a comrade, near ta a year after the fact.

The white man, he got the box part on top a the stand and he's carryin a crate a plates like they weighed as much as him. He eases em down, grabs one, and the glass catches the sun. He grins at me like he spects me ta grin back. I look away. I dunno what interests a white man in a group a folk tillin this field a death.

There's five a us on this patch—five live ones, that is—and maybe a two hundred dead. And those's the ones we kin count. It don't take inta consideration the ones the animals got, leavin bones scattered all over every which way. Or the ones that blowed up when they's hit by cannon, or those that was burned when the Rebs tried ta light the breastworks, tryin ta start a fire that consumed all like they done in the Wilderness. Ain't too many burned here. One a the boys who's diggin, he worked burial in the Wilderness, and he say the smell a smoke's still fresh in the air.

I couldn't work there no more than I kin work here. I'm new ta this crew, so they give me the worst job. I shoulda been diggin. The land talks but it don't say as much as bodies.

I picks up the litter, and drags it ta the hole Dawson's dug. A leg bone rolls off, gets buried under some dried grass. I stare for a minute. I don't wanna touch it again, but I guess I will after I deliver the litter ta Dawson.

He's leanin on his shovel, starin at the molderin pile a blue cloth that I piled on the bottom a the litter. It's harder ta look at the skulls, with their empty eyes and sad little grins. The skulls, they show you youse pickin up bits a men. The cloth could be nothin more than garbage left by the retreatin army.

Dawson reaches down ta help me with the litter when I get close ta the hole. This one's deep, the dirt darker below than it is up top. He's been diggin a while, but he don't got blisters like I'd get if I spent the mornin makin that hole. His hands got calluses on em—he used ta work the land.

I worked the house until the war done started. I was younger then, wasn't quite ready ta be the butler or the reg'lar manservant, but I was trainin. The Missus, she say I had ta learn ta talk better, and I was doin that when they fought the first battle at Mannassas, north a here.

The Missus, she pack up everythin, put it in storage—not that it helped when they burned the city—and she and the little ones went ta live with relatives west a here. Master died at Gettysburg —the real butler told me that when I saw him las week. I was gonna go north, but Luce stopped me. She was pregnant then too, but lost the baby when it was too late for us ta leave. Not enough food, I guess. Her body couldn't handle a baby and survivin at the same time.

I tended her, doin odd jobs, sayin I was free, even though the Missus made it clear she spected all a us ta be around when she got back. Gave us a roof at least till it was burned from under us.

Now we's really and truly free, have been for near two weeks, ever since Grant and Lee signed some papers in Appomatox, not too far from here. They's Union soldiers everwhere—ta keep the peace, they say, tho havin soldiers didn't help ole Mister Lincoln none. Luce been cryin bout him for more'n a week, like he was someone she knew personal.

Thins's changed, and under the good's sumpin bad comin. I kin feel it. It's the way them Rebs look at us when we's walkin down the street, not carryin nothin a theirs, not sayin "yessir" and "nosir," at least when we's thinkin a it. Some habits get ground in good. I still bob my head like a good darkie most a the time, and I hates it more with each bob, like it takes a little piece a me, grinds it up, and loses it forever.

The North's still the Promised Land, least ta me and Luce. We's gonna raise our kids where there's no battlefields, no burned-out buildins, and no hatred in white folks eyes.

So I's workin here.

And now a white man thinks I'm worth photographin.

He's a strange critter, that white man. He been crouchin behind the black curtain, pointin the box ever which way tryin ta see what direction's best. We been pretendin he's not there, waitin for the white boss hired us ta come back and make him go way. Least

I been. Finally, I says that ta Dawson as we tilt the litter.

He laughs. "Ain't no one but us till sundown. No white boy's gonna get his hands in this, Yank or not."

The bodies tumble off the edge, revealin sun-yellow bones mixed in with the cloth. The boots and brass buttons, medals and watches is mostly gone. Guess someone could come and steal from the dead but didn't have the stomach ta bury em. Maybe a white man woulda done this job if there'd been real pickins ta get from it.

A small cloud a dust rises from below and a faint stink a rot. One a the skulls tumbles ta the edge, lands upside down. Looks disrespectful ta me, but I ain't crawlin in there ta right no white boy's head. I done enough a that with ones that was alive.

"I guess I better dig a new hole," Dawson says.

I look around us. They's bodies everwhere. "It'll take most the day ta fill this one."

I don't wanna do bodies by myself. Sooner or later I gotta touch one, really touch one, and then it'll go bad for all a us.

Dawson looks at me long. His eyes are pale green, got from some white man who thought his slave women was good enough for more than scrubbin or pickin. Finally, I's the one who looks away. He ain't touchin no more bodies. He moved up ta diggin when I got hired. He ain't comin back ta this job.

So's I pick up my litter and move ta the next patch a ground. They's a trench jus ahead a me. That's the Reb line. They dug in, didn't let Grant get inta Richmond, not then anyway.

Name a this battle here was Cold Harbor. They ain't no harbor nowhere near round, just little streams, swamps, and high ridges. Lots a windy roads. Ain't no accurate maps, that's why they say Grant lost. Didn't know the land, didn't know how ta fight here.

All I member was the way hope turned sour in my stomach when I found out the Yanks done gone around Richmond, went ta Petersburg and tried ta work their way up. I member thinkin, *hopin*, they was gonna bust through and free us all. Wasn't that long ago they finally got ta Richmond, and then wasn't the way I thought it'd be tall.

They's a lot a bodies here, most a em recnizable. All tangled where they fell, legs under em, arms splayed out, skinless hands clawin toward the sky. I sit the litter next ta the biggest pile and wipe the sweat off my face. The mornin's still cold, but what's facin me's got me hot.

I look for that white man. He's still messin with his camera, yellin sumpin at Kershaw and the rest a the crew. Wants em ta pose. I ain't gonna pose. Not with no litter a bodies and open graves all around. Who wants ta look at that six months from now? Who wants ta think about this ever again?

The canvas stretched across the litter is stained with old blood from its days in the field hospital and goo from the bodies. This time, they ain't none that's just dissolved ta cloth, like my first site. I used that cloth ta hold skulls so the bleached bone didn't touch my fingers. Then I sit it on the litter and let it fall inta the hole, just like the rest a the stuff.

I wish I ain't done that.

I bend over the first body. Uniform is patched and ripped, thin on the elbows and knees. Don't know how they wore that stuff in the Virginia heat. Last May-June it was hotter than holy hell, a sticky deadly heat that was killin old folks in Richmond. Don't know how men marched in it. Don't know how they fought, how they used rifles, barrels turnin hot against they hands, fires burnin all around. Don't know how they come even this far.

My throat gets tight and I makes myself swallow. Then I crouch and slide my hands under that heavy coat. The bones shift and the back a the wool is wet with sumpin I don't want ta think about. I lift and put the body on the litter. Fortunately, all the pieces stay together.

I do the same with the next one, but my luck has run out. The right arm, crossed over the chest as if he was tryin ta cover his heart, slides off, and I catch it, fingers slippin through a hole in the sleeve, catchin bone.

It's soft and smooth and—

he's hungry, so hungry his stomach's cramping. Dust is thick around him, and all he can hear—all he's heard for days—is cannon and musketry rattling like a storm that doesn't quit. Sweat's in his eyes—at least he thinks that's sweat. Orders are to take the line, go over the breastworks, find the weapons, get another five miles before nightfall.

Five miles and they can't even take one.

He doesn't even know where his friends are. Two fell on the march here, in sun so hot it seemed to broil human flesh. The sandy plain was heated to the intensity of a blast furnace. If he survives this, he'll tell his son that he's been to hell and no man should live in such a way that he has to spend eternity there. His son. Wide blue eyes and pudgy fingers. He'll be a boy when the war's over, not a baby. A boy—

". . . looked like some kind of fit," the white man's sayin. He's left his camera and is bent over me. He's younger'n me, his hair stickin up like he ain't never seen the butt enda a comb. He smells a sweat and chemicals.

"Weren't no fit." Dawson's got me braced. He's moved me away from the bodies. I kin see his chin from here, stubble already growin, the stubborn set a his jaw. Worked with him only a mornin and I kin already read him.

"You should give him some water, or feed him," the white man says. "I saw things like this during the war. Strong men—"

"He don't need water," Dawson says.

I set up, wipe my hand in the grass. I kin still feel that bone on my skin, still feel that boy's life like it was my own. He weren't more than twenty, a wife and son back home. New baby he seen only once—a Christmas leave he was lucky enough ta get. The wife cried when he left.

What if it's the last time I see you? she said, clingin, makin his dress shirt wet with her tears.

Now, April, he said, *You just gotta believe we're gonna spend the rest of our lives together.*

But I kin feel inside the fear eatin at him, the lies he told durin the whole stay so she wouldn't worry unduly, the way he tried ta memorize his baby's face so it'd be the last thin he'd see.

And it was.

I puts my head in my hands, but they smell a rot, and I cain't stomach it. The white man, he's still worryin but Dawson, he's got his arms crossed.

"How come you ain't tole me you got the Sight?" he ask.

"Ain't none yo bidness."

The white man, he frownin like we ain't speakin English.

"It my bidness when you cain't do yo job." Dawson say.

"I cain."

"You faint then ever time you touch sumpin?"

"I done the whole mornin. I just need some cloth or gloves or sumpin. That's all."

He grunts, sighs, looks ta the rest a the crew. They's thousands a dead round here, days, maybe weeks a work, and he ain't got a lot a men. We all need the money. He know that. He prob'ly know why too. He prob'ly got the same dream.

"I have gloves," the white man says.

"He don't need fancy gloves," Dawson says.

"I kin use cloth." I don't want no debt ta no white man.

"My gloves'll work better," he says. "They're not fancy. I used them for carrying. I have another pair."

I need the job more'n I need my pride. But I don't say nothin. The white man, he take that for a yes, and runs ta his wagon.

"Who he?" I ask.

Dawson shrugs. "You got the Sight bad."

"It come down through the family."

He nod. "It ain't forward Sight?"

I shake my head. "Only what was."

His smile's sad. "I knows what was. I was hopin you could see what would be."

"I'm hopin that too."

He get up, his knees crackin. "I ain't givin up the shovel."

"I know," I say. It's work with the bodies or go home. I jus gots ta be more careful.

He go back ta his new hole. I look at the bodies stretched out around me, skulls turned toward the mornin sun. All a em got stories. All a em gots wives and families and little boys with liquid blue eyes who ain't never goin ta hear the story a this place.

Coz these boys fought n died, me and Luce and the baby still inside her, we got a chance. Coz these boys fought n died, I's gettin paid this day stead a doin this work for some Massa who says he own me. Coz these boys fought n died, my child kin grow up in my house with my wife in my family.

Coz these boys fought n died.

The white man, he run back ta me and crouch like I'm sick and he gotta be real careful. He got thick gloves, leather, better than any I ever had. He hand em ta me.

"I've heard about the Sight," he says ta me. "I've never met anyone with it before."

I doubt that, but he prob'ly never know'd.

"You see everything from their perspective, don't you? The whole battle. Everything. Even the moment they die."

I slip on the gloves. They's soft. I kin work with em on.

"You think," he ask, "maybe we could try to photograph what you see?"

Then I pulls the gloves off. I cain't owe this man no favor. "No."

"Why not?"

"You see anythin when I was down? Hear anythin?"

He frowns. They's a small crease in his forehead that's gonna grow deeper the older he gets. "No."

"No one does cept the person with the Sight. It ain't sumpin someone else kin share."

His shoulders slump. I hand him the gloves. His face turns bright red. "Oh, no," he says. "Those weren't a bribe. I just wanted to help, that's all."

"Why?"

"You need the work, don't you?" They's some understandin in his eyes. Not enough. But some. It ain't like them Reb eyes, all hatey and nasty. They's a kindness here.

"That box a your'n, it make you see things clear, don't it?"

They's a little smile on his face, sad, but not as sad as Dawson's. "Not as clear as your Sight, I suspect."

That's true nuff.

"I would like to capture what you see," he says. "Maybe some day, I could hire you and we could experiment—"

"No," I says.

"Why not?" he asks.

Dawson put the body, the one I touched, on the litter. The boy's skull is small. They's a nick in the front and a hole in the back the size a my fist. His wife ain't never gonna see this body, ain't never gonna know just how he died. She's gonna tell her boy what a hero Daddy was and how glorious he died, fightin for the cause.

She ain't gonna know about the lies he told and the fear eatin his belly and the last days in the dirt and the heat and the stink.

"Coz sometimes," I says, "you kin see too clear."

He stares at me for a long minute. His eyes is the same green as Dawson's. I'm thinkin maybe I'm gonna have ta splain what I mean when he stands up.

"This is thankless work," he says, maybe meanin ta be kind.

I look at the bodies stretched from here ta the grove where the Cold Harbor tavern still stands. Bodies waitin for someone ta tend em, waitin for someone ta care.

"It ain't thankless," I say. "It jus hard."

The Gallery of His Dreams

Let him who wishes to know what war is look at this series of illustrations. . . . It was so nearly like visiting the battlefield to look over these views, that all the emotions excited by the actual sight of the stained and sordid scene, strewed with rags and wrecks, came back to us, and we buried them in the recesses of our cabinet as we would have buried the mutilated remains of the dead they too vividly represented.

—Oliver Wendell Holmes

1838

BRADY LEANED AGAINST a hay bale and felt the blades dig into his back. He smelled of pig dung and his own sweat, and his muscles ached. His da had gone to the pump to wash up, and then into the cow shed, but Brady claimed he needed a rest. His da, never one to argue with relaxation, let him sit against the hay bales. Brady didn't dare stay too long; if his ma saw him, she would be on the front porch, yelling insults unintelligible through her Irish brogue.

He did need to think, though. Milking cows and cleaning the pigpen didn't give him enough time to make plans. He couldn't stay on the farm the rest of his life, he knew that. He hated the work, the animals, the smell, and the long hours that all led to a poor, subsistence living. His da thought the farm a step up from the hovel he had grown up in and certainly an improvement from Brady's grandfather's life back in the Old Country. Brady often wished he could see what his da's or his grandfather's life had really been like. But he had to trust their memories, memories that, at least in his grandfather's case, had become more and more confusing as the years progressed.

Brady pulled a strand of hay from the bale, sending a burst of sharp fresh summer-scent around him. He wanted more than a ruined farm and a few livestock in upstate New York. Mr. Hanley, his teacher, had pulled Brady aside on the day he left school, and reminded him that in the United States of America even farmboys could become great men. Mr. Hanley used to start the school day by telling the boys that the late President Thomas Jefferson defined the nation's creed when he wrote that all men were created equal, and President Andrew Jackson had proven the statement true with his election not ten years before.

Brady didn't want to be president. He wanted to do something different, something he couldn't even imagine now. He wanted to be great—and he wanted to be remembered.

1840

The spring thaw had turned the streets of New York City into rivers.

Brady laughed as he jumped from one sidewalk board to the next, then turned and waited for Page to jump. Page hesitated a moment, running a slender hand through his beard. Then he jumped and landed, one tattered shoe in the cold water, one out. Brady grabbed his friend's arm, and pulled him up.

"Good Lord, William, how far away is this man's home?"

"He's not just any man," Page said, shaking the water off his legs. "He's a painter, and a damn fine one."

Brady smiled. Page was a painter himself and had, a few months earlier, opened a studio below their joint apartment. Brady helped with the rent on the studio as a repayment for Page's help in moving Brady from the farm. Being a clerk at A. T. Stewart's largest store was an improvement over farm life—the same kind of improvement that Brady's father had made. Only Brady wasn't going to stop there. Page had promised to help by showing Brady how to paint. While Brady had an eye for composition, he lacked the firm hand, the easy grace of a portraitist. Page had been polite; he hadn't said that Brady was hopeless. But they both knew that Mathew B. Brady would never make his living with a paintbrush in his hand.

Brady braced himself against a wooden building as he stepped over a submerged portion of sidewalk. "You haven't said what this surprise is."

"I don't know what the surprise is. Samuel simply said that he had learned about it in France and that we would be astonished." Page slipped into a thin alley between buildings and then pulled open a door. Brady followed, and found himself staring up a dark flight of stairs. Page was already halfway up, his wet shoe squeaking with each step. Brady gripped the railing and took the stairs two at a time.

Page opened the door, sending light across the stairs. Brady reached the landing just as Page bellowed, "Samuel!" Brady peered inside, nearly choking on the scent of linseed and turpentine.

Large windows graced the walls, casting dusty sunlight on a room filled with canvases. Dropcloths covered most of the canvases and some of the furniture scattered about. A desk, overflowing with papers, stood under one window. Near that a large wooden box dwarfed a rickety table. A stoop-shouldered long-haired man braced the table with one booted foot.

"Over here, Page, over here. Don't dawdle. Help me move this thing. The damn table is about to collapse."

Page scurried across the room, bent down and grabbed an edge of the box. The man picked up the other side and led the way to his desk. He balanced the box with one hand and his knee while his other hand swept the desk clean. They set the box down and immediately the man pulled out a handkerchief and wiped away the sweat that had dripped into his bushy eyebrows.

"I meant to show you in a less dramatic fashion," he said, then looked up. Brady whipped his hat off his head and held it with both hands. The man had sharp eyes, eyes that could see right through a person, clear down to his dreams.

"Well?" the man said.

Brady nodded. He wouldn't be stared down. "I'm Mathew B. Brady, sir."

"Samuel F. B. Morse." Morse tucked his handkerchief back into his pocket and clasped his hands behind his back. "You must be the boy Page has been telling me about. He assumes you have some sort of latent talent."

Brady glanced at Page. Page blushed, the color seeping through the patches of skin still visible through his beard.

"Hmmm," Morse said as he stalked forward. He paced around Brady, studied him for a moment. "You're what, eighteen?"

"Almost, sir."

"If you had talent, you'd know it by now." Morse shook his head. His suit smelled faintly of mothballs. "No, no. You're one of the lucky ones, blessed with drive. A man with talent merely has a head start. A man with drive succeeds."

Morse stalked back to his desk, stepping on the papers that littered the floor. "Drive but no talent. I have the perfect machine for you." He put his hand on the box. "Ever hear of Louis Daguerre? No, of course not. What would a farmboy know of the latest scientific discoveries?"

Brady started, then shot another look at Page. Perhaps Page had said something about Brady's background. Page ignored him and had come closer to Morse.

"Daguerre found a way to preserve the world in one image. Look." He handed Page a small metal plate. As Page tilted it toward the light, Brady saw the Unitarian Church he walked past almost every day.

"This is a daguerreotype," Morse said. "I made this one through the window of the third floor staircase at New York University."

"That is the right view." Page's voice held awe. "You used no paints."

"I used this," Morse said, his hand pounding on the box's top. "It has a lens here—" and he pointed at the back end from which a glass-topped cylinder protruded "—and a place here for the plates. The plates are silver on copper which I treat with iodine and expose to light through the lens. Then I put the plate in another box containing heated mercury and when I'm done—an image! An exact reproduction of the world in black and white."

Brady touched the cool edge of the plate. "It preserves memories," he said, thinking that if such a device had existed before, he could have seen his father's hovel, his grandfather's home.

"It does more than that, son," Morse said. "This is our future. It will destroy portrait painting. Soon everything will be images on metal, keepsakes for generations to come."

Page pulled back at the remark about portrait painting. He

went to the window, looked at the street below. "I suppose that's why you brought us up here. To show me that I'll be out of work soon?"

"No, lad." Morse laughed and the sound boomed and echoed off the canvas-covered walls. "I want to save you, not destroy you. I'm opening a school to teach this new process and I invite you to join. Fifty dollars tuition for the entire semester and I promise you'll be a better portraitist when you're done than you are now."

Page gave Morse a sideways look. Page's back was rigid and his hands were clenched in trembling fists. Brady could almost feel his friend's rage. "I paint." Page spoke with a slow deliberation. "I have no need for what will clearly become a poor man's art."

Morse did not seem offended by Page's remark. "And you, young Brady. Will you use your drive to acquire a talent?"

Brady stared at the plate and mysterious box. Fifty dollars was a lot of money, but he already had twenty set aside for a trip home. Page did say he had an eye for composition. And if a man with an eye for composition, a lot of drive and a little talent took Daguerre's Box all over the world, he would be able to send his memories back to the people left behind.

Brady smiled. "Yes," he said. "I'll take your class."

He would postpone the trip to see his parents, and raise the rest of the money somehow. Page whirled away from the window as if Brady had betrayed him. But Brady didn't care. When they got home, he would explain it all. And it was so simple. He had another improvement to make.

1840

That night, Brady dreamed. He stood in a large cool room, darkened and hidden in shadows. He bumped into a wall and found himself touching a ribbed column—a Doric column, he believed. He took cautious steps forward, stumbled, then caught himself on a piece of painted wood. His hands slid up the rough edges until he realized he was standing beside a single-horse carriage. He felt his way around to the back. The carriage box had no windows, but the back stood wide open. He climbed inside. The faint rotten-egg smell of sulphur rose. He bumped against a box and glass rattled. A wagon filled with equipment. He climbed out, feeling like he was snooping. There was more light now. He saw a wall ahead of him, covered with portraits.

The darkness made the portraits difficult to see, but he

thought he recognized the light and shadow work of a Daguerre portrait and yet—and yet—something differed, distorted, perhaps, by the dream. And he knew he was in a dream. The cool air was too dry, the walls made of a foreign substance, the lights (what he could see of them), glass-encased boxes on the ceiling. The portraits were of ghastly things: dead men and stark fields, row after row of demolished buildings. On several, someone had lettered his last name in flowing white script.

"They will make you great," said a voice behind him. He turned, and saw a woman. At least he thought it was a woman. Her hair was cropped above her ears, and she wore trousers.

"Who will make me great?" he asked.

"The pictures," she said. "People will remember them for generations."

He took a step closer to her, but she smiled and touched his palm. The shadows turned black and the dream faded into a gentle, restful sleep.

1849

Brady leaned against the hand-carved wooden railing. The candles on the large chandelier burned steady, while the candelabras flickered in the breezes left by the dancing couples. A pianist, a violinist and a cello player—all, Mr. Handy had assured him, very well respected—played the newest European dance, the waltz, from one corner of the huge ballroom. Mothers cornered their daughters along the wall, approving dance cards, and shaking fans at impertinent young males. The staircase opened into the ballroom, and Brady didn't want to cross the threshold. He had never been to a dance like this before. His only experiences dancing had been at gatherings Page had taken him to when he first arrived in New York. He knew none of the girls, except Samuel Handy's daughter Juliet, and she was far too pretty for Brady to approach.

So he watched her glide across the floor with young man after young man, her hooped skirts swaying, her brown hair in ringlets, her eyes sparkling, and her cheeks flushed. Handy had told him that at the age of four, she had been presented to President Jackson. She had been so beautiful, Handy said, that Jackson had wanted to adopt her. Brady was glad he hadn't seen her as a child, glad he had seen the mature beauty. When he finished taking the portraits of her father, he would ask if he could take one of her. The wet-plate process would let him make copies, and he would keep one in his own rooms, just so that he could show his friends how very lovely she was.

The waltz ended, and Juliet curtsied to her partner, then left the floor. Her dance card swung from her wrist and the diamonds around her neck caught the candlelight. Too late, Brady realized she was coming to see him.

"I have one spot left on my dance card," she said as she stopped in front of him. She smelled faintly of lilacs, and he knew he would have to keep a sprig near her portrait every spring. "And I was waiting for you to fill it."

Brady blushed. "I barely know you, Miss Juliet."

She batted his wrist lightly with her fan. "Julia," she said. "And I know you better than half the boys here. You have spent three days in my daddy's house, Mr. Brady, and your conversation at dinner has been most entertaining. I was afraid that I bored you."

"No, no," he said. The words sounded so formal. How could he joke with his female clients and let this slip of a girl intimidate him? "I would love to take that slot on your dance card, Miss Juliet."

"Julia," she said again. "I hate being named after a stupid little minx who died for nothing. I think when a woman loves, it is her duty to love intelligently, don't you?"

"Yes," Brady said, although he had no idea what she was talking about. "And I'm Mathew."

"Wonderful, Mathew." Her smile added a single dimple to her left cheek. She extended her card to him and he penciled his name in for the next dance, filling the bottom of the first page. The music started—another waltz—and she took his hand. He followed her onto the floor, placed one hand on her cinched waist, and held the other lightly in his own. They circled around the floor, the tip of her skirt brushing against his pants leg. She didn't smile at him. Instead her eyes were very serious and her lips were pursed and full.

"You don't do this very often, do you, Mathew?"

"No," he said. In fact, he felt as if he were part of a dream—the musicians, the beautifully garbed women, the house servants blending into the wallpaper. Everything at the Handy plantation had an air of almost too much sensual pleasure. "I work, probably too much."

"I have seen what you do, Mathew, and I think it is a wondrous magic." A slight flush crept into her cheeks, whether from the exertion or her words, Brady couldn't tell. She lowered her voice. "I dreamed about you last night. I dreamed I was in a beautiful large gallery with light clearer than sunlight, and hundreds of people milled about, looking at your portraits on the wall. They all talked about you, how marvelous your work was, and how it influenced them. You're a great man, Mathew, and I am flattered at the interest you have shown in me."

The music stopped and she slipped from his arms, stopping to chat with another guest as she wandered toward the punch table. Brady stood completely still, his heart pounding against his chest. She had been to the gallery of his dreams. She knew about his future. The musicians began another piece, and Brady realized how foolish he must look, standing in the center of the dance floor. He dodged whirling couples and made his way to the punch table, hoping that he could be persuasive enough to convince Julia Handy to let him replace all those other names on the remaining half of her dance card.

1861

He woke up with the idea, his body sweat-covered and shimmering with nervous energy. If he brought a wagon with him, it would work: a wagon like the one he had dreamed about the night he had met Morse.

Brady moved away from his sleeping wife and stepped onto the bare hardwood. The floor creaked. He glanced at Julia, but she didn't awaken. The bedroom was hot; Washington in July had a muggy air. If the rumors were to be believed the first battle would occur in a matter of days. He had so little time. He had thought he would never come up with a way to record the war.

He had started recording history with his book, *The Gallery of Illustrious Americans.* He had hoped to continue by taking portraits of the impending war, but he hadn't been able to figure out how. The wet plates had to be developed right after the portrait had been taken. He needed a way to take the equipment with him. The answer was so simple, he was amazed he had to dream it.

But that dream had haunted him for years now. And when he had learned the wet-plate process, discovered that the rotten-egg smell of sulphur was part of it, the dream had come back to him as vividly as an old memory. That had been years ago. Now, with the coming war, he found himself thinking of the portraits of demolished buildings, and the woman's voice, telling him he would be great.

He would have to set up a special war fund. The president had given him a pass to make portraits of the army on the field, but had stressed that Brady would have to use his own funds. As Lincoln told Brady with only a hint of humor, the country was taking enough gambles already.

Small price, Brady figured, to record history. He was, after all, a wealthy man.

1861

Julia had hoped to join the picnickers who sat on the hills overlooking the battlefield, but Brady was glad he had talked her out of it. He pulled the wet plate out of his camera, and placed the plate into the box. The portrait would be of smoke and tiny men clashing below him. He glanced at the farmhouse, and the army that surrounded it. They seemed uneasy, as if this battle wasn't what they expected. It wasn't what he had expected, either. The confusion, the smoke, even the heat made sense. The screaming did not.

Brady put the plate in its box, then set the box in his wagon. Before the day was out, he would return to Washington, set the plates and send portraits to the illustrated magazines. The wagon was working out better than he expected. The illustrations would probably earn him yet another award.

The cries seemed to grow louder, and above them, he heard a faint rumbling. He checked the sky for clouds and saw nothing. The smoke gave the air an acrid tinge and made the heat seem even hotter. A bead of sweat ran down the side of his face. He grabbed the camera and lugged it back to the wagon, then returned for the tripod. He was proud of himself; he had expected to be afraid and yet his hands were as steady as they had been inside his studio.

He closed up the back of the wagon, waved his assistant, Tim O'Sullivan, onto the wagon, and climbed aboard. O'Sullivan sat beside him and clucked the horse onto Bull Run road. The army's advance had left ruts so deep that the wagon tilted at an odd angle. The rumble was growing louder. Overhead, something whistled and then a cannonball landed off to one side, spraying dirt and muck over the two men. The horse shrieked and reared; Brady felt the reins cut through his fingers. The wagon rocked, nearly tipped, then righted itself. Brady turned, and saw a dust cloud rising behind him. A mass of people was running toward him.

"Lord a mercy," he whispered, and thrust the reins at O'Sullivan. O'Sullivan looked at them as if he had never driven the wagon before. "I'm going to get the equipment. Be ready to move on my signal."

O'Sullivan brought the horse to a stop and Brady leapt off the side. He ran to the back, opened the door, grabbed his camera, and set up just in time to take portraits of soldiers running past. Both sides—Union and Confederate—wore blue, and Brady couldn't tell which troops were scurrying past him. He could smell the fear, the human sweat, see the strain in the men's eyes. His heart had moved to his throat, and he had to concentrate to shove a wet plate into the camera. He uncapped the lens, hoping that the scene wouldn't change too much, that in his precious three seconds he would capture more than a blur.

Mixed with the soldiers were women, children, and well-dressed men—some still clutching picnic baskets, others barely holding their hats. All ran by. A few loose horses galloped near Brady; he had to hold the tripod steady. He took portrait after portrait, seeing faces he recognized—like that silly newspaper correspondent Russell, the man who had spread the word about Brady's poor eyesight—mouths agape, eyes wide in panic. As Brady worked, the sounds blended into each other. He couldn't tell the human screams from the animal shrieks and the whistle of mortar. Bullets whizzed passed, and more than one lodged in the wagon. The wagon kept lurching, and Brady knew that O'Sullivan was having trouble holding the horse steady.

Suddenly the wagon rattled away from him. Brady turned, knocked over the tripod himself, and watched in horror as people trampled his precious equipment. He started to get down, to save the camera, then realized that in their panic, the people would run over him. He grabbed what plates he could, shoved them into the pocket of his great coat, and joined the throng, running after the wagon, shouting at O'Sullivan to stop.

But the wagon didn't stop. It kept going around the winding, twisting corners of the road, until it disappeared in the dust cloud. Another cannon ball landed beside the road and Brady cringed as dirt spattered him. A woman screamed and fell forward, blood blossoming on her back. He turned to help her, but the crowd pushed him forward. He couldn't stop even if he wanted to.

This was not romantic; it was not the least bit pretty. It had cost him hundreds of dollars in equipment and might cost him his life if he didn't escape soon. This was what the history books had never told him about war, had never explained about the absolute mess, the dirt and the blood. Behind him, he heard screaming, someone shouting that the black cavalry approached, the dreaded black cavalry of the Confederacy, worse than the Four Horses of the Apocalypse, if the illustrated newspapers were to be believed, and Brady ran all the harder. His feet slipped in the ruts in the road and he nearly tripped, but he saw other people down, other people trampled, and he knew he couldn't fall.

He rounded a corner, and there it was, the wagon, on its side, the boxes spilling out, the plates littering the dirt road. O'Sullivan was on his hands and knees, trying to clean up, his body shielded only because the carriage wall made the fleeing people reroute.

Brady hurried over the carriage side, ignoring the split wood, the bullet holes and the fact that the horse was missing. Tears were running down the side of O'Sullivan's face, but the man seemed oblivious to them. Brady grabbed O'Sullivan's arm, and pulled him up. "Come on, Tim," he said. "Black cavalry on the hills. We've got to get away."

"The plates—" O'Sullivan said.

"Forget the plates. We've got to get out of here."

"The horse spooked and broke free. I think someone stole her, Mat."

O'Sullivan was shouting, but Brady could barely hear him. His lungs were choked and he thought he was going to drown in dust. "We have to go," he said.

He yanked O'Sullivan forward, and they rejoined the crowd. They ran until Brady could run no longer; his lungs burned and his side ached. Bullets continued to penetrate, and Brady saw too many men in uniform motionless on the side of the road.

"The crowd itself is a target," he said, not realizing he had spoken aloud. He tightened his grip on O'Sullivan's arm and led him off the road into the thin trees. They trudged straight ahead, Brady keeping the setting sun to his left, and soon the noises of battle disappeared behind them. They stopped and Brady leaned against a thick oak to catch his breath. The sun had gone down and it was getting cool.

"What now?" O'Sullivan asked.

"If we don't meet any Rebs, we're safe," Brady said. He took off his hat, wiped the sweat off his brow with his sleeve, and put his hat back on. Julia would have been very angry with him if he had lost that hat.

"But how do we get back?" O'Sullivan asked.

An image of the smashed equipment rose in Brady's mind

along with the broken, overturned horseless wagon. "We walk, Tim." Brady sighed. "We walk."

1861

Julia watched as he stocked up the new wagon. She said nothing as he lugged equipment inside, new equipment he had purchased from Anthony's supply house on extended credit. He didn't want to hurt his own business by taking away needed revenue, and the Anthonys were willing to help—especially after they had seen the quality of his war work for the illustrated newspapers.

"I can't come with you, can I?" she asked as he tossed a bedroll into the back.

"I'm sorry," Brady said, remembering the woman scream and fall beside him, blood blossoming on her back. His Julia wouldn't die that way. She would die in her own bed, in the luxury and comfort she was used to. He took her hands. "I don't want to be apart from you, but I don't know any other way."

She stroked his face. "We have to remember—" she said. The tears that lined the rims of her eyes didn't touch her voice. "—that this is the work that will make you great."

"You have already made me great," he said, and kissed her one final time.

1863

Brady pushed his blue-tinted glasses up on his nose and wiped the sweat off his brow with the back of his hand. The Pennsylvania sun beat on his long black waistcoat, baking his clothes against his skin. The corpse, only a few hours dead, was already gaseous and bloated, straining its frayed Union uniform. The too-florid smell of death ripened the air. If it weren't for the bodies, human and equine, the farmer's land would seem peaceful, not the site of one of the bloodiest battles of the war.

Brady tilted the corpse's head back. Underneath the gray mottled skin, a young boy's features had frozen in agony. Brady didn't have to alter the expression: he never did. The horror was always real. He set the repeating rifle lengthwise across the corpse, and stood up. A jagged row of posed corpses stretched before him. O'Sullivan had positioned the wagon toward the side of the field and was struggling with the tripod. Brady hurried to help his assistant, worried, always worried about destroying more equipment. They had lost so much trying to photograph the war. He should have known from the first battle how difficult this would be. He had sold nearly everything, asked Julia to give up even the simplest comforts, borrowed against his name from the Anthonys for equipment to record this. History. His country's folly and its glory. And the great, terrible waste of lives. He glanced back at the dead faces, wondered how many people would mourn.

"I think we should put it near the tree." O'Sullivan lugged the top half of the tripod at an angle away from the corpse row. "The light is good—the shade is on the other side. Mathew?"

"No." Brady backed up a few steps. "Here. See the angle? The bodies look random now, but you can see the faces."

He squinted, wishing he could see the faces better. His eyesight had been growing worse; in 1851 it had been so bad that the press thought he would be blind in a decade. Twelve years had passed and he wasn't blind yet. But he wasn't far from it.

O'Sullivan arranged the black curtain, then Brady swept his assistant aside. "Let me," he said.

He climbed under the curtain. The heat was thicker; the familiar scent of chemicals cleared the death from his nose. He peered through the lens. The image was as he had expected it to be, clear, concise, well composed. The light filtered through, reflected oddly through the blue tint on his glasses, and started a sharp ache in his skull. He pulled out, into the sun. "Adjust as you need to. But I think we have the image."

Brady turned away from the field as O'Sullivan prepared the wet plate and then shoved it into the camera. Sweat trickled down the back of Brady's neck into his woolen coat. He was tired, so tired, and the war had already lasted two years longer than anyone expected. He didn't know how many times he had looked on the faces of the dead, posed them for the camera the way he had posed princes and presidents a few years before. If he had stayed in New York, like the Anthonys, everything would have been different. He could have spent his nights with Julia . . .

"Got it," O'Sullivan said. He held the plate gingerly, his face flushed with the heat.

"You develop it," Brady said. "I want to stay here for a few minutes."

O'Sullivan frowned; Brady usually supervised every step of the battle images. But Brady didn't explain his unusual behavior. O'Sullivan said nothing. He clutched the plates and went in the back of the black-covered wagon. The wagon rocked ever so gently as he settled in.

Brady waited until the wagon stopped rocking, then clasped

his hands behind his back and walked through the trampled, blood-spattered grass. The aftermath of battle made him restless: the dead bodies, the ruined earth, the shattered wagons. Battles terrified him, made him want to run screaming from the scene. He often clutched his equipment around him like a talisman—if he worked, if he didn't think about it, he would stave off the fear until the shooting stopped. He tripped over an abandoned canteen. He crouched, saw the bullet hole in its side.

"You stay, even though it appalls you."

The woman's voice startled him so badly he nearly screamed. He backed up as he stood, and found himself facing a thin, short-haired woman wearing pants, a short-sleeved shirt and (obviously) no undergarments. She looked familiar.

"That takes courage." She smiled. Her teeth were even and white.

"You shouldn't be here," he said. His voice shook and he clenched his fists to hide his shaking. "Are you looking for someone in particular? I can take you to the General."

"I'm looking for you. You're the man they call Brady of Broadway?"

He nodded.

"The man who sells everything, bargains his studio to photograph a war?"

Her comment was too close to his own thoughts—and too personal. He felt a flush rise that had nothing to do with the heat. "What do you want?"

"I want you to work for me, Mathew Brady. I will pay for your equipment, take care of your travel, if you shoot pictures for me when and where I say."

She frightened him, a crazy woman standing in a field of dead men. "I run my own business," he said.

She nodded, the smile fading just a little. "And it will bankrupt you. You will die forgotten, your work hidden in crates in government warehouses. That's not why you do this, is it, Mr. Brady."

"I do this so that people can see what really happens here, so that people can travel through my memories to see this place," he said. The ache in his head grew sharper. This woman had no right to taunt him. "I do this for history."

"And it's history that calls you, Mr. Brady. The question is, will you serve?"

"I already serve," he snapped—and found himself speaking to air. Heat shimmered in front of him, distorting his view of the field for a moment. Then the tall grass and the broken picket fence returned, corpses hovering at the edge of his vision like bales of hay.

He took off his glasses and wiped his eyes. The strain was making him hallucinate. He had been too long in the sun. He would go back to the wagon, get a drink of water, lie in the shade. Then, perhaps, the memory of the hallucination would go away.

But her words haunted him as he retraced his steps: *I will pay for your equipment, take care of your travel.* If only someone would do that. He had spent the entire sum of his fortune and still saw no end ahead. She hadn't been a hallucination, she had been a dream. A wish for a different, easier life that no one would ever fulfill.

1865

The day after Appomatox—the end of the war, Brady dreamed:

He walked the halls of a well-lit place he had never seen before. His footsteps echoed on the shiny floor covering. Walls, made of a smooth material that was not wood or stone, smelled of paint and emollients. Ceiling boxes encased the lamps—and the light did not flicker but flowed cleaner than gaslight. Most of the doors lining the hallway were closed, but one stood open. A sign that shone with a light of its own read:

MATHEW B. BRADY EXHIBIT
OFFICIAL PHOTOGRAPHER:
UNITED STATES CIVIL WAR
(1861–1865)

Inside, he found a spacious room twice the size of any room he had ever seen, with skylights in the ceiling and Doric columns creating a hollow in the center. A camera, set up on its tripod, had its black curtain thrown half back, as if waiting for him to step inside. Next to it stood his wagon, looking out of place and ancient without its horse. The wagon's back door also stood open, and Brady saw the wooden boxes of plates inside, placed neatly, so that a path led to the darkroom. The darkroom looked odd: no one had picked up the sleeping pallets, and yet the chemical baths sat out, ready for use. He would never have left the wagon that way. He shook his head, and turned toward the rest of the room.

Three of the long, wide walls were bare. On the fourth, framed pictures crowded together. He walked to them, saw that they were his portraits, his work from Bull Run, Antietam, Gettysburg. He even saw a picture of General Lee in his confederate gray. Beneath the portrait, the attribution read *By Brady (or assistant)*, but Brady had never taken such a portrait, never developed one, never posed one. A chill ran up his back when he realized he hadn't squinted to read the print. He reached up, touched the bridge of his nose. His glasses were gone. He hadn't gone without glasses since he had been a boy. In the mornings, he had to grab his glasses off the nightstand first, then get out of bed.

His entire wartime collection (with huge gaps) framed, on exhibit. Four thousand portraits, displayed for the world to see, just as he had hoped. He reached out to the Lee portrait. As his finger brushed the smooth wood—

—he found himself beneath the large tree next to the Appomatox farmhouse where the day before Lee and Grant had signed the peace treaty. The farmhouse was a big white blur against the blue of the April sky. He grabbed his glasses (somehow they had fallen to his lap) and hooked the frames around his ears. The world came into sharper focus, the blue tint easing the glare of the sun. He knew what he had to do. Even though he had arrived too late to photograph the historic signing of the treaty, he could still photograph General Lee one last time in his uniform.

Brady got up and brushed the grass off his pants. His wagon stood beside the farmhouse. The wagon looked proper—dust-covered, mud-spattered, with a few splintered boards and a cock-eyed wheel that he would have to fix very soon—not clean and neat as it had in his dream. The horse, tied to another tree, looked tired, but he would push her with him to Richmond, to General Lee, to complete the exhibit.

Three empty walls, he thought as he went to find his assistant. He wondered why his earlier portraits weren't mounted there. Perhaps the wall's awaiting something else. Something better.

1866

Brady held his nephew Levin's shoulders and propelled him toward the door. The ticket taker at the desk in the lobby of the New York Historical Society waved them past.

"How many today, John?" Brady asked.

"We had a few paying customers yesterday," the large man said, "but they all left after looking at the first wall."

Brady nodded. The society had said they would close the

exhibit of his war portraits if attendance didn't go up. But despite the free publicity in the illustrated newspapers and the positive critical response, the public was not attending.

Levin had already gone inside. He stood, hands behind his back, and stared at the portraits of destruction he had been too young to remember. Brady had brought Levin to the exhibit to discourage the boy and make him return to school. He had arrived a few days before, declaring that he wanted to be a photographer like his Uncle Mat. Brady had said twelve was too young to start learning the trade, but Julia had promised Levin a place to stay if no one demanded that he return to school. So far, no one had.

Brady went inside too. The lighting was poor, and the portraits were scattered on several small walls. No Doric columns, no wide empty spaces. This was a cramped showing, like so many others he had had, but it shared the emptiness of the gallery in his dreams.

He stared at the portraits, knowing them by heart. They ran in order, from the first glorious parade down Pennsylvania Avenue—taken from his Washington studio—to the last portrait of Lee after Appomatox. Each portrait took him back to the sights and sounds of the moment: the excitement of the parade, the disgust at the carnage, the hopelessness in Lee's eyes. It was here: the recent past, recorded as faithfully as a human being could. One of his reviewers had said that Brady had captured time and held it prisoner in his little glass plates. He certainly did in his mind. Sometimes all it took was a smell—decaying garbage, horse sweat—and he was back on the battlefield, fighting to live while he took his portraits.

From outside the door, he heard the murmur of voices. He turned in time to see John talking to a woman in widow's weeds. John pointed at Brady. Brady smiled and nodded, knowing he was being identified as the artist behind the exhibit.

The woman pushed open the glass doors and stood in front of Brady. She was slight and older than he expected—in her forties or fifties—with deep lines around her eyes and the corners of her mouth.

"I've come to plead with you, Mr. Brady," she said. Her voice was soft. "I want you to take these portraits away. Over there, you have an image of my husband's body, and in the next room, I saw my son. They're dead, Mr. Brady, and I buried them. I want to think about how they lived, not how they died."

"I'm sorry, ma'am," Brady said. He didn't turn to see which

portraits she had indicated. "I didn't mean to offend you. These portraits show what war really is, and I think it's something we need to remember lest we try it again."

Levin had stopped his movement through the gallery. He hadn't turned toward the conversation, but Brady could tell the boy was listening from the cocked position of his head.

"We'll remember, Mr. Brady," the woman said. She smoothed her black skirt. "My whole family has no choice."

She turned her back and walked out, her steps firm and proud. The street door closed sharply behind her. John got up from his chair.

"You've gotten this before," Brady said.

"Every day," John said. "People want to move forward, Mathew. They don't need more reminders of the past."

Brady glanced at his nephew. Levin had moved into one of the back rooms. "Once Levin is done looking at the exhibit, I'll help you remove it," Brady said. "No sense hurting your business to help mine."

He sighed and glanced around the room. Four years of work. Injured associates, ruined equipment, lost wealth and a damaged business. He had expected acclaim, at least, if not a measure of additional fame. One of his mother's aphorisms rose in his mind: a comment she used to make when he would come inside, covered with dirt and dung. "How the mighty hath fallen," she'd say. She had never appreciated his dreams nor had she lived long enough to see them come true. Now her shade stood beside him, as clearly as she had stood on the porch so many years ago, and he could hear the "I-told-you-so" in her voice.

He shook the apparition away. What his mother had never realized was that the mighty had farther to fall.

1871

That morning, he put on his finest coat, his best hat, and he kissed Julia with a passion he hadn't shown in years. She smiled at him, her eyes filled with tears, as she held the door open for him. He stepped into the hallway, and heard the latch snick shut behind him. Nothing looked different: the gas lamps had soot marks around the base of the chimneys; the flowered wallpaper peeled in one corner; the stairs creaked as he stepped on them, heading down to the first floor and the street. Only he felt different: the shuddery bubble in his stomach, the tension in his back, the lightheadedness threatening the sureness of his movements.

He stopped on the first landing and took a breath of the musty hotel air. He wondered what they would think of him now, all the great men he had known. They came back to him, like battlefield ghosts haunting a general. Samuel Morse, his large dark eyes snapping, his gnarled hands holding the daguerreotypes, his voice echoing in the room, teaching Brady that photography would cause a revolution—a revolution, boy!—and he had to ride the crest.

"I did," Brady whispered. His New York studio, so impressive in the 1850s, had a portrait of Morse hanging near the door for luck. Abraham Lincoln had gazed at that portrait. So had his assassin, John Wilkes Booth. Presidents, princes, actors, assassins had all passed through Brady's door. And he, in his arrogance, had thought his work art, not commerce. Art and history demanded his presence at the first Battle of Bull Run. Commerce had demanded he stay home, take *carte de visites,* imperials and portraits of soldiers going off to war, of families about to be destroyed, of politicians, great and small.

No. He had left his assistants to do that, while he spent their earnings, his fortune and his future chasing a dream.

And this morning, he would pay for that dream.

So simple, his attorney told him. He would sign his name to a paper, declare bankruptcy, and the government would apportion his assets to his remaining creditors. He could still practice his craft, still attempt to repay his debts, still *live,* if someone wanted to call that living.

He adjusted his jacket one final time and stepped into the hotel's lobby. The desk clerk called out his customary good morning, and Brady nodded. He would show no shame, no anger. The doorman opened the door and cool, manure-tinged air tickled Brady's nostrils. He took a deep breath and walked into the bustle of the morning: Mathew Brady, photographer. A man who had joked with Andrew Jackson, Martin Van Buren, and James Buchanan. A man who had raised a camera against bullets, who had held more dead and dying than half the physicians on the battlefield. Brady pushed forward, touching the brim of his hat each time he passed a woman, nodding at the gentlemen as if the day were the best in his life. Almost everyone had seen his work, in the illustrated papers, in the exhibits, in the halls of Congress itself. He had probably photographed the sons of most of the people who walked these streets. Dead faces, turned toward the sun.

The thought sobered him. These people had lost husbands,

fathers, children. Losses greater than his. And they had survived, somehow. Somehow.

He held the thought as he made his way through the morning, listening to the attorney mumble, the government officials drone on, parceling out his possessions like clothing at an orphan's charity. The thought carried him out the door, and back onto the street before the anger burst through the numbness:

The portraits were his children. He and Julia had none—and he had nothing else. Nothing else at all.

"Now, are you ready to work with me?"

The female voice was familiar enough that he knew who he would see before he looked up: the crazy woman who haunted him, who wanted him to give everything he could to history.

As if he hadn't given enough.

She stood before him, the winter sunlight backlighting her, and hiding her features in shadow. The Washington crowd walked around her, unseeing, as if she were no more than a post blocking the path.

"And what do I get if I help you?" he asked, his voice sounding harsher than he had ever heard it.

"Notice. Acclaim. Pictures on walls instead of buried in warehouses. The chance to make a very real difference."

He glanced back at the dark wooden door, at the moving figures faint in the window, people who had buried his art, given it to the Anthonys, separated it and segregated it and declared it worthless. His children, as dead as the ones he had photographed.

"And you'll pay my way?" he asked.

"I will provide your equipment and handle your travel, if you take photographs for me when and where I say."

"Done," he said, extending a hand to seal the bargain, thinking a crazy, mannish woman like this one would close a deal like a gentleman. She took his hand, her palm soft, unused to work, and as she shook, the world whirled. Colors and pain and dust bombarded him. Smells he would briefly catch and, by the time he identified them, disappear. His head ached, his eyes throbbed, his body felt as if it were being torn in fifteen different directions. And when they stopped, he was in a world of blackness, where hot rain fell like fire from the sky.

"I need you to photograph this," she said, and then she disappeared. In her place, his wagon stood, the only friend in a place of strangeness. The air smelled of burning buildings, of sticky wet, of decay. Death. He recognized it from the battlefields years ago.

The horizon was black, dotted with orange flame. The trees rose stunted against the oppression. People—Orientals, he realized with some amazement—ran by him, their strange clothing ripped and torn, their faces burned, peeling, shining with the strange heat. They made no sound as they moved: all he heard was the rain slapping against the road.

He grabbed an old man, stopped him, felt the soft, decaying flesh dissolve between his fingers. "What is this place?" he asked.

The old man reached out a trembling hand, touched Brady's round eyes, his white skin. "Amelican—" the old man took a deep breath and exhaled into a wail that became a scream. He wrenched his arm from Brady's grasp, and started to run. The people around him screamed too, and ran, as if they were fleeing an unseen enemy. Brady grabbed onto his wagon, rocking with the force of the panicked crowd, and hurried to the far side.

People lay across the grass like corpses on the battlefield. Only these corpses moved. A naked woman swayed in the middle of the ground, her body covered with burns except for large flower-shaped patches all over her torso. And beside him lay three people, their faces melted away, their eyes bubbling holes in their smooth, shiny faces.

"What is this?" he cried out again.

But the woman who had brought him here was gone.

One of the faceless people grabbed his leg. He shook the hand away, trembling with the horror. The rich smell of decay made him want to gag.

He had been in this situation before—in the panic, among the decay, in the death—and he had found only one solution.

He reached inside his wagon and pulled out the camera. This time, though, he didn't scout for artistic composition. He turned the lens on the field of corpses, more horrifying than anything he'd seen under the Pennsylvania sun, and took portrait after portrait after portrait, building an artificial wall of light and shadow between himself and the black rain, the foul stench, and the silent, grasping hands of hundreds of dying people.

1871

And hours—or was it days?—later, after he could no longer move the tripod alone, no longer hold a plate between his fingers, after she appeared and took his wet plates and his equipment and his wagon, after he had given water to more people than he could count, and tore his suit and felt the sooty raindrops dig into his skin, after all that, he found himself standing on the same street in Washington, under the same sunlit winter sky. A woman he had never seen before peered at him with concern on her wrinkled face and asked, "Are you all right, sir?"

"I'm fine," he said and felt the lightheadedness that had threatened all morning take him to his knees on the wooden sidewalk. People surrounded him and someone called him by name. They took his arms and half carried him to the hotel. He dimly realized that they got him up the stairs—the scent of lilacs announcing Julia's presence—and onto the bed. Julia's cool hand rested against his forehead and her voice, murmuring something soothing, washed over him like a blessing. He closed his eyes—

And dreamed in jumbled images:

Flowers burned into naked skin; row after row after row of bodies stretched out in a farmer's field, face after face tilted toward the sun; and the faces blend into troops marching under gray skies, General Grant's dust-covered voice repeating that war needs different rules, different players, and General Lee, staring across a porch on a gray April morning, wearing his uniform for the last time saying softly that being a soldier is no longer an occupation for a gentleman. And through it all, black rain fell from the gray skies, coating everything in slimy heat, burning through skin, leaving bodies ravaged, melting people's clothes from their frames—

Brady gasped and sat up. Julia put her arm around him. "It's all right, Mathew," she said. "You were dreaming."

He put his head on her shoulder, and closed his eyes. Immediately, flower-burned skin rose in his vision and he forced his eyelids open. He still wore his suit, but there was no long gash in it and the fabric was dry. "I don't know what's wrong with me," he said.

"You just need rest."

He shook his head and got up. His legs were shaky, but the movement felt good. "Think of where we would be if I hadn't gone to Bull Run," he said. "We were rich. We had what we wanted. I would have taken portraits, and we would have made more money. We would have an even nicer studio and a home, instead of this apartment." He smiled a little. "And now the government will sell everything they can, except the portraits. Portraits that no one wants to see."

Julia still sat at the edge of the bed. Her black dress was

wrinkled, and her ringlets mussed. She must have held him while he slept.

"You know," he said, leaning against the windowsill. "I met a woman just after the Battle of Gettysburg, and she told me that I would die forgotten with my work hidden in government warehouses. And I thought she was crazy; how could the world forget Brady of Broadway? I had dreams of a huge gallery, filled with my work—"

"Dreams have truth," Julia said.

"No," Mathew said. "Dreams have hope. Dreams without hope are nightmares." He swept his hand around the room. "This is a nightmare, Julia."

She bowed her head. Her hands were clasped together so tightly her knuckles had turned white. Then she raised her head, tossing her ringlets back, and he saw the proud young woman he had married. "So how do we change things, Mathew?"

He stared at her. Even now, she still believed in him, thought that together they could make things better. He wanted to tell her that they would recapture what they had lost; he wanted to give her hope. But he was forty-eight years old, nearly blind, and penniless. He didn't have time to rebuild a life from nothing.

"I guess we keep working," he said, quietly. But even as he spoke, a chill ran down his back. He had worked for the crazy woman and she had taken him to the gates of hell. And he had nothing to show for it except strange behavior and frightening memories. "I'm sorry, Julia."

"I'm not." She smiled that cryptic smile she had had ever since he married her. "The reward is worth the cost."

He nodded, feeling the rain still hot on his skin, hearing voices call for help in a language he could not understand. He wondered if any reward was worth the sacrifices made for it.

He didn't think so.

1871

Six weeks later, Brady dreamed:

The exhibit room was colder than it had been before, the lighting better. Brady stood beside his wagon and clutched its wooden frame. He stepped around the wagon, saw that the doors to the exhibit were closed, and he was alone in the huge room. He touched his eyes. The glasses were missing, and he could see, just as he had in the previous dreams. His vision was clear, clearer than it had ever been.

No portraits had been added to the far wall. He walked toward his collection and then stopped. He didn't want to look at his old work. He couldn't bear the sight of it, knowing the kind of pain and loss those portraits had caused. Instead he turned and gasped.

Portraits graced a once-empty wall. He ran toward them, nearly tripping over the boards of the wagon. Hundreds of portraits framed and mounted at odd angles glinted under the strange directed lights, the lights that never flickered. He stood closer, saw scenes he hoped he would forget: the flowered woman; the three faceless people, their eyes boiling in their sockets; a weeping man, his skin hanging around him like rags. The portraits were clearer, cleaner than the war portraits from the other wall. No dust had gotten in the fluid, no cracked wet plates, no destroyed glass. Clean, crisp portraits, on paper he had never seen before. But it was all his work, clearly his work.

He made himself look away. The air had a metallic smell. The rest of the wall was blank, as were the other two. More pictures to take, more of hell to see. He had experienced the fire and the brimstone, the burning rain—Satan's tears. He wondered what else he would see, what else she would make him record.

He touched the portrait of the men with melted faces. If he had to trade visions like this for his eyesight and his wealth, he wouldn't make the trade. He would die poor and blind at Julia's side.

The air got colder.

He woke up screaming.

1873

Brady stared at the plate he held in his hand. His subject had long since left the studio, but Brady hadn't moved. He remembered days when subject after subject had entered the studio, and his assistants had had to develop the prints while Brady staged the sittings.

"I'll take that, Uncle."

Brady started. He hadn't realized that Levin was in the room. He wondered if Levin had been watching him stand there, doing nothing. Levin hadn't said anything the past few years, but he seemed to notice Brady's growing strange behaviors. "Thank you, Levin," Brady said, making sure his voice was calm.

Levin kept his eyes averted as he grabbed the covered plate and took it into the darkroom for developing. Levin had grown tall in the seven years that he'd been with Brady. Far from the self-assured twelve-year-old who had come to work for his uncle, Levin had become a silent man who came alive only behind the camera lens. Brady couldn't have survived without him, especially after he had to let the rest of his staff go.

Brady moved the camera, poured the collodion mixture back into its jar and covered the silver nitrate. Then he washed his hands in the bowl filled with tepid water that sat near the chemical storage.

"I have another job for you. Can you be alone on Friday at four?"

This time, Brady didn't jump, but his heart did. It pounded against his ribcage like a child trying to escape a locked room. His nerves had been on edge for so long. Julia kept giving him hot teas and rubbing the back of his neck, but nothing seemed to work. When he closed his eyes he saw visions he didn't want to see.

He turned, slowly. The crazy woman stood there, her hands clasped behind her back. Since she hadn't appeared in almost two years, he had managed to convince himself that she wasn't real—that he had imagined her.

"Another job?" he asked. He was shaking. Either he hadn't imagined the last one, or he was having another nightmare. "I'm sorry. I can't."

"Can't?" Her cheeks flushed. "You promised, Mathew. I need you."

"You never told me you were going to send me to hell," he snapped. He moved away from the chemicals, afraid that in his anger, he would throw them. "You're not real, and yet the place you took me stays in my mind. I'm going crazy. You're a sign of my insanity."

"No," she said. She came forward and touched him lightly. Her fingertips were soft, and he could smell the faint perfume of her body. "You're not crazy. You're just faced with something from outside your experience. You had dreams about the late War, didn't you? Visions you couldn't escape?"

He was about to deny it, when he remembered how, in the first year of his return, the smell of rotted garbage took him back to the Devil's Hole; how the whinny of a horse made him duck for cover; how he stored his wagon because being inside it filled him with a deep anxiety. "What are you telling me?"

"I come from a place you've never heard of," she said. "We have developed the art of travel in an instant and our societal norms are different from yours. The place I sent you wasn't hell. It was a war zone, after the Uni—a country had used a new kind of weapon on another country. I want to send you to more places like that, to photograph them, so that we can display those photographs for people of my society to see."

"If you can travel in an instant—" and he remembered the whirling world, the dancing colors and sounds as he traveled from his world to another "—then why don't you take people there? Why do you need me?"

"Those places are forbidden. I received special dispensation. I'm working on an art project, and I nearly lost my funding because I saw you in Gettysburg."

Brady's shaking eased. "You risked everything to see me?"

She nodded. "We're alike in that way," she said. "You've risked everything to follow your vision too."

"And you need me?"

"You're the first and the best, Mathew. I couldn't even get funding unless I guaranteed that I would have your work. Your studio portraits are lovely, Mathew, but it's your war photos that make you great."

"No one wants to see my war work," Brady said.

Her smile seemed sad. "They will, Mathew. Especially if you work with me."

Brady glanced around his studio, smaller now than it had ever been. Portraits of great men still hung on the walls along with actors, artists, and people who just wanted a remembrance.

"At first it was art for you," she said, her voice husky. "Then it became a mission, to show people what war was really like. And now no one wants to look. But they need to, Mathew."

"I know," he said. He glanced back at her, saw the brightness in her face, the trembling of her lower lip. This meant more to her than an art project should. Something personal, something deep, got her involved. "I went to hell for you, and I never even got to see the results of my work."

"Yes, you did," she said.

"Uncle!" Levin called from the next room.

The woman vanished, leaving shimmering air in her wake. Brady reached out and touched it, felt the remains of a whirlwind. She knew about his dreams, then. Or was she referring to the work he had done inside his wagon on the site, developing plates before they dried so that the portraits would be preserved?

"Did I hear voices?" Levin came out of the back room, wiping his hands on his smock.

Brady glanced at Levin, saw the frown between the young man's brows. Levin was really worried about him. "No voices," Brady said. "Perhaps you just heard someone calling from the street."

"The portrait is done." Levin looked at the chemicals, as if double-checking his uncle's work.

"I'll look at it later," Brady said. "I'm going home to Julia. Can you watch the studio?"

Levin nodded.

Brady grabbed his coat off one of the sitting chairs and stopped at the doorway. "What do you think of my war work, Levin? And be honest, now."

"Honest?"

"Yes."

Brady waited. Levin took a deep breath. "I wish that I were ten years older so that I could have been one of your assistants, Uncle. You preserved something that future generations need to see. And it angers me that no one is willing to look."

"Me, too," Brady said. He slipped his arms through the sleeves of his coat. "But maybe—" and he felt something cautious rise in his chest, something like hope "—if I work just a little harder, people will look again. Think so, Levin?"

"It's one of my prayers, Uncle," Levin said.

"Mine, too," Brady said, and let himself out the door. He whistled a little as he walked down the stairs. Maybe the woman was right; maybe he had a future, after all.

1873

Friday at four, Brady whirled from his studio to a place so hot that sweat appeared on his body the instant he stopped whirling. His wagon stood on a dirt road, surrounded by thatched huts. Some of the huts were burning, but the flames were the only movement in the entire village. Far away, he could hear a chop-chop-chopping sound, but he could see nothing. Flies buzzed around him, not landing, as if they had more interesting places to go. The air smelled of burning hay and something fetid, something familiar. He swallowed and looked for the bodies.

He grabbed the back end of the wagon, and climbed inside. The darkness was welcome. It took a moment for his eyes to get used to the gloom, then he grabbed his tripod and his camera and carried them outside. He pushed his glasses upon his nose, but his finger encountered skin instead of metal. He could see. He squinted and wondered how she did that—gave him his eyesight for such a short period of time. Perhaps it was his reward for going to hell.

A hand extended from one of the burning huts. Brady stopped beside it, crouched, and saw a man lying face down in the dust, the back of his head blown away. Bile rose in Brady's throat, and he swallowed to keep his last meal down. He assembled the camera, uncapped the lens and looked through, seeing the hand and the flames flickering in his narrow, rounded vision. Then he climbed out from under the curtain, went back into the wagon and prepared a plate.

This time he felt no fear. Perhaps knowing that the woman (why had she never told him her name?) could flash him out of the area in an instant made him feel safer. Or perhaps it was his sense of purpose, as strong as it had been at the first Battle of Bull Run, when the bullets whizzed by him, and his wagon got stampeded by running soldiers. He had had a reason then, a life then, and he would get it back.

He went outside and photographed the dead man in the burning hut. The chop-chop-chopping sound was fading, but the heat seemed to intensify. The stillness in the village was eerie. The crackles of burning buildings made him jump. He saw no more bodies, no evidence other than the emptiness and the fires that something had happened in this place.

Then he saw the baby.

It was a toddler, actually. Naked, and shot in the back, the body lying at the edge of a ditch. Brady walked over to the ditch and peered in, then stepped back and got sick for the first time in his professional career.

Bodies filled the ditch—women, children, babies, and old men—their limbs flung back, stomachs gone, faces shot away. Blood flowed like a river, added its coppery scent to the smell of burning hay and the reek of decay. What kind of places was she taking him to, where women and children died instead of soldiers?

He grabbed his camera, his shield, and set it up, knowing that this would haunt him as the hot, slimy rain haunted him. He prepared more plates and photographed the toddler over and over, the innocent baby that had tried to crawl away from the horror and had been shot in the back for its attempts at survival.

And as he worked, his vision blurred, and he wondered why the sweat pouring into and out of his eyes never made them burn.

1875

Brady stared at the $25,000 check. He set it on the doily that covered the end table. In the front room, he heard Levin arguing with Julia.

"Not today," she said. "Give him at least a breath between bad news."

Brady touched the thin paper, the flowing script. The government had given him one-quarter of the wealth he had lost going into the war, one-tenth of the money he spent photographing history. And too late. The check was too late. A month earlier, the War Department, which owned the title to the wet plates, sold them all to the Anthonys for an undisclosed sum. They had clear, legal title, and Edward Anthony had told Brady that they would never, ever sell.

He got up with a sigh and brushed aside the half-open bedroom door. "Tell me what?" he asked.

Levin looked up—guiltily, Brady thought. Julia hid something behind her back. "Nothing, Uncle," Levin said. "It can wait."

"You brought something and I want to know what it is." Brady's voice was harsh. It had been too harsh lately. The flashbacks on his travels, the strain of keeping silent—of not telling Julia the fantastical events—and the reversal after reversal in his own life were taking their toll.

Julia brought her hand out from behind her back. She clutched a stereoscope. The small device shook as she handed it to Brady.

He put the lenses up to his eyes, feeling the frame clink against his glasses. The three dimensional view inside was familiar: the war parade he had taken over ten years ago, as the soldiers rode down Pennsylvania Avenue. Brady removed the thick card from the viewer. The two portraits stood side by side, as he expected. He even expected the flowery script on the side, stating that the stereoscopic portrait was available through the Anthonys' warehouse. What he didn't expect was the attribution at the bottom, claiming that the photography had been done by the Anthonys themselves.

He clenched his fists and turned around, letting the device fall to the wooden floor. The stereoscope clinked as it rolled, and Brady stifled an urge to kick it across the room.

"We can go to Congressman Garfield," Levin said, "and maybe he'll help us."

Brady stared at the portrait. He could take the Anthonys to court. They did own the rights to the wet plates, but they should have given him proper attribution. It seemed a trivial thing to fight over. He had no money, and what influence he had would be better spent getting the plates back than fighting for a bit of name recognition. "No," Brady said. "You can go to the newspapers, if you like, Levin, but we won't get James to act for us. He's done his best already. This is our fight. And we'll keep at it, until the bitter end if we have to."

Julia clenched her hands together and stared at him. It seemed as if the lines around her mouth had grown deeper. He remembered the first time he danced with her, the diamonds around her neck glittering in the candlelight. They had sold those diamonds in 1864 to fund the Petersburg expedition—the expedition in which half of his equipment was destroyed by Confederate shells. *You are going to be a great man,* she had told him. The problem was, he had never asked her what she meant by great. Perhaps she thought of her wealthy father as a great man. Perhaps she stayed with Brady out of wifely loyalty.

She came over to him and put her arm around him. "I love you, Mathew," she said. He hugged her close, so close that he worried he would hurt her. He wouldn't have been able to do anything without her. None of his work, none of his efforts would have been possible—especially in the lean years—if she hadn't believed in him.

"I'm sorry," he whispered into her shoulder.

She slipped out of his embrace and held him so that she could look into his eyes. "We'll keep fighting, Mathew. And in the end, we'll win."

1877

And the assignments kept coming. Brady began to look forward to the whirling, even though he often ended up in hell. His body was stronger there; his eyesight keener. He could forget, for a short time, the drabness of Washington, the emptiness of his life. On the battlefields, he worked—and he could still believe that his work had meaning.

One dark, gray day, he left his studio and found himself hiding at the edge of a forest. His wagon, without a horse, leaned against a spindly tree. The air was thick and humid. Brady's black suit clung to his skin, already damp. Through the bushes he could see soldiers carrying large rifles, surrounding a church. Speaking a language he thought he understood—Spanish?—they herded children together. Then, in twos and threes, the soldiers marched the children inside.

The scene was eerily quiet. Brady went behind the wagon, grabbed his tripod and set up the camera. He stepped carefully on the forest bed; the scuffing noise of his heavy leather shoes seemed to resound like gunshots. He took portrait after portrait, concentrating on the soldiers' faces, the children's looks of resignation. He wondered why the soldiers were imprisoning the children, and what they planned to do to the town he could see just over the horizon. And a small trickle of relief ran through him that here, at least, the children would be spared.

Once the children were inside, the soldiers closed the heavy doors and barred them. Someone had already boarded up the windows. Brady put another plate into his camera to take a final portrait of the closed church before following the army to their nasty work at the village. He looked down, checking the plates the woman had given him, when he heard a whoosh. A sharp, tingling scent rose in his nostrils, followed by the smell of smoke. Automatically he opened the lens—just as a soldier threw a burning torch at the church itself.

Brady screamed and ran out of the bushes. The soldiers saw him—and one leveled a rifle at him. The bullets ratt-a-tatted at him, the sound faster and more vicious than the repeating rifles from the war. Brady felt his body jerk and fall, felt himself roll over, bouncing with each bullet's impact. He wanted to crawl to the church, to save the children, but he couldn't move. He couldn't do anything. The world was growing darker—and he saw a kind of light—and his mother? waiting for him—

And then the whirling began. It seemed slower, and he wasn't sure he wanted it to start. It pulled him away from the light, away from the mother he hadn't seen since he left the farm at sixteen, away from the church and the burning children (he thought he could hear their screams now—loud, terrified, piercing—) and back to the silence of his studio.

He wound up in one of his straight-backed chairs. He tried to stand up, and fell, his glasses jostling on the edge of his nose. Footsteps on the stairs ran toward him, then hands lifted him. Levin.

"Uncle? Are you all right?"

"Shot," Brady whispered. "The children. All dead. Must get the children."

He pushed Levin aside and groped for something, anything to

hold on to. "I have to get back!" he yelled. "Someone has to rescue those children!"

Levin grabbed his shoulders, forced Brady back to the chair. "The war is over, Uncle," Levin said. "It's over. You're home. You're safe."

Brady looked up at Levin and felt the shakes begin. She wouldn't send him back. She wouldn't let him save those children. She knew all along that the church would burn and she wanted him to photograph it, to record it, not to save it. He put his hands over his face. He had seen enough atrocities to last him three lifetimes.

"It's all right," Levin said. "It's all right, Uncle."

It wasn't all right. Levin was becoming an expert at this, at talking Brady home. And to his credit, he never said anything to Julia. "Thank you," Brady said. His words were thin, rushed, as if the bullet holes still riddled his body and sucked the air from it.

He patted Levin on the shoulder, then walked away—walked—to the end of the studio, his room, his home. Perhaps the crazy woman didn't exist. Perhaps what Levin saw was truth. Perhaps Brady's mind was going, after all.

"Thank you," he repeated, and walked down the stairs, comforted by the aches in his bones, the blurry edge to his vision. He was home, and he would stay—

Until she called him again. Until he had his next chance to be young, and working, and doing something worthwhile.

1882

Brady sat in front of the window, gazing into the street. Below, carriages rumbled past, throwing up mud and chunks of ice. People hurried across the sidewalk, heads bowed against the sleet. The rippled glass was cold against his fingers, but he didn't care. He could hear Levin in the studio, talking with a prospective client. Levin had handled all of the business this past week. Brady had hardly been able to move.

The death of Henry Anthony shouldn't have hit him so hard. The Anthony Brothers had been the closest thing Brady had to enemies in the years since the war. Yet, they had been friends once, and companions in the early days of the art. All of photography was dying; Morse was gone. Henry Anthony dead. And three of Brady's assistants, men he had trained to succeed him, dead in the opening of the West.

Levin opened the door and peeked in. "Uncle, a visitor," he said.

Brady was about to wave Levin away when another man stepped inside. The man was tall, gaunt, wearing a neatly pressed black suit. He looked official. "Mr. Brady?"

Brady nodded but did not rise.

"I'm John C. Taylor. I'm a soldier, sir, and a student of your work. I would like to talk with you, if I could."

Brady pushed back the needlepoint chair beside him. Taylor sat down, hat in his hands.

"Mr. Brady, I wanted to let you know what I've been doing. Since the end of the war, I've tried to acquire your work. I have secured, through various channels, over 7,000 negatives of your best pictures."

Brady felt the haze that surrounded him lift somewhat. "And you would like to display them?"

"No, sir, actually, I've been trying to preserve them. The plates the government bought from you years ago have been sitting in a warehouse. A number were destroyed due to incautious handling. I've been trying to get them placed somewhere else. I have an offer from the Navy Department—I have connections there—and I wanted your approval."

Brady laughed. The sound bubbled from inside of him, but he felt no joy. He had wanted the portraits for so long and finally, here was someone asking for his approval. "No one has asked me what I wanted before."

Taylor leaned back. He glanced once at Levin, as if Brady's odd reaction had made Taylor wary.

"My uncle has gone through quite an odyssey to hold on to his plates," Levin said softly. "He has lost a lot over the years."

"From the beginning," Brady said. "No one will ever know what I went through in securing the negatives. The whole world can never appreciate it. It changed the course of my life. Some of those negatives nearly cost me that life. And then the work was taken from me. Do you understand, Mr. Taylor?"

Taylor nodded. "I've been tracking these photographs for a long time, sir. I remembered them from the illustrated papers, and I decided that they needed to be preserved, so that my children's children would see the devastation, would learn the follies we committed because we couldn't reason with each other."

Brady smiled. A man who did understand. Finally. "The government bought my portraits of Webster, Calhoun and Clay. I got paid a lot of money for those paintings that were made from my photographs. Not my work, mind you. Paintings of my work. Page would have been so happy."

"Sir?"

Brady shook his head. Page had left his side long ago. "But no one wants to see the war work. No one wants to see what you and I preserved. I don't want the Navy to bury the negatives. I want them to display the work, reproduce it or make it into a book that someone can see."

"First things first, Mr. Brady," Taylor said. "The Navy has the negatives I've acquired, but we need to remove the others from the War Department before they're destroyed. And then you, or your nephew, or someone else can go in there and put together a showing."

Brady reached over and gripped Taylor's hands. They were firm and strong—a young man's hands on an older man's body. "If you can do that," Brady said. "You will have made all that I've done worthwhile."

1882

Julia huddled on the settee, a blanket over her slight frame. She had grown gaunt, her eyes big saucers on the planes of her face. Her hands shook as she took the letter from Brady. He had hesitated about giving it to her, but he knew that she would ask and she would worry. It would be better for her frail heart to know than to constantly fret. She leaned toward the lamp. Brady watched her eyes move as she read.

He already knew the words by heart. The letter was from General A. W. Greeley, in the War Department. He was in charge of the government's collection of Brady's work. After the opening amenities, he had written:

> *The government has stated positively that their negatives must not be exploited for commercial purposes. They are the historical treasures of a whole people and the government has justly refused to establish a dangerous system of "special privilege" by granting permission for publication to individuals. As the property of the people, the government negatives are held in sacred trust.*

Where no one could see them, and not even Brady himself could use them. He wondered what Taylor thought—Taylor who would have received the letter in Connecticut by now.

Julia looked up, her eyes dotted with tears. "What do they think, that you're going to steal the plates from them like they stole them from you?"

"I don't know," Brady said. "Perhaps they really don't understand what they have."

"They understand," Julia said, her voice harsh. "And it frightens them."

1883

In his dreams, he heard the sounds of people working. Twice he had arrived at the door to his gallery, and twice it had been locked. Behind the thin material, he heard voices—"Here, Andre. No, no. Keep the same years on the same wall space"—and the sounds of shuffling feet. This time, he knocked and the door opened a crack.

Ceiling lights flooded the room. It was wide and bright—brighter than he imagined a room could be. His work covered all the walls but one. People, dressed in pants and loose shirts like the woman who hired him, carried framed portraits from one spot to the next, all under the direction of a slim man who stood next to Brady's wagon.

The man looked at Brady. "What do you want?"

"I just wanted to see—"

The man turned to one of the others walking through. "Get rid of him, will you? We only have a few hours, and we still have one wall to fill."

A woman stopped next to Brady and put her hand on his arm. Her fingers were cool. "I'm sorry," she said. "We're preparing an exhibit."

"But I'm the artist," Brady said.

"He says—"

"I know what he says," the man said. He squinted at Brady, then glanced at a portrait that hung near the wagon. "And so he is. You should be finishing the exhibit, Mr. Brady, not gawking around the studio."

"I didn't know I had something to finish."

The man sighed. "The show opens tomorrow morning, and you still have one wall to fill. What are you doing here?"

"I don't know," Brady said. The woman took his arm and led him out the door.

"We'll see you tomorrow night," she said. And then she smiled. "I like your work."

And then he woke up, shivering and shaking in the dark beside Julia. Her even breathing was a comfort. He drew himself into a huddle and rested his knees against his chest. One wall to fill by tomorrow? He wished he understood what the dreams meant. It had taken him nearly twenty years to fill all the other walls. And then he thought that perhaps dream time worked differently than real time. Perhaps dream time moved in an instant the way he did when the woman whirled him away to another place.

It was just a dream, he told himself, and by the time he fell back to sleep, he really believed it.

1884

By the time the wagon appeared beside him, Brady was shaking. This place was silent, completely silent. Houses stood in neat rows on barren, brown treeless land. Their white formations rested like sentries against the mountains that stood in the distance. A faint smell, almost acrid, covered everything. The air was warm, but not muggy, and beads of sweat rose on his arms like drops of blood.

Brady had arrived behind one of the houses. Inside, a family sat around the table—a man, a woman and two children. They all appeared to be eating—the woman had a spoon raised to her mouth—but no one moved. In the entire time he had been there, no one had moved.

He went into his wagon, removed the camera and tripod, then knocked on the door. The family didn't acknowledge him. He pushed the door open and stepped inside, setting up the camera near a gleaming countertop. Then he walked over to the family. The children were laughing, gazing at each other. Their chests didn't rise and fall, their eyes didn't move. The man had his hand around a cup full of congealed liquid. He was watching the children, a faint smile on his face. The woman was looking down, at the bowl filled with a soggy mush. The hand holding the spoon—empty except for a white stain in the center—had frozen near her mouth. Brady touched her. Her skin was cold, rigid.

They were dead.

Brady backed away, nearly knocking over the tripod. He grabbed the camera, felt its firmness in his hands. For some reason, these specters frightened him worse than all the others. He couldn't tell what killed them or how they died. It had become increasingly difficult, at the many varied places he had been, but he could at least guess. Here, he saw nothing—and the bodies didn't even feel real.

He climbed under the dark curtain, finding a kind of protection from his own equipment. Perhaps, near his own stuff, whatever had killed them would avoid him. He took the photograph, and then carried his equipment to the next house, where a frozen woman sat on a sofa, looking at a piece of paper. In each house, he photographed the still lives, almost wishing for the blood, the fires, the signs of destruction.

1885

Brady folded the newspaper and set it down. He didn't wish to disturb Julia, who was sleeping soundly on the bed. She seemed to get so little rest. Her face had become translucent, the shadows under her eyes so deep that they looked like bruises.

He couldn't share the article with her. A year ago, she might have laughed. But now, tears would stream down her cheeks and she would want him to hold her. And when she woke up, he would hold her, because they had so little time left.

She didn't need to see the paragraph that stood out from the page as if someone had expanded the type:

> *. . . and with his loss, all of photography's pioneers are dead. In the United States alone we have lost, in recent years, Alexander Gardiner, Samuel F. B. Morse, Edward and Henry Anthony, and Mathew B. Brady. Gardiner practiced the craft until his death, going west and sending some of the best images back home. The Anthonys sold many of their fine works in stereoscope for us all to see. Morse had other interests and quit photography to pursue them. Brady lost his eyesight after the War, and closed his studios here and in New York . . .*

Perhaps he was wrong. Perhaps they wouldn't laugh together. Perhaps she would be as angry as he was. He hadn't died. He hadn't. No one allowed him to show his work anymore. He hadn't even been to the gallery of his dreams since that confusing last dream, years ago.

Brady placed the newspaper with the others near the door. Then he crawled onto the bed and pulled Julia close. Her small body was comfort, and in her sleep, she turned and held him back.

1886

One morning, he whirled into a place of such emptiness it chilled his soul. The buildings were tall and white, the grass green, and the flowers in bloom. His wagon was the only black thing on the surface of this place. He could smell lilacs as he walked forward, and he thought of Julia resting at their apartment—too fragile now to even do her needlepoint.

This silence was worse than at the last place. Here it felt as if human beings had never touched this land, despite the buildings. He felt as if he were the only person alive.

He walked up the stone steps of the first building and pushed open the glass door. The room inside was empty—as empty as his gallery had been when he first dreamed it. No dust or footprints marred the white floor, no smudges covered the white walls. He looked out the window and, as he watched, a building twenty yards away shimmered and disappeared.

Brady shoved his hands in his pockets and scurried outside. Another, squarer building also disappeared. The shimmering was different, more ominous than the shimmering left by his benefactress. In these remains, he could almost see the debris, the dust from the buildings that had once been. He could feel the destruction and knew that these places weren't reappearing somewhere else. He ran to his wagon, climbed inside, and peered out at the world from the wagon's edge. And, as he watched, building after building winked out of existence.

He clutched the camera to him, but took no photographs. The smell of lilacs grew stronger. His hands were cold, shaking. He watched the buildings disappear until only a grassy field remained.

"You can't even photograph it."

Her appearance didn't surprise him. He expected her, after seeing the changes, perhaps because he had been thinking of her. Her hair was shoulder-length now, but other than that, she hadn't changed in all the years since he last saw her.

"It's so clean and neat." Her voice shook. "You can't even tell that anyone died here."

Brady crawled out of the wagon and stood beside her. He felt more uneasy here than he had felt under the shelling at the first Battle of Bull Run. There at least he could hear the whistle, feel the explosions. Here the destruction came from nowhere.

"Welcome to war in my lifetime, Mathew." She crossed her arms in front of her chest. "Here we get rid of everything, not just a person's body, but all traces of their home, their livelihood—and, in most cases, any memories of them. I lost my son like this and I couldn't remember that he had existed until I started work on this project." She smiled just a little. "The time travel gives unexpected gifts, some we can program for, like improved eyesight or health, and some we can't, like improved memories. The scientists say it has something to do with molecular rearrangement, but that makes no sense to you, since most people didn't know what a molecule was in your day."

He stood beside her, his heart pounding in his throat. She turned to him, took his hand in hers.

"We can't go any farther than this, Mathew."

He frowned. "I'm done?"

"Yes. I can't thank you in the ways that I'd like. If I could, I'd send you back, give you money, let you rebuild your life from the war on. But I can't. We can't. But I can bring you to the exhibit when it opens, and hope that the response is what we expect. Would you like that, Mathew?"

He didn't know exactly what she meant, and he wasn't sure he cared. He wanted to keep making photographs, to keep working here with her. He had nothing else. "I could still help you. I'm sure there are a number of things to be done."

She shook her head, then kissed his forehead. "You need to go home to your Julia, and enjoy the time you have left. We'll see each other again, Mathew."

And then she started to whirl, to shimmer. Brady reached for her and his hand went through her into the heated air. This shimmer was different; it had a life to it. He felt a thin relief. She had traveled beyond him, but not out of existence. He leaned against the edge of his wagon and stared at the lilac bushes and the wind blowing through the grasses, trying to understand what she had just told him. He and the wagon sat alone, in a field where people had once built homes and lived quiet lives. Finally, at dusk, he too shimmered out of the blackness and back to his own quiet life.

1887

Only Levin and Brady stood beside the open grave. The wind ruffled Brady's hair, dried the tear tracks on his cheeks. He hadn't realized how small Julia's life had become. Most of the people at the funeral had been his friends, people who had come to console him.

He could hear the trees rustling behind him. The breeze carried a scent of lilacs—how appropriate, Julia dying in the spring so that her flower would bloom near her grave. She had been so beautiful when he met her, so popular. She had whittled her life down for him, because she had thought he needed her. And he had.

Levin took Brady's arm. "Come along, Uncle," Levin said.

Brady looked up at his nephew, the closest thing to a child he and Julia had ever had. Levin's hair had started to recede, and he too wore thick glasses.

"I don't want to leave her," Brady said. "I've left her too much already."

"It's all right, Uncle," Levin said as he put his arm around Brady's waist and led him through the trees. "She understands."

Brady glanced back at the hole in the ground, at his wife's coffin, and at the two men who had already started to shovel dirt on top. "I know she understands," he said. "She always has."

1887

That night, Brady didn't sleep. He sat on the bed he had shared with Julia, and clutched her pillow against his chest. He missed her even breathing, her comfortable presence. He missed her hand on his cheek and her warm voice, reassuring him. He missed holding her, and loving her, and telling her how much he loved her.

It's all right, Uncle, Levin had said. *She understands.*

Brady got up, set the pillow down and went to the window. She had looked out so many times, probably feeling alone, while he pursued his dreams of greatness. She had never said what she thought these past few years, but he saw her look at him, saw the speculation in her eyes when he returned from one of his trips. She had loved him too much to question him.

Then he felt it: the odd sensation that always preceded a whirling. But he was done—he hadn't left in over a year. He was just tired, just—

spinning. Colors and pain and dust bombarded him. Smells he would briefly catch and, by the time he identified them, they had disappeared. His head ached, his body felt as if it were being torn in fifteen different directions. And when he stopped, he stood in the gallery of his dreams . . . only he knew that he was wide awake.

It existed then. It really existed.

And it was full of people.

Women wore long clingy dresses in a shining material. Their hair varied in hue from brown to pink, and many had jewelry stapled into their noses, their cheeks and, in one case, along the rim of the eye. The men's clothes were as colorful and as shiny. They wore makeup, but no jewelry. A few people seemed out of place, in other clothes—a woman in combat fatigues from one of the wars Brady had seen, a man in dust-covered denim pants and a ripped shirt, another man dressed in all black leaning against a gallery door. All of the doors in the hallway were open and people spilled in and out, conversing or holding shocked hands to their throats.

The conversation was so thick that Brady couldn't hear separate voices, separate words. A variety of perfumes overwhelmed him and the coolness seemed to have left the gallery. He let the crowd push him down the hall toward his own exhibit and as he passed, he caught bits and pieces of other signs:

. . . IMAGE ARTIST . . .
. . . (2000–2010) . . .
. . . HOLOGRAPHER, AFRICAN BIOLOGICAL . . .
. . . ABC CAMERAMAN, LEBANON . . .
. . . PHOTOJOURNALIST, VIETNAM CONFLICT . . .
. . . (1963) . . .
. . . NEWS REELS FROM THE PACIFIC THEATER . . .
. . . OFFICIAL PHOTOGRAPHER, WORLD WAR I . . .
. . . (1892– . . .
. . . INDIAN WARS . . .

And then his own:

MATHEW B. BRADY EXHIBIT
OFFICIAL PHOTOGRAPHER:
UNITED STATES CIVIL WAR
(1861–1865)

The room was full. People stood along the walls, gazing at his portraits, discussing and pointing at the fields of honored dead. One woman turned away from the toddler who had been shot in the back; another from the burning church. People looked inside Brady's wagon, and more than a few stared at the portraits of him, lined along the Doric columns like a series of somber, aging men.

He caught a few words:

"Fantastic composition" . . . "amazing things with black and white" . . . "almost looks real" . . . "turns my stomach" . . . "can't imagine working with such primitive equipment" . . .

Someone touched his shoulder. Brady turned. A woman

smiled at him. She wore a long purple gown and her brown hair was wrapped around the top of her head. It took a moment for him to recognize his benefactress.

"Welcome to the exhibit, Mathew. People are enjoying your work."

She smiled at him and moved on. And then it hit him. He finally had an exhibit. He finally had people staring at his work, and seeing what had really happened in all those places during all that time. She had shown him this gallery all his life, whirled him here when he thought he was asleep. This was his destiny, just as dying impoverished in his own world was his destiny.

"You're the artist?" A slim man in a dark suit stood beside Brady.

"This is my work," Brady said.

A few people crowded around. The scent of soap and perfume nearly overwhelmed him.

"I think you're an absolutely amazing talent," the man said. His voice was thin, with an accent that seemed British but wasn't. "I can't believe the kind of work you put into this to create such stark beauty. And with such bulky equipment."

"Beauty?" Brady could barely let the word out of his throat. He gazed around the room, saw the flowered woman, the row of corpses on the Gettysburg battlefield.

"Eerie," a woman said. "Rather like late Goya, don't you think, Lavinia?"

Another woman nodded. "Stunning, the way you captured the exact right light, the exact moment to illuminate the concept."

"Concept?" Brady felt his hands shake. "You're looking at war here. People died in these portraits. This is history, not art."

"I think you're underestimating your work," the man said. "It is truly art, and you are a great, great artist. Only an artist would see how to use black and white to such a devastating effect—"

"I wasn't creating art," Brady said. "My assistants and I, we were shot at. I nearly died the day the soldiers burned that church. This isn't beauty. This is war. It's truth. I wanted you to see how ugly war really is."

"And you did it so well," the man said. "I truly admire your technique." And then he walked out of the room. Brady watched him go. The women smiled, shook his hand, told him that it was a pleasure to meet him. He wandered around the room, heard the same types of conversation and stopped when he saw his benefactress.

"They don't understand," he said. "They think this was done

for them, for their appreciation. They're calling this art."

"It is art, Mathew," she said softly. She glanced around the room, as if she wanted to be elsewhere.

"No," he said. "It actually happened."

"A long time ago." She patted his hand. "The message about war and destruction will go home in their subconscious. They will remember this." And then she turned her back on him and pushed her way through the crowd. Brady tried to follow her, but made it as far as his wagon. He sat on its edge and buried his face in his hands.

He sat there for a long time, letting the conversation hum around him, wondering at his own folly. And then he heard his name called in a voice that made his heart rise.

"Mr. Brady?"

He looked up and saw Julia. Not the Julia who had grown pale and thin in their small apartment, but the Julia he had met so many years ago. She was slender and young, her face glowing with health. No gray marked her ringlets, and her hoops were wide with a fashion decades old. He reached out his hands. "Julia."

She took his hands and sat beside him on the wagon, her young-girl face turned in a smile. "They think you're wonderful, Mr. Brady."

"They don't understand what I've done. They think it's art—" he stopped himself. This wasn't his Julia. This was the young girl, the one who had danced with him, who had told him about her dream. She had come from a different place and a different time, the only time she had seen the effects of his work.

He looked at her then, really looked at her, saw the shine in her blue eyes, the blush to her cheeks. She was watching the people look at his portraits, soaking in the discussion. Her gloved hand clutched his, and he could feel her wonderment and joy.

"I would be so proud if this were my doing, Mr. Brady. Imagine a room like this filled with your vision, your work."

He didn't look at the room. He looked at her. This moment, this was what kept her going all those years. The memory of what she thought was a dream, of what she hoped would become real. And it was real, but not in any way she understood. Perhaps, then, he didn't understand it either.

She turned to him, smiled into his face. "I would so like to be a part of this," she said. She thought it was a dream; otherwise she would have never spoken so boldly. No, wait. She *had* been bold when she was young.

"You will be," Brady said. And until that moment, he never

realized how much a part of it she had been, always standing beside him, always believing in him even when he no longer believed in himself. She had made the greater sacrifice—her entire life for his dream, his vision, his work.

"Julia," he said, thankful for this last chance to touch her, this last chance to hold her. "I could not do this without you. You made it all possible."

She leaned against him and laughed, a fluted sound he hadn't heard in decades. "But it's your work that they admire, Mr. Brady. Your work."

"They call me an artist."

"That's right." Her words were crisp, sure. "An artist's work lives beyond him. This isn't our world, Mr. Brady. In the other rooms, the pictures move."

The pictures move. He had been given a gift, to see his own future. To know that the losses he suffered, the reversals he and Julia had lived through weren't all for nothing. How many people got even that?

He tucked her arm in his. He had to be out of this room, out of this exhibit he didn't really understand. They stood together, her hoop clearing a path for them in the crowd. He stopped and surveyed the four walls—filled with his portraits, portraits of places most of these people had never seen—his memories that they shared and made their own.

Then he stepped out of the exhibit into a future in which he would never take part, perhaps to gain a perspective he had never had before.

And all the while, Julia remained beside him.

—For Dean

Three thousand copies of this book have been printed by the Maple-Vail Book Manufacturing Group, Binghamton, NY, for Golden Gryphon Press, Urbana, IL. The typeset is Elante, printed on 55# Sebago. The binding cloth is Arrestox B. Typesetting by The Composing Room, Inc., Kimberly, WI.